Lisa Gardner is the internationally bestselling thriller author of chart-toppers which include *Gone, Hide* and *Say Goodbye*. She lives in New England with her family.

Find out more at http://lisagardner.com

LOVE YOU MORE

Brian Darby lies dead on the kitchen floor. His wife, state trooper Tessa Leoni, claims to have shot him in self-defence; she bears bruising, which backs up her tale. But where is their six-year-old daughter? A homicide investigation ratchets into a statewide search for a missing child, led by veteran Detective D.D. Warren and Bobby Dodge. Would a trained police officer shoot her own husband? And would a mother harm her own child? Meanwhile, Tessa Leoni is walking a tight-rope, with nowhere to turn and no one to trust. She must use every ounce of her training to do what must be done. No sacrifice is too great, no action unthinkable. A mother knows who she loves. And all others will be made to pay.

Books by Lisa Gardner
Published by The House of Ulverscroft:

THE NEXT ACCIDENT
THE SURVIVORS CLUB
THE KILLING CLUB
ALONE
GONE
HIDE
SAY GOODBYE
THE NEIGHBOUR
LIVE TO TELL

2

14

WITHDRAWN

LISA GARDNER

LOVE YOU MORE

Complete and Unabridged

CHARNWOOD
Leicester

First published in Great Britain in 2011 by
Orion Books
an imprint of The Orion Publishing Group Ltd
London

First Charnwood Edition
published 2012
by arrangement with
The Orion Publishing Group Ltd
London

The moral right of the author has been asserted

British Library CIP Data

Gardner, Lisa.
   Love you more.
   1. Warren, D. D. (Fictitious Character)- -Fiction.
   2. Police- -Massachusetts- -Boston- -Fiction.
   3. Abused wives- -Fiction. 4. Mariticide- -
   Massachusetts- -Fiction. 5. Missing children- -
   Fiction. 6. Missing persons- -Investigation- -
   Massachusetts- -Boston- -Fiction. 7. Detective
   and mystery stories. 8. Large type books.
   I. Title
   813.6–dc23

   ISBN 978–1–4448–1083–7

Published by
F. A. Thorpe (Publishing)
Anstey, Leicestershire

Set by Words & Graphics Ltd.
Anstey, Leicestershire
Printed and bound in Great Britain by
T. J. International Ltd., Padstow, Cornwall

This book is printed on acid-free paper

Prologue

Who do you love?

It's a question anyone should be able to answer. A question that defines a life, creates a future, guides most minutes of one's days. Simple, elegant, encompassing.

Who do you love?

He asked the question, and I felt the answer in the weight of my duty belt, the constrictive confines of my armored vest, the tight brim of my trooper's hat, pulled low over my brow. I reached down slowly, my fingers just brushing the top of my Sig Sauer, holstered at my hip.

'Who do you love?' he cried again, louder now, more insistent.

My fingers bypassed my state-issued weapon, finding the black leather keeper that held my duty belt to my waist. The Velcro rasped loudly as I unfastened the first band, then the second, third, fourth. I worked the metal buckle, then my twenty pound duty belt, complete with my sidearm, Taser, and collapsible steel baton released from my waist and dangled in the space between us.

'Don't do this,' I whispered, one last shot at reason.

He merely smiled. 'Too little, too late.'

'Where's Sophie? What did you do?'

'Belt. On the table. Now.'

'No.'

1

'GUN. On the table. NOW!'

In response, I widened my stance, squaring off in the middle of the kitchen, duty belt still suspended from my left hand. Four years of my life, patrolling the highways of Massachusetts, swearing to defend and protect. I had training and experience on my side.

I could go for my gun. Commit to the act, grab the Sig Sauer, and start shooting.

Sig Sauer was holstered at an awkward angle that would cost me precious seconds. He was watching, waiting for any sudden movement. Failure would be firmly and terribly punished.

Who do you love?

He was right. That's what it came down to in the end. Who did you love and how much would you risk for them?

'GUN!' he boomed. 'Now, dammit!'

I thought of my six-year-old daughter, the scent of her hair, the feel of her skinny arms wrapped tight around my neck, the sound of her voice as I tucked her in bed each night. 'Love you, Mommy,' she always whispered.

Love you, too, baby. Love you.

His arm moved, first tentative stretch for the suspended duty belt, my holstered weapon.

One last chance . . .

I looked my husband in the eye. A single heartbeat of time.

Who do you love?

I made my decision. I set down my trooper's belt on the kitchen table.

And he grabbed my Sig Sauer and opened fire.

1

Sergeant Detective D.D. Warren prided herself on her excellent investigative skills. Having served over a dozen years with the Boston PD, she believed working a homicide scene wasn't simply a matter of walking the walk or talking the talk, but rather of total sensory immersion. She felt the smooth hole bored into Sheetrock by a hot spiraling twenty-two. She listened for the sound of neighbors gossiping on the other side of thin walls because if she could hear them, then they'd definitely heard the big bad that had just happened here.

D.D. always noted how a body had fallen, whether it was forward or backward or slightly to one side. She tasted the air for the acrid flavor of gunpowder, which could linger for a good twenty to thirty minutes after the final shot. And, on more than one occasion, she had estimated time of death based on the scent of blood — which, like fresh meat, started out relatively mild but took on heavier, earthier tones with each passing hour.

Today, however, she wasn't going to do any of those things. Today, she was spending a lazy Sunday morning dressed in gray sweats and Alex's oversized red flannel shirt. She was camped at his kitchen table, clutching a thick clay coffee mug while counting slowly to twenty.

She'd hit thirteen. Alex had finally made it to

the front door. Now he paused to wind a deep blue scarf around his neck.

She counted to fifteen.

He finished with the scarf. Moved on to a black wool hat and lined leather gloves. The temperature outside had just crept above twenty. Eight inches of snow on the ground and six more forecasted to arrive by end of the week. March didn't mean spring in New England.

Alex taught crime-scene analysis, among other things, at the Police Academy. Today was a full slate of classes. Tomorrow, they both had the day off, which didn't happen much and warranted some kind of fun activity yet to be determined. Maybe ice skating in the Boston Commons. Or a trip to the Isabelle Stewart Gardner Museum. Or a lazy day where they snuggled on the sofa and watched old movies with a big bowl of buttered popcorn.

D.D.'s hands spasmed on the coffee mug. Okay, no popcorn.

D.D. counted to eighteen, nineteen, twent —

Alex finished with his gloves, picked up his battered black leather tote, and crossed to her.

'Don't miss me too much,' he said.

He kissed her on the forehead. D.D. closed her eyes, mentally recited the number twenty, then started counting back down to zero.

'I'll write you love letters all day, with little hearts over the 'i's,' she said.

'In your high school binder?'

'Something like that.'

Alex stepped back. D.D. hit fourteen. Her mug trembled, but Alex didn't seem to notice.

4

She took a deep breath and soldiered on. *Thirteen, twelve, eleven* . . .

She and Alex had been dating a little over six months. At that point where she had a whole drawer to call her own in his tiny ranch, and he had a sliver of closet space in her North End condo. When he was teaching, it was easier for them to be here. When she was working, it was easier to be in Boston. They didn't have a set schedule. That would imply planning and further solidify a relationship they were both careful to not overly define.

They enjoyed each other's company. Alex respected her crazy schedule as a homicide detective. She respected his culinary skills as a third-generation Italian. From what she could tell, they looked forward to the nights when they could get together, but survived the nights when they didn't. They were two independent-minded adults. She'd just hit forty, Alex had crossed that line a few years back. Hardly blushing teens whose every waking moment was consumed with thoughts of each other. Alex had been married before. D.D. simply knew better.

She lived to work, which other people found unhealthy, but what the hell. It had gotten her this far.

Nine, eight, seven . . .

Alex opened the front door, squaring his shoulders against the bitter morning. A blast of chilled air shot across the small foyer, hitting D.D.'s cheeks. She shivered, clutched the mug more tightly.

'Love you,' Alex said, stepping across the threshold.

'Love you, too.'

Alex closed the door. D.D. made it down the hall just in time to vomit.

* * *

Ten minutes later, she remained sprawled on the bathroom floor. The decorative tiles were from the seventies, dozens and dozens of tiny beige, brown, and harvest gold squares. Looking at them made her want to puke all over again. Counting them, however, was a pretty decent meditative exercise. She inventoried tiles while she waited for her flushed cheeks to cool and her cramped stomach to untangle.

Her cellphone rang. She eyed it on the floor, not terribly interested, given the circumstances. But then she noted the caller and decided to take pity on him.

'What?' she demanded, her usual greeting for former lover and currently married Massachusetts State Police Detective Bobby Dodge.

'I don't have much time. Listen sharp.'

'I'm not on deck,' she said automatically. 'New cases go to Jim Dunwell. Pester him.' Then she frowned. Bobby couldn't be calling her about a case. As a city cop, she took her orders from the Boston turret, not state police detectives.

Bobby continued as if she'd never spoken: 'It's a fuckup, but I'm pretty sure it's *our* fuckup, so I need you to listen. Stars and stripes are next door, media across the street. Come in from the

6

back street. Take your time, notice *everything*. I've already lost vantage point, and trust me, D.D., on this one, you and I can't afford to miss a thing.'

D.D.'s frown deepened. 'What the hell, Bobby? I have no idea what you're talking about, not to mention it's my day off.'

'Not anymore. BPD is gonna want a woman to front this one, while the state is gonna demand their own skin in the game, preferably a former trooper. The brass's call, our heads on the block.'

She heard a fresh noise now, from the bedroom. Her pager, chiming away. Crap. She was being called in, meaning whatever Bobby was babbling about had merit. She pulled herself to standing, though her legs trembled and she thought she might puke again. She took the first step through sheer force of will and the rest was easier after that. She headed for the bedroom, a detective who'd lost days off before and would again.

'What do I need to know?' she asked, voice crisper now, phone tucked against her shoulder.

'Snow,' Bobby muttered. 'On the ground, trees, windows . . . hell. We got cops tramping everywhere — '

'Get 'em out! If it's my fucking scene, get 'em all out.'

She found her pager on the bedside table — yep, call out from Boston operations — and began shucking her gray sweatpants.

'They're out of the house. Trust me, even the bosses know better than to contaminate a

7

homicide scene. But we didn't know the girl was missing. The uniforms sealed off the house, but left the yard fair play. And now the grounds are trampled, and I can't get vantage point. We need vantage point.'

D.D. had sweats off, went to work on Alex's flannel shirt.

'Who's dead?'

'Forty-two-year-old white male.'

'Who's missing?'

'Six-year-old white female.'

'Got a suspect?'

Long, long pause now.

'Get here,' Bobby said curtly. 'You and me, D.D. Our case. Our headache. We gotta work this one quick.'

He clicked off. D.D. scowled at the phone, then tossed it on the bed to finish pulling on her white dress shirt.

Okay. Homicide with a missing child. State police already on-site, but Boston jurisdiction. Why the hell would the state police —

Then, fine detective that she was, D.D. finally connected the dots.

'Ah shit!'

D.D. wasn't nauseous anymore. She was pissed off.

She grabbed her pager, her creds, and her winter jacket. Then, Bobby's instructions ringing in her head, she prepared to ambush her own crime scene.

2

Who do you love?

I met Brian at a Fourth of July cookout. Shane's house. The kind of social invite I generally refused, but lately had realized I needed to reconsider. If not for my own sake, then for Sophie's.

The party wasn't that large. Maybe thirty people or so, other state troopers and families from Shane's neighborhood. The lieutenant colonel had made an appearance, a small coup for Shane. Mostly, however, the cookout attracted other uniformed officers. I saw four guys from the barracks standing by the grill, nursing beers and harassing Shane as he fussed over the latest batch of brats. In front of them were two picnic tables, already dominated by laughing wives who were mixing up batches of margaritas in between tending various children.

Other people lingered in the house, prepping pasta salads, catching the last few minutes of the game. Chitchatting away as they took a bite of this, a drink of that. People, doing what people do on a sunny Saturday afternoon.

I stood beneath the shade of an old oak tree. At Sophie's request, I was wearing an orange-flowered sundress and my single dressy pair of gold sparkling flip-flops. I still stood with my feet slightly apart, elbows tight to my unarmed sides, back to the tree. You can take the girl out of the job, but not the job out of the girl.

I should mingle, but didn't know where to start. Take a seat with the ladies, none of whom I knew, or head to where I would be more comfortable, hanging with the guys? I rarely fit in with the wives and couldn't afford to look like I was having fun with the husbands — then the wives would stop laughing and shoot daggers at me.

So I stood apart, holding a beer I'd never drink as I waited for the event to wind down to a point where I could politely depart.

Mostly, I watched my daughter.

A hundred yards away, she giggled ecstatically as she rolled down a grassy knoll with half a dozen other kids. Her hot pink sundress was already lawn-stained and she had chocolate chip cookie smeared across her cheek. When she popped up at the bottom of the hill, she grabbed the hand of the little girl next to her and they chugged back up as fast as their three-year-old legs could carry them.

Sophie always made friends instantly. Physically, she looked like me. Personality-wise, she was completely her own child. Outgoing, bold, adventurous. If she had her way, Sophie would spend every waking moment surrounded by people. Maybe charm was a dominant gene, inherited from her father, because she certainly didn't get it from me.

She and the other toddler arrived at the top of the hill. Sophie lay down first, her short dark hair contrasting deeply against a patch of yellow dandelions. Then, a flash of chubby arms and flailing legs as she started to roll, her giggles pealing against the vast blue sky.

She stood up dizzily at the bottom and caught me watching her.

'Love you, Mommy!' she cried, and dashed back up the hill.

I watched her run away and wished, not for the first time, that I didn't have to know all the things a woman like me had to know.

★　★　★

'Hello.'

A man had peeled off from the crowd, making his approach. Late-thirties, five ten, hundred and eighty, buzz-cut blonde hair, heavily muscled shoulders. Maybe another cop, given the venue, but I didn't recognize him.

He held out his hand. Belatedly, I offered my own.

'Brian,' he said. 'Brian Darby.' He jerked his head toward the house. 'I live down the street. You?'

'Umm. Tessa. Tessa Leoni. I know Shane from the barracks.'

I waited for the inevitable comments men made when meeting a female officer. *A cop? I'd better be on good behavior, then.* Or, *Ooooh, where's your gun?*

And those were the nice guys.

Brian, however, just nodded. He was holding a Bud Light in one hand. He tucked his other hand in the pocket of his tan shorts. He wore a blue collared shirt with a gold emblem on the pocket, but I couldn't make it out from this angle.

'Got a confession,' he said.

I braced myself.

'Shane told me who you were. Though, to give me some credit, I asked first. Pretty woman, standing alone. Seemed smart to do a little recon.'

'What did Shane say?'

'He assured me that you're totally out of my league. Naturally, I took the bait.'

'Shane's full of shit,' I offered.

'Most of the time. You're not drinking your beer.'

I looked down, as if noticing the bottle for the first time.

'Part of my recon,' Brian continued easily. 'You're holding a beer, but not drinking it. Would you prefer a margarita? I could get you one. Though,' he eyed the gaggle of wives, who were well into the third pitcher and laughing accordingly, 'I'm a little afraid.'

'It's okay.' I loosened my stance, shook out my arms. 'I don't really drink.'

'On call?'

'Not today.'

'I'm not a cop, so I won't pretend to know the life, but I've been hanging out with Shane a good five years now, so I like to think I understand the basics. Being a trooper is way more than patrolling highways and writing tickets. Ain't that right, Shane?' Brian boomed his voice, letting the common lament of any state trooper carry over the patio. At the grill, Shane responded by

12

raising his right hand and flipping off his neighbor.

'Shane's a whiner,' I said, letting my voice carry, as well.

Shane flipped me off, too. Several of the guys laughed.

'How long have you been working with him?' Brian asked me.

'A year. I'm a rookie.'

'Really? What made you want to be a cop?'

I shrugged, uncomfortable again. One of those questions everyone asked and I never knew how to answer. 'Seemed like a good idea at the time.'

'I'm a merchant marine,' Brian offered up. 'I work on oil tankers. We ship out a couple of months, then are home a couple of months, then out a couple of months. Screws with the personal life, but I like the work. Never boring.'

'A merchant marine? What do you do . . . protect against pirates, things like that?'

'Nah. We run from Puget Sound up to Alaska and back. Not too many Somali pirates patrolling that corridor. Plus, I'm an engineer. My job's to keep the ship running. I like wires and gears and rotors. Guns, on the other hand, scare the crap out of me.'

'I don't care for them much myself.'

'Funny comment, coming from a police officer.'

'Not really.'

My gaze had returned automatically to Sophie, checking in. Brian followed my line of sight. 'Shane said you had a three-year-old. Holey moley, she looks just like you. No taking

13

the wrong kid home from this party.'

'Shane said I had a kid, and you still took the bait?'

He shrugged. 'Kids are cool. I don't have any, but that doesn't mean I'm morally opposed. Father in the picture?' he added casually.

'No.'

He didn't look smug at that news, more like contemplative. 'That's gotta be tough. Being a full-time cop and raising a child.'

'We get by.'

'Not doubting you. My father died when I was young. Left my mother to raise five kids on her own. We got by, too, and I respect the hell out of her for it.'

'What happened to your father?'

'Heart attack. What happened to her father?' He nodded toward Sophie, who now appeared to be playing tag.

'Better offer.'

'Men are stupid,' he muttered, sounding so sincere that I finally laughed. He flushed. 'Did I mention I have four sisters? These are the things that happen when you have four sisters. Plus, I have to respect my mom twice as much because not only did she survive being a single mother, but she survived being a single mother with four girls. And I never saw her drink anything stronger than herbal tea. How about them apples?'

'She sounds like a rock,' I agreed.

'Since you don't drink, maybe you're also an herbal tea kind of gal?'

'Coffee.'

'Ah, my personal drug of choice.' He looked me in the eye. 'So, Tessa, maybe some afternoon, I could buy you a cup. Your neighborhood or my neighborhood, just let me know.'

I studied Brian Darby again. Warm brown eyes, easygoing smile, solidly built shoulders.

'Okay,' I heard myself say. 'I would like that.'

* * *

Do you believe in love at first sight? I don't. I'm too studied, too cautious for such nonsense. Or maybe, I simply know better.

I met Brian for coffee. I learned that when he was home, his time was his own. It made it easy to hike together in the afternoons, after I'd recovered from the graveyard shift and before I picked up Sophie from daycare at five. Then we caught a Red Sox game on my night off, and before I knew it, he was joining Sophie and me for a picnic.

Sophie did fall in love at first sight. In a matter of seconds, she'd climbed onto Brian's back and demanded giddyup. Brian obediently galloped his way across the park with a squealing three-year-old clutching his hair and yelling 'Faster!' at the top of her lungs. When they were done, Brian collapsed on the picnic blanket while Sophie toddled off to pick dandelions. I assumed the flowers were for me, but she turned to Brian instead.

Brian accepted the dandelions tentatively at first, then positively beaming when he realized the entire wilted bouquet was just for him.

15

It became easy, after that, to spend the weekends at his house with a real yard, versus my cramped one-bedroom apartment. We would cook dinner together, while Sophie ran around with his dog, an aging German shepherd named Duke. Brian bought a plastic kiddy pool for the deck, hung a toddler's swing from the old oak tree.

One weekend when I got jammed up, he came over and stocked my fridge to get Sophie and me through the week. And one afternoon, after I'd worked a motor vehicle accident that left three kids dead, he read to Sophie while I stared at the bedroom wall and fought to get my head on straight.

Later I sat curled up against him on the couch and he told me stories of his four sisters, including the time they'd found him napping on the sofa and covered him in makeup. He'd spent two hours biking around the neighborhood in glittering blue eye shadow and hot pink lipstick before he happened to catch his reflection in a window. I laughed. Then I cried. Then he held me tighter and we both said nothing at all.

Summer slid away. Fall arrived, and just like that, it was time for him to ship out. He'd be gone eight weeks, back in time for Thanksgiving, he assured me. He had a good friend who always looked after Duke. But, if we wanted . . .

He handed me the key to his house. We could stay. Even girl the place up if we wanted to. Maybe some pink paint in the second bedroom, for Sophie. Couple of prints on the wall. Princess rubber duckies in the bathroom. Whatever it took to make us comfortable.

I kissed his cheek, returned the key to the palm of his hand.

Sophie and I were fine. Always had been, always would be. See you in eight weeks.

Sophie, on the other hand, cried and cried and cried.

Couple of months, I tried to tell her. Hardly any time at all. Just a matter of weeks.

Life was duller with Brian gone. An endless grind of getting up at one p.m., retrieving Sophie from daycare by five, entertaining her until her bedtime at nine, with Mrs. Ennis arriving at ten so I could patrol from eleven to seven. The life of a single working mom. Struggling to stretch a dime into a dollar, cramming endless errands into an already overscheduled day, fighting to keep my bosses happy while still meeting my young daughter's needs.

I could handle it, I reminded myself. I was tough. I'd gotten through my pregnancy alone, I'd given birth alone. I'd endured twenty-five long, lonely weeks at the live-in Police Academy, missing Sophie with every breath I took but determined not to quit because becoming a state police officer was the best shot I had to provide a future for my daughter. I'd been allowed to return home to Sophie every Friday night, but I also had to leave her crying with Mrs. Ennis every Monday morning. Week after week after week, until I thought I'd scream from the pressure. But I did it. Anything for Sophie. Always for Sophie.

Still, I started checking e-mail more often

because if Brian was in port he'd send us a quick note, or attach a silly picture of a moose in the middle of some Alaskan main street. By the sixth week, I realized I was happier the days he e-mailed, tenser the days he didn't. And Sophie was, too. We huddled together over the computer each night, two pretty girls waiting to hear from their man.

Then finally, the call. Brian's ship had docked in Ferndale, Washington. He'd be discharged the day after tomorrow, and would be catching the red-eye back to Boston. Could he take us to dinner?

Sophie selected her favorite dark blue dress. I wore the orange sundress from the Fourth of July cookout, topped with a sweater in deference to the November chill.

Sophie, keeping lookout from the front window, spotted him first. She squealed in delight and raced down the apartment steps so fast I thought she'd fall. Brian barely caught her at the end of the walk. He scooped her up, whirled her around. She laughed and laughed and laughed.

I approached more quietly, taking the time for a last minute tuck of my hair, buttoning my light sweater. I stepped through the front door of the apartment complex. Shut it firmly behind me.

Then I turned and studied him. Took him in from eight feet away. Drank him up.

Brian stopped twirling Sophie. Now he stood at the end of the walk, my child still in his arms, and he studied me, too.

We didn't touch. We didn't say a word. We didn't have to.

Later, after dinner, after he brought us back to his place, after I tucked Sophie into the bed across the hall, I walked into his bedroom. I stood before him, and let him peel the sweater from my arms, the sundress from my body. I placed my hands against his bare chest. I tasted the salt on the column of his throat.

'Eight weeks was too long,' he muttered thickly. 'I want you here, Tessa. Dammit, I want to know I'm coming home to you always.'

I placed his hands upon my breasts, arching into the feel of his fingers.

'Marry me,' he whispered. 'I mean it, Tessa. I want you to be my wife. I want Sophie to be my daughter. You and her should be living here with me and Duke. We should be a family.'

I tasted his skin again. Slid my hands down his body, pressed the full length of my bare skin against his bare skin. Shivered at the contact. Except it wasn't enough. The feel of him, the taste of him. I needed him against me, I needed him above me, I needed him inside me. I needed him everywhere, right now, this instant.

I dragged him down to the bed, wrapping my legs around his waist. Then he was sliding inside my body and I groaned, or maybe he groaned, but it didn't really matter. He was where I needed him to be.

At the last moment, I caught his face between my hands so I could look into his eyes as the first wave crashed over us.

'Marry me,' he repeated. 'I'll be a good husband, Tessa. I'll take care of you and Sophie.'

He moved inside of me and I said: 'Yes.'

3

Brian Darby died in his kitchen. Three shots, tightly clustered midtorso. D.D.'s first thought was that Trooper Leoni must've taken her firearms training seriously, because the grouping was textbook perfect. As new recruits learned at the Academy — never go for the head and never shoot to wound. Torso is the high percentage shot and if you're discharging your weapon, you'd better be in fear for your life or someone else's, meaning you're shooting to kill.

Leoni had gotten the job done. Now, what the hell had happened to drive a state trooper to shoot her husband? And where was the kid?

Currently, Trooper Leoni was sequestered in the front sunroom, being tended by EMTs for an ugly gash in her forehead and even uglier black eye. Her union rep was already with her, a lawyer on his way.

A dozen other state troopers had closed ranks outside, standing stiff-legged on the sidewalk where they could give their Boston colleagues working the scene, and the overexcited press reporting the scene, thousand-yard stares.

That left most of the Boston brass and most of the state police brass to squabble amongst themselves in the white command van now parked at the elementary school next door. The homicide unit supervisor from the Suffolk County DA was presumably playing referee,

20

no doubt reminding the Massachusetts State Police superintendent that the state really couldn't oversee an investigation involving one of its own officers, while also reminding the commissioner of Boston Police that the state's request for a state police liaison was perfectly reasonable.

In between bouts of marking turf, the head muckety-mucks had managed to issue an Amber Alert for six-year-old Sophie Leoni, brown hair, blue eyes, approximately forty-six inches tall, weighing forty-five pounds, and missing her top two front teeth. Most likely wearing a pink, long-sleeved pajama set dotted with yellow horses. Last seen around ten-thirty the previous evening, when Trooper Leoni had allegedly checked on her daughter before reporting for her eleven p.m. patrol shift.

D.D. had a lot of questions for Trooper Tessa Leoni. Unfortunately, she did not have access: Trooper Leoni was in shock, the union rep had squawked. Trooper Leoni required immediate medical attention. Trooper Leoni was entitled to appropriate legal counsel. She had already provided an initial statement to the first responder. All other questions would have to wait until her attorney deemed appropriate.

Trooper Leoni had a lot of needs, D.D. thought. Shouldn't one of those include working with the Boston cops to find her kid?

For the moment, D.D. had backed off. Scene this busy, there were plenty of other matters that required her immediate attention. She had Boston district detectives swarming the scene,

21

Boston homicide detectives working the evidence, various uniformed officers canvassing the neighborhood, and — given that Trooper Leoni had shot her husband with her service Sig Sauer — the firearms discharge investigation team had been automatically dispatched, flooding the small property with even more miscellaneous police personnel.

Bobby had been right — in official lingo, this case was a cluster-fuck.

And it was all hers.

D.D. had arrived thirty minutes ago. She'd parked six blocks away, on bustling Washington Street versus a quieter side street. Allston-Brighton was one of the most densely populated neighborhoods in Boston. Filled to the brim with students from Boston College, Boston University, and Harvard Business School, the area was dominated by academics, young families, and support staff. Expensive place to live, which was ironic given that college students and academics rarely had any money. End result was street after street of tired, three-story apartment buildings, each carved into more units than the last. Families were piled in, with twenty-four-hour convenience stores and Laundromats sprouting up to meet the continuous demand.

This was the urban jungle in D.D.'s mind. No wrought-iron balustrades or decorative brickwork like Back Bay or Beacon Hill. Here, you paid a fortune for the honor of renting a strictly utilitarian box-like apartment in a strictly utilitarian box-like building. Parking was first come first serve, which meant most of the masses spent half their time cruising for spaces. You fought your way to work, you fought your way home, then ended the day eating a microwavable dinner in a standing room only kitchenette, before falling asleep on the world's smallest futon.

Not a bad area, however, for a state trooper. Easy access to Mass Pike, the main artery bisecting the state. East on the Pike hit 1–93, west brought you to 128. Basically, in a matter of minutes, Leoni could access three major hunting grounds for the trooper on patrol. Smart.

D.D. also liked the house, an honest to goodness single-family dwelling plunked down in the thick of Allston-Brighton, with a tidy row of three-story apartment buildings on one side and a sprawling brick elementary school to the other. Thankfully, being Sunday, the school was closed, allowing the current mass of law enforcement to take over the parking lot while sparing them from further drama caused by panicky parents overrunning the scene.

Quiet day in the neighborhood. At least it had been.

Trooper Leoni's vintage two-bedroom bungalow was built into a hillside, white-dormered structure stacked over a redbricked two-car garage. A single flight of concrete steps led from the street-level sidewalk up to the front door and one of the largest yards D.D. had ever seen in downtown Boston.

Good family home. Just enough space to raise a kid inside, perfect lawn for a dog and a swing set outside. Even now, walking the lot in the dead of winter, D.D. could picture the cookouts, the playdates, the lazy evenings hanging on the back deck.

So many things that could go right in a house like this. So what had gone wrong?

She thought the yard might hold the key. Big, sprawling, and completely unprotected in the midst of population overload.

Cut through the school parking lot, walk onto this property. Emerge from behind four different apartment buildings, walk onto this property. You could access the Leoni residence from the back street, as D.D. had done, or by walking up the concrete steps from the front street, as most of the Massachusetts state police seem to have done. From the back, the front, the right and left, the property was easy to enter and easier to exit.

Something every uniformed officer must have figured out, because instead of studying a pristine sweep of white snow, D.D. was currently looking at the largest collection of boot imprints ever amassed in a quarter acre.

She hunched deeper into her winter field coat and exhaled a frustrated puff of frosty breath. Fucking morons.

Bobby Dodge appeared on the back deck, probably still searching for his vantage point. Given the way he was frowning down at the mucked-up snow, his thoughts mirrored her own. He caught sight of her, adjusted his black brimmed hat against the early March chill, and walked down the deck stairs to the yard.

'Your troopers trampled my crime scene,' D.D.

24

called across the way. 'I won't forget that.'

He shrugged, burying his hands in his black wool coat as he approached. A former sniper, Bobby still moved with the economy of motion that came from spending long hours holding perfectly still. Like a lot of snipers, he was a smaller guy with a tough, sinewy build that matched his hard-planed face. No one would ever describe him as handsome, but plenty of women found him compelling.

Once upon a time, D.D. had been one of those women. They'd started out as lovers, but discovered they worked better as friends. Then, two years ago Bobby had met and married Annabelle Granger. D.D. hadn't taken the wedding well; the birth of their daughter had felt like another blow.

But D.D. had Alex now. Life was on the up. Right?

Bobby came to a halt before her. 'Troopers protect lives,' he informed her. 'Detectives protect evidence.'

'Your troopers screwed my scene. I don't forgive. I don't forget.'

Bobby finally smiled. 'Missed you, too, D.D.'

'How's Annabelle?'

'Fine, thanks.'

'And the baby?'

'Carina's already crawling. Can barely believe it.'

D.D. couldn't either. Crap, they were getting old.

'And Alex?' Bobby asked.

'Good, good.' She waved her gloved hand,

done with small talk. 'So what d'ya think happened?'

Bobby shrugged again, taking his time answering. While some investigators felt a need to work their homicide scenes, Bobby liked to study his. And while many detectives were prone to jabber, Bobby rarely spoke unless he had something useful to say.

D.D. respected him immensely, but was careful never to tell him that.

'At first blush, it would appear to be a domestic situation,' he stated finally. 'Husband attacked with a beer bottle, Trooper Leoni defended with her service weapon.'

'Got a history of domestic disturbance calls?' D.D. asked.

Bobby shook his head; she nodded in agreement. The lack of calls meant nothing. Cops hated to ask for help, especially from other cops. If Brian Darby had been beating his wife, most likely she'd taken it in silence.

'You know her?' D.D. asked.

'No. I left patrol shortly after she started. She's only been on the force four years.'

'Word on the street?'

'Solid officer. Young. Stationed out of the Framingham barracks, working the graveyard shift, then racing home to her kid, so not one to mingle.'

'Works *only* the graveyard shift?'

He arched a brow, looking amused. 'Scheduling's a competitive world for troopers. Rookies get to spend an entire year on graveyard before they can bid for another time slot. Even then,

26

scheduling is awarded based on seniority. Four-year recruit? My guess is she had another year before she could see daylight.'

'And I thought being a detective sucked.'

'Boston cops are a bunch of crybabies,' Bobby informed her.

'Please, at least we know better than to disturb crime-scene snow.'

He grimaced. They resumed their study of the trampled yard.

'How long have they been married?' D.D. asked now.

'Three years.'

'So she was already on the force and she already had the kid when she met him.'

Bobby didn't answer, as it wasn't a question.

'In theory, he would've known what he was getting into,' D.D. continued out loud, trying to get a preliminary feel for the dynamics of the household. 'A wife who'd be gone all night. A little girl who'd require evening and morning care.'

'When he was around.'

'What do you mean?'

'He worked as a merchant marine.' Bobby pulled out a notepad, glanced at a line he'd scribbled. 'Shipped out for sixty days at a time. Sixty out, sixty home. One of the guys knew the drill from statements Trooper Leoni had made around the barracks.'

D.D. arched a brow. 'So wife has a crazy sched-ule. Husband has a crazier schedule. Interesting. Was he a big guy?' D.D. hadn't lingered over the body, given her tender stomach.

'Five ten; two hundred ten, two hundred twenty pounds,' Bobby reported. 'Muscle, not flab. Weight lifter, would be my guess.'

'A guy who could pack a punch.'

'In contrast, Trooper Leoni's about five four, hundred and twenty pounds. Gives the husband a clear advantage.'

D.D. nodded. A trooper had training in hand-to-hand combat, of course. But a smaller female against a larger male was still stacked odds. And a husband, to boot. Plenty of female officers learned on-the-job skills they didn't practice on the home front; Trooper Leoni's black eye wasn't the first D.D. had seen on a female colleague.

'Incident happened when Trooper Leoni first came home from work,' Bobby said now. 'She was still in uniform.'

D.D. arched a brow, let that sink in. 'She was wearing her vest?'

'Under her blouse, SOP.'

'And her belt?'

'Drew her Sig Sauer straight from the holster.'

'Shit.' D.D. shook her head. 'This is a mess.'

Not a question, so again Bobby didn't answer.

The uniform, not to mention the presence of a trooper's duty belt, changed everything. For starters, it meant Trooper Leoni had been wearing her vest at the time of the attack. Even a two hundred and twenty pound male would have a hard time making an impact against an officer's body armor. Second, a trooper's duty belt held plenty of tools other than a Sig Sauer that would've been appropriate for defense. For

28

example, a collapsible steel baton, or police-issued Taser or pepper spray or even the metal handcuffs.

Fundamental to every officer's training was the ability to quickly size up the threat and respond with the appropriate level of force. A subject yells at you, you didn't pull your gun. A subject hits you, you still didn't necessarily pull your weapon.

But Trooper Leoni had.

D.D. was starting to understand why the state union rep was so eager to get Tessa Leoni appropriate legal counsel, and so insistent that she *not* talk to the police.

D.D. sighed, rubbed her forehead. 'I don't get it. So battered wife syndrome. He hit her one too many times, she finally cracked and did something about it. That explains his body in the kitchen and her visit with the EMTs in the sunroom. But what about the kid? Where's the girl?'

'Maybe this morning's fight started last night. Stepdad started pounding. Girl fled the scene.'

They looked at the snow, where any trace of small footsteps had been thoroughly eradicated.

'Calls went out to the local hospitals?' D.D. asked. 'Uniforms are checking with the neighbors?'

'It's a full Amber Alert, and no, we're not stupid.'

She stared pointedly at the snow. Bobby shut up.

'What about birth father?' D.D. tried. 'If Brian Darby is the stepdad, then where's Sophie's birth father and what does he have to say about all this?'

'No birth father,' Bobby reported.

'I believe that's biologically impossible.'

'No name listed on the birth certificate, no guy mentioned around the barracks, and no male role model visiting every other weekend.' Bobby shrugged. 'No birth father.'

D.D. frowned. 'Because Tessa Leoni didn't want him in the picture, or because he didn't want to be in the picture? And oh yeah, in the last couple of nights, did those dynamics suddenly change?'

Bobby shrugged again.

D.D. pursed her lips, starting to see multiple possibilities. A birth father intent on reclaiming parental rights. Or an overstretched household, trying to juggle two intense careers and one small child. Option A meant the biological father might have kidnapped his own child. Option B meant the stepdad — or birth mother — had beat that child to death.

'Think the girl is dead?' Bobby asked now.

'Hell if I know.' D.D. didn't like to think about the girl. A wife shooting her husband, fine. A missing kid . . . This case was gonna suck.

'Can't hide a body in the ground,' she considered out loud. 'Too frozen for digging. So if the girl *is* dead . . . Most likely her remains have been tucked somewhere inside the house. Garage? Attic? Crawl space? Old freezer?'

Bobby shook his head.

D.D. took his word for it. She hadn't ventured into the house beyond the kitchen and sunroom, but given the number of uniforms currently combing through the eleven hundred square foot space, they should've been able to dismantle the structure board by board.

'I don't think this has anything to do with the birth father,' Bobby stated. 'If the birth father was back in the picture making noise, those would be the first words out of Tessa Leoni's mouth. *Contact my rat bastard ex-boyfriend, who's been threatening to take my daughter from me.* Leoni's said no such thing — '

'Because the union rep has shut her down.'

'Because the union rep doesn't want her to make statements that incriminate herself. Totally fair game, however, to make statements that incriminate others.'

Couldn't argue with that logic, D.D. thought. 'Fine, forget birth father for a second. Sounds like the current household was dysfunctional enough. To judge by Trooper Leoni's face, Brian Darby is a wife beater. Maybe he hit his stepdaughter, too. She died, Trooper Leoni came home to the body, and they both panicked. Stepfather has done a terrible thing, but Trooper Leoni let him, making her party to the crime. They take the body for a drive and dump it. Then get home, get into a fight, and the stress of the whole situation leads Tessa to snap.'

'Trooper Leoni helped dump her own daughter's body,' Bobby said, 'before returning home and shooting her husband?'

D.D. regarded him squarely. 'Make no assumptions, Bobby. You of all people know that.'

31

He didn't say anything, but met her stare.

'I want Trooper Leoni's cruiser,' D.D stated.

'I believe the brass is ironing that out.'

'His car, too.'

'Two thousand and seven GMC Denali. Your squad already has it.'

D.D. raised a brow. 'Nice car. Merchant mariners make that kind of money?'

'He was an engineer. Engineers always make that kind of money. I don't think Trooper Leoni hurt her own child,' Bobby said.

'You don't?'

'Spoke to a couple of the troopers who worked with her. They had nothing but good things to say about her. Loving mom, dedicated to her daughter, yada yada yada.'

'Yeah? They also know her husband was using her for a punching bag?'

Bobby didn't say anything right away, which was answer enough. He turned back to the scene. 'Could be an abduction,' he insisted stubbornly.

'Unfenced lot, bordered by a couple hundred strangers . . . ' D.D. shrugged. 'Yeah, if just the six-year-old were missing, I'd absolutely run the perverts up the flagpole. But what are the odds of a stranger creeping into the home the same evening/morning the husband and wife have a fatal argument?'

'Make no assumptions,' Bobby repeated, but didn't sound any more convinced than she had.

D.D. resumed studying the churned-up yard, which might have once contained footprints relative to their present discussion and now

32

didn't. She sighed, hating it when good evidence went bad.

'We didn't know,' Bobby murmured beside her. 'Call came in as an officer in distress. That's what the troopers responded to. Not a homicide scene.'

'Who made the call?'

'I'm guessing she made the initial phone call — '

'Tessa Leoni.'

'Trooper Leoni. Probably to a buddy in the barracks. The buddy summoned the cavalry and the call was picked up by operations. At that point, most of the troopers responded, with the lieutenant colonel bringing up the rear. Now, once Lieutenant Colonel Hamilton got here — '

'Realized it was less of a crisis, more of a cleanup,' D.D. muttered.

'Hamilton did the sensible thing and notified Boston turret, given the jurisdiction.'

'While also summoning his own detectives.'

'Skin in the game, babe. What can I say?'

'I want transcripts.'

'Somehow, as official state police liaison, I have a feeling that will be the first of many things I will fetch for you.'

'Yes, state police liaison. Let's talk about that. You're the liaison, I'm the head detective. I take that to mean I call the shots, you run the plays.'

'Have you ever worked any other way?'

'Now that you mention it, never. So first task, find me the girl.'

'Don't I wish.'

'Fine. Second task — get me access to Trooper Leoni.'

'Don't I wish,' Bobby repeated.

'Come on, you're the state police liaison. Surely she'll talk to the state police liaison.'

'Union rep is telling her to shut up. Her lawyer, once he arrives, will most likely second that command. Welcome to the blue wall, D.D.'

'But I also wear the fucking uniform!'

Bobby looked pointedly at her heavy field jacket, emblazoned *BPD*. 'Not in Trooper Leoni's world.'

4

I was on my first solo patrol for all of two hours when I received my debut domestic disturbance call. Incident came from dispatch as a verbal domestic — basically the occupants of apartment 25B were arguing so loudly, their neighbors couldn't sleep. Neighbors got mad, neighbors called the cops.

On the surface, nothing too exciting. Trooper shows up, occupants of 25B shut up. And probably drop a bag of burning dog poo on the neighbor's front stoop the next morning.

But at the Academy they had drilled into us — there is no such thing as a typical call. Be aware. Be prepared. Be safe.

I sweated through my dark blue BDUs all the way to apartment 25B.

New troopers work under the supervision of a senior officer for their first twelve weeks. After that, we patrol alone. No wingman for companionship, no partner to watch your back. Instead, it's all about dispatch. Second you're in your cruiser, second you exit your vehicle, second you stop for a cup of coffee, second you pull over to pee, you tell dispatch all about it. Operations is your lifeline and when something goes wrong, it's operations that will send the cavalry — your fellow state troopers — to the rescue.

In the classroom, this had sounded like a plan.

But at one in the morning, getting out of my cruiser in a neighborhood I didn't know, approaching a building I'd never seen, to confront two people I'd never met, it was easy to consider other facts, too. For example, while there are approximately seventeen hundred state troopers, only six hundred or so are on patrol at the same time. And these six hundred troopers are covering the entire state of Massachusetts. Meaning we're spread out all over the place. Meaning that when things go wrong, it's not a five-minute fix.

We're all one big family, but we're still very much alone.

I approached the building as I had been trained, my elbows glued to my waist to protect my service weapon, my body turned slightly to the side to form a smaller target. I angled away from the windows and kept to one side of the door, where I would be out of direct line of fire.

The most frequent call-out received by a uniformed officer is situation unknown. At the Academy, we were advised to treat all calls like that. Danger is everywhere. All people are suspect. All suspects are liars.

This is the way you work. For some officers, this also becomes the way they live.

I mounted three steps to a tiny front stoop, then paused to take a deep breath. Command presence. I was twenty-three years old, average height and unfortunately pretty. Chances were, whoever opened that door was going to be older than me, bigger than me, and rougher than me. Still my job to control the situation. Feet wide.

Shoulders back. Chin up. As the other rookies liked to joke, never let 'em see you sweat.

I stood to the side. I knocked. Then I quickly threaded my thumbs into the waistband of my dark blue pants, so my hands couldn't tremble.

No sounds of disturbance. No sounds of footsteps. Lights blazed, however; the occupants of 25B were not asleep.

I knocked again. Harder this time.

No sound of movement, no sign of the residents.

I fidgeted with my duty belt, debated my options. I had a call, a call required a report, a report required contact. So I drew myself up taller and knocked *hard*. *BAM. BAM. BAM.* Pounded my knuckles against the cheap wooden door. I was a state trooper, dammit, and I would not be ignored.

This time, footsteps.

Thirty seconds later, the door silently swung open.

The female occupant of unit 25B did not look at me. She stared at the floor as the blood poured down her face.

★ ★ ★

As I learned that night, and many nights since, the basic steps for handling domestic violence remain the same.

First, the officer secures the scene, a swift, preliminary inspection to identify and eliminate any potential threats.

Who else is in the home, Officer? May I walk

37

through the house? Trooper, is that your weapon? I'm going to need to take your firearm, Trooper. Are there any other guns on the property? I'm also going to need your duty belt. Unhook it, easy . . . Thank you. I'm going to request that you remove your vest. Do you require assistance? Thank you. I will take that now. I need you to move into the sunroom. Have a seat right here. Stay put. I'll be back.

Scene secured, the officer now inspects the female party for signs of injury. At this stage, the officer makes no assumption. The individual is neither a suspect nor a victim. She is simply an injured party and is handled accordingly.

Female presents with bloody lip, black eye, red marks on throat, and bloody laceration high on right forehead.

Many battered women will argue that they're okay. Don't need no ambulance. Just get the hell out and leave 'em alone. Be all better by morning.

The well-trained officer ignores such statements. There is evidence of a crime, triggering the larger wheels of criminal justice into motion. Maybe the battered woman is the victim, as she claims, and will ultimately refuse to press charges. But maybe she is the instigator — maybe the injuries were sustained while the female beat the crap out of an unknown party, meaning she is the perpetrator of a crime and her injuries and statement need to be documented for the charges that will soon be filed by that unknown party. Again, make no assumptions. The trooper will alert dispatch of the

38

situation, request backup and summon the EMTs.

Other bodies will now start to arrive. Uniforms. Medical personnel. Sirens will sound in the horizon, official vehicles pouring down the narrow funnel of city streets while the neighbors gather outside to catch the show.

The scene will become a very busy place, making it even more important for the first responder to document, document, document. The trooper will now conduct a more detailed visual inspection of the scene, making notes and snapping initial photographs.

Dead male, late-thirties, appears to be five ten, two hundred ten to two hundred twenty pounds. Three GSWs midtorso. Discovered faceup two feet to the left of the table in the kitchen.

Two wooden kitchen chairs toppled. Remnants of broken green glass under chairs. One shattered green bottle — labeled Heineken — located six inches to the left of the table in the kitchen.

Sig Sauer semiauto discovered on top of forty-two inch round wooden table. Officer removed cartridge and emptied chamber. Bagged and tagged.

Family room cleared.

Upstairs two bedrooms and bath cleared.

More uniforms will assist, questioning neighbors, securing the perimeter. The female party will remain sequestered away from the action, where she will now be tended by the medical personnel.

Female EMT, checking my pulse, gently

probing my eye socket and cheekbone for signs of fracture. Asking me to remove my ponytail so she can better tend my forehead. Using tweezers to remove the first piece of green glass which will later be matched to the shattered beer bottle.

'How do you feel, ma'am?'

'Head hurts.'

'Do you have any recollection of blacking out or losing consciousness?'

'Head hurts.'

'Do you feel nauseous?'

'Yes.' Stomach rolling. Trying to hold it together, against the pain, the confusion, the growing disorientation that this can't be happening, shouldn't be happening . . .

The EMT further examining my head, finding the growing lump at the back of my skull.

'What happened to your head, ma'am?'

'What?'

'The back of your head, ma'am. Are you sure you didn't lose consciousness, take a fall?'

Me, looking at the EMT blankly. 'Who do you love?' I whisper.

The EMT does not reply.

Next up, taking an initial statement. A good trooper will note both what the subject says and *how* she says it. People in a genuine state of shock have a tendency to babble, offering fragments of information but unable to string together a coherent whole. Some victims disassociate. They speak in flat, clipped tones about an event that in their own minds already didn't happen to them. Then there are the professional liars — the ones who pretend to

40

babble or disassociate.

Any liar will sooner or later overreach. Add a little too much detail. Sound a bit too composed. Then the well-trained investigator can pounce.

'Can you tell me what happened here, Trooper Leoni?' A Boston district detective takes the first pass. He is older, hair graying at the temples. He sounds kind, going for the collegial approach.

I don't want to answer. I have to answer. Better the district detective than the homicide investigator who will follow. My head throbs, my temples, my cheek. My face is on fire.

Want to throw up. Fighting the sensation.

'My husband . . . ' I whisper. My gaze drops automatically to the floor. I catch my mistake, force myself to look up, meet the district detective's eye. 'Sometimes . . . when I worked late. My husband grew angry.' Pause. My voice, growing stronger, more definite. 'He hit me.'

'Where did he hit you, Officer?'

'Face. Eye. Cheek.' My fingers finding each spot, reliving the pain. Inside my head, I'm stuck in a moment of time. Him, looming above. Me, cowering on the linoleum, genuinely terrified.

'I fell down,' I recite for the district detective. 'My husband picked up a chair.'

Silence. The district detective waiting for me to say more. Spin a lie, tell the truth.

'I didn't hit him,' I whisper. I've taken enough of these statements. I know how this story goes. We all do. 'If I didn't fight back,' I state mechanically, 'he'd wear out, go away. If I did . . . It was always worse in the end.'

41

'Your husband picked up a chair, Trooper Leoni? Where were you when he did this?'

'On the floor.'

'Where in the house?'

'The kitchen.'

'When your husband picked up the chair, what did you do?'

'Nothing.'

'What did he do?'

'Threw it.'

'Where?'

'At me.'

'Did it hit you?'

'I . . . I don't remember.'

'Then what happened, Trooper Leoni?' *The district detective leaning down, peering at me more closely. His face is a study of concern. Is my eye contact wrong? My story too detailed? Not detailed enough?*

All I want for Christmas is my two front teeth, my two front teeth, my two front teeth.

The song sounds in my head. I want to giggle. I don't.

Love you, Mommy. Love you.

'I threw the chair back at him,' *I tell the district detective.*

'You threw the chair back at him?'

'He got . . . angrier. So I must have done something, right? Because he became angrier.'

'Were you in full uniform at this time, Trooper Leoni?'

I meet his eye. 'Yes.'

'Wearing your duty belt? And your body armor?'

'Yes.'

'Did you reach for anything on your duty belt? Take steps to defend yourself?'

Still looking him in the eye. 'No.'

The detective regards me curiously. 'What happened next, Trooper Leoni?'

'He grabbed the beer bottle. Smashed it against my forehead. I . . . I managed to fend him off. He stumbled, toward the table. I fell. Against the wall. My back against the wall. I needed to find the doorway. I needed to get away.'

Silence.

'Trooper Leoni?'

'He had the broken bottle,' I murmur. 'I needed to get away. But . . . trapped. On the floor. Against the wall. Watching him.'

'Trooper Leoni?'

'I feared for my life,' I whisper. 'I felt my sidearm. He charged . . . I feared for my life.'

'Trooper Leoni, what happened?'

'I shot my husband.'

'Trooper Leoni — '

I meet his gaze one last time. 'Then I went looking for my daughter.'

5

By the time D.D. and Bobby finished circling around to the front of the property, the EMTs were retrieving a stretcher from the back of the ambulance. D.D. glanced their way, then identified the Boston uniform standing outside the crime-scene tape with the murder book. She approached him first.

'Hey, Officer Fiske. You've logged every single uniform entering this joint?' She gestured to the notebook in his hand, where he was collecting the names of all personnel to cross the crime-scene tape.

'Forty-two officers,' he said, without batting an eyelash.

'Jesus. Is there a single cop left on patrol in the greater Boston area?'

'Doubt it,' Officer Fiske said. Kid was young and serious. Was it just D.D. or were they getting younger and more serious with each passing year?

'Well, here's the problem, Officer Fiske. While you're collecting names here, other cops are entering and exiting from the rear of the property, and that's really pissing me off.'

Officer Fiske's eyes widened.

'Got a buddy?' D.D. continued. 'Radio him to grab a notebook, then take up position behind the house. I want names, ranks, and badge numbers, all on record. And while you two are at

44

it, get the word out: Every state trooper who showed up at this address needs to report to Boston HQ by end of day to have an imprint made of his or her boots. Failure to comply will result in immediate desk duty. You heard it straight from the state liaison officer.' She jerked her thumb at Bobby, who stood beside her rolling his eyes.

'D.D. — ' he started.

'They trampled my scene. I don't forgive. I don't forget.'

Bobby shut up. She liked that about him.

Having both secured her scene and stirred the pot, D.D. next approached the EMTs, who now had the stretcher positioned between them and were preparing to climb the steep stairs to the front door.

'Hang on,' D.D. called out.

The EMTs, one male, one female, paused as she approached.

'Sergeant Detective D.D. Warren,' D.D. introduced herself. 'I'm the one in charge of this circus. You getting ready to transport Trooper Leoni?'

A heavyset woman at the head of the stretcher nodded, already turning back toward the stairs.

'Whoa, whoa, whoa,' D.D. said quickly. 'I need five minutes. Got a couple of questions for Trooper Leoni before she goes on her merry way.'

'Trooper Leoni has sustained a significant head wound,' the female answered firmly. 'We're taking her to the hospital for a CT scan. You got your job, we got ours.'

45

The EMTs took a step closer to the stairs. D.D. moved to intercept.

'Is Trooper Leoni at risk for bleeding out?' D.D. pressed. She glanced at the woman's name tag, adding belatedly, 'Marla.'

Marla did not appear impressed. 'No.'

'Is she in any immediate physical danger?'

'Swelling of the brain,' the EMT rattled off, 'bleeding of the brain . . . '

'Then we'll keep her awake and make her recite her name and date. Isn't that what you guys do for a concussion? Count to five, forward and backward, name, rank, and serial number, yada yada yada.'

Beside her, Bobby sighed. D.D. was definitely toeing a line. She kept her attention focused on Marla, who appeared even more exasperated than Bobby.

'Detective — ' Marla started.

'Kid missing,' D.D. interrupted. 'Six-year-old girl, God knows where and in what kind of danger. I just need five minutes, Marla. Maybe that's a lot to ask from you and your job and from Trooper Leoni and her injuries, but I don't think that's nearly enough to ask for a six-year-old child.'

D.D. was good. Always had been. Always would be. Marla, who appeared to be mid-forties and probably had at least one or two kids at home, not to mention how many little nieces and nephews, caved.

'Five minutes,' she said, glancing over at her partner. 'Then we're taking her out, ready or not.'

'Ready or not,' D.D. agreed, and sprinted for the stairs.

'Eat your Wheaties this morning?' Bobby muttered as he jogged up behind her.

'You're just jealous.'

'Why am I jealous?'

'Because I always get away with this shit.'

'Pride goeth before the fall,' Bobby murmured.

D.D. pushed opened the front door of the house. 'For six-year-old Sophie's sake, let's hope not.'

★ ★ ★

Trooper Leoni was still sequestered in the sunroom. D.D. and Bobby had to pass through the kitchen to get there. Brian Darby's body had been removed, leaving behind bloodstained hardwoods, a pile of evidence placards, and a thick dusting of fingerprint powder. The usual crime-scene detritus. D.D. covered her mouth and nose with her hand as she skirted through. She was still two paces ahead of Bobby and hoped he didn't notice.

Tessa Leoni looked up at Bobby and D.D.'s entrance. She held an ice bag against half of her face, which still didn't cover the blood on her lip or the oozing gash in her forehead. As D.D. walked into the sunroom, the female officer lowered the pack to reveal an eye that had already swollen shut and turned eggplant purple.

D.D. suffered a moment of shock, despite herself. Whether she believed Leoni's initial statement or not, the female trooper had definitely taken a beating. D.D. quickly glanced at the officer's hands, trying to ascertain any signs of defensive wounds. Trooper Leoni caught the motion, and covered her knuckles with the ice pack.

For a moment, the two women studied each other. Trooper Leoni seemed young to D.D., especially wearing her state blues. Long dark hair, blue eyes, heart-shaped face. Pretty girl despite the bruises and maybe more vulnerable because of them. Immediately, D.D. felt herself set on edge. Pretty and vulnerable almost always tried her patience.

D.D. surveyed the other two occupants of the room.

Standing beside Leoni was a super-sized state trooper, his shoulders thrown back in his best tough-guy stance. Conversely, sitting across from her, was a petite gray-suited older gentleman with a yellow legal pad balanced delicately on one knee. Union rep standing, D.D. determined. Union-appointed lawyer sitting. So the gang was all here.

The union rep, a fellow state trooper, spoke first.

'Trooper Leoni isn't answering questions,' he stated, jutting out his chin.

D.D. glanced at his badge. 'Trooper Lyons — '

'She has provided an initial statement,' Trooper Lyons continued stiffly. 'All other questions will have to wait until she's been treated by a doctor.' He glanced behind D.D. to the doorway. 'Where are the EMTs?'

'Getting their gear,' D.D. said soothingly. 'They'll be right up. Of course Trooper Leoni's injuries are a priority. Nothing but the best for a fellow officer.'

D.D. moved to the right, making room for Bobby to stand beside her. A united front of city and state law enforcement. Trooper Lyons didn't look impressed.

The lawyer had risen to standing. Now he held out a hand. 'Ken Cargill,' he said by way of introduction. 'I'll be representing Trooper Leoni.'

'Sergeant Detective D.D. Warren,' D.D. introduced herself, then Bobby.

'My client is not taking questions at this time,' Cargill told them. 'Once she has received the proper medical attention and we understand the full extent of her injuries, we'll let you know.'

'Understand. Not here to push. EMTs said they needed a few minutes to prepare the stretcher, grab some fluids. Thought we could use that time to cover a few basics. We got a full Amber Alert out for little Sophie, but I gotta be honest.' D.D. spread her hands in a helpless gesture. 'We have no leads. As I'm sure Trooper Leoni knows, in these kinds of cases, every minute counts.'

At the mention of Sophie's name, Trooper Leoni stiffened on the sofa. She wasn't looking at D.D., or at any of the men in the room. She had her gaze locked on a spot on the worn green carpet, hands still tucked beneath the ice pack.

'I searched everywhere,' Leoni said abruptly. 'The house, the garage, the attic, his vehicle — '

'Tessa,' Trooper Lyons interjected. 'Don't do this. You don't have to do this.'

'When was the last time you saw your daughter?' D.D. asked, seizing the opening while she had it.

'Ten forty-five last night,' the officer answered automatically, as if speaking by rote. 'I always check on Sophie before reporting for duty.'

D.D. frowned. 'You left here at ten forty-five for your eleven o'clock shift? You can make it from here to the Framingham barracks in fifteen minutes?'

Trooper Leoni shook her head. 'I don't drive to the barracks. We drive our cruisers home, so the moment we take the wheel, we start our patrols. I called the desk officer from my cruiser and declared Code 5. He assigned me my patrol area and I was good to go.'

D.D. nodded. Not being a state trooper, D.D. didn't know these things. But she was also playing a game with Trooper Leoni. The game was called establish the suspect's state of mind. That way, when Trooper Leoni inevitably said something useful, and her eager-beaver attorney sought to block that admission by claiming his client was suffering from a concussion and therefore mentally incapacitated, D.D. could point out how lucidly Leoni had answered other, easily verifiable questions. For example, if Leoni had been able to accurately recollect what time she'd called the desk officer, where she'd gone on patrol, etc., etc., then why assume she was suddenly mistaken about how she'd shot her own husband?

These were the kind of games a skilled detective knew how to play. Couple of hours ago, D.D. might not have used them on a fellow officer. She might have been willing to cut poor battered Trooper Leoni some slack, show her the kind of preferential treatment one female officer was inclined to give another. But that was before the state troopers had trampled her crime scene and placed D.D. squarely on the other side of their blue wall.

D.D. did not forgive. She did not forget.

And she did not want to be working a case right now involving a small child. But that was not something she could talk about, not even to Bobby.

'So you checked your daughter at ten forty-five . . . ' D.D. prodded.

'Sophie was asleep. I kissed her on the cheek. She . . . rolled over, pulled the covers up.'

'And your husband?'

'Downstairs. Watching TV.'

'What was he watching?'

'I didn't notice. He was drinking a beer. That distracted me. I wished . . . I preferred it when he didn't drink.'

'How many beers had he had?'

'Three.'

'You counted?'

'I checked the empties lined up next to the sink.'

'Your husband have a problem with alcohol?' D.D. asked bluntly.

Leoni finally looked up at D.D., peering at her with one good eye, as the other half of her

51

face remained a swollen, pulpy mess. 'Brian was home sixty days at a stretch with nothing to do. I had work. Sophie had school. But he had nothing. Sometimes, he drank. And sometimes . . . Drinking wasn't good for him.'

'So your husband, who you wished didn't drink, had had three beers and you still left him alone with your daughter.'

'Hey — ' Trooper Lyons started to interrupt again.

But Tessa Leoni said, 'Yes, ma'am. I left my daughter with her drunken stepdad. And if I had known . . . I would've killed him then, goddammit. I would've shot him last night!'

'Whoa — ' Attorney was out of the chair. But D.D. didn't pay any attention to him and neither did Leoni.

'What happened to your daughter?' D.D. wanted to know. 'What did your husband do to her?'

Leoni was already shrugging her shoulders. 'He wouldn't tell me. I got home, went upstairs. She should've been in bed. Or maybe playing on the floor. But . . . nothing. I searched and I searched and I searched. Sophie was gone.'

'He ever hit her?' D.D. asked.

'Sometimes, he got frustrated with me. But I never saw him hit her.'

'Lonely? You're gone all night. He's alone with her.'

'No! You're wrong. I would've known! She would've told me.'

'Then you tell me, Tessa. What happened to your daughter?'

'I don't know! Dammit. She's just a little girl. What kind of man hurts a child? What kind of man would *do* such a thing?'

Trooper Lyons placed his hands on her shoulders, as if trying to soothe. Trooper Leoni, however, shrugged him off. She rose to her feet, obviously agitated. The movement, however, proved too much; almost immediately, she lurched to one side.

Trooper Lyons caught her arm, lowering her carefully back to the love seat while skewering D.D. with an angry stare.

'Steady,' he said gruffly to Tessa Leoni, while continuing to glare at D.D. and Bobby.

'You don't understand, you don't understand,' the mother/trooper was murmuring. She didn't look pretty or vulnerable anymore. Her face had taken on an unhealthy pallor; she looked like she was going to vomit, her hand patting the empty seat beside her. 'Sophie's so brave and adventurous. But she's scared of the dark. Terrified. Once, when she was nearly three, she climbed into the trunk of my cruiser and it closed and she screamed and screamed and screamed. If you could've heard her scream. Then you would know, you'd understand . . . '

Leoni turned to Trooper Lyons. She grabbed his beefy hands, peering up at him desperately. 'She's gotta be safe, right? You would keep her safe, right? You would take care of her? Bring her home. Before dark, Shane. Before dark. Please, please, I'm begging you, *please*.'

Lyons didn't seem to know how to respond or handle the outburst. He remained holding

Leoni's shoulders, meaning D.D. was the one who grabbed the waste bucket and got it under the ashen-faced woman just in time. Leoni puked until she dry-heaved, then puked a little more.

'My head,' she groaned, already sagging back into the love seat.

'Hey, who's disrupting our patient? Anyone who's not an EMT, out!' Marla and her partner had returned. They muscled into the room, Marla giving D.D. a pointed glance. D.D. and Bobby took the hint, turning toward the adjoining kitchen.

But Leoni, of all people, grabbed D.D.'s wrist. The strength in her pale hand startled D.D., brought her up short.

'My daughter needs you,' the officer whispered, as the EMTs took her other hand and started administering the IV.

'Of course,' D.D. said stupidly.

'You must find her. Promise me!'

'We'll do our best — '

'*Promise me!*'

'Okay, okay,' D.D. heard herself say. 'We'll find her. Of course. Just . . . get to the hospital. Take care of yourself.'

Marla and her partner moved Leoni to the backboard. The female officer was still thrashing, trying to push them away, trying to pull D.D. closer. It was hard to say. In a matter of seconds, the EMTs had her strapped down and were out the door, Trooper Lyons following stoically in her wake.

The lawyer stayed behind, holding out a card

as they stepped from the sunroom back into the home. 'I'm sure you understand none of that was admissible. Among other things, my client never waived her rights, and oh yes, she's suffering from a *concussion*.'

Having gotten his say, the lawyer also departed, leaving D.D. and Bobby standing alone next to the kitchen. D.D. didn't have to cover her nose anymore. She was too distracted from the interview with Officer Leoni to notice the smell.

'Is it just me,' D.D. said, 'or does it look like someone took a meat mallet to Tessa Leoni's face?'

'And yet there's not a single cut or scrape on her hands,' Bobby provided. 'No broken nails or bruised knuckles.'

'So someone beat the shit out of her, and she never lifted a hand to stop it?' D.D. asked skeptically.

'Until she shot him dead,' Bobby corrected mildly.

D.D. rolled her eyes, feeling perplexed and not liking it. Tessa Leoni's facial injuries appeared real enough. Her fear over her daughter's disappearance genuine. But the scene . . . the lack of defensive wounds, a trained officer who went first for her gun when she had an entire duty belt at her disposal, a female who'd just given such an emotional statement while studiously avoiding all eye contact . . .

D.D. was deeply uncomfortable with the scene, or maybe, with a fellow female officer who'd grabbed her arm and basically begged

D.D. to find her missing child.

Six-year-old Sophie Leoni, who was terrified of the dark.

Oh God. This case was gonna hurt.

'Sounds like she and the husband got into it,' Bobby was saying. 'He overwhelmed her, knocked her to the floor, so she went for her gun. Only afterward did she discover her daughter missing. And realize, of course, that she'd just killed the only person who could probably tell her where Sophie is.'

D.D. nodded, still considering. 'Here's a question: What's a trooper's first instinct — to protect herself or to protect others?'

'Protect others.'

'And what's a mother's first priority? Protect herself or protect her child?'

'Her child.'

'And yet, Trooper Leoni's daughter is missing, and the first thing she does is notify her union rep and find a good lawyer.'

'Maybe she's not a very good trooper,' Bobby said.

'Maybe, she's not a very good mother,' D.D. replied.

6

I fell in love when I was eight years old. Not the way you think. I had climbed the tree in my front yard, taking a seat on the lower branch and staring down at the tiny patch of burnt-out lawn below me. Probably, my father was at work. He owned his own garage, opening up shop by six most mornings and not returning till after five most nights. Probably, my mother was asleep. She passed the days in the hushed darkness of my parents' bedroom. Sometimes, she'd call to me and I'd bring her little things — a glass of water, a couple of crackers. But mostly, she waited for my father to come home.

He'd fix dinner for all of us, my mother finally shuffling out of her dark abyss to join us at the little round table. She would smile at him, as he passed the potatoes. She would chew mechanically, as he spoke gruffly of his day.

Then, dinner completed, she would return to the shadows at the end of the hall, her daily allotment of energy all used up. I'd wash dishes. My father would watch TV. Nine p.m., lights out. Another day done for the Leoni family.

I learned early on not to invite over classmates. And I learned the importance of being quiet.

Now it was hot, it was July, and I had another endless day stretching out before me. Other kids were probably living it up at summer camp, or

57

splashing away at some community pool. Or maybe, the really lucky ones, had happy, fun parents who took them to the beach.

I sat in a tree.

A girl appeared. Riding a hot pink scooter, blonde braids flapping beneath a deep purple helmet as she flew down the street. At the last moment, she glanced up and spotted my skinny legs. She screeched to a halt beneath me, peering up.

'My name is Juliana Sophia Howe,' she said. 'I'm new to this neighborhood. You should come down and play with me.'

So I did.

Juliana Sophia Howe was also eight years old. Her parents had just moved to Framingham from Harvard, Mass. Her father was an accountant. Her mother stayed home and did things like tend the house and cut the crusts off peanut butter and jelly sandwiches.

By mutual agreement, we always played at Juliana's house. She had a bigger yard, with real grass. She had a Little Mermaid sprinkler head and a Little Mermaid slip and slide. We could play for hours, then her mother would serve us lemonade with pink curly straws and thick slices of red watermelon.

Juliana had an eleven-year-old brother, Thomas, who was a real 'pain in the ass.' She also had fifteen cousins and tons of aunts and uncles. On the really hot days, her whole family would gather at her grandma's house by the South Shore and they would go to the beach. Sometimes, she got to ride the carousel, and

Juliana considered herself an expert on grabbing the brass ring, though she hadn't actually gotten it yet — but she was close.

I didn't have cousins, or aunts and uncles or a grandmother near the South Shore. Instead, I told Juliana how my parents had made a baby when I was four years old. Except the baby was born blue and the doctors had to bury him in the ground, and my mother had to come home from the hospital and move into her bedroom. Sometimes, she cried in the middle of the day. Sometimes, she cried in the middle of the night.

My father told me I was not to talk about it, but one day, I'd found a shoe box tucked behind my father's bowling ball in the hall closet. In the box had been a little blue cap and a little blue blanket and a pair of little blue booties. There was also a picture of a perfectly white newborn baby boy with bright red lips. At the bottom of the picture, someone had written *Joseph Andrew Leoni*.

So I guess I had a little brother Joey, but he had died and my father had been working and my mother had been crying ever since.

Juliana thought about this. She decided we should have a proper mass for baby Joey, so she got out her rosary beads. She showed me how to loop the dark green beads around my fingers and say a little prayer. Next, we needed to sing a song, so we sang 'Away in the Manger,' because it was about a baby and we sort of knew the words. Then it was time for the eulogy.

Juliana did the honors. She'd heard one before, at her grandfather's funeral. She thanked the Lord for taking care of baby Joey. She said it was good he did not suffer. She said she was sure he was having a great time playing poker in heaven, and looking down upon us all.

Then, she took both of my hands in her own, and told me she was very sorry for my loss.

I started to cry, big noisy sobs that horrified me. But Juliana just patted my back. There, there, she said. Then she cried with me, and her mom came up to check on us because we were making such a racket. I thought Juliana would tell her mother everything. Instead, Juliana announced that we needed emergency chocolate chip cookies. So her mother went downstairs and made us a batch.

Juliana Sophia Howe was that kind of friend. You could cry on her shoulder and trust her to keep your secrets. You could play in her yard and count on her to give you her best toys. You could stay in her house and depend on her to share her family.

When I went into labor all alone, I pictured Juliana holding my hand. And when I finally held my daughter for the first time, I named her in honor of my childhood friend.

Juliana, unfortunately, doesn't know any of these things.

She has not spoken to me in over ten years.

For while Juliana Sophia Howe was the best thing that ever happened to me, turned out, I was the worst thing that ever happened to her.

Sometimes, love is like that.

★ ★ ★

In the back of the ambulance, the female EMT administered intravenous fluids. She had produced a pan just in time for me to vomit again.

My cheek burned. My sinus cavities had filled with blood. I needed to hold it together. Mostly, I wanted to close my eyes and let the world slip away. The light hurt my eyes. The memories seared my brain.

'Tell me your name,' the EMT instructed, forcing me back to attention.

I opened my mouth. No words came out.

She offered me a sip of water, helped clean my cracked lips.

'Tessa Leoni,' I finally managed.

'What is today's date, Tessa?'

For a second, I couldn't answer. No numbers appeared in my head and I started to panic. All I could picture was Sophie's empty bed.

'March thirteen,' I finally whispered.

'Two plus two?'

Another pause. 'Four.'

Marla grunted, adjusting the line carrying clear fluids to the back of my hand. 'Nice shiner,' she remarked.

I didn't answer.

'Almost as pretty as the bruise covering half your ass. Husband like steel-toed boots?'

I didn't answer, just pictured my daughter's smiling face.

The ambulance slowed, maybe ready to turn into the emergency room. I could only hope.

Marla studied me a second longer. 'I don't get it,' she said abruptly. 'You're a cop. You've received special training, you've handled these kinds of calls yourself. Surely you of all people oughtta know . . . ' She seemed to catch herself. 'Well, guess that's the way these things go, right? Domestic violence happens across all social groups. Even those who should know better.'

The ambulance came to a stop. Thirty seconds later, the back doors flew open and I rolled into daylight.

I didn't look at Marla anymore. I kept my eyes on the gray March sky rushing past overhead.

Inside the hospital, there was a lot of activity at once. An emergency room nurse charged forward to meet us, ushering us into an exam room. There was paperwork to be filled out, including the omnipresent HEPA form advising me of my right to privacy. As the nurse assured me, my doctor would not discuss my case with anyone, not even other members of law enforcement, as that would violate doctor-patient confidentiality. What she did not say, but I already knew, was that my medical charts were considered neutral and could be subpoenaed by the DA. Meaning any statements I made to the doctor, which were recorded in those charts . . .

Always a loophole somewhere. Just ask a cop.

Paperwork completed, the nurse turned to the next matter at hand.

Last night, I had spent fifteen minutes donning my uniform. First, basic black panties, then a black sports bra, then a silk undershirt to keep the next layer — heavy body armor — from chafing my skin. I'd rolled on black dress socks, then my navy blue trousers with their electric blue accent stripes. Next I'd laced up my boots,

62

because I'd already learned the hard way I couldn't reach my feet once I'd donned my vest. So socks, trousers, boots, then back to the top half, adding my bulky vest, which I covered with a state police turtleneck in deference to the weather, then topped with my official light blue blouse. I had to adjust the vest under my turtleneck, then work to get three layers — silk undershirt, turtleneck, and blouse — tucked into my pants. Next I belted my slacks with a broad black belt to hold them in place. Then I got my gear.

Twenty pound black leather duty belt, which I wrapped over my pants belt, and attached with four Velcro keepers. Next taking my Sig Sauer semiauto from the gun safe in the bedroom closet and inserting it into the holster on my right hip. Clipping my cellphone to the front of my duty belt, then attaching my police pager to the clip on my right shoulder. Checking my radio on my left hip, inspecting my two extra ammo clips, the steel baton, pepper spray, one pair of cuffs, and Taser. Then slipping three ink pens into the sewn inserts on my left shirt-sleeve.

Finally, the pièce de résistance, my official state trooper hat.

I always paused to study my reflection in the mirror. A state trooper's uniform is not just a look, but a feel. The weight of my duty belt pulling at my hips. The bulk of my body armor, flattening out my chest, broadening my shoulders. The tight band of my hat, pulled down low onto my forehead and casting an impenetrable shadow across my eyes.

Command presence. Never let them see you sweat, baby.

The nurse stripped my uniform from me. She removed my light blue blouse, my turtleneck, body armor, undershirt, bra. She pulled off my boots, unrolled my socks, unclasped my belt, and tugged my trousers down my legs, before doing the same with my underwear.

Each item was removed, then bagged and tagged as evidence in the case the Boston cops would be building against me.

Finally, the nurse removed my gold stud earrings, my watch, and my wedding band. Can't wear jewelry for the CT scan I was told as she stripped me bare.

The nurse handed me a hospital gown, then bustled away with her evidence bags and my personal possessions. I didn't move. Just lay there, feeling the loss of my uniform, the shame of my own nakedness.

I could hear a TV down the hall broadcasting my daughter's name. Next would come an image of her school photo, snapped just this October. Sophie wore her favorite yellow ruffled top. She was turned slightly sideways, looking back at the camera with her big blue eyes, an excited smile on her face because she loved pictures and she especially wanted this photo, her first since she'd lost her top front tooth, and the tooth fairy had brought her a whole dollar which she couldn't wait to spend.

My eyes burned. There is pain, then there was pain. All the words I could not speak. All the images I couldn't get out of my head.

The nurse returned. She stuck my arms in the Johnny gown, then had me roll to the side so she could tie it in the back.

Two technicians arrived. They whisked me away to the CT scan, my gaze locked on the blur of ceiling tiles whizzing by overhead.

'Pregnant?' one asked.

'What?'

'Are you pregnant?'

'No.'

'Claustrophobic?'

'No.'

'Then this will be a breeze.'

I was wheeled into another sterile room, this one dominated by a large, donut-shaped machine. The technicians didn't let me stand, but hoisted me from the gurney directly onto the table.

I was instructed to lie absolutely still while the donut-shaped X-ray moved around my head, taking cross sections of my skull. A computer would then combine the two-dimensional X-ray images to form a three-dimensional model.

In thirty minutes, the doctor would have a graphic image of my brain and my bones, including any swelling, bruising, or bleeding.

The technicians made it sound very easy.

Lying alone on the table, I wondered how deep the scanner could peer. I wondered if it could see all the things I saw every time I closed my eyes. Blood, appearing on the wall behind my husband, then streaking down to the kitchen floor. My husband's eyes, widening in surprise as he looked down, seemed to actually notice the red stains blooming across his muscled chest.

Brian sliding down, down, down. Me, now standing over him, and watching the light dim in his eyes.

'I love you,' I had whispered to my husband, right before the light fled. 'I'm sorry. I'm sorry. I love you . . . '

There is pain, then there was pain.

The machine started to move. I closed my eyes and I allowed myself one last memory of my husband. His final words, as he died on our kitchen floor.

'Sorry,' Brian had gasped, three bullets in his torso. 'Tessa . . . love you . . . more.'

7

With Brian Darby's body removed, and Tessa Leoni whisked off to the hospital, the immediate practicalities of the homicide investigation began to wind down while the search for six-year-old Sophie Leoni ramped up.

With that in mind, D.D. summoned the taskforce officers to the white command van and began cracking the whip.

Witnesses. D.D. wanted a short list from all the uniformed officers of any and all neighbors worth a second interview. She then assigned six homicide detectives to begin those interviews ASAP. If someone was a credible witness or potential suspect, she wanted them identified and talking in the next three minutes.

Cameras. Boston was riddled with them. City installed them to monitor traffic. Businesses installed them for security. D.D. formed a three-man team whose job was to do nothing but identify all cameras in a two mile radius and skim through all video footage from the past twelve hours, starting with the video cameras closest to the house and working out.

Known associates. Friends, family, neighbors, teachers, babysitters, employers; if someone had ever set foot on the property, D.D. wanted their name on her desk in the next forty-five minutes. In particular, she wanted all teachers, playmates, and caretakers of Sophie Leoni rounded up and cranked through the wringer. Full background checks, a search of their homes if the detective could talk his way through the door. Officers needed to be eliminating friends and identifying foes and they needed to be doing it now, now, now.

Other people out there knew this family. Enemies from the husband's job, felons snagged in Trooper Leoni's patrols, maybe partners in torrid affairs, or longtime personal confidantes. Other people knew Brian Darby and Tessa Leoni. And one of those people might know what had happened to a six-year-old girl who'd last been seen sleeping in her own bed.

Time was not on their side. Get out, hit the streets, beat the clock, D.D. ordered her crew.

Then she shut up and sent them back to work.

The Boston detectives scrambled. The brass nodded. She and Bobby returned to the house.

D.D. trusted her fellow investigators to begin the enormous task of sifting through all the nuances of an entire family's existence. What she wanted most for herself, however, was to live and breathe the victims' final hours. She wanted to absorb the crime scene into her DNA. She wanted to inundate herself with the tiniest little domestic details, from paint choices to decorative knickknacks. She wanted to set and reset the scene a dozen different ways in her mind, and she wanted to populate it with a little girl, a merchant marine father, and a state trooper mother. This one house, these three lives, these past ten hours. Everything came down to that. A home, a family, a collision course of multiple lives with tragic consequences.

D.D. needed to see it, feel it, live it. Then she could dissect the family down to its deepest darkest truth, which in turn would bring her Sophie Leoni.

D.D.'s stomach flip-flopped queasily. She tried not to think about it as she and Bobby once again entered the bloodstained kitchen.

By mutual consent, they started upstairs, which featured two dormered bedrooms, separated by a full bath. The bedroom facing the street appeared to be the master, dominated by a queen-sized bed with a simple wooden headboard and dark blue comforter. Bedding immediately struck D.D. as more his than hers. Nothing else in the room changed her opinion.

The broad dresser, a beat-up oak, screamed of bachelor days. It was topped by an old thirty-six inch TV which was tuned to ESPN. Plain white walls, stark wood floors. Not so much a domestic retreat, as a way station, D.D. thought. A place to sleep, change clothes, then exit.

D.D. tried the closet. Three-fourths of it yielded sharply pressed men's shirts, arranged by color. Then came half a dozen neatly hanging blue jeans. Then a mishmash of cotton slacks and tops, two state police uniforms, one dress uniform, and one orange flower-printed sundress.

'He took up more space in the closet,' D.D. reported to Bobby, who was examining the dresser.

'Men have been killed for less,' he agreed.

'Seriously. Check this out. Color-coded shirts,

pressed blue jeans. Brian Darby was beyond anal-retentive and bordering on just plain freaky.'

'Brian Darby was also getting seriously huge. Look at this.' Bobby held up a framed eight-by-ten portrait with his gloved hands. D.D. finished inspecting the empty gun safe she'd found in the left-hand corner of the closet, then crossed to him.

The framed picture featured Tessa Leoni in the orange sundress with a white sweater, holding a small bouquet of tiger lilies. Brian Darby stood beside her in a brown sports jacket, a single tiger lily pinned to his collar. A little girl, presumably Sophie Leoni, stood in front of both of them, wearing a dark green velvet dress with a ring of lilies in her hair. All three were beaming at the camera, happy family celebrating a happy day.

'Wedding photo,' D.D. murmured.

'That would be my guess. Now look at Darby. Check out his shoulders.'

D.D. obediently checked out the former groom and now dead husband. Good-looking guy, she decided. Had a military/cop vibe going on with the buzz-cut blonde hair, chiseled chin, squared shoulders. But the impression was balanced by warm brown eyes, crinkling at the corners from the impact of his smile. He looked happy, relaxed. Not the kind of guy you'd immediately suspect of battering his wife — or, for that matter, ironing his blue jeans.

D.D. handed the picture back to Bobby. 'I don't get it. So he was happy on his wedding day. That doesn't mean anything.'

70

'Nah. He was *smaller* on his wedding day. That Brian Darby is a fit one eighty. Bet he worked out, kept active. Dead Brian Darby, on the other hand . . . '

D.D. remembered what Bobby had told her earlier. 'Big guy, you said. Two ten, two twenty, probably a weight lifter. So not that he got married and he got fat. You're saying, he got married and he *muscled up.*'

Bobby nodded.

D.D. thought about the picture again. 'It's not easy to be in a relationship where the woman is the one who carries a gun,' she murmured.

Bobby didn't touch that statement, and she was grateful.

'We should find his gym,' he said now. 'Check out his regimen. Inquire about known supplements.'

' 'Roid rage?'

'Worth asking about.'

They moved out of the master, into the adjoining bath. This room, at least, had a splash of personality. A brightly striped shower curtain was drawn around an old claw-foot tub. A yellow-duckie area rug dotted the tiled floor. Layers of blue and yellow towels warmed up wooden towel racks.

This room also displayed more signs of life — a Barbie toothbrush lying on the edge of the sink, a pile of purple hair elastics in a basket on the back of the toilet, a clear plastic spit cup declaring 'Daddy's Little Princess.'

D.D. checked the medicine cabinet. She found three prescription bottles, one made out to Brian

Darby for Ambien, a sleep aid. One made out to Sophie Leoni, involving some kind of topical eye ointment. A third for Tessa Leoni, hydrocodone, a painkiller.

She showed the bottle to Bobby. He made a note.

'Have to follow up with the doc. See if she had an injury, maybe something from the job.'

D.D. nodded. Rest of the medicine cabinet held a plethora of lotions, shaving creams, razors, and colognes. Only thing of note, she thought, was the fairly impressive stash of first-aid supplies. Lotta Band-Aids, she thought, in a lotta different sizes. A battered wife, stockpiling for inevitable repairs, or just life as an active family? She checked under the sink, found the usual mix of soap, toilet paper, feminine hygiene products, and cleaning supplies.

They moved on.

The next room clearly belonged to Sophie. Soft pink walls, with stenciled flowers in pale green and baby blue. A flower-shaped rug. A wall of bright white cubbies brimming with dolls, dresses, and glittering ballet shoes. Tessa and Brian lived in a dorm. Little Sophie, on the other hand, inhabited a magical garden complete with bunnies running along the floorboards and butterflies painted around the windows.

It was beyond obscene, D.D. thought, to stand in the middle of such a space, and start looking for signs of blood.

Her hand was pressed to her stomach. She didn't even notice it as she carefully began her first visual inspection of the bed.

'Luminol?' she murmured.

'No hits,' Bobby responded.

Per protocol, the crime-scene techs had sprayed Sophie Leoni's sheets with luminol, which reacted with bodily fluids such as blood and semen. The lack of hits meant the sheets were clean. Which didn't mean Sophie Leoni had never been sexually assaulted; just meant she hadn't been recently assaulted on this set of linens. The crime-scene techs would also check the laundry, even pull bedding out of the washing machine if necessary. Unless someone knew to clean all items in bleach, it was amazing what the luminol could find on 'clean' linens.

More things D.D. didn't want to know while standing in the middle of a magical garden.

She wondered who had painted this room. Tessa? Brian? Or maybe the three of them working together back in the days when the love was still new and the family felt fresh and committed to one another.

She wondered just how many nights had passed before Sophie woke up to the first sound of a distinct smack, a muffled scream. Or maybe Sophie hadn't been sleeping at all. Maybe she'd been sitting at the kitchen table, or playing with a doll in the corner.

Maybe she'd run to her mother the first time. Maybe . . .

Ah, Jesus Christ. D.D. did not want to be working this case right now.

She fisted her hands, turned toward the window, and focused on the weak March daylight.

Bobby had stilled next to the wall. He was studying her, but didn't say a word.

Once more, she was grateful.

'We should find out if there's a favorite snuggle toy,' she said at last.

'Rag doll. Green dress, brown yarn hair, blue button eyes. Named Gertrude.'

D.D. nodded, scanning the room slowly. She identified a night-light — *Sophie's terrified of the dark* — but no snuggle toy. 'I don't see it.'

'Neither did the first responder. So far, we're operating under the assumption the doll is missing, too.'

'Her pajamas?'

'Trooper Leoni said her daughter was wearing a long-sleeved set, pink with yellow horses. No sign of them.'

D.D. had a thought. 'What about her coat, hat, and snow boots?'

'Don't have that in my notes.'

For the first time, D.D. felt a glimmer of hope. 'Missing coat and hat means she was roused out of bed in the middle of the night. Not given the time to change, but the chance to bundle up.'

'No need to bundle up a corpse,' Bobby remarked.

They left the room and pounded down the stairs. Inspected the coat closet, then the bin of shoes and winter accessories tucked by the front door. No little kid coat. No little kid hat. No little kid boots.

'Sophie Leoni was bundled up!' D.D. declared triumphantly.

'Sophie Leoni left the house alive.'

'Perfect. Now, all we gotta do is find her before nightfall.'

* * *

They returned upstairs long enough to examine the windows for signs of forced entry. Finding none, they headed downstairs for the same drill. Both doors featured relatively new hardware and bolt locks, none of which showed signs of tampering. The windows in the sunroom, they discovered, were so old and moisture-warped they refused to budge.

All in all, the house appeared secure. To judge from the look on Bobby's face, he hadn't expected anything different and neither had D.D. Sad rule in missing kid cases — most of the time, the trouble came from inside the home, not outside it.

They toured the family room, which reminded D.D. of the bedroom. Plain walls, wooden floors topped by a beige area rug. The black leather L-shaped sofa seemed more like a his purchase than a hers. A fairly new-looking laptop computer sat at one end of the couch, still plugged into the wall. Room also boasted a flat-screen TV, mounted above a sleek entertain-ment unit that housed a state-of-the-art audio system, Blu-ray DVD player, and Wii gaming console.

'Boys and their toys,' D.D. remarked.

'Engineer,' Bobby said again.

D.D. examined a small art table set up in the corner for Sophie. On one side of the table sat a stack of blank white paper. In the middle was a caddy filled with crayons. That was it. No works in progress on the table. No displays of completed genius on the walls. Very organized, she thought, especially for a six-year-old.

The starkness of the home was starting to wig her out. People did not live like this and people with kids definitely should not live like this.

They crossed into the kitchen, where D.D. stood as far away from the outline of the corpse as she could. Bloodstain, shattered glass, and toppled chairs aside, the kitchen was as meticulous as the rest of the house. Also tired and dated. Thirty-year-old dark wood cabinets, plain white appliances, stained Formica counter-top. First thing Alex would do to this house, D.D. thought, was gut and modernize the kitchen.

But not Brian Darby. He spent his money on electronics, a leather sofa, and his car. Not the house.

'They made an effort for Sophie,' D.D. murmured out loud, 'but not for each other.'

Bobby looked at her.

'Think about it,' she continued. 'It's an old vintage house that's still an old vintage house. As you keep pointing out, he's an engineer, meaning he's probably got some basic skills with power tools. Combined household income is a good two hundred grand a year, plus Brian Darby has this whole sixty days of vacation thing going on. Meaning they have some expertise, some time, and some resources they could spend on the home. But they don't. Only in Sophie's room.

She gets the fresh paint, new furniture, pretty bedding, etc. They made an effort for her, but not for themselves. Makes me wonder in how many other areas of their life that same rule applied.'

'Most parents focus on their kids,' Bobby observed mildly.

'They haven't even hung a picture.'

'Trooper Leoni works long hours. Brian Darby ships out for months at a time. Maybe, when they're home, they have other priorities.'

D.D. shrugged. 'Like what?'

Bobby nodded. 'Come on. I'll show you the garage.'

★　★　★

The garage freaked D.D. out. The broad, two-bay space was lined on all three sides with the craziest Peg-Board system she'd ever seen. Seriously, floor to ceiling of Peg-Boards, which were then fitted with shelving brackets and bike holders and plastic bins for sporting goods and even a custom golf bag holder.

D.D. took in the space and was struck by two things at once: Brian Darby did apparently have a lot of outdoor hobbies, and he needed professional help for his anal-retentiveness.

'The floor is clean,' D.D. said. 'It's March, it's snowy, and the entire city has been sanded within an inch of its life. How can the floor be this clean?'

'He parked his car on the street.'

'He parked his sixty thousand dollar SUV on

77

one of the busiest streets in Boston rather than dirty his garage?'

'Trooper Leoni also parked her cruiser out front. Department likes us to keep our vehicles visible in the neighborhood — presence of a cop car is viewed as a deterrent.'

'This is nuts,' D.D. stated. She crossed to one wall, where she found a large broom and dustpan racked side by side. Next to them sat two plastic garbage cans and a blue bin for recycling. Recycling bin revealed half a dozen green beer bottles. Garbage cans were already empty — the bags probably having been removed by the crime-scene techs. D.D. strolled by his and her dirt bikes, plus a pink number that clearly belonged to Sophie. She found a row of backpacks and a shelf dedicated to hiking boots of various weights and sizes, including a pink pair for Sophie. Hiking, biking, golfing, she determined.

Then, on the other side of the garage, she got to add skiing to the list. Six pairs of skis, three alpine, three cross country. And three sets of snowshoes.

'If Brian Darby was home, he was moving,' D.D. added to her mental profile.

'Wanting the family with him,' Bobby commented, gesturing to the wife and child sets that rounded out each trio.

'But,' D.D. mused, 'Tessa already commented — she had work, Sophie had school. Meaning, Brian was often alone. No loving family to join him, no appreciative female audience to be dazzled by his manly prowess.'

'Stereotyping,' Bobby warned.

D.D. gestured around the garage. 'Please. This is a stereotype. Engineer. Anal-retentive. If I stay in here much longer, my head will hurt.'

'You don't iron your jeans?' he asked.

'I don't label my power tools. Seriously, check this out.' She'd arrived at the workbench, where Brian Darby had arranged his power tools on a shelf bearing names for each item.

'Nice tools.' Bobby was frowning. 'Very nice tools. An easy grand worth.'

'And yet he doesn't fix up the house,' D.D. lamented. 'So far, I'm siding with Tessa on this.'

'Maybe it's not about the doing,' Bobby said. 'Maybe it's about the buying. Brian Darby likes having toys. Doesn't mean he plays with them.'

D.D. considered it. Certainly an option, and would explain the pristine condition of the garage. Easy to keep it clean if you never parked in it, never worked in it, never retrieved any of the gear from it.

But then she shook her head. 'Nah, he didn't gain thirty pounds in muscle sitting around all day. Speaking of which, where's the weight set?'

They looked around. Of all the toys, no dumbbells or free weight systems.

'Must belong to a gym,' Bobby said.

'We'll have to check that out,' D.D. concurred. 'So Brian is a doer. But his wife and child are also busy. So maybe he does some stuff on his own to pass the time. Unfortunately, he still comes home to an empty house, which leaves him restless. So first he cleans the place within an inch of its life . . . '

79

'Then,' Bobby finished, 'he tosses back a couple of beers.'

D.D. was frowning. She walked toward the far corner, where the concrete floor appeared darker. She bent down, touched the spot with her fingertips. Felt damp.

'Leak?' she murmured, trying to inspect the corner wall where moisture might be penetrating, but of course, the cinder-block surface was obscured by more Peg-Board.

'Could be.' Bobby crossed to where she knelt. 'This whole corner is built into the hillside. Could have drainage issues, even a leak from a pipe above.'

'Have to watch it, see if it grows.'

'Concerned the house will fall down on your watch?'

She looked at him. 'No, concerned it's not water from a leak. Meaning, it came from something else, and I want to know what.'

Unexpectedly, Bobby smiled. 'I don't care what the other staties say: Trooper Leoni is lucky to have you on her case, and Sophie Leoni is even luckier.'

'Oh, fuck you,' D.D. told him crossly. She straightened, more discomfited by praise than she was ever riled by criticism. 'Come on. We're heading out.'

'The pattern of the water stain told you where Sophie is?'

'No. Given that Tessa Leoni's lawyer hasn't magically called with permission to interview her yet, we're gonna focus on Brian Darby. I want to talk to his boss. I want to know exactly what kind of man needs to color-code his closet and Peg-Board his garage.'

'A control freak.'

'Exactly. And when something or someone undermines that control — '

'Just how violent does he get,' Bobby finished for her. They stood in the middle of the garage.

'I don't think a stranger abducted Sophie Leoni,' D.D. stated quietly.

Bobby paused a heartbeat. 'I don't think so either.'

'Meaning it's him, or it's her.'

'He's dead.'

'Meaning, maybe Trooper Leoni finally wised up.'

8

A woman never forgets the first time she is hit.

I was lucky. My parents never whacked me. My father never slapped my face for talking back, or spanked my behind for willful disobedience. Maybe because I was never that disobedient. Or maybe, because by the time my father got home at night, he was too tired to care. My brother died and my parents became shells of their former selves, using up all their energy just getting through the day.

By the time I was twelve, I'd come to terms with the morbid little household that passed as my own. I got into sports — soccer, softball, track team, anything that would keep me late after school and minimize the hours I spent on the homefront. Juliana liked sports, too. We were the Bobbsey twins, always in uniform, always rushing off somewhere.

I took some hits on the playing field. A line drive to the chest that knocked me flat on my back. I realized for the first time that you really do see stars when the breath has been knocked from your lungs and your skull ricochets against the hard earth.

Then there were miscellaneous soccer injuries, a head butt to the nose, cleats to the knee, the occasional elbow to the gut. Take it from me, girls can be tough. We dish out and man up with the best of them, particularly in the heat of battle, trying to score one for our team.

But those injuries were nothing personal. Just the kind of collateral damage that happens when you and your opponent both want the ball. After the game, you shook hands, slapped each other on the butt, and meant it.

First time I really had to fight was at the Academy. I knew I would receive rigorous training in hand-to-hand combat and I was looking forward to it. A lone female living in Boston? Hand-to-hand combat was an excellent idea, whether I made it as a trooper or not.

For two weeks, we practiced drills. Basic defensive stances for protecting our face, our kidneys, and, of course, our sidearms. Never forget your weapon, we were lectured again and again. Most cops who lose their gun are then shot and killed with that gun. First line of defense, subdue the offending party before ever getting within arm's length. But in the event things go sour and you find yourself in a personal combat situation, protect your weapon, and strike hard first chance you get.

Turned out, I didn't know how to deliver a punch. Sounded easy enough. But I fisted my hand wrong, had a tendency to overuse my arm, versus throwing my whole body behind the blow by rotating at the waist. So there were a couple more weeks, teaching all of us, even the big guys, how to pack a punch.

Six weeks into it, the instructors decided we'd had enough drills. Time to practice what they'd preached.

They divvied us up into two teams. We all

donned protective padding and, to start, were armed with padded bars the instructors affectionately referred to as pogo sticks. Then, they turned us loose.

Don't believe for a second I got to fight another woman of my approximate size and weight. That would be too easy. As a female officer, I was expected to handle anything and anyone. So the trainers made their picks deliberately random. I ended up across from another recruit, named Chuck, who was six one, two hundred and forty pounds, and a former football player.

He didn't even try to hit me. He just ran straight at me and knocked me flat on my ass. I went down like a ton of bricks, remembering once more that line drive to my chest as I struggled to regain my breath.

The instructor blew his whistle. Chuck offered me a hand up, and we tried again.

This time, I was aware of my fellow recruits watching. I registered my instructor's scowl at my disappointing performance. I fixated on the fact this was supposed to be my new life. If I couldn't defend myself, if I couldn't do this, I couldn't become a trooper. Then what would I do? How would I earn enough money for Sophie and me to live? How would I provide for my daughter? What would happen to us?

Chuck rushed. This time, I stepped to the side and slammed my pogo stick into his gut. I had approximately half a second to feel good about myself. Then two hundred and forty pounds of Chuck straightened, laughed, and came back at me.

It got ugly after that. To this day, I don't recall it all. I remember starting to feel genuinely panicked. That I was blocking and moving, and putting my shoulder behind the blow, and still Chuck kept coming and Chuck kept coming. Two hundred and forty pounds of linebacker against my one hundred and twenty pounds of desperate new motherhood.

The padded end of his pogo stick connecting with my face. My head snapped back as my nose absorbed the blow. I staggered, eyes flooding with instant tears, off balance, half-blinded, wanting to fall, but realizing frantically that I couldn't go down. He'd kill me. That's how it felt. Couldn't go down or I'd be dead.

Then, at the last second, I did fall, into a tight little ball that I then sprang out of, straight into the towering giant's legs. I caught him at the knees, jerked sideways, and toppled him like a redwood.

The instructor blew the whistle. My class-mates cheered.

I staggered to standing, touching gingerly at my nose.

'That's gonna leave a mark,' my instructor informed me cheerfully.

I crossed to Chuck, offered him a hand up.

He accepted gratefully enough. 'Sorry 'bout the face,' he said, looking sheepish. Poor big guy, having to take on the girl.

I assured him it was all right. We were all doing what we had to do. Then we got to square off against new partners and do it all over again.

Later that night, curled up alone in my dorm

room, I finally cradled my nose with my hand and cried. Because I didn't know if I could go through that again. Because I wasn't sure if I was really prepared for a new life where I had to hit and be hit. Where I might honestly have to fight for my life.

At that moment, I didn't want to be a trooper anymore. I just wanted to go home to my baby girl. I wanted to hold Sophie and inhale the scent of her shampoo. I wanted to feel her chubby little hands pressed against my neck. I wanted to feel my ten-month-old daughter's unconditional love.

Instead, I got pummeled the next day, and the day after that. I endured bruised ribs, whacked shins, and aching wrists. I learned to take a blow. I learned to deliver in kind. Until by the end of the twenty-five-week course, I came out of the gate swinging with the best of them, covered in purple welts but ready to rumble.

Tiny, fast, and tough.

Giant Killer, my fellow recruits called me, and I was proud of the nickname.

I remembered those days now, as the doctor examined the results from the CT scan, then gently probed the mass of swollen purple flesh around my eye.

'Fracture of the zygomatic bone,' he murmured, adding for my benefit: 'Your cheek is broken.'

More perusing of film images, more inspection of my skull. 'No sign of hematoma or contusion of the brain. Nausea? Headache?'

I murmured yes to both.

'Name and date.'

I managed my name, blanked on the date.

Doctor's turn to nod. 'Given the clear CT scan, it would seem you have only a concussion to go with your fractured zygomatic. And what happened here?' He finished with my head, moving to my torso, where the yellow and green remnants of a fading bruise covered half my ribs.

I didn't answer, just stared at the ceiling.

He palpitated my stomach. 'Does this hurt?'

'No.'

He rotated my right arm, then my left, searching for further signs of damage. He found it on my left hip, another deep purple bruise, this time in the shape of a rounded arc, like what might be formed from the toe of a work boot.

I'd seen bruises in the shape of men's rings, watch faces, even an imprint of a quarter on a female who'd been slugged by a boyfriend holding a roll of coins. Judging by the doctor's face, he'd seen it all, as well.

Dr. Raj smoothed my gown back in place, retrieved my medical chart, made some notes.

'Cheek fracture will heal best if left alone,' he stated. 'We'll keep you overnight to monitor the concussion. If your nausea and headache have subsided by morning, chances are you may go home.'

I didn't say anything.

The doctor stepped closer, cleared his throat.

'There is a bump on your left sixth rib,' he stated. 'A fracture I suspect did not heal correctly.'

He paused as if waiting for me to say

something, perhaps a statement he could enter into my medical chart: *Patient says husband knocked her down and kicked her in the ribs. Patient says husband has a favorite baseball bat.*

I said nothing, because statements became records, and records became evidence that could be used against you.

'Did you wrap your ribs yourself?' the doctor asked.

'Yes.'

The doctor grunted, my one admission filling in all his blanks.

The doctor saw me as a victim, just as the EMT had seen me as a victim. They were both wrong. I was a survivor and I was currently walking a tightrope where I absolutely, positively could not afford to fall.

Dr. Raj studied me again. 'Rest is the best medicine for healing,' he said finally. 'Given your concussion, I cannot prescribe a narcotic, but I will have a nurse bring you some ibuprofen for the pain.'

'Thank you.'

'In the future,' he said, 'should you injure your ribs, please come to me immediately. I would like to see them better wrapped.'

'I'll be all right,' I said.

Dr. Raj did not appear convinced. 'Rest,' he repeated. 'The pain and the swelling will subside soon enough. Though I have a feeling you already know that by now.'

The doctor departed.

My cheek burned. My head throbbed. But I was satisfied.

I was awake, I was lucid. And finally, I was alone.

Time to plan.

My fingers fisted against the sheets. I studied the ceiling tiles with my one good eye, and used my pain to steel my resolve.

A woman remembers the first time she is hit. But with any luck, she also remembers the first time she fights back and wins.

I am the Giant Killer.

Just gotta think. Just gotta plan. Just gotta get one step ahead.

I could do this. I would do this.

All I want for Christmas is my two front teeth, my two front teeth, my two front teeth.

Then, I rolled onto my side, curled up in a ball, and wept.

9

When D.D. wasn't overseeing an interagency taskforce charged with solving a murder and rescuing a child, she led a three-man squad in Boston's homicide unit. Her first squadmate, Phil, was the quintessential family man, married to his high school sweetheart and raising four kids. Her other squadmate, Neil, was a lanky redhead who'd formerly served as an EMT before joining the BPD. He had a tendency to handle the autopsies for the team, spending so much time at the morgue that he was now dating the ME, Ben Whitley.

D.D. had a whole taskforce at her disposal; she still preferred to go with what she knew. She put Neil in charge of Brian Darby's autopsy, currently scheduled for Monday afternoon. In the meantime, Neil could start pestering the medical staff overseeing Tessa Leoni's care to determine the extent of her current injuries as well as any medical history of past 'accidents.' She assigned Phil, their data cruncher, to run the computer background checks on Brian Darby and Tessa Leoni. And, of course, get her the information on Brian Darby's employer, immediately.

Turned out, Brian worked for Alaska South Slope Crude, otherwise known as ASSC. Head offices were in Seattle, Washington, and not open on Sunday. This did not suit D.D. She chewed the inside of her cheek while sitting in the command van, nursing a bottle of water. The initial crush of officers had subsided. Most of the neighbors had drifted off, leaving the usual assortment of 'didn't see nothing, don't know anything' mutterings in their wake. Now only the media remained, still ensconced across the street, still clamoring for a press conference.

D.D. was probably going to have to do something about that, but she wasn't ready yet. She wanted something to happen first. Maybe a breaking lead she could dangle in front of the hungry hordes. Or a new piece of information that would enable the media to work on her behalf. Something. Anything.

Crap, she was tired. Really, truly, bone deep, could curl up on the command center floor and fall asleep right now sort of tired. She couldn't get used to it. The intense bouts of nausea followed by the nearly deadening sense of fatigue. Five weeks late and her body already wasn't her own.

What was she going to do? How could she tell Alex, when she still didn't know how she felt about it herself?

What was she going to do?

Bobby, who'd been in earnest conversation with his lieutenant colonel, finally broke away and took a seat beside her. He stretched out his legs.

'Hungry?' he asked.

'What?'

'It's after two, D.D. We need lunch.'

She looked at him blankly, not quite believing it was after two and definitely not ready to deal

91

with all the current issues that surrounded mealtimes.

'You okay?' He asked it evenly.

''Course I'm okay! Just . . . preoccupied. In case you haven't noticed, we're still missing a six-year-old girl.'

'Then I have a gift for you.' Bobby held out a piece of paper. 'The lieutenant colonel just had this faxed over. It's from Tessa Leoni's file, and it includes an emergency contact other than her husband.'

'What?'

'Mrs. Brandi Ennis. Guess she watched Sophie when Trooper Leoni was on patrol and Brian Darby out to sea.'

'Hot damn.' D.D. grabbed the paper, skimmed the contents, then flipped open her phone.

Brandi Ennis answered on the first ring. Yes, she'd seen the news. Yes, she wanted to talk. Immediately. At her home would be fine. She provided an address.

'Give us fifteen minutes,' D.D. assured the elderly-sounding woman. Then she and Bobby were out the door.

★   ★   ★

Twelve minutes later, D.D. and Bobby pulled up in front of a squat brick apartment building. Peeling white trim around small windows. Crumbling concrete on the front stoop.

Low-income housing, D.D. decided, which was probably still a stretch for most of its inhabitants.

92

A couple of kids were playing in the snow out front, trying to fashion a sad-looking snowman. They spotted two cops getting out of their car and immediately bolted inside. D.D. grimaced. Countless hours of community relations later, and the next generation was still as suspicious of the police as the first. It didn't make any of their lives easier.

Mrs. Ennis lived on the second floor, Unit 2C. Bobby and D.D. took the stairs up, knocking lightly on the scarred wooden door. Mrs. Ennis opened before D.D.'s fist had even dropped down, obviously waiting for them.

She gestured them inside a small but tidy studio apartment. Kitchen cabinets to the left, kitchen table to the right, brown floral sleeper sofa straight ahead. The TV was on, blaring away on top of a cheap microwave stand. Mrs. Ennis took a second to cross the space and snap it off. Then she asked them politely if they'd like some tea or coffee.

D.D. and Bobby declined. Mrs. Ennis bustled at the cabinets anyway, putting on a pot of water, getting down a package of Nilla wafers.

She was an older woman, probably late sixties, early seventies. Steel gray hair cut no-nonsense short. Wearing a dark blue running suit over a petite, stoop-shouldered frame. Her gnarled hands shook slightly as she opened the box of cookies, but she moved briskly, a woman who knew what she was about.

D.D. took a moment to wander the space, just in case Sophie Leoni was magically sitting on the sofa with her gap-tooth smile, or maybe playing with duckies in the bath, or even tucked inside the lone closet to hide from her abusive parents.

As she closed the closet door, Mrs. Ennis said calmly, 'You may sit now, Detective. I don't have the child, nor would I ever do that to her poor mother.'

Sufficiently chastised, D.D. shed her heavy winter coat and took a seat. Bobby was already munching on a Nilla wafer. D.D. eyed them. When her stomach did not flip-flop in protest, she reached out carefully. Simple foods such as crackers and dry cereal had been good to her thus far. She took several experimental bites, then decided she might be in luck, because now that she thought about it, she was starving.

'How long have you known Tessa Leoni?' D.D. asked.

Mrs. Ennis had taken a seat, clutching a mug of tea. Her eyes appeared red, as if she'd been crying earlier, but she seemed composed now. Ready to talk.

'I first met Tessa seven years ago, when she moved into the building. Across the hall, apartment 2D. Also a studio, though she changed to a one bedroom not long after Sophie was born.'

'You met her before Sophie was born?' D.D. asked.

'Yes. She was three, four months pregnant. Just this little thing with this little belly. I heard a crash and came out into the hallway. Tessa had been trying to carry a box filled with pots and pans up the stairs and it had broken on her. I offered to help, which she declined, but I picked up her chicken fryer anyway and that's how it began.'

'You became friends?' D.D. clarified.

'I would have her over for dinner on occasion and she would return the favor. Two lone females in the building. It was nice to have some company.'

'And she was already pregnant?'

'Yes, ma'am.'

'She talk much about the father?'

'She never mentioned him at all.'

'What about dating, social life, visits from her family?'

'No family. No boys either. She worked at a coffee shop, trying to save her money for the baby's birth. It's not an easy thing, expecting a baby all alone.'

'No male companionship?' D.D. pressed. 'Maybe she went out late a couple of nights, hung out with friends . . . '

'She doesn't have friends,' Mrs. Ennis said emphatically.

'She doesn't have friends?' D.D. repeated.

'It's not her way,' Mrs. Ennis said.

D.D. glanced over at Bobby, who also appeared intrigued by this news.

'What is her way?' D.D. asked at last.

'Independent. Private. Her baby mattered to her. From the beginning, that's what Tessa talked about and that's what she worked for. She understood being a single mother was going to be tough. Why, it was sitting here at this very table she came up with the idea to become a cop.'

'Really?' Bobby spoke up. 'Why a trooper?'

'She was trying to plan ahead — she couldn't very well support a child working in a coffee shop her whole life. So we started to discuss her options. She had a GED. She couldn't see herself behind a desk, but some kind of job where she could do things, be active, appealed to her. My son had become a firefighter. We talked about that, and next thing I knew, Tessa had homed in on joining the police force. She looked up applications, did all sorts of research. Pay scale was good, she met the initial requirements. Then, of course, she found out about the Academy and the wind went out of her sails. That's when I volunteered to babysit. Hadn't even met little Sophie yet, but I said I'd take her. If Tessa could get that far into the recruitment process, I'd assist with childcare.'

D.D. was looking at Bobby. 'How long's the state Police Academy again?'

'Twenty-five weeks,' he supplied. 'Live in dorms, only allowed home on the weekends. Not easy if you're a solo parent.'

'I will have you know,' Mrs. Ennis said stiffly, 'we all did just fine. Tessa completed her application before giving birth. She was accepted into the next recruitment class, when Sophie was nine months old. I know Tessa was nervous. I was, too. But it was also exciting.' The older woman's eyes flashed. She considered D.D. 'Are you a single woman? Have any children of your own? There's something invigorating about embarking on a new chapter in your life, taking a risk that might provide a whole new future for you and your child.

'Tessa was always serious, but now she was dedicated. Diligent. She knew what she was up against, a single mother trying to become a police officer. But she also believed that becoming a state police trooper was the best shot she had for her and Sophie. She never wavered. And that woman, once she puts her mind to something . . . '

'Single, dedicated parent,' D.D. murmured.

'Very.'

'Loving?'

'Always!' Mrs. Ennis said emphatically.

'What about when she graduated from the Academy,' Bobby spoke up. 'You come to cheer her on?'

'Even bought a new dress,' Mrs. Ennis confirmed.

'Anyone else there in her corner?'

'Just us girls.'

'She'd have to start on patrol right away,' Bobby continued. 'Working the graveyard shift then coming home to a small child . . . '

'She had thought to put Sophie in daycare, but I wouldn't hear of it. Sophie and I had done just fine during our Academy days. Easy enough for me to cross the hall and sleep on Tessa's sofa instead of my own. Then when Sophie was awake, I'd bring her back over to my place until after lunch so Tessa could get some rest. It was hardly a bother to entertain Sophie for a few hours. Lord, that child . . . All smiles and giggles and kisses and hugs. We should all be so lucky to have a little Sophie in our lives.'

'Happy child?' D.D. asked.

'And funny and feisty. Beautiful little girl. 'Bout broke my heart when they moved away.'

'When was that?'

'When she met her husband, Brian. He swept both her and Sophie off their feet. Regular Prince Charming. Least Tessa deserved, after working so hard on her own. And Sophie, too. Every girl should have a chance to be Daddy's Little Princess.'

'Did you like Brian Darby?' D.D. asked.

'Yes,' Mrs. Ennis stated, though her tone was noticeably more reserved.

'How did they meet?'

'Through the job, I believe. Brian was a friend of another trooper.'

D.D. looked at Bobby, who nodded and made the note.

'He spend much time here?'

Mrs. Ennis shook her head. 'Too small; it was easier for them to go to his place. There was a spell when I didn't see Tessa or Sophie too much. And I was happy for them, of course, of course. Though . . . ' Mrs. Ennis sighed. 'I don't have grandkids of my own. Sophie, she's like my own, and I miss her.'

'But you still help out?'

'When Brian ships out. Those couple of months I come over, spend the night with Sophie, just like the old days. In the morning, I get her off to school. I'm also listed as an emergency contact, because with Tessa's job, she can't always be immediately available. So snow days, maybe Sophie isn't feeling too good. I handle those days. And it's no bother. As I said, Sophie's like my own.'

D.D. pursed her lips, regarded the elderly woman.

'How would you describe Trooper Leoni as a mother?' she asked.

'There isn't anything she wouldn't do for Sophie,' Mrs. Ennis replied immediately.

'Trooper Leoni ever drink?'

'No, ma'am.'

'Gotta be stressful, though. Working, then coming home to a child. Sounds to me she never had a moment to herself.'

'Never heard her complain,' Mrs. Ennis said stubbornly.

'Ever get a call just because Tessa's having a bad day, could use a little break?'

'No, ma'am. If she wasn't working, she wanted to be with her daughter. Sophie's her world.'

'Until she met her husband.'

Mrs. Ennis was silent for a moment. 'Honestly?'

'Honestly,' D.D. said.

'I think Tessa loved Brian because Sophie loved Brian. Because, at least in the beginning, Brian and Sophie got along so well.'

'In the beginning,' D.D. prodded.

The older woman sighed, looked down at her tea. 'Marriage,' she said, a weight of emotion behind the word. 'It always starts out so fresh . . . ' She sighed again. 'I can't tell you what goes on behind closed doors, of course.'

'But . . . ' D.D. prodded again.

'Brian and Tessa and Sophie made one

another happy in the beginning. Tessa would come home with stories of hikes and picnics and bike rides and cookouts, all the good stuff. They played well together.

'But marriage is more than playing. It also became Brian shipping out, and now Tessa's in a house with a yard and the lawn mower is broken or the leaf blower is broken and she's gotta figure it all out because he's gone and she's here and houses have to be taken care of, just like kids and dogs and state police jobs. I saw her . . . I saw her get frazzled more. Life with Brian home was better for her, I think. But life with Brian gone grew a lot harder. She had more to deal with, more to take care of, than when it had just been her and Sophie in a little one-bedroom apartment.'

D.D. nodded. She could see that. There was a reason she didn't have a yard, a plant, or a goldfish.

'And for Brian?'

'Of course, he never confided in me,' Mrs. Ennis said.

'Of course.'

'But, from comments Tessa made . . . He worked when he shipped out. Twenty-four/seven, apparently, no days off. So when he came home, he didn't always want to go straight to house chores or lawn tending or even child rearing.'

'He wanted to play,' D.D. stated.

'Man needed some time to relax. Tessa changed the schedule, so the first week he was home, I'd still come over to help Sophie in the mornings. But Brian didn't like that either —

said he couldn't relax with me in the house. So we went back to the old routine. They were trying,' Mrs. Ennis spoke up earnestly. 'But their schedules were tough. Tessa had to work when she had to work and she didn't always come home when she was supposed to come home. Then Brian disappeared for sixty days, then reappeared for sixty days . . . I don't think it was easy on either of them.'

'Ever hear them fight?' D.D. asked.

Mrs. Ennis studied her tea. 'Not fight . . . I could feel the tension. Sophie sometimes . . . When Brian came home, she'd have a couple of days where she'd be unusually quiet. Then he'd leave again, and she'd perk up. A father who came and went, that's not easy for a child to understand. And the stress of the household . . . kids can feel that.'

'He ever hit her?'

'Heavens no! And if I so much as suspected such a thing, I would've reported him myself.'

'To whom?' D.D. asked curiously.

'Tessa, of course.'

'He ever hit her?'

Mrs. Ennis hesitated. D.D. eyed the older woman with renewed interest.

'I don't know,' the older woman said.

'You don't know?'

'Sometimes, I noticed some bruising. Once or twice, not so long ago, Tessa seemed to limp. But when I asked her about it — she fell down the icy steps, had a minor accident snowshoeing. They're an active family. Sometimes, active people get injured.'

'But not Sophie.'

'Not Sophie!' Mrs. Ennis said fiercely.

'Because you would've done something about that.'

For the first time, the woman's mouth trembled. She looked away, and in that moment, D.D. could see the woman's shame.

'You did suspect he was hitting her,' D.D. stated levelly. 'You worried Tessa was being abused by her husband, and you did nothing about it.'

'Six, eight weeks ago . . . It was clear something had happened, she wasn't moving well, but was also refusing to acknowledge it. I tried to bring it up . . . '

'What did she say?'

'That she fell down the front steps. She'd forgotten to salt them, it was all her fault . . . ' Mrs. Ennis pursed her lips, clearly skeptical. 'I couldn't figure it out,' the older woman said at last. 'Tessa's a police officer. She's had training, she carries a gun. I told myself, if she really needed help, she'd tell me. Or maybe another officer. She spends all day with the police. How could she not ask for help?'

Million dollar question, D.D. thought. She could tell from the look on Bobby's face he thought the same. He leaned forward, caught Mrs. Ennis's attention.

'Did Tessa ever mention Sophie's biological father? Maybe he contacted her recently, showed interest in his child?'

Mrs. Ennis shook her head. 'Tessa never spoke of him. I always assumed the man didn't have any interest in being a father. He had a better offer, she said, and left it at that.'

'Tessa ever mention being worried about an arrest she'd made recently?'

Mrs. Ennis shook her head.

'What about trouble on the job, maybe with another trooper? Couldn't have been easy to be the only female in the Framingham barracks.'

Again, Mrs. Ennis shook her head. 'She never spoke of work. Least not to me. Tessa was proud of her job, though. I could see that, just watching her leave for patrol each night. Maybe she picked the state police because she thought it would help her child, but it helped her, too. A strong job for a strong woman.'

'You think she could've shot her husband?' D.D. asked bluntly.

Mrs. Ennis wouldn't answer.

'What if he hurt her child?'

Mrs. Ennis looked up sharply. 'Oh dear Lord. You can't mean . . . ' She covered her mouth with her hand. 'You think Brian killed Sophie? You think she's dead? But the Amber Alert . . . I thought she was just missing. Maybe run off because of the confusion . . . '

'What confusion?'

'The news said there was an incident. Left one dead. I thought maybe there was a break-in, a struggle. Maybe Sophie ran away, to be safe.'

'Who would break in?' D.D. asked.

'I don't know. It's Boston. Burglars, gangsters . . . These things happen.'

'There's no sign of break-in,' D.D. said quietly, giving Mrs. Ennis time to let that news settle in.

'Tessa has confessed to shooting her husband. What we're trying to determine is what led up to that event, and what happened to Sophie.'

'Oh my Lord. Oh my . . . Oh my . . . ' Mrs. Ennis's hands moved from her mouth to her eyes. Already, she had started crying. 'But I never thought . . . Even if Brian had . . . lost his temper a few times, I never suspected things had gotten so bad. I mean, he went away, right? If things had gotten so bad, why didn't she and Sophie just leave him when he was away? I would've helped. Surely she knew that!'

'Excellent question,' D.D. agreed softly. 'Why didn't she and Sophie just leave once he'd shipped out?'

'Sophie ever talk much about school?' Bobby spoke up. 'Did she seem happy there, or have any concerns?'

'Sophie loved school. First grade. Mrs. DiPace. She'd just started reading all the Junie B. Jones novels with a little help. I mean reading, just like that. She's a bright child. And a good girl, too. I can . . . I can get you the principal's name, teachers, I have the whole school list since I dropped her off half the time. Everyone only ever has wonderful things to say about her, and oh my, just . . . '

Mrs. Ennis was out of her seat, walking in a tight circle before she seemed to remember what she needed to do. She crossed to a little end table next to the sofa, opened the top drawer, and started pulling out information.

'What about after-school activities?' D.D. asked.

'They had an after-school art program. Every Monday. Sophie loved that.'

'Parents volunteer as part of that?' Bobby probed.

D.D. nodded, following his train of thought. Parents who they could grind through more background checks.

Mrs. Ennis returned to them, holding several pieces of paper — a school calendar, contact information for administrative personnel, a phone tree of other parents to notify in the event of snow days.

'Can you think of anyone who might want to harm Sophie?' D.D. asked as gently as she could.

Mrs. Ennis shook her head, her face still stricken.

'If she ran away, can you think of where she'd hide?'

'In the tree,' Mrs. Ennis said immediately. 'When she wanted time alone, she always climbed the big oak in the backyard. Tessa said she used to do the same thing as a child.'

Bobby and D.D. nodded. They had both studied the bare limbed tree. Six-year-old Sophie had not been perched among the branches.

'How do you get to the house?' D.D. thought to ask, as she and Bobby rose out of their chairs.

'The bus.'

'Has Sophie ever ridden it with you? Does she understand mass transit?'

'We have been on the bus. I don't think she would know how . . . ' Mrs. Ennis paused, her dark eyes brightening. 'But she does know her coins. The last few times we rode, she counted out the money. And she's very adventurous. If she thought she needed to get on the bus for some reason, I could see her trying it alone.'

'Thank you, Mrs. Ennis. If you think of anything else . . . ' D.D. handed the woman her card.

Bobby had opened the door. At the last moment, just as D.D. was exiting into the hall, Bobby turned back.

'You said another officer introduced Tessa and Brian. Do you remember who that was?'

'Oh, it was at a cookout . . . ' Mrs. Ennis paused, searched her memory banks. 'Shane. That's what Tessa called him. She'd gone to Shane's house.'

Bobby thanked the woman, then followed D.D. down the stairs.

'Who's Shane?' D.D. asked, the moment they were outside, puffing out frosty breaths of air and tugging on their gloves.

'I'm guessing Trooper Shane Lyons, out of the Framingham barracks.'

'The union rep!' D.D. stated.

'Yep. As well as the officer who made the initial call.'

'Then that's who we'll be interviewing next.' D.D. glanced at the distant horizon, noticed for the first time the rapidly fading daylight, and felt her heart sink. 'Oh no. Bobby . . . It's nearly dark!'

'Then we'd better work faster.'

Bobby turned down the walk. D.D. followed quickly behind him.

10

I was dreaming. In a hazy sort of way, I understood that, but didn't jolt myself awake. I recognized the fall afternoon, the golden wisps of memory, and I didn't want to leave it. I was with my husband and daughter. We were together, and we were happy.

In my dream/memory, Sophie is five years old, her dark hair pulled into a stubby ponytail beneath her helmet as she rides her pink bike with big white training wheels through the neighborhood park. Brian and I trail behind her, holding hands. Brian's face is relaxed, his shoulders down. It's a beautiful fall day in Boston, the sun is out, the leaves are bright copper, and life is good.

Sophie comes to the top of a hill. She waits for us to catch up, wanting an audience. Then, with a squeal, she kicks off against the pavement and sails her bike down the small incline, pedaling madly for maximum speed.

I shake my head at my daughter's madcap ways. Never mind that my stomach clenched the moment she took off. I know better than to let anything show on my face. My nervousness only encourages her, 'scaring Mommy' a favorite game both she and Brian like to play.

'I want to go faster!' Sophie announces at the bottom.

'Find a bigger hill,' Brian says.

I roll my eyes at both of them. 'That was plenty fast, thank you very much.'

'I want to take off my training wheels.'

I pause, do a little double-take. 'You want to remove your training wheels?'

'Yes.' Sophie is adamant. 'I want to ride like a big girl. On two wheels. Then I'll be faster.'

I'm not sure what I think. When did I lose my training wheels? Five, six, I don't remember. Probably sooner versus later. I was always a tomboy. How can I blame Sophie for sharing the same trait?

Brian is already beside Sophie's bike, checking out the setup.

'Gonna need tools,' he declares, and that quickly, it's settled. Brian trots home for a set of wrenches, Sophie bounds around the park, announcing to all strangers and at least half a dozen squirrels that she's going to ride on two wheels. Everyone is impressed, particularly the squirrels, who chatter at her, before scampering up trees.

Brian returns within fifteen minutes; he must have run the whole way to our house and back and I feel a rush of gratitude. That he loves Sophie that much. That he understands a five-year-old's impulsiveness so well.

Removing training wheels turns out to be remarkably easy. Within minutes, Brian has tossed the wheels into the grass, and Sophie is back on her bike, feet flat on the ground as she tightens the straps of her red helmet and regards us solemnly.

'I'm ready,' she declares.

And I have a moment, my hand pressed

108

against my stomach, thinking, *But I'm not*. I'm really not. Wasn't it just yesterday that she was this tiny little baby that fit on the curve of my shoulder? Or maybe a careening ten-month-old, taking that first wild step? How did she get this tall and where did all those years go and how do I get them back?

She's my whole world. How will I handle it if she falls?

Brian is already stepping forward. He instructs Sophie to mount her bike. He has one hand on the handlebars, keeping them straight, another hand on the back of the banana seat to hold the bike steady.

Sophie sits on the seat, both feet on the pedals. She appears both somber and fierce. She's going to do this, it's only a question of how many crashes until she gets it right.

Brian is talking to her. Murmuring some instructions I can't hear, because it's easier if I stand back, distance myself from what is about to happen. Mothers hold close, fathers let go. Maybe that's the way of the world.

I try to remember again my first experience without training wheels. Did my father help me? Did my mother come out to witness the event? I can't remember. I want to. Any kind of memory of my father providing words of advice, my parents paying attention.

But I come up blank. My mother is dead. And my father made it clear ten years ago that he never wanted to see me again.

He doesn't know he has a granddaughter named Sophie. He doesn't know his only child became a state police officer. His son died. His daughter, he threw away.

Brian has Sophie lined up. The bike is trembling a little. Her nervousness. Maybe his. They are both wired, intent. I remain on the sidelines, unable to speak.

Sophie starts to peddle. Beside her, Brian breaks into a jog, hands on the bike, assisting with balance as Sophie gains momentum. She's going faster. Faster, faster.

I hold my breath, both hands clenched into fists. Thank God for the helmet. It's all I can think. Thank God for the helmet and why didn't I cocoon my entire child in bubble wrap before letting her mount up?

Brian lets go.

Sophie surges forward, pedaling strong. Three feet, four feet, six, eight. Then, at the last second she glances down, seems to realize that Brian is no longer beside her, that she really is on her own. In the next instant, the handlebars twist and down she goes. A startled cry, an impressive crash.

Brian is already there, on his knees beside her before I can take three steps. He untangles Sophie from her bike, gets her to standing, inspects each limb.

Sophie's not crying. Instead, she turns to me, as I hustle down the bike path toward her.

'Did you see me?' my wild child squeals. 'Mommy, did you see me?'

'Yes, yes, yes,' I hasten to assure her, finally arriving at the scene and inspecting my child for damage. She's safe; I've lost twenty years off my life.

'Again!' my child demands.

Brian laughs as he straightens out her bike and helps her climb aboard. 'You're crazy,' he tells her, shaking his head.

Sophie simply beams.

By the end of the afternoon, she's sailing around the park, training wheels nothing but a distant memory. Brian and I can no longer stroll behind her; she's too fast for us. Instead, we climb up on a picnic table, where we can sit and watch her bike exuberant laps.

We're holding hands again, snuggled shoulder to shoulder against the late afternoon chill. I place my head on his shoulder as Sophie goes racing by.

'Thank you,' I say.

'She's a nut,' he answers.

'I don't think I could've done that.'

'Hell, my heart's still hammering in my chest.'

That surprises me enough to straighten and look at him. 'She scared you?'

'Are you kidding? That first spill.' He shakes his head. 'No one tells you how terrifying it is to be a parent. And we're just beginning. She's gonna want a trick bike next, you know. She'll be leaping down stairs, standing on handlebars. I'm going to need that hair stuff for men, what's it called, that gets the gray out?'

'Just for Men?'

'Yep. First thing when we get home, I'm ordering a case.'

I laugh. He puts his arm around my shoulders.

'She really is amazing,' he says, and all I can do is nod, because he's exactly right. She's

Sophie and she's the best thing that ever happened to either of us.

'I'm sorry about this weekend,' Brian says, one, two minutes later.

I nod against his shoulder, accepting his words without looking at him.

'I don't know what I was thinking,' he continues. 'Guess I got caught up in the moment. It won't happen again.'

'It's okay,' I say and I mean it. At this stage of the marriage, I still accept his apologies. At this stage of the marriage, I still believe in him.

'I'm thinking of joining a gym,' Brian says shortly. 'Got enough time on my hands, figured I could spend it getting into shape.'

'You're in good shape.'

'Yeah. But I want to get back to weight lifting. Haven't done that since my college days. And let's face it.' Sophie zooms past our picnic table. 'At the rate she's going, I'm going to need all my strength to keep up.'

'Whatever you want to do,' I tell him.

'Hey, Tessa.'

'What?'

'I love you.'

In my dream/memory, I smile, curve my arms around my husband's waist. 'Hey, Brian. Love you, too.'

★ ★ ★

I woke up hard, a noise jerking me from the golden past to the sterile present. That afternoon, the solid feel of my husband's arms,

112

the bright sound of Sophie's exuberant laugh. The lull before the storm, except I hadn't known it then.

That afternoon Brian and I had returned home with an exhausted child. We'd put her to bed early. Then, after a leisurely dinner, we'd made love and I'd fallen asleep thinking I was the luckiest woman in the world.

It would be a year before I told my husband I loved him again. Then he would be dying on our freshly scrubbed kitchen floor, his chest plugged with the bullets from my gun, his face a sad mirror of my own regrets.

In the seconds before I ran through the house, tore apart the house, searching frantically for the daughter I hadn't found yet.

More noises penetrated my consciousness. Distant beeps, rapid footsteps, someone yelling for something. Hospital noises. Loud, insistent. Urgent. It returned me once and for all to the present. No husband. No Sophie. Just me, alone in a hospital room, wiping tears from the unbruised half of my face.

For the first time, I realized there was something in my left hand. I drew my hand up so I could inspect the find with my one good eye.

It was a button, I realized. Half an inch in diameter. Navy blue frayed thread still looped through double-holes. Could be from pants, or a blouse, maybe even a state police uniform.

But it wasn't. I recognized the button the instant I saw it. I could even picture the second button that should be sewn right beside it, twin plastic rounds forming blue eyes on my daughter's favorite doll.

And for a second, I was so angry, so filled with rage my knuckles turned white and I couldn't speak.

I hurtled the button across the room, where it smacked against the privacy curtain. Then, just as quickly, I was sorry I'd done such an impulsive thing. I wanted it back. Needed it back. It was a tie to Sophie. One of my only links to her.

I tried to sit up, intent on retrieval. Immediately, the back of my skull roared to life, my cheek throbbing in a fresh spike of pain. The room wavered, tilted sickeningly, and I could feel my heart rate sky-rocket from sudden, excruciating distress.

Dammit, dammit, dammit.

I forced myself to lie down, take a steadying breath. Eventually, the ceiling righted and I could swallow without gagging. I lay perfectly still, acutely aware of my own vulnerability, the weakness I couldn't afford.

This was why men beat women, of course. To prove their physical superiority. To demonstrate they were bigger and stronger than us, and that no amount of special training would ever change that. They were the dominant gender. We might as well submit now and surrender.

Except I didn't need to be smashed over the head with a beer bottle to understand my physical limitations. I didn't need a hairy-knuckled fist exploding in my face to realize that some battles couldn't be won. I'd already spent my whole life coming to terms with the fact that

I was smaller, more vulnerable than others. I'd still survived the Academy. I'd still spent four years patrolling as one of the state's few female troopers.

And I'd still given birth, all alone, to an amazing daughter.

Like hell I would submit. Like hell I would surrender.

I was crying again. The tears shamed me. I wiped my good cheek again, careful not to touch my black eye.

Forget the fucking duty belt, our instructors had told us the first day of Academy training. Two most valuable tools an officer has are her head and her mouth. Think strategically, speak carefully, and you can control any person, any situation.

That's what I needed. To regain control, because the Boston cops would be returning soon, and then I was probably doomed.

Think strategically. Okay. Time.

Four, five o'clock?

It would be dark soon. Night falling.

Sophie . . .

My hands trembled. I supressed the weakness.

Think strategically.

Stuck in a hospital. Can't run, can't hide, can't attack, can't defend. So I had to get one step ahead. Think strategically. Speak carefully.

Sacrifice judiciously.

I remembered Brian again, the beauty of that fall afternoon, and the way you can both love a man and curse him all in one breath. I knew what I had to do.

I found the bedside phone, and I dialed.

'Ken Cargill, please. This is his client, Tessa Leoni. Please tell him I need to make arrangements for my husband's body. Immediately.'

11

Trooper Shane Lyons agreed to meet Bobby and D.D. at the BPD headquarters in Roxbury after six. That gave them enough time to stop for dinner. Bobby ordered up a giant hoagie, double everything. D.D. nursed a bowl of chicken noodle soup, liberally topped with crumbled saltines.

Sub shop had a TV blaring in the corner, the five o'clock news leading with the shooting in Allston-Brighton and the disappearance of Sophie Marissa Leoni. The girl's face filled the screen, bright blue eyes, huge, gap-tooth smile. Beneath her photo ran the hotline number, as well as an offer of a twenty-five thousand dollar reward for any tips that might lead to her recovery.

D.D. couldn't watch the newscast. It depressed her too much.

Eight hours after the first call out, they weren't making sufficient progress. One neighbor had reported seeing Brian Darby driving away in his white GMC Denali shortly after four p.m. yesterday. After that, nothing. No visual sightings. No phone calls logged on the landline or messages on his cell. Where Brian Darby had gone, what he'd done, who he might have seen, no one had any idea.

Which brought them to six-year-old Sophie. Yesterday had been a Saturday. No school, no

117

playdates, no appearances in the yard, no sightings in local cameras or magical tips pouring in through the hotline. Friday, she'd been picked up from school at three p.m. After that, it was anybody's guess.

Tessa Leoni had reported in for her eleven p.m. graveyard shift on Saturday night. Three neighbors had noticed her cruiser departing; one had noticed its reappearance after nine the next morning. Dispatch had a full roster of duty calls, verifying Trooper Leoni had worked her shift, turning in the last batch of paperwork shortly after eight a.m. Sunday morning.

At which point, the entire family fell off the grid. Neighbors didn't see anything. Neighbors didn't hear anything. No fighting, no screaming, not even gunshots, though that made D.D. suspicious because how you could *not* hear a 9mm fire off three rounds was beyond her. Maybe people just didn't want to hear what they didn't want to hear. That seemed more likely.

Sophie Leoni had now been declared missing since ten this morning. Sun was down, thermostat was plunging, and four to six inches of snow were reportedly on their way.

The day had been bad. The night would be worse.

'I gotta make a call,' Bobby said. He'd finished his sandwich, was balling up the wrapping.

'Gonna tell Annabelle you're working late?'

He gestured outside the sub shop window, where the first flakes had started to fall. 'Am I wrong?'

'She okay with your schedule?' D.D. asked.

He shrugged. 'What can she do? The job's the job.'

'What about Carina? Soon she'll figure out Daddy disappears and doesn't always return home to play. Then there's the missed recitals, school plays, soccer games. *I scored one for the team, Dad! Except you weren't there.*'

Bobby regarded her curiously. 'The job's the job,' he repeated. 'Yeah, there are times it sucks, but then, most jobs do.'

D.D. scowled. She looked down, poked at her soup. The saltines had absorbed the broth, creating a lumpy mess. She didn't feel like eating anymore. She was tired. Discouraged. She was thinking of a little girl they probably wouldn't find alive. She was thinking of elderly Mrs. Ennis's comments on how hard it was for Trooper Leoni to juggle her job, a house, and a kid.

Maybe female law enforcement officers weren't meant to lead lives of domestic bliss. Maybe if Trooper Leoni hadn't tried for the whole husband and white picket fence, D.D. wouldn't have been called out this morning and a cute, innocent child wouldn't now be missing.

Good Lord, what was D.D. supposed to tell Alex? How was she, a career detective and self-admitted workaholic, supposed to *feel* about this?

She poked at her soup one last time, then pushed it away. Bobby was still standing there, apparently waiting for her to say something.

'You ever picture me as a mom?' she asked him.

'No.'

'You didn't even have to think about that.'

'Don't ask the question if you don't want the answer.'

She shook her head. 'I've never pictured myself as a mom. Moms . . . sing lullabies and carry around Cheerios and make funny faces just to get their babies to smile. I only know how to make my squad smile and that involves fresh coffee and maple-frosted donuts.'

'Carina likes peekaboo,' Bobby said.

'Really?'

'Yeah. I put my hand over my eyes, then jerk it away and cry, *'Peekaboo!'* She can do that for hours. Turns out I can do that for hours, too. Who knew?'

D.D. covered her eyes with her palm, then whipped her hand away. Bobby disappeared. Bobby reappeared. Other than that, it didn't do much for her.

'I'm not your baby,' Bobby said by way of explanation. 'We're genetically programmed to want to make our children happy. Carina beams, and . . . I can't even describe it. But my whole day has been worth it, and whatever silly thing makes her look like that, I'm gonna do it again. What can I tell you? It's crazier than love. Deeper than love. It's . . . being a parent.'

'I think Brian Darby murdered his stepdaughter. I think he killed Sophie, then Tessa Leoni returned home and shot him.'

'I know.'

'If we're genetically programmed to want to

120

make our offspring happy, how come so many parents hurt their own kids?'

'People suck,' Bobby said.

'And that thought gets you out of bed each morning?'

'I don't have to hang out with people. I have Annabelle, Carina, my family, and my friends. That's enough.'

'Gonna have a second Carina?'

'Hope so.'

'Why, you're an optimist, Bobby Dodge.'

'In my own way. I take it you and Alex are getting serious?'

'Guess that's the question.'

'Does he make you happy?'

'I'm not someone who gets happy.'

'Then does he make you content?'

She thought of her morning, wearing Alex's shirt, sitting at Alex's table. 'I could spend more time with him.'

'It's a start. Now, if you'll excuse me, I'm gonna call my wife and probably make some goo-goo noises for my daughter.'

Bobby stepped away from the table. 'Can I listen in?' D.D. called after him.

'Absolutely not,' he called back.

Which was just as well, because her stomach was cramping uneasily again and she was thinking of a little bundle in blue or maybe a little bundle in pink and wondering what a little Alex or little D.D. might look like, and if she could love a child as much as Bobby obviously loved Carina, and if that love alone could be enough.

Because domestic bliss rarely worked out for female cops. Just ask Tessa Leoni.

* * *

By the time Bobby finished his call, the early evening snow had turned the roads into a snarled mess. They used lights and sirens all the way, but it still took them over forty minutes to hit Roxbury. Another five minutes to find parking, and Trooper Shane Lyons had been cooling his heels for at least a quarter of an hour by the time they entered the lobby of BPD headquarters. The burly officer stood as they walked in, still dressed in full uniform, hat pulled low on his brow, black leather gloves encasing both hands.

Bobby greeted the officer first, then D.D. An interrogation room would appear disrespectful, so D.D. found an unoccupied conference room for them to use. Lyons took a seat, removing his hat, but leaving on his coat and gloves. Apparently, he was planning on a short conversation.

Bobby offered him a Coke, which he accepted. D.D. stuck to water, while Bobby nursed a black coffee. Preliminaries settled, they got down to business.

'You didn't seem surprised to hear from us,' D.D. started off.

Lyons shrugged, twirled his Coke can between his gloved fingers. 'I knew my name would come up. Had to complete my duties as union rep, first, however, which was my primary responsibility at the scene.'

'How long have you known Trooper Leoni?' Bobby asked.

'Four years. Since she started at the barracks. I was her senior officer, overseeing her first twelve weeks of patrol.' Lyons took a sip of his soda. He appeared uncomfortable, every inch the reluctant witness.

'You worked closely with Trooper Leoni?' D.D. prodded.

'First twelve weeks, yes. But after that, no. Troopers patrol alone.'

'Socialize much?'

'Maybe once a week. On duty officers will try to meet up for coffee or breakfast. Breaks up our shifts, maintains camaraderie.' He looked at D.D. 'Sometimes, the Boston cops even join us.'

'Really?' D.D. did her best to sound horrified.

Lyons finally smiled. 'Gotta back each other up, right? So good to keep the lines of communication open. But having said that, most of a trooper's shift is spent alone. Especially graveyard. It's you, the radar gun, and a highway full of drunks.'

'What about at the barracks?' D.D. wanted to know. 'You and Tessa hang out, grab a bite to eat after work?'

Lyons shook his head. 'Nah. A trooper's cruiser is his — or her — office. We only return to the barracks if we make an arrest, need to process an OUI, that kind of thing. Again, most of our time is on the road.'

'But you assist one another,' Bobby spoke up. 'Especially if there's an incident.'

'Sure. Last week, Trooper Leoni pinched a guy

for operating under the influence on the Pike, so I arrived to help. She took the guy to the barracks to administer the breathalyzer and read him his rights. I stayed with his vehicle until the truck came to tow it away. We backed each other up, but we hardly stood around talking about our spouses and kids while she stuffed a drunk in the back of her cruiser.' Lyons pinned Bobby with a look. 'You must remember how it is.'

'Tell us about Brian Darby,' D.D. spoke up again, redirecting Lyons's stare.

The state trooper didn't answer right away, but thinned his lips, appearing to be wrestling with something inside himself.

'I'm damned if I do, damned if I don't,' he muttered abruptly.

'Damned for what, Trooper?' Bobby asked evenly.

'Look.' Lyons set down his soda. 'I know I'm screwed here. I'm supposed to be an excellent judge of character, goes with the job. But then, this situation with Tessa and Brian. Hell, either I'm a total idiot who didn't know my neighbor had rage management issues, or I'm an asshole who set up a fellow officer with a wife beater. Honest to God . . . If I'd known, if I'd suspected . . . '

'Let's start with Brian Darby,' D.D. said. 'What did you know about him?'

'Met him eight years ago. We were both in a neighborhood hockey league. Played together every other Friday night; he seemed like a nice guy. Had him over a couple of times for dinner and beer. Still seemed like a nice guy. Worked a

124

crazy schedule as a merchant marine, so he got my job, too. When he was around, we'd get together — play hockey, go sking, maybe a day hike. He liked sports and I do, too.'

'Brian was an active guy,' Bobby said.

'Yeah. He liked to keep moving. Tessa did, too. Frankly, I thought they'd be a good fit. That's why I set them up. Figured even if they didn't end up dating, they could be hiking buddies, something.'

'You set them up,' D.D. repeated.

'Invited them both to a summer cookout. Let them take it from there. Come on, I'm a guy. That's as involved as a guy gets.'

'They leave the party together?' Bobby asked.

Lyons had to think about it. 'Nah. They met later for drinks, something like that. I don't know. But next thing I knew, Tessa and her daughter were moving in with him, so I guess it worked.'

'You attend the wedding?'

'No. Didn't even hear about it until it was all over. I think I noticed Tessa was suddenly wearing a ring. When I asked, she said they'd gotten married. I was a little startled, thought it was kind of quick, and okay, maybe I was surprised they didn't invite me, but . . . ' Lyons shrugged. 'It's not like we were that close or I was that involved.'

It seemed important for him to establish the point. He wasn't *that* close to the couple, not *that* involved in their lives.

'Tessa ever talk about the marriage?' D.D. asked.

'Not to me.'

'So to others?'

'I can only speak for myself.'

'And you're not even doing that,' D.D. stated bluntly.

'Hey. I'm trying to tell you the truth. I don't spend my Sundays dining at Brian and Tessa's house or having them over to my place after church. We're friends, sure. But, we got our own lives. Hell, Brian wasn't even in town half the year.'

'So,' D.D. said slowly. 'Your hockey buddy Brian Darby ships out half the year, leaving behind a fellow trooper to juggle the house, the yard, and a small child, all by herself, and you just go your own way. Have your own life, don't need to get bogged down with theirs?'

Trooper Lyons flushed. He looked at his Coke, his square jaw noticeably clenched.

Good-looking guy, D.D. thought, in a ruddy face sort of way. Which made her wonder: Did Brian Darby start bulking up because his wife carried a gun? Or because his wife started calling a hunky fellow trooper for help around the house?

'I might have fixed the lawn mower,' Lyons muttered.

D.D. and Bobby waited.

'Kitchen faucet leaked. Took a look at that, but out of my league, so I gave her the name of a good plumber.'

'Where were you last night?' Bobby asked quietly.

'Patrolling!' Lyons looked up sharply. 'For

chrissake, I haven't been home since eleven last night. I got three kids of my own, you know, and if you don't think I'm not picturing them every time Sophie's photo flashes across the news . . . Shit. Sophie's just a kid! I still remember her rolling down the hill in my backyard. Then last year, climbing the old oak. Not even my eight-year-old son could catch up with her. She's half monkey, that one. And that smile, and ah . . . Dammit.'

Trooper Lyons covered his face with his hand. He appeared unable to speak, so Bobby and D.D. gave him a moment.

When he finally got himself together, he lowered his hand, grimacing. 'You know what we called Brian?' he said abruptly. 'His nickname on the hockey team?'

'No.'

'Mr. Sensitive. The man's favorite movie is *Pretty Woman*. When his dog, Duke, died, he wrote a poem and ran it in the local paper. He was that kind of guy. So no, I didn't think twice about introducing him to a fellow officer with a small child. Hell, I thought I was doing Tessa a favor.'

'You and Brian still play hockey together?' Bobby asked.

'Not so much. My schedule changed; I work most Friday nights.'

'Brian looks bigger now than when he got married. Like he's bulked up.'

'I think he joined a gym, something like that. He talked about lifting weights.'

'You ever work out with him?'

Lyons shook his head.

D.D.'s pager went off. She glanced at the display, saw it was the crime-scene lab and excused herself. When she left the conference room, Bobby was grilling Trooper Lyons on Brian Darby's exercise regimen and/or possible supplements.

D.D. got out her cellphone and dialed the crime lab. Turned out they had some initial findings from Brian's white GMC Denali. She listened, nodded, then ended the call in time to bolt for the ladies' room, where she managed to keep the soup down, but only after splashing a great deal of cold water on her face.

She rinsed her mouth. Ran more cold water over the back of her hands. Then she studied her pale reflection and informed herself that like it or not, she would get this done.

She would survive this evening. She would find Sophie Leoni.

Then she would go home to Alex, because they had a couple of things to talk about.

*　*　*

D.D. marched back into the conference room. She didn't wait, but led with the big guns because Trooper Lyons was stonewalling them, and frankly, she didn't have time for this bullshit anymore.

'Preliminary report on Brian Darby's vehicle,' she said sharply.

She flattened her hands on the table in front of Trooper Lyons and leaned down, till she was mere inches from his face.

'They found a collapsible shovel tucked into a rear compartment, still covered in dirt and bits of leaves.'

Lyons didn't say anything.

'Found a brand-new air freshener as well, melon scented, the kind that plugs into a socket. Lab geeks thought that was strange, so they took it out.'

Lyons didn't say anything.

'Odor became apparent in less than fifteen minutes. Very strong, they said. Very distinct. But being geeks, they call in a cadaver dog just to be sure.'

The officer paled.

'Decomp, Trooper Lyons. As in, the lab gurus are pretty damn certain a dead body was placed in the back of Brian Darby's vehicle in the past twenty-four hours. Given the presence of the shovel, they further surmise the body was driven to an unknown location and buried. Brian got a second home? Lake house, hunting lodge, ski cabin? Maybe if you finally start talking to us, we can at least bring home Sophie's body.'

'Ah no . . . ' Lyons paled further.

'Where did Brian take his stepdaughter?'

'I don't know! He doesn't have a second home. Least nothing he ever told me about!'

'You failed them. You introduced Brian Darby to Tessa and Sophie, and now Tessa is in a hospital beaten to a pulp and little Sophie's most likely dead. *You* set these wheels in motion. Now man up, and help us find Sophie's body. Where would he take her? What would he do? Tell us all of Brian Darby's secrets.'

'He didn't have secrets! I swear . . . Brian was a stand-up guy. Sailed the ocean blue, then returned home to his wife and stepdaughter. Never heard him raise his voice. Certainly, never saw him raise a fist.'

'*Then what the hell happened?*'

A heartbeat pause. Another long, shuddering breath.

'There is . . . There is another option,' Lyons said abruptly. He looked at both of them, face still ashen, hands flexing and unflexing around his Coke. 'Not really talking out of school,' he babbled. 'I mean, you'll find out sooner or later from Lieutenant Colonel Hamilton. He's the one who told me. Plus, it's a matter of record.'

'Trooper Lyons! Spit it out!' D.D. yelled.

So he did. 'What happened this morning . . . Well, let's just say, this wasn't the first time Trooper Leoni has killed a man.'

12

First thing I learned as a female police officer was that men were not the enemy I feared them to be.

A bunch of drunken rednecks at a bar? If my senior officer, Trooper Lyons, got out of the cruiser, they escalated immediately to more aggressive acts of machismo. If I appeared on the scene, however, they dropped their posturing and began to study their boots, a bunch of sheepish boys caught in the act by Mom. Rough-looking long-haul truckers? Can't say *yes, ma'am,* or *no, ma'am* fast enough if I'm standing beside their rigs with a citation book. Pretty college boys who've tossed back a few too many brews? They stammer, hem and haw, then almost always end up asking me out on a date.

Most men have been trained since birth to respond to a female authority figure. They view someone like me either as the mom they have been prepped to obey, or maybe, given my age and appearance, as a desirable woman worthy of being pleased. Either way, I'm not a direct challenge. Thus, the most belligerent male can afford to step down in front of his buddies. And in situations overloaded with testosterone, my fellow troopers often called me directly for backup, counting on my woman's touch to defuse the situation, as it generally did.

Male parties might flirt a little, fluster a little,

or both. But inevitably, they did what I said.

Females on the other hand . . .

Pull over the soccer mom doing ninety-five in her Lexus, and she'll instantly become verbally combative, screeching shrilly about her need for speed in front of her equally entitled-looking two-point-two kids. Doing a civil standby, assisting while a guy under a restraining order fetches his last few things from the apartment, and the battered girlfriend will inevitably come flying at me, demanding to know why I'm letting him pack his own underwear and cursing and screaming at me as if I'm the one responsible for every bad thing that's ever happened in her life.

Men are not a problem for a female trooper.

It's the women who will try to take you out, first chance they get.

★   ★   ★

My lawyer had been prattling away at my bedside for twenty minutes when Sergeant Detective D.D. Warren yanked back the privacy curtain. The state police liason, Detective Bobby Dodge, was directly behind her. His face was impossible to read. Detective Warren, however, wore the hungry look of a jungle cat.

My lawyer's voice trailed off. He appeared unhappy with the sudden appearance of two homicide detectives, but not surprised. He'd been trying to explain to me my full legal predicament. It wasn't good, and the fact I had yet to give a full statement to the police, in his expert opinion, made it worse.

132

Currently, my husband's death was listed as a questionable homicide. Next course of action would be for the Suffolk County DA, working in conjunction with the Boston police, to determine an appropriate charge. If they thought I was a credible victim, a poor battered wife with a corroborating history of visits to the emergency room, they could view Brian's death as justifiable homicide. I shot him, as I claimed, in self-defense.

But murder was a complicated business. Brian had attacked with a broken bottle; I had retaliated with a gun. The DA could argue that while I was clearly defending myself, I'd still used unnecessary force. The pepper spray, steel baton, and Taser I carried on my duty belt all would've been better choices, and for my trigger-happy ways, I'd be charged with man-slaughter.

Or, maybe they didn't believe I'd feared for my life. Maybe they believed Brian and I had been fighting and I'd shot and killed my husband in the heat of the moment. Homicide without premeditation, or Murder 2.

Those were the best-case scenarios. There was, of course, another scenario. One where the police determined my husband was not a violent wife beater, but instead, found me to be a master manipulator who shot my husband with premeditated malice and forethought. Murder 1.

Otherwise known as the rest of my life behind bars. Game over.

These were the concerns that had brought my lawyer to my bedside. He didn't want me fighting the police for my husband's remains. He wanted me to issue a statement to the press, a victimized wife extolling her innocence, a desperate mother pleading for her young daughter's safe return. He also wanted me to start playing nicely with the detectives handling my case. As he pointed out, battered woman's syndrome was an affirmative defense, meaning the burden of proof rested on my bruised shoulders.

Marriage, it turned out, boiled down to he said, she said, long after one of the spouses was dead.

Now the homicide detectives were back and my lawyer rose awkwardly to assume a defensive stance beside my bed.

'As you can see,' he began, 'my client is still recovering from a concussion, not to mention a fractured cheekbone. Her doctor has ordered her to remain overnight for observation, and to get plenty of rest.'

'Sophie?' I asked. My voice came out strained. Detective Warren appeared too harsh to be approaching a mother with bad news. But then again . . .

'No word,' she said curtly.

'What time is it?'

'Seven thirty-two.'

'After dark,' I murmured.

The blonde detective stared at me. No compassion, no sympathy. I wasn't surprised. There were so few women in blue, you'd think we'd help each other out. But women were funny that way. So willing to turn on one of their own,

134

especially a female perceived as weak, such as one who served as her husband's personal punching bag.

I couldn't imagine Detective Warren ever tolerating domestic abuse. If a man hit her, I bet she'd hit back twice as hard. Or taser him in the balls.

Detective Dodge was on the move. He'd commandeered two low-slung chairs and positioned them next to the bed. He gestured for D.D. to take a seat, both of them pulling up close. Cargill took the hint and perched on the edge of his own chair, still looking uncomfortable.

'My client isn't up to answering a lot of questions, just yet,' he said. 'Of course, she wants to do anything she can to assist in the search for her daughter. Is there information you need relevant to that investigation?'

'Who is Sophie's biological father?' Detective Warren asked. 'And where is he?'

I shook my head, a motion that immediately caused me to wince.

'I need a name,' Warren said impatiently.

I licked my dry lips, tried again. 'She doesn't have a father.'

'Impossible.'

'Not if you're a slut and an alcoholic,' I said.

Cargill shot me a startled glance. The detectives, however, appeared intrigued.

'You're an alcoholic?' Bobby Dodge asked evenly.

'Yes.'

'Who knows?'

'Lieutenant Colonel Hamilton, some of the guys.' I shrugged, trying not to move my bruised cheek. 'I sobered up seven years ago, before I joined the force. It hasn't been an issue.'

'Seven years ago?' D.D. repeated. 'When you were pregnant with your daughter?'

'That's right.'

'How old were you when you got pregnant with Sophie?'

'Twenty-one. Young and stupid. I drank too much, partied too hard. Then one day, I was pregnant and it turned out the people I thought were my friends only hung out with me because I was part of the circus. Minute I left the show, I never saw any of them again.'

'Male associates?' D.D. asked.

'Won't help you. I didn't sleep with men I knew. I slept with men I didn't know. Generally older men who were interested in buying a young stupid girl plenty of alcohol. I got drunk. They got laid. Then we each went our own way.'

'Tessa,' my lawyer began.

I held up a hand. 'It's old news, and nothing that matters. I don't know Sophie's dad. I couldn't have worked it out if I tried, and I didn't want to try. I got pregnant. Then I grew up, wised up, and sobered up. That's what matters.'

'Sophie ever ask?' Bobby asked.

'No. She was three when I met Brian. She started calling him Daddy within a matter of weeks. I don't think she remembers anymore that we ever lived without him.'

'When did he first hit you?' D.D. asked. 'One

month into the marriage? Six? Maybe a whole year?'

I didn't say anything, just stared up at the ceiling. I had my right hand under the thin green hospital blanket, gripping the blue button a nurse had retrieved for me.

'We're going to need to see your medical records,' D.D. stated. She was staring at my lawyer, challenging him.

'I fell down the stairs,' I said, my lips twisting into a funny smile, because it was actually the truth, but they, of course, would interpret it as the appropriate lie. Irony. God save me from irony.

'Excuse me?'

'The bruise on my ribs . . . Should've de-iced the outdoor steps. Oops.'

Detective Warren gave me an incredulous look. 'Sure. You fell. What, three, four times?'

'I think it was only twice.'

She didn't appreciate my sense of humor. 'Ever report your husband for battery?' she pressed.

I shook my head. Made the back of my skull ping-pong with pain while filling my good eye with tears.

'What about to a fellow trooper? Say, Trooper Lyons. Sounds like he's good at helping out around the house.'

I didn't say anything.

'Female friend?' Bobby spoke up. 'What about a minister, or a call to a hotline? We are asking these things to help you, Tessa.'

The tears built up more. I blinked them away.

'Wasn't that bad,' I said finally, staring up at the white ceiling tiles. 'Not in the beginning. I thought . . . I thought I could control him. Get things back on track.'

'When did your husband start lifting weights?' Bobby asked.

'Nine months ago.'

'Looks like he packed on some pounds. Thirty pounds over nine months. Was he using supplements?'

'He wouldn't say.'

'But he was bulking up. Actively working on increasing muscle mass?'

Miserably, I nodded my head. All the times I told him he didn't need to work out that hard. That he already looked good, was plenty strong. I should've known better, his obsessive need for tidiness, his compulsive drive to organize even the soup cans. I should've read the signs. But I hadn't. As the saying goes, the wife is always the last to know.

'When did he first hit Sophie?' D.D. asked.

'He did not!' I fired to life.

'Really? You're seriously gonna tell me, with your bashed-up skull and shattered cheek, that your brute of a dead husband hit you and only you, for as long as you both shall live?'

'He loved Sophie!'

'But he didn't love you. That was the problem.'

'Maybe he was on steroids.' It was something. I looked at Bobby.

''Roid rage doesn't discriminate,' D.D. drawled. 'Then he'd definitely whack both of you.'

138

'I'm just saying . . . He'd only been home from his last tour a couple of weeks, and this time . . . this time something had definitely changed.' That much wasn't a lie. In fact, I hoped they would trace that thread. I could use a couple of crack detectives on my side. Certainly, Sophie deserved investigators smarter than me coming to the rescue.

'He was more violent,' Bobby stated carefully.

'Angry. All the time. I was trying to understand, hoping he'd settle back in. But it wasn't working.' I twisted the top blanket with one hand, squeezed the button beneath the blanket with the other. 'I just . . . I don't know how it got to this. And that's the truth. We loved each other. He was a good husband and a good father. Then . . . ' More tears. Honest ones this time. I let a single drop trace down my cheek. 'I don't know how it got to this.'

The detectives fell quiet. My lawyer had relaxed beside me. I think he liked the tears, and probably the mention of possible steroid abuse, as well. That was a good angle.

'Where's Sophie?' D.D. asked, less hostile now, more intent.

'Don't know.' Another honest answer.

'Her boots are gone. Coat, too. Like someone bundled her up, took her away.'

'Mrs. Ennis?' I spoke up hopefully. 'She's Sophie's caretaker — '

'We know who she is,' D.D. interjected. 'She doesn't have your child.'

'Oh.'

'Does Brian have a second home? Old ski

lodge, fishing shack, anything like that?' Bobby this time.

I shook my head. I was getting tired, feeling my fatigue in spite of myself. I needed to get my endurance up. Build up my strength for the days and nights to come.

'Who else might know Sophie, remove her from your home?' D.D. insistent, not letting it go.

'I don't know — '

'Brian's family?' she persisted.

'He has a mother, four sisters. The sisters are scattered, his mother lives in New Hampshire. You'd have to ask, but we never saw them that much. His schedule, mine.'

'Your family?'

'I don't have a family,' I said automatically.

'That's not what the police file said.'

'What?'

'What?' my lawyer echoed.

Neither detective looked at him. 'Ten years ago. When you were questioned by the police for the death of nineteen-year-old Thomas Howe. According to the paperwork, it was your own father who supplied the gun.'

I stared at D.D. Warren. Just stared and stared and stared.

'Those records are sealed,' I said softly.

'Tessa . . . ' my lawyer began again, not sounding happy.

'But I told Lieutenant Colonel Hamilton about the incident when I first started on the force,' I stated levelly. 'I didn't want there to be any misunderstandings.'

140

'You mean, like one of your fellow officers discovering you'd shot and killed a kid?'

'Shot and killed a kid?' I mimicked. 'I was sixteen. *I* was the kid! Why the hell do you think they sealed the records? Anyway, the DA never brought charges, ruling it justifiable homicide. Thomas assaulted me. I was just trying to get away.'

'Shot him with a twenty-two,' Detective Warren continued as if I'd never spoken. 'Which you just so happened to have on you. Also, no signs of physical assault — '

'You have been speaking to my father,' I said bitterly. I couldn't help myself.

D.D. tilted her head, eyeing me coolly. 'He never believed you.'

I didn't say anything. Which was answer enough.

'What happened that night, Tessa? Help us understand, because this really doesn't look good for you.'

I clutched the button tighter. Ten years was a long time. And yet, not long enough.

'I was spending the night at my best friend's house,' I said at last. 'Juliana Howe. Thomas was her older brother. The last few times I'd been over, he'd made some comments. If we were alone in a room together, he stood too close, made me feel uncomfortable. But I was sixteen. Boys, particularly older boys, made me uncomfortable.'

'Then why'd you spend the night?' D.D. wanted to know.

'Juliana was my best friend,' I said quietly, and

141

in that moment I felt it all again. The terror. Her tears. My loss.

'You brought a gun,' the detective continued.

'My father gave me the gun,' I corrected. 'I'd gotten a job in the food court at the mall. I often worked till eleven, then had to walk out to my car in the dark. He wanted me to have some protection.'

'So he gave you a gun?' D.D. sounded incredulous.

I smiled. 'You'd have to know my father. Picking me up in person would have meant getting involved. Handing me a twenty-two semiauto I had no idea how to use, on the other hand, got him off the hook. So that's what he did.'

'Describe that night.' Bobby spoke up quietly.

'I went to Juliana's house. Her brother was out; I was happy. We made popcorn and had a Molly Ringwald movie marathon — *Sixteen Candles*, followed by *Breakfast Club*. I fell asleep on the sofa. When I woke up all the lights were off and someone had put a blanket over me. I assumed Juliana had headed up to bed. I was just going to follow when her brother walked through the front door. Thomas was drunk. He spotted me. He . . . '

Both detectives and my lawyer waited.

'I tried to get around him,' I said finally. 'He cornered me against the sofa, pressed me down into it. He was bigger, stronger. I was sixteen. He was nineteen. What could I do?'

My voice trailed off again. I swallowed.

'May I have some water?' I asked.

My lawyer found the pitcher bedside, poured

142

me a glass. My hand was shaking when I raised the plastic cup. I figured they couldn't blame me for the show of nerves. I drank the whole cup, then set it down again. Given how long it had been since I'd last given a statement, I had to think this through. Consistency was everything, and I couldn't afford a mistake this late in the game.

Three pairs of eyes waited for me.

I took another deep breath. Gripped the blue button and thought about life, the patterns we made, the cycles we couldn't escape.

Sacrifice judiciously.

'Just about when . . . Thomas was going to do what he was going to do, I felt my purse, against my hip. He had me pinned with the weight of his body while he worked on the zipper of his jeans. So I reached down with my right hand. I found my purse. I got the gun. And when he wouldn't get off me, I pulled the trigger.'

'In the living room of your best friend's house?' Detective Warren said.

'Yes.'

'Must've made a helluva mess.'

'Twenty-two's not that big of a gun,' I said.

'What about your best friend? How'd she take all this?'

I kept my gaze on the ceiling. 'He was her brother. Of course she loved him.'

'So . . . DA clears you. Court seals the records. But your father, your best friend. They never forgave you, did they.'

She made it a statement, not a question, so I didn't answer.

'Is that when you started drinking?' Detective Dodge asked.

I nodded wordlessly.

'Left home, dropped out of school . . . ' he continued.

'I'm hardly the first officer with a misspent youth,' I retorted stiffly.

'You got pregnant,' Detective Warren said. 'Grew up, wised up, and sobered up. That's a lotta sacrifice for a kid,' she commented.

'No. That's love for my daughter.'

'Best thing that ever happened to you. Only family you have left.'

D.D. still sounded skeptical, which I guess was warning enough.

'You ever hear of decomposition odor analysis?' the detective continued, her voice picking up. 'Arpad Vass, a research chemist and forensic anthropologist, has developed a technique for identifying the more than four hundred body vapors that emanate from decaying flesh. Turns out, these vapors get trapped in soil, fabrics — even, say, the carpet in the back of a vehicle. With the use of an electronic body sniffer, Dr. Vass can identify the molecular signature of body decomp left behind. For example, he can scan carpet that has been removed from a vehicle and actually see the vapors formed into the shape of a child's dead body.'

I made a noise. Might have been a gasp. Might have been a moan. Beneath the sheet, my hand tightened.

'We just sent Dr. Vass the carpet from your

144

husband's SUV. What's he gonna find, Tessa? Is this going to be your last glimpse of your daughter's body?'

'Stop. That is insensitive and inappropriate!' My lawyer was already on his feet.

I didn't really hear him. I was remembering pulling back the covers, gazing, horrified, at Sophie's empty bed.

All I want for Christmas is my two front teeth . . .

'What happened to your daughter!' Detective Warren demanded to know.

'He wouldn't tell me.'

'You came home? She was already gone?'

'I searched the house,' I whispered. 'The garage, sunroom, attic, yard. I searched and searched and searched. I demanded that he tell me what he did.'

'What happened, Tessa? What did your husband do to Sophie?'

'I don't know! She was gone. Gone! I went to work and when I came home . . . ' I stared at D.D. and Bobby, feeling my heart beat wildly again. Sophie. Vanished. Just like that.

All I want for Christmas is my two front teeth, my two front teeth . . .

'What did he do, Trooper Leoni? Tell us what Brian did.'

'He ruined our family. He lied to me. He betrayed us. He destroyed . . . everything.'

Another deep breath. I looked both detectives in the eye: 'And that's when I knew he had to die.'

145

13

'What do you think of Tessa Leoni?' Bobby asked five minutes later, as they headed back to HQ.

'Liar, liar, pants on fire,' D.D. said crossly.

'She seems deliberate with her replies.'

'Please. If I didn't know any better, I'd say she doesn't trust cops.'

'Well, advanced rates of alcoholism, suicide, and domestic violence aside, what's not to love?'

D.D. grimaced, but got his point. Law enforcement officers weren't exactly walking advertisements for well-adjusted human beings. Lotta cops graduated from the school of hard knocks. And most of them swore that's what it took to work these streets.

'She changed her story,' D.D. said.

'Noticed that myself.'

'We've gone from her shooting her husband first, then discovering that her daughter was missing, to she discovered Sophie was missing first, then ended up killing her husband.'

'Different timelines, same results. Either way Trooper Leoni was beaten to a pulp, and either way, six-year-old Sophie is gone.'

D.D. shook her head. 'Inconsistency about one detail makes you have to question all details. If she lied about the timeline, what other pieces of her story are false?'

'A liar is a liar is a liar,' Bobby said softly.

She glanced over at him, then tightened her

hands on the wheel. Tessa's sob story had gotten to him. Bobby had always had a weakness for damsels in distress. Whereas D.D. had been spot-on with her first impression of Tessa Leoni: pretty and vulnerable, which was trying D.D.'s nerves.

D.D. was tired. It was after eleven and her new, high maintenance body was begging for sleep. Instead, she and Bobby were returning to Roxbury for the first taskforce meeting. Clock was still ticking. Media needed a statement. DA demanded an update. Brass just wanted the homicide case closed and the missing child found, right now.

In the old days, D.D. would be brewing six pots of coffee and eating half a dozen donuts to get through the night. Now, instead, she was armed with a fresh bottle of water and a package of saltines. They weren't getting the job done.

She'd texted Alex as they were leaving the hospital: *Won't see you tonight, sorry bout tomorrow.* He'd texted back: *Saw the news. Good luck.*

No guilt, no whining, no recriminations. Just genuine support.

His text made her weepy, which she blamed squarely on her condition, because no man had made D.D. Warren cry in at least twenty years and like hell she'd start now.

Bobby kept looking at her ubiquitous water bottle, then at her, then at her water bottle. If he did it again, she was going to dump the contents of said bottle over his head. The thought cheered her up, and she'd almost pulled herself together by the time they found parking.

Bobby grabbed a fresh cup of black coffee, then they headed upstairs to the homicide unit. D.D. and her fellow detectives were lucky. BPD headquarters had been built only fifteen years ago, and while the location was still subject to debate, the building itself was modern and well maintained. The homicide unit appeared less *NYPD Blue* and more MetLife Insurance Company. Sensible dividers carved out brightly lit work spaces. Broad expanses of gray metal files were covered in green plants, family photos, and personal knickknacks. A Red Sox foam finger was mounted here, a Go Pats banner hung there.

The secretary had a thing for cinnamon potpourri, while the detectives had a fetish for coffee, so the space even smelled nice — a cinnamon, coffee blend that made one of the newer guys nickname the reception area Starbucks. In typical cop fashion, the nickname stuck and now the secretary had Starbucks stickers, napkins, and paper cups all positioned on the front counter, which had confused more than one witness arriving to make a statement.

D.D. found her squad and a leader from each investigative team already gathered in the conference room. She moved to the head of the table, next to the large white board that would become their case bible for the coming days. She set down her water, picked up a black marker, and they were off and running.

The search for Sophie Leoni was highest priority. Hotline was ringing nonstop and had generated two dozen tips which officers were chasing down as they spoke. Nothing significant as of yet. Canvassing of neighbors, local businesses, and community medical centers was proceeding along the same lines — some leads, but nothing significant as of yet.

Phil had run background on Sophie's caretaker, Brandi Ennis, which had come back clean. Coupled with D.D. and Bobby's personal interview, they felt they could rule her out as a suspect. Initial backgrounds on the school administration and Sophie's teacher raised no red flags. They were starting on parents next.

The video team had studied seventy-five percent of the outtakes from various cameras within a two-mile radius of the Leoni residence. They had yet to see any sign of Sophie, Brian Darby, or Tessa Leoni. Their search had broadened to include any visual of Brian Darby's white GMC Denali.

Given the crime lab's findings that a body had most likely been placed in the back of Darby's vehicle, retracing the last twenty-four hours of the Denali was their best lead. D.D. assigned two detectives to pore through credit card records to see if they could determine the last time the Denali had been fueled up. Based on that date and how many gallons were currently left in the tank, they could work out the largest possible distance Brian Darby would've been able to drive with a body in the back of his vehicle. Also, the same two detectives would check for any parking tickets, speeding citations, or Fast Lane/E-Z Pass (toll booth) records that might help place the Denali Friday night through Sunday morning.

Finally, D.D. would leak details about the Denali to the press, encouraging eye witnesses to phone in with new details.

Phil agreed to search for any properties that might be owned by Brian Darby or a family member. His initial background reports on the family hadn't revealed any red flags. Brian Darby had no arrests or warrants under his name. Couple of speeding tickets scattered over the past fifteen years, other than that he appeared to be a law-abiding citizen. He'd worked the past fifteen years for the same company, ASSC, as a merchant marine. He had a two hundred thousand dollar mortgage on the home, a thirty-four thousand dollar loan on the Denali, four grand in consumer debt, and over fifty grand in the bank, so not a bad financial picture.

Phil had also made initial contact with Brian Darby's boss, who agreed to a phone interview tomorrow morning at eleven a.m. By phone, Scott Hale had expressed shock at Darby's death, and total disbelief the man had beat his wife. Hale had also been dismayed by Sophie's disappearance and was going to ask ASSC to increase the amount of money currently being offered as a reward.

D.D., who'd written across the top of the board, *Did Brian Darby Beat His Wife?* added a check to the No column.

Which made her other squadmate, Neil, raise his hand for the Yes column. Neil had spent the day at the hospital, where he'd subpoenaed Tessa

Leoni's medical records. While there wasn't a long history of 'accidents,' today's admittance alone had revealed multiple injuries from multiple time frames. Tessa Leoni presented with bruised ribs, probably from an incident at least one week ago (the fall down the front steps, D.D. had retorted, already rolling her eyes). The doctor had also made a notation he was concerned that one fractured rib had healed improperly due to 'inadequate medical attention,' which would support Tessa's assertion that she didn't seek outside assistance, but dealt with the consequences of each beating on her own.

In addition to her concussion and fractured cheekbone, her medical chart listed a multitude of contusions, including a bruise in the shape of a rounded work boot.

'Does Brian Darby have steel-toed work boots?' D.D. asked excitedly.

'Went back to the house and retrieved one pair,' Neil said. 'Asked the lawyer if we could match the boots against the bruise on Leoni's hip. He considered that an invasion of privacy and requested we get a warrant.'

'Invasion of privacy!' D.D. snorted. 'This is the sort of discovery that helps her. Establishes pattern of abuse, meaning she won't end up in jail for twenty to life.'

'He didn't argue that. Just said she was under doctor's orders to rest, so he wanted to wait until she's recovered from her concussion.'

'Please! Then the bruise is faded and we've lost our match and she's lost her corroboration. Screw the lawyer. Get a warrant. Get it done.'

151

Neil agreed, though it would have to wait till midmorning, as he'd be starting his day at the ME's office with the autopsy of Brian Darby. The autopsy was now scheduled for seven a.m., given that Tessa Leoni was requesting the return of her husband's remains ASAP, in order to plan an appropriate funeral.

'What?' D.D. exclaimed.

'Not kidding,' Neil said. 'Her lawyer called the ME this afternoon, wanting to know how soon Tessa could get the body back. Don't ask me.'

But D.D. stared at the lanky redhead anyway. 'Brian Darby's shooting is a questionable death. Of course his body must be autopsied, which Tessa knows as well as anyone.' She turned her gaze to Bobby. 'State Troopers learn homicide one-oh-one right?'

Bobby made a show of scratching his head. 'What? They cram ninety classes into twenty-five weeks of Academy training, and we're supposed to graduate knowing basic investigative steps?'

'So why would she ask for the body back?' D.D. asked him. 'Why even make that call?'

Bobby shrugged. 'Maybe she thought the autopsy had already been performed.'

'Maybe she thought she'd get lucky,' Neil spoke up. 'She's a fellow member of law enforcement. Maybe she thought the ME would honor her request and return her husband's body without the basic post-mortem.'

D.D. chewed her lower lip. She didn't like it. Pretty and vulnerable aside, Tessa Leoni was a cool customer, amazingly lucid when she needed to be. If Tessa had made the call, there had to be a reason.

D.D. turned back to Neil. 'What did the ME tell her?'

'Nothing. The ME was speaking to her lawyer, not Trooper Leoni. Ben reminded the lawyer that an autopsy had to be performed, which Cargill didn't refute. My understanding is that they settled on a compromise — Ben would perform the autopsy first thing, to speed up the return of Darby's body to his family.'

'So autopsy is happening sooner,' D.D. mused, 'and body is being returned sooner. When will Darby's body be released?'

Neil shrugged. 'After the autopsy, an assistant will need to suture and clean up the corpse. Maybe as soon as end of day Monday, or Tuesday afternoon.'

D.D. nodded, still turning the matter around in her head, but not seeing the angle. For some reason, Tessa Leoni wanted her husband's body sooner versus later. They would have to come back to that, as there must be a reason. There was always a reason.

D.D. returned to her taskforce. She demanded some good news. Nobody had any. She demanded some fresh leads. Nobody had any.

She and Bobby volunteered what they'd learned about Tessa Leoni's misspent youth. Having to shoot to kill once in self-defense was bad luck. Twice seemed dangerously close to a pattern of behavior, though from a legal perspective, it would take three times to be the charm.

D.D. wanted to learn more about the shooting of Thomas Howe. First thing in the morning, she and Bobby would track down the officer in charge of the investigation. If possible, they'd also contact the Howe family and Tessa's father. Last but not least, they wanted to identify Brian Darby's gym and check out his exercise regimen and the possibility of steroid abuse. Man had bulked up relatively quickly, Mr. Sensitive becoming Mr. Tempermental. It was worth checking out.

With that, D.D. jotted down the next steps and handed out homework. Video team needed to complete their marathon viewing of Boston cameras. Phil needed to complete background reports, conduct property searches, and interview Brian Darby's boss. Neil had autopsy duty as well as securing a warrant for matching Brian Darby's boot against Tessa Leoni's bruised hip.

Fuel squad got to play with gas consumption and Boston maps, creating a maximum search area for Sophie Leoni, while the hotline officers would continue running down old leads and mining for fresh information.

D.D. needed reports from today's interviews on her desk within the hour. Get to documenting, she ordered her team, then return for duty at oh-dark-thirty. Sophie Leoni remained missing, which meant no rest for the weary.

The detectives filed out.

D.D. and Bobby stayed behind to brief the superintendent of homicide, then consult with the Suffolk County DA. Neither man was interested in details, as much as they wanted results. It was D.D.'s fun-filled job as lead detective to inform them she had not determined the events leading up to Brian Darby's shooting, nor located six-year-old Sophie Leoni. But hey, pretty much every cop in Boston was currently working the case, so the taskforce was bound to have something . . . sometime.

The DA, who'd gone positively bug-eyed at the revelation that Tessa Leoni had already pleaded self-defense once before, agreed to D.D.'s request for more time before determining criminal charges. Given the differences between building a case for manslaughter versus Murder 1, additional information would be ideal and a deep bore into Tessa Leoni's misspent youth a necessity.

They'd keep the media focused on the search for Sophie, and away from the particulars of Brian Darby's death.

Twelve thirty-three in the morning, D.D. finally slunk back to her own office. Her boss was satisfied, the DA appeased, her taskforce engaged. And so it went, another day in another high profile case. The cogs of the criminal justice system churning round and round.

Bobby took the seat across from her. Without a word, he picked up the first typed report from the pile on her desk and began to read.

After another moment, D.D. joined him.

14

When Sophie was almost three, she locked herself in the trunk of my police cruiser. This happened before I ever met Brian, so I had only myself to blame.

We were living across the hall from Mrs. Ennis at the time. It was late fall, when the sun faded earlier and the nights were growing colder. Sophie and I had been outside, where we'd walked to the park and back. Now it was dinnertime, and I was fussing in the kitchen while assuming she was playing in the family room, where the TV was blaring *Curious George*.

I'd made a small salad, part of my program to introduce more vegetables into my child's diet. Then I'd grilled two chicken breasts and baked Ore-Ida French fries — my compromise, Sophie could have her beloved fries as long as she ate some salad first.

This project took me twenty, twenty-five minutes. But a busy twenty-five minutes. I was occupied and apparently not paying attention to my toddler because when I walked into the family room to announce it was time for dinner, my child wasn't there.

I didn't panic right away. I'd like to say it was because I was a trained police officer, but it had more to do with being Sophie's mom. Sophie started running at thirteen months and hadn't slowed down since. She was the child who disappeared in grocery stores, bolted away from park swing sets, and made a quick beeline through a sea of legs in a crowded mall, whether I was following or not. In the past six months, I'd already lost Sophie several times. In a matter of minutes, however, we always found each other again.

I started with the basics — a quick walk through our tiny one bedroom. I called her name, then for good measure, checked the cupboards in the bathroom, both closets, and under the bed. She wasn't in the apartment.

I checked the front door, which, sure enough, I'd forgotten to bolt, meaning the entire apartment complex had just become fair game. I crossed the hall, cursing myself silently and feeling the growing frustration that comes from being an overstretched single parent, responsible for all things at all times, whether I was up to the challenge or not.

I knocked on Mrs. Ennis's door. No, Sophie wasn't there, but she swore she'd just seen Sophie playing outside.

Outside I went. Sun had gone down. Streetlights blazed, as well as the spotlights on the front of the apartment building. It was never truly dark in a city like Boston. I took that to heart as I walked around the squat brick complex, calling my daughter's name. When no laughing child came running around the corner, no high-pitched giggles erupted from a nearby bush, I grew more concerned.

I started to shiver. It was cold, I didn't have a

jacket, and given that I remembered seeing Sophie's raspberry-colored fleece hanging next to the door in our apartment, she didn't have a coat either.

My heart accelerated. I took a deep, steadying breath, trying to fight a growing well of dread. The whole time I'd been pregnant with Sophie, I'd lived in a state of fear. I hadn't felt the miracle of life growing in my body. Instead, I saw the photo of my dead baby brother, a marble white newborn with bright red lips.

When I'd gone into labor, I didn't think I'd be able to breathe through the terror clutching my throat. I would fail, my baby would die, there was no hope, no hope, no hope.

Except, then there was Sophie. Perfect, mottled red, screaming loudly Sophie. Warm and slippery and achingly beautiful as I cradled her against my breast.

My daughter was tough. And fearless and impulsive.

You didn't panic with a kid like Sophie. You strategized: What would Sophie do?

I returned to the apartment complex, performed a quick door-to-door canvass. Most of my neighbors weren't home from work yet; the few that answered hadn't seen Sophie. I moved fast now, footsteps with purpose.

Sophie liked the park and might head there, except we'd already spent an afternoon playing on the swings and even she'd been ready to leave at the end. She liked the corner store and was positively fascinated by the Laundromat — she loved to watch the clothes spin.

I decided to head back upstairs. Another quick walk-through of our apartment to determine if anything else might be missing — a special toy, her favorite purse. Then I'd grab my car keys and tour the block.

I made it just inside the door, then discovered what she'd taken: The keys to my police cruiser were no longer sitting in the change dish.

This time, I hauled ass out of the apartment and down the front steps. Toddlers and police cruisers didn't mix. Forget the radio, lights, and sirens in the front. I had a shotgun in the trunk.

I ran to the passenger's side, peering in from the sidewalk. The interior of the cruiser appeared empty. I tried the door, but it was locked. I walked around more carefully, heart pounding, breathing shallow as I inspected each door and window. No sign of activity. Locked, locked, locked.

But she'd taken the keys. Think like Sophie. What button might she have hit on the key fob? What might she have done?

Then I heard her. A *thump, thump, thump* from the trunk. She was inside, banging against the lid.

'Sophie?' I called out.

The thumping stopped.

'Mommy?'

'Yes, Sophie. Mommy's here. Honey,' my voice had risen shrilly, despite my best intentions. 'Are you all right?'

'Mommy,' my child replied calmly from inside the locked trunk. 'Stuck, Mommy. Stuck.'

I closed my eyes, exhaling my pent-up breath.

159

'Sophie, honey,' I said as firmly as I could. 'I need you to listen to Mommy. Don't touch anything.'

' 'Kay.'

'Do you still have the keys?'

'Mmm-hmm.'

'Are they in your hand?'

'No touching!'

'Well, you can touch the keys, honey. Hold the keys, just don't touch anything else.'

'Stuck, Mommy. Stuck.'

'I understand, honey. Would you like to get out?'

'Yes!'

'Okay. Hold the keys. Find a button with your thumb. Push it.'

I heard a click as Sophie did as she was told. I ran to the front door to check. Of course, she'd hit the lock key.

'Sophie, honey,' I called back. 'Button next to it! Hit that one!'

Another click, and the front door unlocked. Expelling another breath, I opened the door, found the latch for the trunk and released it. Seconds later, I was standing above my daughter, who was curled up as a pink puddle in the middle of the metal locker holding my backup shotgun and a black duffel bag filled with ammo and additional policing gear.

'Are you all right?' I demanded to know.

My daughter yawned, held out her arms to me. 'Hungry!'

I scooped her out of the trunk, placed her on her feet on the sidewalk, where she promptly shivered from the chill.

'Mommy,' she started to whine.

'Sophie!' I interrupted firmly, feeling the first edge of anger now that my child was out of immediate danger. 'Listen to me.' I took the keys from her, held them up, shook them hard. 'These are *not* yours. You *never* touch these keys. Do you understand? No touching!'

Sophie's lower lip jutted out. 'No touching,' she warbled. The full extent of what she'd done seemed to penetrate. Her face fell, she stared at the sidewalk.

'You do not leave the apartment without telling me! Look me in the eye. Repeat that. Tell Mommy.'

She looked up at me with liquid blue eyes. 'No leave. Tell Mommy,' she whispered.

Reprimand delivered, I gave in to the past ten minutes of terror, scooped her back into my arms, and held her tight. 'Don't scare Mommy like that,' I whispered against the top of her head. 'Seriously, Sophie. I love you. I never want to lose you. You are my Sophie.'

In response her tiny fingers dug into my shoulders, clutched me back.

After another moment, I set her down. I should've set the bolt lock, I reminded myself. And I'd have to move my keys to the top of a cabinet, or perhaps add them to the gun safe. More things to remember. More management in an already overstretched life.

My eyes stung a little, but I didn't cry. She was my Sophie. And I loved her.

'Weren't you scared?' I asked as I took her

hand and led her back to the apartment for our now cold dinner.

'No, Mommy.'

'Not even locked in the dark?'

'No, Mommy.'

'Really? You're a brave girl, Sophie Leoni.'

She squeezed my hand. 'Mommy come,' she said simply. 'I know. Mommy come for me.'

★ ★ ★

I reminded myself of that evening now, as I lay trapped in a hospital room, surrounded by beeping monitors and the constant hum of a busy medical center. Sophie was tough. Sophie was brave. My daughter was not terrified of the dark, as I'd let the detectives believe. I wanted them to fear for her, and I wanted them to feel for her. Anything that would make them work that much harder, bring her home that much sooner.

I needed Bobby and D.D., whether they believed me or not. My daughter needed them, especially given that her superhero mother currently couldn't stand without vomiting.

It went against the grain, but there it was: My daughter was in jeopardy, lost in the dark. And there wasn't a damn thing I could do about it.

One a.m.

I fisted my hand around the blue button, held it tight.

'Sophie, be brave,' I whispered in the semi-darkened room, willing my body to heal

162

faster. 'Mommy's coming. Mommy will always come for you.'

Then I forced myself to review the past thirty-six hours. I considered the full tragedy of the days behind. Then I contemplated the full danger of the days ahead.

Work the angles, anticipate the obstacles, get one step ahead.

Brian's autopsy had been moved to first thing in the morning. A Pyrrhic victory — I had gotten my way, and in doing so, had certainly stuck my own head in the noose.

But it also fast-forwarded the timeline, took some of the control from them and gave it back to me.

Nine hours, I figured. Nine hours to physically recover, then ready or not, the games began.

I thought of Brian, dying on the kitchen floor. I thought of Sophie, snatched from our home.

Then I allowed myself one last moment to mourn my husband. Because once upon a time, we'd been happy.

Once upon a time, we'd been a family.

15

D.D. made it back to her North End condo at two-thirty in the morning. She collapsed on her bed, fully clothed, and set her alarm for four hours' sleep. She woke up six hours later, glanced at the clock, and immediately panicked.

Eight-thirty in the morning? She never overslept. Never!

She bolted out of bed, gazed wild-eyed around her room, then grabbed her cellphone and dialed. Bobby answered after the second ring, and she expelled in a breathless rush: 'I'm coming I'm coming I'm coming. I just need forty minutes.'

'Okay.'

'Must have screwed up the alarm. Just gotta shower, change, breakfast. I'm on my way.'

'Okay.'

'Fuck! The traffic!'

'D.D.,' Bobby said, more firmly. 'It's okay.'

'It's eight-thirty!' she shouted back, and to her horror realized she was about to cry. She plopped back on the edge of her bed. Good God, she was a mess. What was happening to her?

'I'm still home,' Bobby said now. 'Annabelle's sleeping, I'm feeding the baby. Tell you what. I'll call the lead detective from the Thomas Howe shooting. With any luck, we can meet in Framingham in two hours. Sound like a plan?'

D.D., sounding meek: 'Okay.'

'Call you back in thirty. Enjoy the shower.'

D.D. should say something. In the old days, she would've definitely said something. Instead, she clicked off her cell and sat there, feeling like a balloon that had abruptly deflated.

After another minute, she trudged to the sleek master bath, where she stripped off yesterday's clothes and stood in a sea of white ceramic tiles, staring at her naked body in the mirror.

She touched her stomach with her fingers, brushed her palms across the smooth expanse of her skin, tried to feel some sign of what was happening to her. Five weeks late, she didn't detect any baby bump or gentle mound. If anything, her stomach appeared flatter, her body thinner. Then again, going from all you can eat buffets to broth and crackers could do that to a girl.

She switched her inspection to her face, where her rumpled blonde curls framed gaunt cheeks and bruised eyes. She hadn't taken a pregnancy test yet. Given her missed cycle, then the intense fatigue interspersed with relentless nausea, her condition seemed obvious. Just her luck to end a three-year sex drought by getting knocked up.

Maybe she wasn't pregnant, she thought now. Maybe she was dying instead.

'Wishful thinking,' she muttered darkly.

But the words brought her up short. She didn't mean that. She couldn't mean that.

She felt her stomach again. Maybe her waist was thicker. Maybe, right over here, she could feel a hint of round . . . Her fingers lingered,

165

cradled the spot gently. And for a second, she pictured a newborn, puffy red face, dark slitted eyes, rosebud lips. Boy? Girl? It didn't matter. Just a baby. An honest to God baby.

'I won't hurt you,' she whispered in the quiet of the bathroom. 'I'm not mommy material. I'm gonna suck at this. But I won't hurt you. I'd never intentionally hurt you.'

She paused, sighed heavily, felt her denial take the first delicate step toward acceptance.

'But you're gonna have to work with me on this. Okay? You're not winning the mommy lottery here. So it's gonna take some compromise on both our parts. Like maybe you could start letting me eat again, and in return, I'll try to get to bed before midnight. It's the best I can do. If you want a better offer, you need to return to the procreation pot and start over.

'Your mommy's trying to find a little girl. And maybe you don't care about that, but I do. Can't help myself. This job's in my blood.'

Another pause. She sighed heavily again, her fingers still stroking her stomach. 'So I gotta do what I gotta do,' she whispered. 'Because the world is a mess, and someone has to clean it up. Or girls like Sophie Leoni will never stand a chance. I don't want to live in a world like that. And I don't want you to grow up in a world like that. So let's do this together. I'm going to shower, then I'm going to eat. How about some cereal?'

Her stomach didn't immediately sour, which she took as a yes. 'Cereal it is. Then back to work for both of us. Sooner we find Sophie, sooner I can take you home to your daddy. Who, at least once upon a time, mentioned wanting kids. Hope that's still true. Ah geez. We're all gonna need a little faith here. All right, let's get this done.'

D.D. turned on the shower spray.

Later, she ate Cheerios, then left her condo without throwing up. Good enough, she decided. Good enough.

*   *   *

Detective Butch Walthers lived up to his name. Heavyset face, massive shoulders, barrel gut of a former linebacker now gone to seed. He agreed to meet Bobby and D.D. at a small breakfast spot around the corner from his house, because it was his day off and as long as he was talking shop, he wanted a meal out of it.

D.D. walked in, hit a solid wall of cooked eggs and fried bacon and nearly walked back out. She'd always loved diners. She'd always loved eggs and bacon. To be reduced to instant nausea now was beyond cruel.

She took several steadying breaths through her open mouth. Then in a fit of inspiration, she fished peppermint gum out of her shoulder bag. Old trick learned from working countless homicide scenes — chewing minty gum overwhelms one's sense of smell. She stuck three sticks into her mouth, felt the sharp peppermint flavor flood the back of her throat, and managed to make it to the rear of the diner, where Bobby was already sitting across from Detective

167

Walthers in a side booth.

Both men stood as she approached. She introduced herself to Walthers, nodded at Bobby, then slid into the booth first, so she could be closest to the window. She was in luck, the double-hung appeared to actually open. She immediately went to work on the latches.

'Little hot,' she commented. 'Hope you don't mind.'

Both men watched her curiously, but said nothing. The diner was hot, D.D. thought defensively, and the rush of crisp March air smelled of snow and nothing else. She leaned closer to the narrow opening.

'Coffee?' Bobby asked.

'Water,' D.D. said.

He arched a brow.

'Already had java,' she lied. 'Don't want the jitters.'

Bobby wasn't buying it. She should've known. She turned to Walthers before Bobby could ask about breakfast. D.D. turning down a meal probably signaled the end of the universe as he knew it.

'Thanks for meeting with us,' D.D. said. 'Especially on your day off.'

Walthers nodded accommodatingly. His bulbous nose was lined with broken red capillaries. Drinker, D.D. deduced. One of the old-time veterans nearing the end of his policing career. If he thought life was hard now, she thought with a trace of sympathy, wait till he tried retirement. So many empty hours to fill with memories of the good old days, and regrets over

168

the ones that got away.

'Surprised to get a call 'bout the Howe shooting,' Walthers said now. 'Worked a lotta cases in my time. Never considered that investigation to be an interesting one.'

'Seemed pretty clear-cut?'

Walthers shrugged. 'Yes and no. Physical evidence was FUBAR, but background on Tommy Howe was straightforward — Tessa Leoni wasn't the first girl he'd attacked; just the first who'd fought back.'

'Really?' D.D. was intrigued.

The waitress appeared, gazing at them expectantly. Walthers ordered the Trailblazer Special with four links of sausage, two fried eggs, and half a plate of home fries. Bobby seconded the order. D.D., feeling brave, went with orange juice.

Now Bobby was definitely staring at her.

'So walk us through the case,' D.D. said to Walthers, the moment the waitress left.

'Call came into nine-one-one. The mom, that's my memory, quite hysterical. First responder found Tommy Howe dead from a single gunshot wound in the family room, the parents and his sister gathered round in their bathrobes. The mother was sobbing, father trying to console, younger sister shell-shocked. Parents didn't know nothing 'bout anything. They'd woken up to a noise, father had gone downstairs, found Tommy's body, and that had been that.

'Sister, Juliana, was the one with the answers, but it took a bit to get them. She'd had a friend sleeping over — '

169

'Tessa Leoni,' D.D. supplied.

'Exactly. Tessa had fallen asleep on the couch while they were watching movies. Juliana had gone upstairs to bed. Shortly after one a.m., she'd also heard a noise. She'd come downstairs and saw her brother and Tessa on the couch. In her own words, she wasn't sure what was going on, but then she heard a gunshot and Tommy staggered back. He fell to the floor, and Tessa got off the sofa, still holding the gun.'

'Juliana saw Tessa shoot her brother?' D.D. asked.

'Yep. Juliana was pretty messed up. She said Tessa claimed Tommy had attacked her. Juliana didn't know what to do. Tommy was bleeding everywhere, she could hear her father coming down the stairs. She panicked, told Tessa to go home, which Tessa did.'

'Tessa ran home in the middle of the night?' Bobby spoke up with a frown.

'Tessa lived on the same street, five houses down. Not a big distance to cover. When the dad made it downstairs, he yelled at Juliana to have her mom call nine-one-one. Which is the scene I walked into. Bloody family room, dead teenager, missing shooter.'

'Where was Tommy shot?'

'Upper left thigh. Bullet nicked his femoral artery and he bled out. Bad luck, if you think about it — dying from a single GSW to the leg.'

'Only one shot?'

'That's all it took.'

Interesting, D.D. thought. At least Brian Darby had earned three in the chest. What a

170

difference twenty-five weeks of intensive firearms training could make.

'So where was Tessa?' D.D. asked.

'After Juliana's statement, I proceeded to the Leoni residence, where Tessa answered on the first knock. She'd showered — '

'No way!'

'Told you the physical evidence was FUBAR. Then again' — Walthers shrugged his burly shoulders — 'she was sixteen years old. By her own admission, she'd been sexually assaulted, before shooting her attacker. Heading straight for the shower — can you blame her?'

D.D. still didn't like it. 'What physical evidence could you recover?'

'The twenty-two. Tessa handed it right over. Her prints were on the handle and ballistics matched the slug that killed Tommy Howe to the gun. We bagged and tagged her discarded clothes. No semen on the underwear — she claimed he didn't, ahem, get to finish what he'd started. But some blood on her clothing, same type as Tommy Howe.'

'Test her hands for powder?'

'Negative — but then, she'd showered.'

'Rape kit?'

'She declined.'

'She declined?'

'She said she'd been through enough. I tried to convince her to let a nurse examine her for bruising, tried to explain it would be in her own best interest, but she wasn't buying it. Girl was shaking like a leaf. You could see — she was done.'

'Where's the father through all this?' Bobby wanted to know.

'He woke up when we entered the home. Apparently figuring out for the first time that his daughter had returned early from her sleepover and that there'd been an incident. He seemed a little . . . checked out. Stood in the kitchen in his boxers and wife-beater T-shirt, arms crossed over his chest, not saying a word. I mean, here's his sixteen-year-old daughter talking about being attacked by a boy, and he's just standing there like a goddamn statue. Donnie,' Walthers snapped his fingers as the name came to him, 'Donnie Leoni. Owned his own garage. Never could figure him out. I was guessing drinking, but never confirmed it.'

'Mother?' D.D. asked.

'Dead. Six months earlier, heart failure. Not a happy household, but . . . ' Again, Walthers shrugged. 'Most of them aren't.'

'So,' D.D. replayed the events in her mind, 'Tommy Howe is dead from a single GSW in his family room. Tessa confesses to the crime, all cleaned up and unwilling to submit to a physical exam. I don't get it. The DA simply took her word for it? Poor traumatized sixteen-year-old girl must be telling the truth?'

Walthers shook his head. 'Between you and me?'

'By all means,' D.D. assured him. 'Between friends.'

'I couldn't make heads or tails of Tessa Leoni. I mean, on the one hand, she was sitting in her kitchen trembling uncontrollably. On the other

172

hand . . . she delivered a precise recounting of every minute of the evening. In all my years, never had a victim recount so many details with such clarity, especially a victim of sexual assault. It bothered me, but what could I say: *Honey, your memory is too good for me to take you seriously?'* Walthers shook his head. 'In this day and age, those kinds of statements can cost a detective his shield, and trust me — I got two ex-wives to support — I need my pension.'

'So why let her off with self-defense? Why not press charges?' Bobby asked, clearly as perplexed as D.D.

'Because Tessa Leoni might have been a questionable victim, but Tommy Howe was the perfect perpetrator. Within twenty-four hours, three different girls phoned in with accounts of being sexually assaulted by him. None of them wanted to make a formal statement, mind you, but the more we dug, the more we discovered Tommy had a clear reputation with the ladies: He didn't take no for an answer. He didn't necessarily use brute force, which is why so many of the girls were reluctant to testify. Instead, sounded like he would ply them with alcohol, maybe even spike their drinks. But a couple of the girls remembered clearly *not* being interested in Tommy Howe, and waking up in his bed anyway.'

'Rohypnol,' D.D. said.

'Probably. We never found any trace of it in his dorm room, but even his buddies agreed that what Tommy wanted, Tommy got, and the girl's feelings on the subject weren't of much interest to him.'

'Nice guy,' Bobby muttered darkly.

'His parents certainly thought so,' Walthers remarked. 'When the DA announced he wasn't pressing charges, tried to explain the mitigating circumstances . . . You would've thought we were claiming the Pope was an atheist. The father — James, James Howe — hit the roof. Screamed at the DA, called my lieutenant to rant how my shitty police work was allowing a cold-blooded murderer to go free. Jim had contacts, he'd get us all in the end.'

'Did he?' D.D. asked curiously.

Walthers rolled his eyes. 'Please, he was corporate middle management for Polaroid. Contacts? He made a decent living, and I'm sure his underlings feared him. But he was only a king of an eight-by-eight cubicle and a two thousand square foot house. Parents.' Walthers shook his head.

'Mr. and Mrs. Howe never believed Tommy attacked Tessa Leoni?'

'Nope. They could never see their son's guilt, which was interesting, 'cause Donnie Leoni could never see his daughter's innocence. I heard through the grapevine that he kicked her out. Apparently, he's one of those guys who believes the girl must be asking for it.' Walthers shook his head again. 'What can you do?'

The waitress reappeared, bearing platters of food. She slid plates in front of Walthers and Bobby, then handed D.D. her glass of juice.

'Anything else?' the waitress asked.

They shook their heads; she departed.

The men dug in. D.D. leaned closer to the cracked window to escape the greasy odor of sausage. She removed her gum, attempted the orange juice.

So Tessa Leoni had shot Tommy Howe once in the leg. If D.D. pictured the scene in her mind, the choreography made sense. Tessa, sixteen years old, terrified, pressed down into the sofa cushions by the weight of a bigger, stronger male. Her right hand fumbling beside her, feeling the lump of her purse digging into her hip. Fishing for her father's twenty-two, finally getting her hand around the grip, wedging it between their bodies . . .

Walthers had been right — damned unlucky for Tommy that he'd died from such a wound. All things considered, unlucky for Tessa, too, as she'd lost her father and her best friend over it.

It sounded like justifiable homicide, given the number of other women willing to corroborate Tommy's history of sexual assault. And yet, for one woman to have now been involved in two fatal shootings . . . First one involving an aggressive teenage boy. Second one involving an abusive husband. First incident a single shot to the leg that just happened to prove fatal. Second incident three shots to the chest, center of the kill zone.

Two shootings. Two incidents of self-defense. Bad luck, D.D. mused, taking a second small sip of orange juice. Or learning curve?

Walthers and Bobby finished up their meals. Bobby grabbed the check, Walthers grunted his thanks. They exchanged cards, then Walthers went his way, leaving Bobby and D.D. standing alone on the sidewalk.

Bobby turned to her the second Walthers disappeared around the corner. 'Something you want to tell me, D.D.?'

'No.'

He clenched his jaw, looked like he might press the matter, then didn't. He turned away, studying the front awning of the diner. If D.D. didn't know better, she'd think his feelings were hurt.

'Got a question for you,' D.D. said, to change the subject and ease the tension. 'I keep coming back to Tessa Leoni, forced to kill two men in two separate incidents of self-defense. I'm wondering, is she that unlucky, or is she that smart?'

That caught Bobby's attention. He turned back to her, expression intent.

'Think about it,' D.D. continued. 'Tessa's hung out to dry at sixteen, ends up pregnant and alone at twenty-one. But then, in her own words, she rebuilds her life. Sobers up. Gives birth to a beautiful daughter, becomes a respectable police officer, even meets a great guy. Until the first time he drinks too much and whacks her. Now what does she do?'

'Cops don't confide in other cops,' Bobby said stiffly.

'Exactly,' D.D. agreed. 'Violates the code of the patrol officer, who's expected to handle all situations alone. Now, Tessa could leave her husband. Next time Brian shipped out, Tessa and Sophie would have a sixty-day window to get settled into their own place. Except, maybe having lived in a cute little house, Tessa doesn't want to return to one-bedroom living. Maybe she likes the house, the yard, the expensive SUV, the fifty grand in the bank.'

'Maybe she doesn't believe moving out will be enough,' Bobby countered levelly. 'Not all abusive husbands are willing to take the hint.'

'All right,' D.D. granted him. 'That, too. Tessa decides she needs a more permanent solution. One that removes Brian Darby from her and Sophie's life forever, while preserving prime Boston real estate. So what does she do?'

Bobby stared at her. 'You're saying that based on her experience with Tommy Howe, Tessa decides to stage an attack where she can shoot her husband in self-defense?'

'I'm thinking that thought should've crossed her mind.'

'Yeah. Except Tessa's injuries aren't staged. Concussion, fractured cheekbone, multiple contusions. Woman can't even stand up.'

'Maybe Tessa goaded her husband into attacking. Not too hard to do. She knew he'd been drinking. Now all she has to do is incite him into whacking her a few times, and she's safe to open fire. Brian gives in to his inner demon, and Tessa takes advantage.'

Bobby frowned, shook his head. 'That's cold. And still doesn't hold water.'

'Why not?'

'Because of Sophie. So Tessa gets her husband to hit her. And Tessa shoots her husband. As you put it yesterday, that explains his body in the kitchen, and her visit with the EMTs in the sunroom. But what about Sophie? Where's Sophie?'

D.D. scowled. Her arm rested across her stomach. 'Maybe she wanted Sophie out of the house in case she witnessed the event.'

'Then she arranges for Sophie to stay with Mrs. Ennis.'

'Wait — maybe that's the problem. She didn't arrange for Sophie to stay with Mrs. Ennis. Sophie saw too much, then Tessa had to squirrel her away so we couldn't question her.'

'Tessa has Sophie in hiding?'

D.D. thought about it. 'It would explain why she was so slow to cooperate. She's not worried about her child — she knows Sophie is safe.'

But Bobby was already shaking his head. 'Come on, Tessa's a trained police officer. She knows the minute she declares her child missing, the whole state goes on Amber Alert. What are the chances of successfully hiding a child whose photo is being beamed over every major news medium in the free world? Who would she even trust with that kind of request — *It's nine a.m. Sunday morning, I just shot my husband, so hey, want to run away with my six-year-old for a bit?* This is a woman we've already established doesn't have close family or friends. Her options would be Mrs. Ennis or Mrs. Ennis, and Mrs. Ennis doesn't have Sophie.

'Furthermore,' Bobby continued relentlessly, 'there's no endgame there. Sooner or later, we're gonna find Sophie. And when we do, we're

178

gonna ask her what she saw that morning. If Sophie did witness Tessa and Brian's confrontation, a few days' delay isn't going to change anything. So why take such a risk with your own kid?'

D.D. pursed her lips. 'Well, when you put it like that . . . ' she muttered.

'Why is this so hard for you?' Bobby asked suddenly. 'A fellow officer is hospitalized. Her young daughter is missing. Most of the detectives are happy to help her out, while you seem hell-bent on finding a reason to string her up.'

'I am not — '

'Is it because she's young and pretty? Are you really so petty?'

'Bobby Dodge!' D.D. exploded.

'We need to find Sophie Leoni!' Bobby yelled right back. In all their years together, D.D. wasn't sure she'd ever heard Bobby yell, but that was okay, because she was shouting, too.

'I know!'

'It's been over twenty-four hours. My daughter was crying at three a.m., and all I could wonder was if somewhere little Sophie was doing the same.'

'I know!'

'I hate this case, D.D.!'

'Me, too!'

Bobby stopped yelling. He breathed heavily instead. D.D. took a moment to expel a frustrated breath. Bobby ran a hand through his short hair. D.D. mopped back her blonde curls.

'We need to talk to Brian Darby's boss,' Bobby

179

stated after another minute. 'We need a list of any friends, associates who might know what he'd do with his stepdaughter.'

D.D. glanced at her watch. Ten a.m. Phil had scheduled the call with Scott Hale for eleven. 'We gotta wait another hour.'

'Fine. Let's start calling gyms. Maybe Brian had a personal trainer. People confess everything to their personal trainers, and we need a confession right about now.'

'You call gyms,' she said.

Bobby eyed her warily. 'Why? What are you going to do?'

'Locate Juliana Howe.'

'D.D. — '

'Divide and conquer,' she interjected crisply. 'Cover twice the ground, get results twice as fast.'

'Jesus. You really are a hard-ass.'

'Used to be what you loved about me.'

D.D. headed for her vehicle. Bobby didn't follow her.

16

Brian and I had our first big fight four months after getting married. Second week in April, an unexpected snowstorm had blanketed New England. I'd been on duty the night before, and by seven a.m. the Mass Pike was a tangled mess of multiple auto accidents, abandoned vehicles, and panicked pedestrians. We were up to our ears in it, graveyard shift swinging into day shift even as additional officers were being summoned and most emergency personnel activated. Welcome to the day in the life of a uniformed officer during a wintry Nor'easter.

At eleven a.m., four hours after I would've normally ended my shift, I managed to call home. No one answered. I didn't worry. Figured Brian and Sophie were outside playing in the snow. Maybe sledding, or building a snowman or digging for giant purple crocuses beneath the crystal blue April snow.

By one, my fellow officers and I had managed to get the worst of the accidents cleared, about three dozen disabled vehicles relocated, and at least two dozen stranded drivers on their way. Clearing the Pike allowed the plows and sand and gravel trucks to finally do their job, which in turn eased our job.

I finally returned to my cruiser long enough to take a sip of cold coffee and check my cellphone, which had buzzed several times at my waist. I was just noticing the long string of calls from Mrs. Ennis when my pager went off at my shoulder. It was dispatch, trying to reach me. I had an emergency phone call they were trying to patch through.

My heart rate spiked. I reached reflexively for the steering wheel of my parked cruiser, as if that would ground me. I had a vague memory of granting permission, of picking up the radio to hear Mrs. Ennis's panicked voice. She'd been waiting for over five hours now. Where was Sophie? Where was Brian?

At first, I didn't understand, but then the pieces of the story emerged. Brian had called Mrs. Ennis at six a.m., when the snow had first started falling. He'd been watching the weather and, in his adrenaline junkie way, had determined this would be a perfect powder ski day. Sophie's daycare was bound to be canceled. Could Mrs. Ennis watch her instead?

Mrs. Ennis had agreed, but she'd need at least an hour or two to get to the house. Brian hadn't been thrilled. Roads would be getting worse, yada yada yada. So instead, he offered to drop Sophie at Mrs. Ennis's apartment on his way to the mountains. Mrs. Ennis had liked that idea better, as it kept her off the bus. Brian would be there by eight. She agreed to have breakfast waiting for Sophie.

Except, it was now one-thirty. No Brian. No Sophie. And no one answering the phone at the house. What had happened?

I didn't know. Couldn't know. Refused to picture the possibilities that immediately leapt into my mind. The way a teenager's body could eject from a car and wrap around a telephone pole. Or the way the steering column of an older, pre-air bag vehicle could cave in a grown adult's chest, leaving a man sitting perfectly still, almost appearing asleep in the driver's seat until you noticed the trickle of blood at the corner of his mouth. Or the eight-year-old girl, who'd just three months ago had to be cut out of the crushed front end of a four-door sedan, her relatively uninjured mother standing there, screaming how the baby had been crying, she'd just turned around to check the baby . . .

These are the things I know. These are the scenes I remembered as I slammed my cruiser into gear, flipped on lights and sirens and fishtailed my way toward my home, thirty minutes away.

My hands were shaking when I finally careened to a halt in front of our brick garage, front end of my cruiser on the sidewalk; back half in the street. I left on my lights, bolting out of the cruiser and up the snow-buried stairs toward the dark home above. My boot hit the first patch of ice and I grabbed the metal railing just in time to keep from plummeting to the street below. Then I crested the hill and was pulling on my front door, working my keys with one hand, banging on the door with the other, even as the dark-eyed windows told me everything I didn't want to know.

Finally, with a sharp wrench of my hand, I twisted the key in the lock, shoved open the door . . .

Nothing. Empty kitchen, vacant family room. I rushed upstairs; both bedrooms unoccupied.

My duty belt jingled loudly at my waist as I rat-tat-tatted back down the stairs into the kitchen. There, I finally paused, took several steadying breaths, and reminded myself I was a trained police officer. Less adrenaline, more intelligence. That's how one solved problems. That's how one stayed in control.

'Mommy? Mommy, you're home!'

My heart practically leapt out of my chest. I turned just in time to catch Sophie as she hurtled herself into my arms, hugged me half a dozen times, and started prattling about her exciting snow day in one long breathless rush that left me dazed and confused all over again.

Then I realized Sophie hadn't returned alone, but that a neighborhood girl was standing in the doorway. She raised her hand in greeting.

'Mrs. Leoni?' she asked, then immediately flushed. 'I mean, Officer Leoni.'

It took a bit, but I managed to sort it out. Brian had definitely gone skiing. But he'd never taken Sophie to Mrs. Ennis's house. Instead, while loading his gear, he'd run across fifteen-year-old Sarah Clemons, who lived in the apartment building next door. She'd been shoveling the front walk, he'd started talking to her, and next thing she knew, she'd agreed to watch Sophie until I got home, so Brian could get out of town faster.

Sophie, who was enamored with teenage girls, had thought this was an exciting change of plans. Apparently, she and Sarah had spent the morning sledding down the street, having a snowball fight, and watching episodes of *Gossip Girl*, which Sarah had TiVo'd.

Brian had never clarified his return, but had informed Sarah that I'd appear home sooner or later. Sophie had caught sight of my cruiser coming down the street and that had been that.

I was home. Sophie was happy, and Sarah was relieved to turn over her unexpected charge. I managed to scrounge up fifty bucks. Then I called Mrs. Ennis, reported back to dispatch, and sent my daughter, who was hopped up on hot chocolate and teenage television shows, outside to build a snowman. I stood on the back deck to supervise, still in uniform, while I placed the first phone call to Brian's cell.

He didn't answer.

After that, I forced myself to return my duty belt to the gun safe in the master bedroom, and carefully turn the combo lock. There are other things I remember. Other things I know.

Sophie and I made it through the evening. I discovered you can want to kill your spouse and still be an effective parent. We ate macaroni and cheese for dinner, played several games of Candy Land, then I stuck Sophie in the tub for her nightly bath.

Eight-thirty p.m., she was sound asleep in bed. I paced the kitchen, the family room, the freezing cold sunroom. Then I returned outside, hoping to burn off my growing rage by raking the snow from the roof and shoveling the side steps and back deck.

At ten p.m., I took a hot shower and changed

into a clean uniform. Did not remove the duty belt from the safe. Did not trust myself with my state-issued Sig Sauer.

At ten-fifteen, my husband finally walked through the front door, carrying a giant bag and his downhill skis. He was whistling, moving with the kind of loose-limbed grace that comes from spending an entire day engaged in intense physical activity.

He leaned his skis against the wall. Set down his ski bag. Tossed his keys on the kitchen table, then was just starting to remove his boots when he spotted me. He seemed to notice my uniform first, his gaze going automatically to the clock on the wall.

'It's that late? Crap, sorry. I must've lost track of time.'

I stared at him, hands on my hips, the epitome of the nagging fishwife. I didn't fucking care.

'Where. Were. You.'

The words came out hard and clipped. Brian looked up, appeared genuinely surprised. 'Skiing. Didn't Sarah tell you that? The girl next door. She brought Sophie home, right?'

'Funny question to ask now, don't you think?'

He hesitated, less certain. 'Is Sophie home?'

'Yes.'

'Did Sarah do okay? I mean, Sophie's okay?'

'Best I can tell.'

Brian nodded, seemed to be considering. 'So . . . why am I in so much trouble?'

'Mrs. Ennis — ' I started.

'Shit!' he exploded, jumping immediately to standing. 'I was supposed to call her. While driving. Except the roads really were crap, and I needed two hands on the wheel, and by the time I got to the highway and better conditions . . . Oh no . . . ' He groaned. Slumped back down in his seat. 'I screwed that up.'

'*You left my child with a stranger! You took off to play, when I needed you here. And you panicked a perfectly wonderful old woman who will probably have to double her heart medicine for the next week!*'

'Yeah,' my husband agreed, mumbling. 'I messed up. I should've called her. I'm sorry.'

'How could you?' I heard myself say.

He went back to work on the laces of his boots. 'I forgot. I was going to drop Sophie off at Mrs. Ennis's house, but then I met Sarah and she's right next door — '

'You left Sophie with a stranger for the entire day — '

'Whoa, whoa, whoa. It was already eight. I figured you'd be home at any time.'

'I worked till after one. And I'd still be working, except Mrs. Ennis called dispatch and had them emergency page me.'

Brian paled and stopped fiddling with his boots. 'Uh-oh.'

'No kidding!'

'Okay. Okay. Yes. Definitely. Not calling Mrs. Ennis was a first-class fuckup. I'm sorry, Tessa. I'll call Mrs. Ennis in the morning and apologize.'

'You don't know how scared I was,' I had to state.

He didn't speak.

'The whole way . . . driving here. Have you ever held an infant's skull in your hands, Brian?'

He didn't speak.

'It's like cradling rose petals. The unfused segments are so paper thin you can see through them, so light that if you exhale, they'll blow out of your cupped hands. These are the things I know, Brian. These are the things I can't forget. Which means, you *don't* screw up with a woman like me, Brian. You *don't* hand over my kid to a stranger, you *don't* ditch my daughter just so you can get out to play. You guard Sophie. Or you get the hell out of our lives. Are we clear on that?'

'I screwed up,' he replied levelly. 'I get that. Is Sophie all right?'

'Yes — '

'Did she like Sarah?'

'Apparently — '

'And you called Mrs. Ennis?'

'Of course!'

'Then at least things turned out all right in the end.' He returned to his boots.

I crossed the kitchen so fast I nearly caught flight. 'You *married* me!' I screamed at my new husband. 'You *chose* me. You *chose* Sophie. How dare you *fail* us!'

'It was a phone call, Tessa. And yes, I will try to do better next time.'

'I thought you'd died! I thought Sophie had died!'

'Well, yeah, then isn't it good that I'm finally home?'

'Brian!'

'I know I screwed up!' He finally gave up on

188

his boots, throwing his hands in the air. 'I'm new at this! I've never had a wife and daughter before, and just because I love you doesn't mean I'm not sometimes stupid. For chrissake, Tessa . . . I'm about to ship out again. I just wanted one last day of fun. Fresh snow. Powder skiing . . . ' He inhaled. Exhaled. Stood up.

'Tessa,' he said more quietly. 'I would never intentionally hurt you or Sophie. I love you both. And I promise to do better next time. Have a little faith, okay? We're both new at this and we're bound to make some mistakes, so please . . . Have a little faith.'

My shoulders sagged. The fight left me. I let go of my anger long enough to feel the relief that my daughter was okay, my husband was safe, and the afternoon had worked out in the end.

Brian pulled me against his chest. I allowed his embrace. I even slid my arms around his waist.

'Be careful, Brian,' I whispered against his shoulder. 'Remember, I'm not like other women.'

For a change, he didn't argue.

* * *

I remembered this moment of my marriage, and others, as the nurse stood back and gestured for me to take my first awkward step. I'd managed to eat dry toast at six a.m. without throwing up. At seven-thirty, they'd moved me to the chair next to my bed to see how I'd do sitting up.

The pain inside my skull had flared the first few minutes, then settled into a dull roar. Half of

189

my face remained swollen and tender, my legs felt shaky, but overall, I'd made progress in the past twelve hours. I could stand, sit, and eat dry toast. World, look out.

I wanted to run, madly, desperately, out of the hospital, where by some miracle I would find Sophie standing on the sidewalk waiting for me. I would swing her into my arms. *Mommy* she would cry happily. And I would hug her and kiss her and tell her how sorry I was for everything and never let her go.

'All right,' the nurse said crisply. 'First step, let's give it a whirl.'

She offered her arm for balance. My knees trembled violently, and I placed a grateful hand on her arm.

That first shuffling step made my head swim. I blinked my eyes several times, and the disorientation passed. Up was up, down was down. Progress.

I inched forward, tiny little hiccups of my feet that slowly but surely took me across the gray linoleum, closer and closer to the bathroom. Then I was inside, gently shutting the door behind me. The nurse had supplied toiletries for showering. Second test of the day — seeing if I could pee and shower on my own. Then the doctor would examine me again.

Then, maybe, just maybe, I could go home.

Sophie. Sitting on the floor of her room, surrounded by painted bunnies and bright orange flowers, playing with her favorite raggedy-haired doll. *Mommy, you're home! Mommy, I love you!*

I stood at the sink and stared at my reflection in the mirror.

The flesh around my eye was so black and engorged with blood, it looked like an eggplant. I could barely make out the bridge of my nose, or the top line of my eyebrow. I thought of those scenes in the early Rocky movies, where they'd razor-opened his swollen flesh just so he could see. I might have to give it a try. Day was still young.

My fingers traveled from my black eye, to the laceration two inches above it, the scab just now forming, pulling at the roots of my hair. Then I reached around to the prominent lump still protruding from the back of my skull. It felt hot and tender to the touch. I let my hand fall away, holding on to the edge of the sink instead.

Eight a.m. Monday morning.

The autopsy would've started an hour ago. The Y-incision down my husband's chest. Cracking apart his ribs. Fishing out three slugs fired from the 9mm Sig Sauer bearing my fingerprints. Then the sound of the saw as they began to remove the top of his skull.

Eight a.m. Monday morning . . .

I thought again of all the moments I'd like to have back. Places I should've said yes, times I should've said no. Then Brian would be alive, maybe waxing his skis for his next big adventure. And Sophie would be home, playing on the floor of her room, Gertrude nestled beside her, waiting for me.

Eight a.m. Monday morning . . .

'Hurry up, D.D. and Bobby,' I murmured. 'My daughter needs you.'

17

Thanks to the wonder of GPS, Bobby identified Brian Darby's gym on his second try. He simply put in Darby's address, then searched for nearby gyms. Half a dozen popped up. Bobby started with the location closest to Brian's house and worked his way out. A national chain turned out to be the winner. Bobby drove there in thirty minutes, and was meeting with Brian's personal trainer eight minutes after that.

'Saw the news,' the petite, dark-haired woman said, already looking worried. Bobby was trying to size her up. She appeared about five feet tall and ninety pounds, more gymnast than trainer. Then she twisted both her hands in an anxious gesture, and half a dozen tendons snaked to life in her forearms.

He revised his initial opinion of Jessica Ryan — tiny, but dangerous. Mini-hulk.

She'd been working out with some middle-aged man sporting a hundred dollar workout shirt and four hundred dollar haircut when Bobby had arrived. When Bobby first approached, Jessica had pointedly given him a cold shoulder, focusing on her obviously well-paying customer. Bobby had flashed his creds, however, and that quickly, Jessica with the tight pink T-shirt and sparkling purple nails was his.

Her disappointed client got to finish his workout with some kid whose neck was bigger than Bobby's thigh. Bobby and Jessica retreated to the employee break room, where Jessica quickly shut the door.

'Is he really dead?' Jessica asked now, biting her lower lip.

'I'm here regarding Brian Darby's death,' Bobby stated.

'And his little girl? They've been showing her picture all over the news. Sophie, right? Have you found her yet?'

'No, ma'am.'

Jessica's big brown eyes welled up. For the second time in the past hour, Bobby was happy he'd left D.D. to work on his own. The first time, because it was either walk away from her or strangle her. Now because there was no way D.D. would've played well with a doe-eyed female trainer prone to glistening tears and hot pink micro-shorts.

Being a happily married man, Bobby was making it a point not to study the micro-shorts or the tight T-shirt. So far, that left him staring at the personal trainer's extremely well-sculpted bicep.

'What do you bench-press?' he heard himself ask.

'One thirty-five,' Jessica replied easily, still dabbing at the corners of her eyes.

'What's that? Twice your weight?'

She blushed.

He realized he'd basically just flirted and shut up. Maybe he shouldn't have left D.D. Maybe no man, happily married or not, should be sequestered alone with a woman like Jessica

Ryan. Which made him wonder if Tessa Leoni had ever met Jessica Ryan. Which made him wonder how Brian Darby had ever lived past the first week of fitness training.

Bobby cleared his throat, took out his spiral notepad and a mini-recorder. He turned on the recorder and placed it on the counter next to the microwave.

'Have you met Sophie?' he asked his interview subject.

'Once. School was canceled so Brian brought her in with him for his workout. She seemed really sweet; she found a set of one pound hand weights and carried them around, mimicking all of Brian's exercises.'

'Brian works out solely with you?'

'I'm his primary personal trainer,' Jessica said with a touch of pride. 'Sometimes, however, our schedules don't mix, then another trainer might fill in for me.'

'And how long has Brian been working out with you?'

'Oh, nearly a year. Well, maybe closer to nine months.'

'Nine months?' Bobby made a note.

'He's done great!' Jessica gushed. 'One of my best clients. His goal was to bulk up. So the first three months I put him on this wicked hard diet. Eliminated his fats and salts and carbs — and he's one of those guys that really loves his refined carbs, too. French toast for breakfast, hoagies for lunch, mashed potatoes for dinner, and a bag of cookies for dessert. Let me tell you, I didn't think he was going to make it through the first

194

two weeks. But once he got his system cleaned out and reset, then we started the next stage: For the past six months, he's been following this regimen I developed from my fitness competitions — '

'Fitness competitions?'

'Yes. Miss Fit New England, four years running.' Jessica flashed him a white smile. 'It's my passion.'

Bobby tore his gaze away from her tanned, toned bicep and returned it to his notebook.

'So I gave Brian a week by week diet of six high-protein meals a day,' Jessica continued perkily. 'We're talking thirty grams of protein per meal, consumed every two to three hours. It's a big commitment of time and resources, but he did awesome! Then I added in a fitness regimen of sixty minutes of cardio followed by sixty minutes of heavy weights.'

'Every day?' Bobby ran. Or had run, before Carina was born. He shifted his notepad two inches lower, in front of his waistline, which come to think about it, had been a bit tight this morning.

'Cardio five to seven times a week, strength training five times a week. And I introduced him to hundreds. He was great at hundreds!'

'Hundreds?'

'Lower weight, but higher rep, to see if you can hit a hundred. If we do it right, you can't on the first try, but continue training, then four weeks later, try again. In the first two months, Brian nailed all his hundreds, forcing me to bump up his weights. Really, amazing results. I mean, not for nothing, but most of my clients talk a good game. Brian was delivering the goods.'

'He appeared to have put on a fair amount of weight in the past year,' Bobby commented.

'He put on a fair amount of *muscle*,' Jessica corrected immediately. 'Three inches to his arms alone. We took measurements every two weeks if you want them. Of course, his work schedule means we missed months at a time, but he kept on track.'

'You mean when he shipped out as a merchant marine?'

'Yeah. He'd disappear for two months at a time. First trip out, totally wrecked him. Lost most of what we'd done. Second time, I prepared an entire program for him to follow, including diet, cardio, and weights. I got a list of all the equipment available on the ship, and tailored it perfectly, so he'd have no excuses. He did much better.'

'So Brian was working hard with you when he was here and hard on the ship when he went away. Any reason he was working so hard?'

Jessica shrugged. 'To look better. To feel better. He was an active guy. When we first started, he wanted to improve his fitness so he could tackle some bigger mountains skiing, biking, that sort of thing. He was active, but thought he should be stronger. We took it from there.'

Bobby set down his notepad, regarded her for a moment. 'So Brian wants to improve his skiing and biking. And in order to do that, he's spending how much money a week . . . ?' He waved his hand around the well-kept room in an obviously well-equipped gym.

'Couple hundred,' Jessica said. 'But there's no price tag for good health!'

'Two hundred a week. And how many hours of training, grocery shopping, food prep . . . '

'You gotta commit if you want results,' Jessica informed him.

'Brian committed. Brian got results. Brian was still following the program. Why? What's he looking for? Forty pounds of muscle later, what was he lacking?'

Jessica regarded him curiously. 'He wasn't still trying to bulk up. However, Brian's not naturally a big guy. When a . . . smaller man . . . '

On behalf of men everywhere, Bobby winced.

'When a smaller man wants to maintain bigger results, he has to keep working. That's the truth. High protein, big weights, day after day. Otherwise, his body is going to return to its preferred size, which in Brian's case was closer to one eighty, not two twenty.'

Bobby considered that information, which, as a smaller guy, wasn't great to hear.

'Sounds like a lot of work,' he said at last. 'Not easy for anyone to maintain, let alone a working parent. Time to time, I bet Brian's schedule got a little busy, his hours squeezed. He ever . . . seek additional assistance?'

Jessica furrowed her brow. 'What do you mean?'

'Products to aid his speed/ability to add muscle?'

197

Jessica frowned harder; then, she got it. 'You mean steroids.'

'I'm curious.'

Immediately, she shook her head. 'I'm not down with that. If I thought he was juicing up, I'd quit. Screw the two hundred a week. I dated a guy into 'roids. No way I'd go down that road again.'

'You were dating Brian?'

'No! I didn't mean *that*. I mean associating with someone abusing steroids. It makes people crazy. The stuff you see on the news — it's not a lie.'

Bobby regarded her levelly. 'And for your own training?'

She met his gaze just as levelly. 'Sweat and tears, baby. Sweat and tears.'

Bobby nodded. 'So you're not a proponent of steroids — '

'No!'

'But what about other trainers in the gym? Or even outside the gym. Brian got some great results very fast. How sure are you that it was all his sweat and tears?'

Jessica didn't answer right away. She chewed her lower lip again, crossing her arms over her chest.

'I don't think so,' she said at last. 'But I couldn't swear to it. Something was going on with Brian. He just got back into town three weeks ago, and this time around . . . He was moody. Dark. Something was on his mind.'

'You ever meet his wife?'

'The state trooper? No.'

'But he talked about her.'

Jessica shrugged. 'They all do.'

'They?'

'Clients. I don't know, being a trainer is like being a hairdresser. The ministers of the grooming services sector. Clients talk. We listen. It's half our job.'

'So what did Brian say?'

Jessica shrugged, obviously uncomfortable again.

'He's dead, Jessica. Killed in his own home. Help me understand why Brian Darby embarked on a major self-improvement program and it still wasn't enough to save him.'

'He loved her,' Jessica whispered.

'Who?'

'Brian loved his wife. Genuinely, deeply, soulfully. I'd kill for a man to love me like that.'

'Brian loved Tessa.'

'Yeah. And he wanted to be stronger for her. For her and Sophie. He needed to be a big man, he used to joke, because guarding two females was four times the work.'

'Guarding?' Bobby asked with a frown.

'Yeah. That's the word he'd used. Guess he'd screwed up once and Tessa had gotten on his case. Sophie was to be guarded. He took it seriously.'

'You ever sleep with Brian?' Bobby asked suddenly.

'No. I don't screw around with my clients.' She shot him a look. 'Asshole,' she muttered.

Bobby flashed his creds again. 'That would be 'Detective Asshole' to you.'

199

Jessica merely shrugged.

'Tessa screw around on Brian? Maybe he discovered something, helped spark his quest to become a bigger man.'

'Not that he ever said. Though . . . ' She paused. 'No guy is gonna admit that to a girl. Especially a pretty one like me. Come on, that's like saying, *I'm a miserable weenie,* up front. Guys make you find that out for yourself.'

Bobby couldn't argue with that logic. 'But Brian didn't think his wife loved him.'

That hesitation again. 'I don't know. I got the impression . . . Tessa's a state trooper, right? A police officer. Kind of sounded like she was tough. Things were her way or the highway. Brian jumped through a lot of hoops. Didn't mean, however, she thought he was the greatest guy on God's green earth. Just meant she expected him to jump through a lot of hoops, especially when it came to Sophie.'

'She had a lot of rules regarding her daughter?'

'Brian worked hard. When he was home, he wanted to play. Tessa, however, wanted him to babysit. Sounds like sometimes they went round and round a bit. But he never said anything bad about her,' Jessica added hastily. 'He wasn't that kind of guy.'

'What kind of guy?'

'Guy who rags on his wife. Trust me' — she rolled her eyes — 'we have plenty of those around here.'

'So why was Brian moody?' Bobby cycled back. 'What happened this last time he was on tour?'

'I don't know. He never said. He just seemed . . . miserable.'

'You think he beat his wife?'

'No!' Jessica appeared horrified.

'She has a medical history consistent with abuse,' Bobby added, just for the sake of argument.

Jessica, however, stood by her man. 'No fucking way.'

'Really?'

'Really.'

'How would you know?'

'Because he was sweet. And sweet guys don't whack their wives.'

'Again, how would you know?'

She stared at him. 'Because I managed to find a wife beater all by myself. Married him for five long years. Till I got smart, got fit, and kicked his ass to the curb.'

She flexed her arms pointedly. Miss Fit New England four times running, indeed. 'Brian loved his wife. He didn't hit her, and he didn't deserve to die. Are we done?'

Bobby reached into his pocket, fished out his card. 'Think about why Brian might have been 'moody' since his last return. And if anything comes to you, give me a call.'

Jessica took his card, while regarding his outstretched arm, which did not look nearly as toned as her own.

'I could help you with that,' she said.

'No.'

'Why not? Cost? You're a detective. I could cut you a deal.'

'You haven't met my wife,' Bobby said.

'She also a cop?'

'Nope. But she's very good with a gun.'

Bobby got his mini-recorder, got his notepad, and got out of there.

18

D.D. didn't have any trouble tracking down Tessa's childhood friend Juliana MacDougall, nee Howe, wife of three years, mother of one, living in a seventeen hundred square foot cape in Arlington. D.D. might have lied a little. Said she was from the high school, tracking down alumnae for an upcoming reunion.

Hey, not everyone wanted to take calls from their local detectives, and even fewer probably wanted to answer yet more questions regarding the shooting that had killed a brother ten years ago.

D.D. got Juliana's address, established she was home, and took a ride over. On the way there, she checked her voice messages, including a cheery morning greeting from Alex wishing her the best with the missing persons case and letting her know he was in the mood to cook homemade alfredo, if she was in the mood to eat it.

Her stomach growled. Then spasmed. Then growled again. Leave it to her to be carrying a baby as contrarian as she was.

She should call Alex. She should make some time this evening, even thirty minutes to sit and talk. She tried to picture the conversation in her mind, but still wasn't sure how it would go.

HER: So remember how you said you and

203

your first wife tried to have a baby a few years ago, but it didn't work out? Turns out, you were *not* the problem in that equation.

HIM:

HER:

HIM:

HER:

It wasn't much of a conversation. Maybe because she didn't have much of an imagination, or any experience with these things. Personally, she was more adept at the 'Don't call me, I'll call you' conversation.

Would he offer to marry her? Should she accept that kind of deal, if not for her sake, then for the baby's? Or did it matter in this day and age? Did she just assume he would help her? Or would he just assume she'd never let him?

Her stomach hurt again. She didn't want to be pregnant anymore. It was too confusing and she wasn't great with big life questions. She preferred more elemental debates, such as why did Tessa Leoni kill her husband, and what did it have to do with her shooting Thomas Howe ten years ago?

Now, there was a question for the ages.

D.D. followed her guidance system into a maze of tiny side streets in Arlington. A left here, two rights there, and she arrived in front of a cheerful red-painted house with white trim and a snow-covered front yard the size of D.D.'s car. D.D. parked by the curb, grabbed her heavy coat, and headed for the door.

Juliana MacDougall answered after the first

ring. She had long, dishwater blonde hair pulled back into a messy ponytail and a fat, drooling baby balanced on her denim-clad hip. She regarded D.D. curiously, then blanked her face completely when D.D. flashed her creds.

'Sergeant Detective D.D. Warren, Boston PD. May I come in?'

'What is this regarding?'

'Please.' D.D. gestured to the inside of the toy-strewn house. 'It's cold out here. I think we'd all be more comfortable talking inside.'

Juliana thinned her lips, then silently held the door open for D.D. to enter. The home boasted a tiny, tiled entryway, opening to a small family room with nice windows and recently refinished hardwood floors. The house smelled like fresh paint and baby powder, a new little family settling into a new little home.

A laundry basket occupied the single dark green sofa. Juliana flushed, then lowered the plastic bin to the floor without ever releasing her grip on her baby. When she finally sat, she perched on the edge of the cushion, her child held in the middle of her lap as the first line of defense.

D.D. sat on the other end of the sofa. She regarded the drooling baby. The drooling baby stared back at her, then shoved its whole fist in its mouth and made a sound that might have been 'Gaa.'

'Cute,' D.D. said, in a voice that was clearly skeptical. 'How old?'

'Nathaniel is nine months.'

'Boy.'

'Yes.'

'Walking?'

'Just learned to crawl,' Juliana said proudly.

'Good boy,' D.D. said, and that quickly was out of baby prattle. Good Lord, how was she ever going to be a mom, when she couldn't even talk to one?

'Do you have a job?' D.D. asked.

'Yes,' Juliana said proudly, 'I'm raising my child.'

D.D. accepted that answer, moved on. 'So,' she announced curtly. 'I imagine you've seen the news. The missing girl in Allston-Brighton.'

Juliana regarded her blankly. 'What?'

'The Amber Alert? Six-year-old Sophie Leoni, missing from her home in Allston-Brighton?'

Juliana frowned, held her baby a little closer. 'What does that have to do with me? I don't know any child from Allston-Brighton. I live in Arlington.'

'When was the last time you saw Tessa Leoni?' D.D. asked.

Juliana's reaction was immediate. She stiffened and looked away from D.D., her blue gaze dropping to the hardwood floor. A square block with the letter 'E' and a picture of an elephant was by her slippered foot. She retrieved the block and offered it to the baby, who took it from her, then tried to cram the whole thing in his mouth.

'He's teething,' she murmured absently, stroking her child's red-flushed cheek. 'Poor little guy hasn't slept in nights, and whimpers to be held all day long. I know all babies go through it, but I didn't think it would be so hard. Seeing my own child in pain. Knowing there's nothing I can do but wait.'

D.D. didn't say anything.

'Sometimes, at night, when he's crying, I rock and cry with him. I know it sounds corny, but it seems to help him. Maybe no one, not even babies, likes to cry alone.'

D.D. didn't say anything.

'Oh my God,' Juliana MacDougall exclaimed abruptly. 'Sophie Leoni. *Sophia* Leoni. She's Tessa's daughter. Tessa had a little girl. Oh. My. God.'

Then Juliana Howe shut up completely, just sitting there with her baby boy, who was still chewing the wooden block.

'What did you see that night?' D.D. asked the young mother gently. No need to define which night. Most likely, Juliana's entire life circled back to that one moment in time.

'I didn't. Not really. I was half asleep, heard a noise, came downstairs. Tessa and Tommy . . . They were on the couch. Then there was a noise, and Tommy stood up, kind of stepped back, then fell down. Then Tessa stood up, saw me, and started crying. She held out her hand, and she was holding a gun. That was the first thing I really noticed. Tessa had a gun. The rest sunk in from there.'

'What did you do?'

Juliana was quiet. 'It's been a long time.'

D.D. waited.

'I don't understand. Why these questions now? I told everything to the police. Last I knew, it was an open-and-shut case. Tommy had a reputation . . . The detective said Tessa wasn't the first girl he'd hurt.'

'What do you think?'

Juliana shrugged. 'He was my brother,' she whispered. 'Honestly, I try not to think about it.'

'Did you believe Tessa that night? That your friend was protecting herself?'

'I don't know.'

'She ever show any interest in Tommy before? Ask about his schedule? Bat her eyelashes in his direction?'

Juliana shook her head, still not looking at D.D.

'But you never spoke to her afterward. You cast her out. Like her father.'

Now Juliana flushed. Her grip tightened on her baby. He whimpered and immediately she let go.

'Something was wrong with Tommy,' she said abruptly.

D.D. waited.

'My parents couldn't see it. But he was . . . mean. If he wanted something, he took it. Even when we were little, if I had a toy and he wanted that toy . . . ' She shrugged again. 'He'd break something, rather than let me keep it. My father would say boys will be boys, and let it go. But I learned. Tommy wanted what he wanted and you didn't get in his way.'

'You think he attacked Tessa.'

'I think when Detective Walthers told us other girls had called about Tommy, I wasn't surprised. My parents were horrified. My father . . . he still doesn't believe. But I could. Tommy wanted what he wanted and you didn't get in his way.'

'Did you ever tell that to Tessa?'

'I haven't spoken to Tessa Leoni in ten years.'

'Why not?'

'Because.' The ubiquitous shrug again. 'Tommy wasn't just my brother — he was my parents' son. And when he died . . . My parents burned up their savings on Tommy's funeral. Then, when my father couldn't go back to work, we lost our house. My parents had to declare bankruptcy. Eventually, they divorced. My mother and I moved in with my aunt. My father had a nervous breakdown. He lives in an institution, where he spends his days going through Tommy's scrapbook. He can't get over it. He just can't. The world is a terrible place, where your child can be killed and the police cover it up.'

Juliana stroked her own baby's cheek. 'It's funny,' she murmured. 'I used to think my family was perfect. That's even what Tessa loved best about me. I came from this great family, not like her family at all. Then, in one night, we turned into them. It wasn't just that I lost my brother, but that my parents lost their son.'

'She ever try to contact you?'

'The last words I spoke to Tessa Leoni were, 'You need to go home right now!' And that's what she did. She took her gun and she ran out of my house.'

'What about seeing her around the neighborhood?'

'Her father kicked her out. Then she was no longer around the neighborhood.'

'You never wondered about her? Never

209

worried about your best friend in the whole wide world, who had to fight off your own brother? You invited her over that night. According to her initial statement, Tessa had asked if Tommy would be home for the evening.'

'I don't remember.'

'Did you tell Tommy she was coming?'

Juliana's lips thinned. Abruptly, she set the baby on the floor, stood up. 'You should go now, Detective. I haven't spoken to Tessa in ten years. I didn't know she had a daughter, and I certainly don't know where she is.'

But D.D. stayed put, sitting on the edge of the sofa, peering up at Tessa's former best friend.

'Why did you leave Tessa in the family room that night?' D.D. pushed. 'If it was a sleepover, why didn't you rouse your best friend to come up to your room? What did Tommy tell you to do?'

'*Stop it!*'

'You suspected, didn't you? You knew what he was up to, and that's why you came downstairs. You feared your brother, you worried about your friend. Did you warn Tessa, Juliana? Is that why she brought the gun?'

'No!'

'You knew your father wouldn't listen. Boys will be boys. Sounds like your mom had already internalized the message. That left you and Tessa. Two sixteen-year-old girls, trying to stand up to one brute of an older brother. Did she think she'd simply scare him off? Wave the gun, and that would be the end of things?'

Juliana didn't respond. Her face was ashen.

'Except the gun went off,' D.D. continued conversationally. 'And Tommy got hit. Tommy *died*. Your entire family fell apart. All because you and Tessa didn't really know what you were doing. Whose idea was it to bring the gun that night?'

'Get out.'

'Yours? Hers? What were the two of you *thinking*?'

'Get out!'

'I'm going to check your phone records. One call. That's all I need. One call placed from Tessa to you and your new little family is going to fall apart, too, Juliana. I'm gonna rip it apart, if I learn you've been holding out on me.'

'*Get out!*' Juliana screamed. On the floor, the baby responded to his mother's tone and started to wail.

D.D. climbed off the sofa. She kept her eyes on Juliana MacDougall, the woman's pale face, heaving shoulders, wild gaze. She looked like a deer caught in the headlights. She looked like a woman trapped by a ten-year-old lie.

D.D. gave one last try: 'What happened that night, Juliana? What aren't you telling me?'

'I loved her,' the woman said suddenly. 'Tessa was my best friend in the whole world, and I loved her. Then my brother died, my family shattered, and my world went to shit. I'm not going back. Not for her, not for you, not for anyone. Whatever happened to Tessa this time around, I don't know and I don't care. Now get out of my home, Detective, and don't bother me or my family again.'

Juliana held open the door. Her baby was still sobbing on the floor. D.D. took the hint and finally departed. The door slammed shut behind her, the dead bolt turning for good measure.

When D.D. turned, however, she could see Juliana through the front window. The woman had picked up her crying son, cradling the baby against her chest. Soothing the child or letting the child soothe her?

Maybe it didn't matter. Maybe that's the way these things worked.

Juliana MacDougall loved her son. As her parents had loved her brother. As Tessa Leoni loved her daughter.

Cycles, D.D. thought. Pieces of a larger pattern. Except she couldn't quite pull it apart, or put it back together.

Parents loved their children. Some parents would go to any length to protect them. And other parents . . .

D.D. started to get a bad feeling.

Then her cellphone rang.

19

Sergeant Detective D.D. Warren and Detective Bobby Dodge came for me at 11:43 a.m. I heard their footsteps in the corridor, fast and focused. I had a split second; I used it to stash the blue button in the back part of the lowest drawer in the hospital bed stand.

My only link to Sophie.

My final unnecessary reminder to play by the rules.

Maybe, one day I could return and retrieve the button. If I was lucky, maybe Sophie and I could do it together, reclaiming Gertrude's missing eye and reattaching it to her dispassionate doll's face.

If I was lucky.

I'd just sat down on the edge of my hospital bed when the privacy curtain was ripped back and D.D. strode into the room. I knew what was coming next and still had to bite my lower lip to hold back my scream of protest.

'*All I want for Christmas is my two front teeth, my two front teeth, my . . .*'

I realized belatedly I was humming the song under my breath. Fortunately, neither of the detectives seemed to notice.

'Tessa Marie Leoni,' D.D. began and I steeled my spine. 'You are under arrest for the murder of Brian Anthony Darby. Please rise.'

More footsteps in the corridor. Most likely the

DA and his assistant, not wanting to miss the big moment. Or maybe some muckety-mucks from the BPD, always attuned to high profile photo ops. Probably some brass from the state police, as well. They wouldn't abandon me just yet, a young, abused female officer. They couldn't afford to appear so insensitive.

The press would be amassing in the parking lot, I realized, impressed by my own detachment as I rose to my feet, presenting both wrists to my colleagues. Shane would arrive shortly, as union rep. Also my lawyer. Or maybe they would meet me at the courthouse, where I would be formally charged with killing my own husband.

I had a flashback to another moment in time, sitting at a kitchen table, my freshly showered hair dripping down my back as a heavyset detective asked over and over again, '*Where'd ya get the gun, why'd ya bring the gun, what made ya fire the gun . . .* '

My father, standing impassively in the doorway, his arms crossed over his dirty white T-shirt. And me, understanding even then that I'd lost him. That my answers didn't matter anymore. I was guilty, I would always be guilty.

Sometimes, that's the price you paid for love.

Detective Warren read me my rights. I didn't speak; what was left to say? She cuffed my wrists, prepared to lead me away, then encountered the first logistical issue. I had no clothes. My uniform had been bagged and tagged as evidence upon my admittance, delivered to the crime lab yesterday afternoon. That left me in a hospital Johnny, and even D.D. understood the political dangers of a Boston cop being photographed dragging away a battered state trooper who was wearing nothing but a hospital gown.

She and Detective Dodge had a quick conference, off to one side of the room. I sat back down on the edge of the bed. A nurse had entered and was watching the proceedings with concern. Now she crossed to me.

'Head?' she asked crisply.

'Hurts.'

She took my pulse, made me track her finger with my eyes, then nodded in satisfaction. Apparently, I was merely in pain, not in crisis. Having assured herself that her patient was in no immediate danger, the nurse retreated out the door.

'Can't use a prison jumpsuit,' D.D. was arguing in low tones with Bobby. 'Her lawyer will argue we biased the judge, bringing her before him in jailhouse orange. Hospital gown presents the same issue, except this time we look like insensitive jerks. We need clothes. Simple nondescript blue jeans, sweater. That sort of thing.'

'Get an officer to swing by her house,' Bobby muttered back.

D.D. regarded him for a second, then turned to study me.

'Got a favorite outfit?' D.D. asked.

'Wal-Mart,' I said, standing up.

'What?'

'Couple blocks over. Size 6 jeans, medium sweater. I'd appreciate underclothes, too, plus socks and shoes.'

215

'I'm not buying you clothes,' D.D. said crossly. 'We'll get some from your house.'

'No,' I said, and sat back down.

D.D. glared at me. I let her. She was arresting me, after all, what did she have to be so angry about? I didn't want clothing from home, personal articles the Suffolk County Jail would seize from me and lock away for the duration of my incarceration. I would rather arrive in a hospital gown. Why not? The look bought me sympathy, and I would take all the help I could get.

Apparently, D.D. figured that out, as well. A uniformed officer was summoned, instructions given. The patrol officer didn't even bat an eye at being told to buy women's clothing. He disappeared out the door, which left me alone with D.D. and Bobby again.

Others must be staying out in the hall. Hospital rooms weren't that big. They might as well wait in the corridor for the show.

I was counting down, though I didn't know to what.

'What did you use?' D.D. asked abruptly. 'Bags of ice? Snow? Funny, you know. I noticed the damp spot on the basement floor, yesterday. I wondered about it.'

I said nothing.

She walked toward me, eyes narrowed, as if studying a particular species of wildlife. I noticed when she walked, she kept one hand splayed over her stomach, the other on her hip. I also noticed that her face was pale with dark circles under her eyes. Apparently, I was keeping the good detective up at night. Score one for me.

I regarded her with my good eye. Dared her to look at the swollen, eggplant purple mess of my face, and pass judgment.

'You ever meet the ME?' she asked now, switching gears, becoming more conversational. She halted in front of me. From my vantage point, perched on the edge of the hospital bed, I had to look up at her.

I didn't speak.

'Ben's good. One of the best we've ever had,' she continued. 'Maybe another ME wouldn't have noticed it. But Ben loves the details. Apparently, the human body is like any other meat. You can freeze it and thaw it, but not without some changes in — how did he put it? — consistency. The flesh on your husband's extremities felt wrong to him. So he took a few samples, stuck them under a microscope, and hell if I understand all the science, but basically determined damage at a cellular level consistent with the freezing of human tissue. You shot your husband, Tessa. Then, you put him on ice.'

I didn't speak.

D.D. leaned closer. 'This is what I don't get, though. Obviously, you were buying time. You needed to get something done. What, Tessa? What were you doing while your husband's corpse lay frozen in the basement?'

I didn't speak. I listened to a song instead, playing in the back of my mind. *All I want for Christmas is my two front teeth, my two front teeth, my two front teeth . . .*

'Where is she?' D.D. whispered, as if reading

217

my mind. 'Tessa, what did you do with your little girl? Where's Sophie?'

'When are you due?' I asked, and D.D. recoiled as if shot, while five feet away, Bobby inhaled sharply.

He hadn't known, I determined. Or maybe he'd known, but not known, in that way men sometimes do. I found this interesting.

'Is he the father?' I asked.

'Shut up,' D.D. said curtly.

Then I remembered. 'No,' I corrected myself, as if she'd never spoken. I looked over at Bobby. 'You're married to another woman, from the state mental institute case, couple years back. And you have a baby now, don't you? Not that long ago. I heard about that.'

He didn't say anything. Just stared at me with cool gray eyes. Did he think I was threatening his family? Was I?

Maybe I just needed to make conversation, because otherwise I might say all the wrong things. For example, I used snow, because it was easy enough to shovel and didn't leave behind trace evidence such as a dozen empty ice bags. And Brian was heavy, heavier than I'd imagined. All that working out, all that pumping up, just so myself and a hit man could lug an extra forty pounds down the stairs and into his precious, never-any-tool-out-of-place garage.

I'd cried when I scooped the snow on top of my husband's dead body. The hot tears formed little holes in the white snow, then I had to pile on more snow and all the while my hands were shaking uncontrollably. I kept myself focused.

One shovel full of snow, then a second, then a third. It took twenty-three.

Twenty-three scoops of snow to bury a grown man.

I'd warned Brian. I'd told him in the beginning that I was a woman who knew too much. You don't mess with a woman who knows the kind of things I know.

Three tampons to plug the bullet holes. Twenty-three scoops of snow to hide the body.

All I want for Christmas is my two front teeth, my two front teeth, my two front teeth . . .

Love you more, he'd told me as he died.

Stupid, sorry son of a bitch.

I didn't speak anymore. D.D. and Bobby also sat in silence for a good ten, fifteen minutes. Three members of law enforcement not making eye contact. Finally, the door banged open and Ken Cargill barged in, black wool coat flapping around him, thinning brown hair mussed. He drew to a halt, then noticed my shackled wrists and turned on D.D. with all the fury of a good defense lawyer.

'What is this!' he cried.

'Your client, Tessa Marie Leoni, has been charged in the death of her husband, Brian Anthony Darby. We have read her her rights, and are now awaiting transport to the courthouse.'

'What are the charges?' Cargill demanded to know, sounding appropriately indignant.

'Murder one.'

His eyes widened. 'Murder with premeditated malice and forethought? Are you out of your mind? Who authorized these charges? Have you

219

even *looked* at my client lately? The black eye, the fractured cheek, and oh yes, the *concussion?*'

D.D. simply stared at him, then turned back to me. 'Ice or snow, Tessa? Come on, if not for us, then for your lawyer's sake, tell him how you froze the body.'

'*What?*'

I wondered if all lawyers went to acting school, or if they just came by it naturally, the way cops did.

The first uniformed officer was back, breathing hard; apparently he'd run all the way through the hospital with the oversized WalMart bag. He thrust it at D.D., who did the honors of explaining my new wardrobe to Cargill.

D.D. unshackled my wrists. I was handed the pile of new clothes, hangers and other sharp objects removed, then allowed to disappear into the bathroom to change. The Boston patrol officer had done a decent job. Wide-leg jeans, stiff as boards with their newness. A green crewneck sweater. A sports bra, plain underwear, plain socks, bright white tennis shoes.

I moved slowly, dragging the bra, then the sweater, over my battered head. The jeans were easier, but tying my shoelaces proved impossible. My fingers were shaking too hard.

Do you know what had been the hardest part about burying my husband?

Waiting for him to bleed out. Waiting for his heart to stop and the last ounce of blood to still and cool in his chest, because otherwise he would drip. He would leave a trail, and even if it was small and I cleaned it up with bleach, the

220

luminol would give it away.

So I sat, on a hard chair in the kitchen, holding a vigil I never thought I'd have to hold. And the whole time, I just couldn't decide, which was worse? Shooting a boy, and running away with the blood still fresh on my hands? Or shooting a man, and sitting there, waiting for his blood to dry so I could clean up properly?

I'd placed three tampons in the holes in the back of Brian's chest, as a safety measure.

'*What are you doing?*' *the man had demanded.*

'*Can't leave a blood trail,*' *I'd said calmly.*

'*Oh,*' *he'd said, and let me go.*

Three bloody tampons. Two front teeth. It's funny, the talismans that can bring you strength.

I hummed the song. I tied my shoes. Then, I stood up, and took one last minute to study myself in the mirror. I didn't recognize my own reflection. That distorted face, hollowed-out cheeks, lank brown hair.

It was good, I thought, to feel like a stranger to myself. It suited all the things about to happen next.

'Sophie,' I murmured, because I needed to hear my daughter's name. 'Sophie, love you more.'

Then I opened the bathroom door and once more presented my wrists.

The cuffs were cool; they slid on with a click.

It was time. D.D. on one side. Bobby on the other. My lawyer bringing up the rear.

We strode into the bright white corridor, the DA pushing away from the wall, ready to lead the parade in triumphant glory. I saw the lieutenant colonel, his gaze steady as he regarded his shackled officer, his face impossible to read. I saw other men in uniform, names I knew, hands I had shook.

They did not look at me, so I returned the favor.

We headed down the corridor, toward the big glass doors and the screaming mob of reporters waiting on the other side.

Command presence. Never let them see you sweat.

The glass doors slid open, and the world exploded in flashing white lights.

20

'We gotta start over,' D.D. was saying an hour and a half later. They'd handed Tessa over to the Suffolk County Sheriff's Department at the courthouse. The DA would present the charges. Her lawyer would enter a plea, bail would be set, and a mittimus prepared by the court, legally granting the county permission to hold Tessa Leoni until the requirements of her bail were met. At which point, Tessa would be either bailed out or transported to the Suffolk County Jail. Given that the DA was going to argue Tessa was a flight risk and request no bail, there was a good chance she was already on her way to the women's detainee unit as they spoke.

That still didn't solve all their problems.

'Our timeline was set by Tessa's initial statement to police,' D.D. was saying now, back at BPD headquarters, where she'd hastily summoned all members of the taskforce. 'We assumed, based upon her accounting of events, that Brian Darby was shot and killed Sunday morning, after a physical altercation with her. According to the ME, however, Darby's body was frozen prior to Sunday morning, and most likely, *unthawed* for Tessa's star-making performance.'

'Can he tell how long it was frozen?' Phil spoke up from the front row.

D.D. let their third squadmate, Neil, answer

223

the question, as he'd been the one attending the autopsy.

'Probably less than twenty-four hours,' Neil provided for the room. 'Ben said he can see cellular damage consistent with freezing in the extremities, but not the internal organs. Meaning the body was on ice, but not long enough to freeze all the way through. Limbs, face, fingers, toes, yes. Deep torso, no. So probably put on ice twelve to twenty-four hours. He can only estimate because the timeline would be affected by room temperature. Then you must factor in at least a few hours for the body to return to room temperature . . . He's guessing — stress guessing — Brian Darby was actually killed Friday night or Saturday morning.'

'So,' D.D. stated, redirecting attention to her. 'We're going to have to recanvass all the neighbors, friends, and family — when was the last time someone saw or spoke to Brian Darby alive? Are we looking at Friday night or Saturday morning?'

'Had a call on his cellphone Friday evening,' another detective, Jake Owens, commented. 'Saw that when I was going through the records yesterday.'

'Long call? Like he talked to someone?'

'Eight or nine minutes, so not just leaving a message. I'll trace the number, have a chat with the recipient.'

'Make sure the person spoke to Brian,' D.D. ordered crisply, 'and it wasn't Tessa, using his phone.'

'I don't get it.' Phil had been doing all the

224

background checks and in many ways knew more about the details of the case than anyone. 'We're thinking Tessa shot her husband, then froze the body — then staged a whole scene for Sunday morning. Why?'

D.D. shrugged. 'Interestingly enough, she wouldn't tell us that.'

'Buying time,' Bobby said, from his place, leaning against the front wall. 'No other good reason. She was buying time.'

'For what?' Phil asked.

'Most likely, to deal with her daughter.'

That brought the room up short. D.D. frowned at him. Obviously, she wasn't happy with his conjecture. That was okay. He wasn't happy to learn she was pregnant from a suspect in a murder investigation. Call him old-fashioned, but that stuck in his craw, and he was feeling pissy about it.

'You think she hurt the daughter?' Phil asked now, his voice wary. He had four kids at home.

'A neighbor saw Brian's Denali leave the house Saturday afternoon,' Bobby said. 'Initially, we assumed Brian was driving the SUV. Given that the lab techs believe a dead body was in the back of the vehicle, we further assumed that Brian had killed his stepdaughter, and was disposing of the evidence. Except, Brian Darby was most likely dead by Saturday afternoon. Meaning he wasn't the one transporting a corpse.'

D.D. thinned her lips, but nodded curtly. 'I think we have to consider the notion that Tessa Leoni killed her entire family. Given that Sophie was at school on Friday, my guess is either Friday night, before Tessa's patrol shift, or Saturday morning after her patrol shift, something terrible happened in the household. Brian's body was put on ice in the garage, while Sophie's body was driven to an undisclosed location and dumped. Tessa reported to work once again Saturday evening. Then Sunday morning, it was showtime.'

'She staged it,' Phil muttered. 'Made it look like her husband had done something to Sophie. Then she and Brian fought and she killed him in self-defense.'

D.D. nodded; Bobby, too.

'What about the facial injuries, though?' Neil spoke up from the back. 'No way she made it through Saturday night patrol with a concussion and fractured face. She couldn't stand yesterday, let alone operate a motor vehicle.'

'Good point,' D.D. concurred. She moved in front of the whiteboard, where she'd written: *Timeline*. Now, she added one bullet — *Tessa Leoni Injuries: Sunday Morning*. 'Wounds gotta be fresh. Can a doctor verify that?' she asked Neil, a former EMT and their resident medical expert.

'Tough with contusions,' Neil answered. 'Everyone heals at a different rate. But I'm gonna guess the severity of the injuries dictates they happened sooner versus later. She wouldn't have been terribly functional after taking such massive blows to the head.'

'Who beat her up?' another officer asked.

'Accomplice,' Phil muttered up front.

226

D.D. nodded. 'In addition to revamping our timeline, this new information also means we need to reconsider the scope of the case. If Brian Darby didn't beat his wife, who did, and why?'

'Lover,' Bobby said quietly. 'Most logical explanation. Why did Tessa Leoni kill her husband and daughter? Because she didn't want to be with them anymore. Why didn't she want to be with them anymore? Because she had met someone new.'

'Hear anything through the grapevine?' D.D. asked him. 'Rumors from the barracks, that sort of thing.'

Bobby shook his head. 'Not that plugged in, though. I'm a detective, not a trooper. We'll need to interview the LT.'

'First thing this afternoon,' D.D. assured him.

'Gotta say,' Phil spoke up, 'this theory fits better with what Darby's boss, Scott Hale, reported. I talked to him at eleven, and he swore up and down that Darby didn't have a violent bone in his body. A tanker crew is pretty tight. You see people sleep deprived, homesick, and stressed out, while maintaining a twenty-four/ seven work schedule. As an engineer, Darby got to deal with all the technical crises, and apparently big things go wrong on big ships — water in the fuel, fried electrical systems, glitches in the control software. Still, Hale never saw Darby lose his composure. In fact, the bigger the problem, the more jazzed Darby was about finding a solution. Hale certainly doesn't believe a guy like that goes home and beats up his wife.'

'Darby was a model employee,' D.D. said.

'Darby was everyone's favorite engineer. And apparently, quite good at Guitar Hero — they have a rec room on board.'

D.D. sighed, crossed her arms over her chest. She glanced over at Bobby, not quite meeting his eye, but looking in his general direction. 'What'd you learn at the gym?' she asked.

'Brian had spent the past nine months following a vigorous exercise regimen designed to bulk up. Personal trainer swore he wasn't doing steroids, just putting in blood, sweat, and tears. She only heard him say good things about his wife, but thought that having a state trooper for a spouse was tough on the guy. Oh, and in the past three weeks, since returning home from his last tour, Darby was definitely in a mood, but not willing to talk about it.'

'What do you mean by 'in a mood'?'

'Personal trainer said he seemed darker, temperamental. She'd asked a couple of times, guessing trouble on the home front, but he wouldn't comment. For what it's worth, that makes him something of a novelty. Apparently, most clients pour out their souls while working out. Go to a gym, enter a confessional.'

D.D. perked up. 'So something was on his mind, but Darby wasn't talking about it.'

'Maybe he discovered his wife was having an affair,' Neil commented from the back. 'You said when he returned, meaning, he'd just left his wife all alone for sixty days . . . '

'In addition to the rec room on the ship,' Phil spoke up, 'there's a computer room for the crew. I'm working on the warrant now to get copies of all of Darby's ingoing and outgoing e-mail. Might find something there.'

'So Tessa meets another man,' D.D. mused, 'decides to off her husband. Why homicide? Why not divorce?'

She posed the question generally, a challenge to the room.

'Life insurance,' an officer spoke up.

'Expediency,' said another. 'Maybe he threatened to fight a divorce.'

'Maybe Darby had something on her, threatened to make trouble if she divorced him.'

D.D. wrote down each comment, seeming particularly interested in the third bulletin. 'By her own admission, Tessa Leoni is an alcoholic, who'd already killed once when she was sixteen. Figure if that's what she's willing to admit to, what *isn't* she willing to say?'

D.D. turned back to the group. 'Okay, then why kill her daughter? Brian's a stepdad, so he doesn't have grounds to challenge for custody. It's one thing to end a marriage. Why kill her own kid?'

Room was slower with this one. Of all people, it was Phil who finally ventured an answer: 'Because her lover doesn't want kids. Isn't that how these things work? Diane Downs, etc., etc. Women kill their children when their children are inconvenient for them. Tessa was looking to start a new life. Sophie could not be part of that life, so Sophie had to die.'

No one had anything to add to that.

'We need to identify the lover,' Bobby murmured.

'We need to find Sophie's body,' D.D. sighed more heavily. 'Prove once and for all just what Tessa Leoni is capable of.'

She set down her marker, looked over the whiteboard.

'All right, people. These are our assumptions: Tessa Leoni killed her husband and child, most likely sometime Friday evening or Saturday morning. She froze her husband's body in the garage. She disposed of her daughter during a Saturday afternoon drive. Then she reported to work — most likely while unthawing her husband's body in the kitchen — before returning home, letting her lover beat the shit out of her, and calling her fellow state troopers. It's some story. Now get out there, and find me some *facts*. I want e-mails and phone messages between her and her lover. I want a neighbor who noticed her unloading ice or shoveling snow. I want to know exactly where Brian Darby's white Denali traveled to on Saturday afternoon. I want Sophie's body. And if this is indeed what happened, I want Tessa Leoni locked up for life. Any questions?'

'Amber Alert?' Phil asked, as he rose to his feet.

'We keep it active until we find Sophie Leoni, one way or the other.'

The taskforce understood what she meant: until they found the child, or until they recovered the child's body. The detectives filed out of the room. Then it was just Bobby and D.D., standing together, alone.

He pushed away from the wall first and

headed for the door.

'Bobby.'

There was just enough uncertainty in her voice to make him turn.

'I haven't even told Alex,' she said. 'All right? I haven't even told Alex.'

'Why not?'

'Because . . . ' She shrugged. 'Because.'

'Are you going to keep the baby?'

Her eyes widened. She motioned frantically to the open door, so he humored her by closing it. 'Now see, this is why I didn't say anything,' she exploded. 'This is precisely the kind of conversation I didn't want to have!'

He remained standing there, staring at her. She had one hand splayed across her lower abdomen. How had he never noticed that before, he the former sniper? The way she cradled her belly, almost protectively. He felt stupid, and realized now he'd never needed to ask the question. He knew the answer just by looking at the way she was standing: She was keeping the baby. That's what had her so terrified.

Sergeant Detective D.D. Warren was going to be a mom.

'It's going to be okay,' he said.

'Oh God!'

'D.D., you have been great at everything you've ever wanted to do. Why should this be any different?'

'Oh God,' she said again, eyes wilder.

'Can I get you anything? Water? A pickle? How about ginger chews? Annabelle lived on ginger chews. Said they settled her stomach.'

231

'Ginger chews?' She paused. Appeared a little less frantic, a little more curious. 'Really?'

Bobby smiled at her, crossed the room, and because it felt like the right thing to do, he gave her a hug. 'Congratulations,' he whispered in her ear. 'Seriously, D.D. Welcome to the ride of your life.'

'You think?' She looked a little misty-eyed, then surprised them both by hugging him back. 'Thanks, Bobby.'

He patted her shoulder. She leaned her head into his chest. Then they both straightened, turned to the whiteboard, and got back to work.

21

I stood, my hands shackled at my waist, as the district attorney read off the charges. According to the DA, I had deliberately and willfully shot my own husband. Furthermore, they had reason to believe I may have also killed my own daughter. At this time, they were entering charges of Murder 1, and requesting I be held without bail, given the severity of the charges.

My lawyer, Cargill, blustered his protest. I was an upstanding state police trooper, with a long and distinguished career (four years?). The DA had insufficient evidence against me, and to believe such a reputable officer and dedicated mother would turn on her entire family was preposterous.

The DA pointed out ballistics had already matched the bullets in my husband's chest to my state-issued Sig Sauer.

Cargill argued my black eye, fractured face, and concussed brain. Obviously, I'd been driven to it.

The DA pointed out that might have made sense, if my husband's body hadn't been frozen after death.

This clearly perplexed the judge, who shot me a startled glance.

Welcome to my world, I wanted to tell him. But I said nothing, showed nothing, because even the smallest gesture, happy, angry, or sad, would lead to the same place: hysteria.

Sophie, Sophie, Sophie.

All I want for Christmas is my two front teeth, my two front teeth, my two front teeth.

I was going to burst into song. Then I would simply scream because that's what a mother wanted to do when she pulled back the covers of her child's empty bed. She wanted to scream, except I'd never had a chance.

There had been a noise downstairs. Sophie, I'd thought again. And I'd sprinted out of her bedroom, running downstairs, racing straight into the kitchen, and there had been my husband, and there had been a man holding a gun against my husband's temple.

'Who do you love?' he'd said, and that quickly, my choices had been laid out for me. I could do what I was told and save my daughter. Or I could fight back, and lose my entire family.

Brian, staring at me, using his gaze to tell me what I needed to do. Because even if he was a miserable fuckup, he was still my husband and, more importantly, he was Sophie's father. The only man she'd ever called Daddy.

He loved her. For all his faults, he loved us both.

Funny, the things you don't fully appreciate until it's too late.

I'd placed my duty belt on the kitchen table.

And the man had stepped forward, ripped my Sig Sauer from the holster, and shot Brian three times in the chest.

Boom, boom, boom.

My husband died. My daughter had disappeared. And me, the trained police officer, stood there, completely shell-shocked, scream still locked in my lungs.

A gavel came down.

The sharp jolt jerked me back to attention. My gaze went instinctively to the clock: 2:43 p.m. Did the time still matter? I hoped it did.

'Bail is set at one million dollars,' the judge declared crisply.

The DA smiled. Cargill grimaced.

'Hold steady,' Shane muttered behind me. 'Everything'll be okay. Hold steady.'

I didn't dignify his empty platitudes with a response. The troopers' union had money set aside for bail, of course, just as it assisted with the hiring of a lawyer for any officer needing legal assistance. Unfortunately, the union's nest egg was hardly a million bucks. That kind of funding would take time, not to mention a special vote. Which probably meant I was out of luck.

Like the union was going to get further involved with a female officer accused of murdering her husband and child. Like my sixteen hundred male colleagues were going to vote affirmative on that one.

I said nothing, I showed nothing, because the scream was bubbling up again, a tightness in my chest that built and built. I wished I had the blue button, wished I'd been able to keep it, because holding it, in a perverse way, had kept me sane. The button meant Sophie. The button meant Sophie was out there, and I just had to find her again.

The court guard approached, placing his hand on my elbow. He jerked me forward and I started to walk, one foot in front of the other, because that's what you did, what you had to do.

Cargill was beside me. 'Family?' he asked quietly.

I understood what he meant. Did I have family to bail me out? I thought of my father, felt the scream rise from my chest into my throat. I shook my head.

'I'll talk to Shane, present your case to the union,' he said, but I could already feel his skepticism.

I remembered my superior officers, not meeting my gaze as I passed down the hospital corridor. The walk of shame. The first of many.

'I can request special treatment at the jail,' Cargill said, speaking rapidly now, for we were approaching the doorway that led to the holding cell, where I would be officially led away. 'You're a state police officer. They'll grant you segregation if you want it.'

I shook my head. I'd been to the Suffolk County Jail; the segregation unit was the most depressing one in the place. I'd get my own cell, but I'd also be locked inside twenty-three hours a day. No privileges such as a gym pass or library hour, and no commons area boasting a finicky TV and world's oldest exercise bike to help pass the time. Funny, the things I was about to consider luxury items.

'Medical eval,' he suggested urgently, meaning I could also request medical time, placing me in the hospital ward.

'With all the other psychos,' I muttered back, because last time I'd toured the prison, all the screamers had been down in Medical, yelling 24/7 to themselves, the guards, the other inmates. Anything, I suppose, to drown out the voices in their heads.

We'd arrived outside the holding cell, the guard giving Cargill a pointed look. For a moment, my frazzled attorney hesitated. He gazed at me with something that might have been sympathy and I wished he hadn't, because it merely made the scream rise from my throat to the dark hollow of my mouth. I had to thin my lips, clench my jaw to keep it from escaping.

I was strong, I was tough. Nothing here I hadn't seen before. Usually I was the one on the other side of the bars, but details, details.

Cargill grabbed hold of my cuffed hands. He squeezed my fingers.

'Ask for me, Tessa,' he murmured. 'You have the legal right to confer with your lawyer at any time. Call, and I will come.'

Then he was gone. The holding-cell door opened. I stumbled inside, joining five other women with faces as pale and detached as my own. As I watched, one drifted over to the stainless steel toilet, pulled up her black spandex miniskirt, and peed.

'What'ya staring at, bitch?' she asked, yawning.

The cell door banged shut behind me.

* * *

Introducing the South Bay shuffle: To execute this time-honored jail transport maneuver, a detainee must link each of her arms through the arm of the person on either side, then clasp her hands at her waist, where her wrists will be cuffed. Once each detainee has been 'pretzeled' with the inmates on either side, ankles are also shackled together and a line of six females can shamble their way to the sheriff's van.

Females sit on one side of the van. Males sit on the other. A clear Plexiglas sheet separates the two. The bleach blonde beside me spent most of the journey making suggestive motions with her tongue. The two hundred and fifty pound, heavily tattooed black male across from us urged her on with his hips.

Three more minutes, and I think they could've completed their transaction. Sadly for their sake, we arrived at the Suffolk County Jail.

The sheriff's van pulled into the unloading bay. A massive metal garage door clanged down and locked tight, sealing in the place. Then the vehicle doors finally opened.

Males disembarked first, exiting the van as a shackled line and entering the sally port. After a few moments, it was our turn.

Stepping out of the van was the hardest. I felt the peer pressure not to stumble or fall, as I would take down the entire line. The fact I was white and wearing new clothes already made me stand out, as most of my fellow detainees appeared to be members of the sex and drugs trade. The cleaner ones probably worked for money. The not so clean ones worked for product.

Most of them had been up all night, and to judge by the various smells, they'd been busy.

Interestingly enough, the orange-haired woman to my right crinkled her nose at my particular odor of hospital antiseptic and brand-new blue jeans. While the girl to my left (eighteen, nineteen years old?) took in my bashed-in face, and said, 'Oh honey, next time, just give him the money, and he'll go easier on you.'

Doors opened. We shuffled our way into the sally port. The doors behind us shut. The doors to the left clanged open.

I could see command central directly ahead of me, staffed by two COs in dark blue BDUs. I kept my head down, afraid of spotting a familiar face.

More hobbling steps, inching our way shoulder to shoulder, hip to hip down a long corridor, past cinder-block walls painted a dirty yellow, inhaling the astringent smell of government institutions everywhere — a mix of sweat, bleach, and human apathy.

We arrived at the 'dirty hold,' another large cell, much like the one at the courthouse. Hard wooden bench lining one wall. Single metal toilet and sink. Two public pay phones. All calls had to be made collect, we were informed, while an automated message would inform the receiver the call originated from the Suffolk County Jail.

We were unshackled. The CO exited. The metal door clanged shut, and that was that.

I rubbed my wrists, then noticed I was the

239

only one who did so. Everyone else was already lining up for the phone. Ready to call whomever to bail them out.

I didn't line up. I sat on the hard wooden bench and watched the hookers and drug dealers, who still had more people who loved them than I did.

The CO called my name first. Even knowing it was coming, I had a moment of panic. My hands gripped the edge of the bench. I wasn't sure I could let go.

I'd handled it so far. I'd handled so much thus far. But now, the processing. Officer Tessa Leoni would officially cease to exist. Inmate #55669021 would take her place.

I couldn't do it. I wouldn't do it.

The CO called my name again. He stood outside the metal door, staring straight at me through the window. And I knew he knew. Of course he knew. They were admitting a female state police officer. Had to be the juiciest scuttlebutt around. A woman charged with killing her husband and suspected of murdering her six-year-old daughter. Exactly the kind of inmate COs loved to hate.

I forced myself to let go of the bench. I drew myself to standing.

Command presence, I thought, a little wildly. Never let them see you sweat.

I made it to the door. The CO snapped on the bracelets, placing his hand upon my elbow. His grip was firm, his face impassive.

'This way,' the CO said, and jerked my arm to the left.

We returned to command central, where I was grilled for basic information: height, weight, DOB, closest relative, contact information, addresses, phone numbers, distinguishing tattoos, etc. Then they took my picture standing in front of the cinder-block wall, holding a sign covered in the number that would be my new identity. The finished product became my new ID card, which I would be required to wear at all times.

Back down the corridor. New room, where they took away my clothing, and I got to squat naked while a female officer pointed a flashlight into all of my orifices. I received a drab brown prison suit — one pair of pants, one shirt — a single pair of flat white sneakers, nicknamed 'Air Cabrals' in deference to the sheriff, Andrea Cabral, and a clear plastic hooter bag. The hooter bag contained a clear toothbrush the size of a pinky, a small clear deodorant, clear shampoo, and white toothpaste. The toiletries were clear to make it harder for inmates to conceal drugs in the containers. The toothbrush was small so it would be less effective when inevitably made into a shiv.

If I desired additional toiletries, say conditioner, hand lotion, lip balm, I had to purchase them from the commissary. Chapstick ran $1.10. Lotion $2.21. I could also buy better tennis shoes, ranging from $28 to $47.

Next, the nurse's office. She checked out my black eye, swollen cheek, and gashed head. Then I got to answer routine medical questions, while being inoculated for TB, always a major consideration for prison populations. The nurse lingered on the psych eval, perhaps trying to determine if I was the kind of woman who might do something rash, like hang myself with overbleached sheets.

The nurse signed off on my medical eval. Then the CO escorted me down the cinderblock hall to the elevator banks. He punched the ninth floor, which held pretrial women. I had two choices, Unit 1-9-1 or Unit 1-9-2. I got 1-9-2.

Sixty to eighty women held at a time in the pretrial units. Sixteen cells to a unit. Two to three women to a cell.

I was led to a cell with only one other female. Her name was Erica Reed. She currently slept on the top bunk, kept her personal possessions on the bottom. I could make myself at home on the butcher block that also served as a desk.

Second the metal door shut behind me, Erica started chewing her discolored fingernails, revealing a row of blackened teeth. Meth addict. Which explained her pale sunken face and lank brown hair.

'Are you the cop?' she asked immediately, sounding very excited. 'Everyone said we were getting a cop! I *hope* you're the cop!'

I realized then that I was in even bigger trouble than I'd thought.

22

Lieutenant Colonel Gerard Hamilton didn't sound thrilled to talk to D.D. and Bobby; more like resigned to his fate. One of his troopers was involved in an 'unfortunate incident.' Of course the investigative team needed to interview him.

As a matter of courtesy, D.D. and Bobby met him in his office. He shook D.D.'s hand, then greeted Bobby with a more familiar hand clasp to the shoulder. It was obvious the men knew each other, and D.D. was grateful for Bobby's presence — Hamilton probably wouldn't have been so collegial otherwise.

She let Bobby take the lead while she studied Hamilton's office. The Massachusetts State Police were notoriously fond of their military-like hierarchy. If D.D. worked in a modest office space decorated as Business-R-Us, then Hamilton's space reminded her of an up-and-coming political candidate's. The wood-paneled walls held black-framed photos of Hamilton with every major Massachusetts politician, including a particularly large snapshot of Hamilton and Mass.'s Republican senator, Scott Brown. She spotted a diploma from UMass Amherst, another certificate from the FBI Academy. The impressive rack of antlers mounted above the LT's desk showcased his hunting prowess, and in case that didn't do the trick, another photo showed Hamilton in green fatigues and an orange hunting vest standing next to the fresh kill.

D.D. didn't dwell on the photo too long. She was getting the impression that Baby Warren was a vegetarian. Red meat bad. Dry cereal, on the other hand, was starting to sound good.

'Of course I know Trooper Leoni,' Hamilton was saying now. He was a distinguished-looking senior officer. Trim, athletic build, dark hair graying at the temples, permanently tanned face from years of outdoor living. D.D. bet the young male officers openly admired him, while the young female officers secretly found him sexy. Was Tessa Leoni one of those officers? And did Hamilton return the sentiment?

'Fine officer,' he continued evenly. 'Young, but competent. No history of incidents or complaints.'

Hamilton had Tessa's file open on his desk. He confirmed Tessa had worked graveyard Friday and Saturday nights. Then he and Bobby reviewed her duty logs, much of which made no sense to D.D. Detectives tracked active cases, cleared cases, warrants, interviews, etc., etc. Troopers tracked, among other things, vehicle stops, traffic citations, call outs, warrants served, property seized, and a whole slew of assists. It sounded less like policing to D.D. and more like basketball. Apparently, troopers were either making calls or assisting other troopers making calls.

Either way, Tessa had particularly robust duty logs, even Friday and Saturday night. On

Saturday's graveyard shift alone, she'd issued two citations for operating under the influence — OUI — which in the second case involved not just taking the driver into custody, but arranging for the suspect's vehicle to be towed.

Bobby grimaced. 'Seen the paperwork yet?' he said, tapping the two OUIs.

'Got it from the captain a couple of hours ago. It's good.'

Bobby looked at D.D. 'Then she definitely didn't have a concussion Saturday night. I can barely complete those forms stone-sober, let alone suffering from a massive head trauma.'

'Take any personal calls Saturday night?' D.D. asked the LT.

Hamilton shrugged. 'Troopers patrol with their personal mobiles, not just their department-issued pager. It's possible she took all sorts of personal calls. Nothing, however, through official channels.'

D.D. nodded. She was surprised troopers were still allowed their cellphones. Many law enforcement agencies were banning them, as uniformed officers, often the first responders to crime scenes, had a tendency to snap personal photos using their mobiles. Maybe they thought the guy who blew his head off looked funny. Or they wanted to share that particular blood spatter with a buddy they had in a different field office. From a legal perspective, however, any crime-scene photo was evidence and subject to full disclosure to the defense. Meaning that if any such photos surfaced *after* the case had been adjudicated, their mere presence would be grounds for a mistrial.

The DA didn't like it very much when that happened. Had a tendency to get downright nasty on the subject.

'Leoni ever reprimanded?' D.D. asked now.

Hamilton shook his head.

'Take a lot of days off, maybe personal time? She's a young mom, spending half her year alone with a kid.'

Hamilton flipped through the file, shook his head. 'Admirable,' he commented. 'Not easy meeting both the demands of the job and the needs of a family.'

'Amen,' Bobby murmured.

They both sounded sincere. D.D. chewed her lower lip. 'How well did you know her?' she asked the LT abruptly. 'Group bonding activities, the gang meeting for drinks, that sort of thing?'

Hamilton finally hesitated. 'I didn't really know her,' he said at last. 'Trooper Leoni had a reputation for being distant. Couple of her performance reviews touched on the subject. Solid officer. Very reliable. Showed good judgment. But on the social front, remained aloof. It was a source of some concern. Even troopers, who primarily patrol alone, need to feel the cohesiveness of the group. The reassurance that your fellow officer always has your back. Trooper Leoni's fellow troopers respected her professionally. But no one really felt they knew her personally. And in this job, where the lines between professional and personal life easily blur . . . '

Hamilton's voice trailed off. D.D. got his point and was intrigued. Law enforcement wasn't a day job. You didn't just punch a clock, perform your duties, and hand off to your coworkers. Law enforcement was a calling. You committed to your work, you committed to your team, and you resigned yourself to the life.

D.D. had wondered if Tessa had been too close to a fellow officer, or even a commanding officer, such as the LT. In fact, it sounded as if she wasn't close enough.

'Can I ask you a question?' Hamilton asked suddenly.

'Me?' Startled, D.D. blinked at the lieutenant colonel, then nodded.

'Do you fraternize with your fellow detectives? Grab a beer, share cold pizza, catch the game at one another's homes?'

'Sure. But I don't have a family,' D.D. pointed out. 'And I'm older. Tessa Leoni . . . you're talking about a young, pretty mom dealing with a barrack of entirely male officers. She's your only female trooper, right?'

'In Framingham, yes.'

D.D. shrugged. 'Not a lot of women in blue. If Trooper Leoni wasn't feeling the brotherly love, can't say I blame her.'

'We never had any complaints of sexual harassment,' Hamilton stated immediately.

'Not all women feel like doing the paperwork.'

Hamilton didn't like this assertion. His face shuttered up, he looked intimidating, harsh even.

'At the barracks level,' he stated crisply, 'we encouraged Leoni's commanding officer to

247

create more opportunities for her to feel included. Let's just say it met with mixed results. No doubt it is difficult to be the lone female in a dominantly male organization. On the other hand, Leoni herself did not appear inclined to bridge the divide. To be blunt, she was perceived as a loner. And even officers who made an effort to befriend her — '

'Such as Trooper Lyons?' D.D. interrupted.

'Such as Trooper Lyons,' Hamilton agreed. 'They tried and failed. Teamwork is about winning the hearts and minds of your fellow officers. In that regard, Trooper Leoni got it half right.'

'Speaking of hearts and minds.' Bobby sounded apologetic, as if sorry to reduce the LT down to the level of gossipmonger. 'Any reports of Leoni being involved with another officer? Or perhaps an officer who was interested in her, whether she returned the interest or not?'

'I did some asking. Trooper Leoni's closest associate seems to be Trooper Shane Lyons, though that relationship is more through the husband than Leoni.'

'Did you know him?' D.D. asked curiously. 'The husband, Brian Darby? Or her daughter, Sophie?'

'I knew them both,' Hamilton answered gravely, surprising her. 'At various cookouts and family functions over the years. Sophie is a pretty little girl. Very precocious, that's my memory.' He frowned, seemed to be wrestling with something inside himself. 'You could tell Trooper Leoni loved her very much,' he said abruptly. 'At least, that's what I always thought when I saw them together. The way Tessa held her daughter, doted on her. The thought . . . '

Hamilton looked away. He cleared his throat, then clasped his hands on the desk before him. 'Sad, sad business,' the LT murmured to no one in particular.

'What about Brian Darby?' Bobby asked.

'Knew him even longer than Tessa. Brian was a good friend of Trooper Lyons. He started appearing at cookouts a good eight, nine years ago. Even joined us a couple of times to see the Boston Bruins, attended poker night every now and then.'

'Didn't know you and Trooper Lyons were so close,' D.D. stated, arching a brow.

Hamilton gave her a stern look. 'If my troopers invite me to a function, I always try to attend. Camaraderie is important, not to mention that informal gatherings are invaluable for keeping the lines of communication open between troopers and the chain of command. Having said that, I probably join Trooper Lyons and his 'posse,' as he calls them, three or four times a year.'

'What did you think of Brian?' Bobby asked.

'Followed hockey, also liked the Red Sox. Made him a stand-up guy in my book.'

'Talk to him much?'

'Hardly at all. Most of our outings were of the male-bonding variety — catching a game, playing a game, or betting on a game. And yes,' he turned to D.D. as if already anticipating her complaint, 'it's possible such activities made

249

Trooper Leoni feel excluded. Though from what I remember, she also follows the Red Sox, with the whole family attending many of the games.'

D.D. scowled. She hated it when she was so transparent.

'And Trooper Leoni's alcoholism,' Bobby asked quietly. 'That ever come up?'

'I was aware of the situation,' Hamilton replied just as evenly. 'To the best of my knowledge, Leoni had successfully completed a twelve-step program and remained on track. Again, no history of incidents or complaints.'

'What about that whole matter of her shooting and killing someone when she was sixteen?' D.D. asked.

'That,' Hamilton said heavily, 'is gonna bite us on the ass.'

The bluntness of his statement took D.D. by surprise. She had a moment, then got it. The press digging deeper into Boston's latest femme fatale, demanding to know what the state police were thinking, hiring a trooper who already had a history of violence . . .

Yep, the LT would have a lot of explaining to do.

'Look,' the commanding officer said now. 'Trooper Leoni was never charged with a crime. She met all of our candidacy requirements. To refuse her application — that would've been discrimination. And for the record, she passed the Academy with flying colors and has performed exemplary in the line of duty. We had no way of knowing, no way of anticipating . . . '

'You think she did it?' D.D. asked. 'You knew her husband, her child. Think Tessa killed them both?'

'I think the longer I stay in this job, the less I'm surprised by all the things that should surprise me.'

'Any talk of marital problems between her and Brian?' Bobby asked.

'I would be the last to know,' Hamilton assured him.

'Noticeable changes in behavior, particularly the past three weeks?'

Hamilton tilted his head to the side. 'Why the past three weeks?'

Bobby merely studied his superior officer. But D.D. understood. Because Brian Darby had only been home for the past three weeks, and according to his personal trainer, he'd returned from his last tour of duty not very happy with life.

'There was one situation that comes to mind,' Hamilton said abruptly. 'Not involving Trooper Leoni, but her husband.'

D.D. and Bobby exchanged a glance.

'Probably six months ago,' Hamilton continued, not really looking at them. 'Let's see . . . November. That sounds right. Trooper Lyons arranged an outing to Foxwoods. Many of us attended, including Brian Darby. Personally, I took in a show, blew my fifty bucks in the casino, and called it a night. But Brian . . . When the time came, we couldn't get him to leave. One more round, one more round, this would be the one. He and Shane ended up in an argument, with Shane physically pulling him off the casino floor. The other guys laughed it off. But . . . It seemed pretty clear to me that Brian Darby should not return to Foxwoods.'

'He had a gambling problem?' Bobby asked with a frown.

'I'd say his interest in gaming appeared higher than average. I'd say that if Shane hadn't yanked him away from the roulette table, Brian would still be sitting there, watching the numbers spin around.'

Bobby and D.D. exchanged glances. D.D. would like this story better if Brian didn't have fifty grand sitting in the bank. Gambling addicts didn't normally leave fifty grand in savings. Still, they studied the lieutenant colonel.

'Have Shane and Brian returned to Foxwoods lately?' Bobby asked.

'You would have to ask Trooper Lyons.'

'Trooper Leoni ever mention any financial stress? Ask for extra shifts, more OT hours, that sort of thing?'

'To judge by the duty logs,' Hamilton said slowly, 'she's been working more hours lately.'

But fifty grand in the bank, D.D. thought. Who needed OT when you had fifty grand in the bank?

'There is something else you probably should know,' Hamilton said quietly. 'I need you to understand, this is strictly off the record. And it may have nothing to do with Trooper Leoni. But . . . You said the past three weeks, and as a matter of fact, we launched an internal investigation exactly two weeks ago: An outside auditor discovered funds had been improperly moved from the union's account. The auditor believes the funds were embezzled, most likely from an inside source. We are trying to locate those monies now.'

D.D. went wide-eyed. 'How nice of you to mention that. And to volunteer it so readily, too.'

Bobby shot her a warning glance.

'How much are we talking?' he asked in a more reasonable tone.

'Two hundred and fifty thousand.'

'Missing as of two weeks ago?'

'Yes. But the embezzlement started twelve months prior, a series of payments made to an insurance company, which it turns out, doesn't exist.'

'But the checks have been cashed,' Bobby stated.

'Each and every one,' Hamilton replied.

'Who signed for them?'

'Hard to make out. But all were deposited into the same bank account in Connecticut, which four weeks ago was closed out.'

'The fake insurance company was a shell,' D.D. determined. 'Set up to receive payments, a quarter of a million dollars' worth, then shut down.'

'That's what the investigators believe.'

'Bank's gotta have information for you,' Bobby said. 'Same bank for all transactions?'

'The bank has been cooperating fully. It supplied us with video footage of a woman in a red baseball cap and dark sunglasses closing out the account. That has become internal affair's biggest lead — they are pursuing a female with inside information on the troopers' union.'

'Such as Tessa Leoni,' D.D. murmured.

The lieutenant colonel didn't argue.

23

If you want someone dead, prison is the perfect place to do it. Just because the Suffolk County Jail was minimum security didn't mean it wasn't filled with violent offenders. The convicted murderer who'd just served twenty years at the state maximum security prison might finish up his or her county sentence here, completing eighteen months for burglary or simple assault that had been in addition to the homicide charge. Maybe my roommate Erica was locked up for dealing drugs, or turning tricks, or petty theft. Or maybe she'd killed the last three women who'd tried to get between her and her meth.

When I asked the question, she just smiled, showing off twin rows of black teeth.

Unit 1-9-2 held thirty-four other women just like her.

As pretrial detainees, we were kept separate from the general inmate population, in a locked-down unit where food came to us, the nurse came to us, and programming came to us. But within the unit, there was plenty of intermingling, creating multiple opportunities for violence.

Erica walked me through the daily schedule. Morning started at seven a.m., with 'count time,' when the CO would conduct head count. Then we would be served breakfast in our cells,

255

followed by a couple of hours 'rec time' — we could leave our cells and roam unshackled around the unit, maybe hang out in the commons area watching TV, maybe shower (three showers located right off the commons area, where everyone could also enjoy that show), or ride the squeaky exercise bike (verbal insults from your fellow detainees not included).

Most women, I quickly realized, spent their time playing cards or gossiping at the round stainless steel tables in the center of the unit. A woman would join a table, pick up one rumor, share two more, then visit a neighbor's cell, where she could be the first to provide the big scoop. And around and around the women went, table to table, cell to cell. The whole atmosphere reminded me of summer camp, where everyone wore the same clothes, slept in bunks, and obsessed over boys.

Eleven a.m., everyone returned to their assigned cell for the second session of count time, followed by lunch. More rec time. Count time again at three. Dinner around five. Final count time at eleven, followed by lights out, which was not to be confused with quiet time. In prison, there was no such thing as quiet time, and in a corrections facility that housed both men and women, there was definitely no such thing as quiet time.

The females, I quickly learned, occupied the top three floors of the Suffolk County 'tower.' Some enterprising woman (or man, I suppose) determined that the plumbing pipes from the upper floors connected to the lower floors.

Meaning that a female detainee — say, my roommate Erica — could stick her head inside the white porcelain toilet bowl and proceed to 'talk' to a random male on the lower floor. Though, talking isn't really what any man wants to do. Think of it more as the prison version of sexting.

Erica would make lewd comments. Nine floors beneath us, a faceless man would groan. Erica would make more lewd comments: *Harder, faster, come on, baby, I'm rubbing my tits for you, can you feel me rubbing my tits for you?* (I made that up: Erica didn't have tits. Meth had dissolved all the fat and tissue from her bones, including her breasts. Black teeth, black nails, no boobs. Erica should be starring in a public service announcement targeting teenage girls: This is your body on meth.)

Faceless man nine floors below us, however, wouldn't know that. In his mind, Erica was probably some buxom blonde, or maybe the hot Latina chick he'd spotted once in Medical. He would whack off happily. Erica would start round two.

As would the woman in the cell beside us, and the cell beside her and the cell beside her. All. Night. Long.

Prison is a social place.

The Suffolk County Jail involves multiple buildings. Sadly, only males in the lower floors of the tower could communicate via the toilets with the females on the top three levels. Obviously, this posed a great hardship for the men in other buildings.

The enterprising males in Building 3, however, figured out that we could peer down at their windows from our cells. As Erica explained to me, first thing in the morning our job was to check for messages posted in the windows of Building 3 — say, an artful arrangement of socks, underwear, and T-shirts forming a series of numbers or letters. Only so much could be spelled out with socks, obviously, so a code had been developed. We would write down the code, which would direct the women of 1-9-2 to various books during library time, where a more complete message could be recovered (*fuck me, fuck me, do me, do me, oh you're so pretty can you feel me get so hard . . .*).

Prison poetry, Erica told me with a sigh. Spelling wasn't her strong suit, she confessed, but she always did her best to write back, leaving behind a fresh note (*yes, yes, YES!*) in the same novel.

In other words, inmates could communicate between units, female pretrial detainees to males in general pop and vice versa. Most likely, then, the entire prison population knew of my presence, and an inexperienced detainee in one unit could gain assistance from a more hardened inmate from another.

I wondered how it would happen.

Say, when my entire unit was escorted down nine floors to the lower-level library. Or the couple of times we'd go to the gym. Or during visitation, which was also a group activity, one huge room filled with a dozen tables where everyone intermingled.

258

Easy enough for a fellow inmate to saddle up beside me, drive a shiv through my ribs, and disappear.

Accidents happen, right? Especially in prison.

I did my best to think it through. If it were me, a female detainee trying to get at a trained police officer, how would I do it? On second thought, maybe not overt violence. One, a cop should be able to fend off an attack. Two, the few times the unit was on the move — walking to the library or the gym or visitation — we were escorted by the SERT team, a bunch of hulking COs prepared to pounce at a moment's notice.

No, if it were me, I'd go with poison.

Time-honored female weapon of choice. Not hard to smuggle in. Each detainee was allowed to spend fifty bucks a week at the canteen. Most seemed to blow their wad on Ramen noodles, tennis shoes, and toiletries. With outside help, no problem stashing a little rat poison in the seasoning packet of the Ramen noodles, the cap of the newly purchased hand lotion, etc., etc.

A moment's distraction and Erica could stir it into my dinner. Or later, out in the commons area when another detainee, Sheera, offered me peanut butter on toast.

Arsenic could be combined into lotions, hair products, toothpaste. Every time I moisturized my skin, washed my hair, brushed my teeth . . .

Is this how you go crazy? Realizing all the ways you could die?

And if you did, how few people would care?

Eight twenty-three p.m. Sitting alone on a thin mattress in front of a thickly barred window. Sun long gone. Gazing out at the frigid darkness beyond the glass, while behind me, the relentless fluorescent lights burned too bright.

And wishing for just an instant that I could bend back those bars, open up the high window and, nine stories above the churning city of Boston, step out into the brisk March night and see if I could fly.

Let it all go. Fall into the darkness there.

I pressed my hand against the glass. Stared into the deep dark night. And wondered if somewhere Sophie was gazing out at the same darkness. If she could feel me trying to reach her. If she knew that I was still here and that I loved her and I was going to find her. She was my Sophie and I would save her, just as I had done when she'd locked herself in the trunk.

But first, we both had to be brave.

Brian had to die. That's what the man had told me, Saturday morning in my kitchen. Brian had been a very bad boy and he had to die. But Sophie and I might live. I just had to do as I was told.

They had Sophie. To get her back, I would take the blame for killing my husband. They even had a few ideas on the subject. I could set things up, argue self-defense. Brian would still be dead, but I'd get off and Sophie would be miraculously found and returned to me. I'd probably have to quit the force, but hey, I'd have my daughter.

Standing in the middle of the kitchen, my ears ringing from gunfire, my nostrils still flared with the scent of gunpowder and blood, this had seemed a good deal. I'd said yes, to anything, to everything.

I'd just wanted Sophie.

'Please,' I'd begged, *begged* in my own home. 'Don't hurt my daughter. I'll do it. Just keep her safe.'

Now, of course, I was starting to realize how foolish I'd been. Brian had to die and someone *else* take the blame for his death? If Brian had to die, why not tamper with his brakes, or cause an 'accident' next time he went skiing? Brian was alone most of the time, plenty of things the man in black could've done other than shoot Brian and order his wife to take the blame. Why that? Why me?

Sophie would be miraculously found? How? Wandering in a major department store, or maybe waking up at a highway rest stop? Obviously the police would question her, and children were notoriously unreliable witnesses. Maybe the man could scare her into saying nothing, but why take that risk?

Not to mention once my daughter was returned to me, what incentive did I have to stay quiet? Maybe I'd go to the police then. Why take that risk?

I was thinking more and more that the kind of person who could shoot a man three times in cold blood probably didn't take unnecessary risks.

I was thinking more and more that the kind of person who could shoot a man three times in cold blood had a lot more going on than he was admitting.

What had Brian done? Why did he need to die?

And did he realize, in the last second of his life, that he'd almost certainly doomed me and Sophie, as well?

I felt the metal bars press against either side of my hand, not round as I'd assumed, but fashioned in a shape similar to the slats in vertical blinds.

The man wanted me in prison, I realized now. He, and the people he no doubt worked for, wanted me out of the way.

For the first time in three days, I smiled.

Turned out, they had a little surprise coming. Because in the bloody aftermath, my ears still ringing, my eyes wide with horror, I'd latched onto one thought. I needed to buy time, I needed to slow things down.

Fifty thousand dollars, I'd offered the man who'd just killed my husband. Fifty thousand dollars if he'd give me twenty-four hours to 'get my affairs in order.' If I was going to take the blame for my husband's death, end up in jail, I had to make arrangements for my daughter. That's what I'd told him.

And maybe he didn't trust me, and maybe he had been suspicious, but fifty grand was fifty grand, and once I explained to him that I could put Brian's body on ice . . .

He'd been impressed. Not shocked. Impressed. A woman who could preserve her husband's body with snow was apparently his kind of gal.

So the nameless hit man had accepted fifty grand, and in return I had twenty-four hours to 'get my story straight.'

Turns out, there's a lot you can do in twenty-four hours. Especially when you're the kind of woman who can dispassionately shovel snow over the man who'd once promised to love her, to take care of her, to never leave her.

I didn't think of Brian now. I wasn't ready, couldn't afford to go to that place. So I focused on what mattered most.

Who do you love?

The hit man was right. That's what life comes down to in the end. Who do you love?

Sophie. Somewhere out there in that same darkness, my daughter. Six years old, heart-shaped face, big blue eyes, and a toothless smile that could power the sun. Sophie.

Brian had died for her. Now I would survive for her.

Anything to get my daughter back.

'I'm coming,' I whispered. 'Be brave, sweetheart. Be brave.'

'What?' Erica said, from the top bunk where she was mindlessly flipping cards.

'Nothing.'

'Window won't break,' she stated. 'No escaping that way!' Erica cackled as if she'd told a great joke.

I turned toward my roommate. 'Erica, the pay phone in the commons area — can I use that to make a call?'

She stopped playing her cards.

'Who you gonna call?' she asked with interest.

'Ghostbusters,' I said, straight-faced.

Erica cackled again. Then she told me what I needed to know.

24

Bobby wanted to stop for dinner. D.D. did not.

'You need to take better care of yourself,' Bobby informed her.

'And you need to stop fussing over me!' she snapped back, as they drove through the streets of Boston. 'I never liked it before and I don't like it now.'

'No.'

'*Excuse me?*'

'I said no. And you can't make me.'

D.D. twisted in the passenger's seat until she could glare straight at him. 'You do realize pregnant women are expected to be hormonal and crazy. Meaning I could kill you now, and as long as there's one mother on the jury, I'd get away with it.'

Bobby smiled. 'Ahh, Annabelle used to say the same thing!'

'Oh, for Pete's sake — '

'You're pregnant,' he interrupted her. 'Men like to fuss over pregnant women. It gives us something to do. We also, secretly, love to fuss over babies. Why, the first time you bring in the infant to meet your squad . . . I bet Phil will knit a pair of booties. Neil . . . I'm guessing he'll provide Looney Tunes Band-Aids and the baby's first bike helmet.'

D.D. stared at him. She hadn't thought of booties, Band-Aids, or bringing the kid to work.

She was still working on baby, let alone Life with Baby.

She had a text from Alex: *Heard about the arrest, how goes the rest of the battle?*

She hadn't answered. She didn't know what to say. Sure, they'd arrested Tessa Leoni, but they'd also failed to find six-year-old Sophie. And the sun had gone down for the second time, now thirty-six hours since the initial Amber Alert, but probably two full days since Sophie had gone missing. Except, most likely the Amber Alert didn't matter. Most likely Tessa Leoni had killed her entire family, including Sophie.

D.D. wasn't working a missing persons case; she was leading a murder investigation to recover a child's body.

She wasn't ready to think about that yet. Not prepared for Alex's gentle, but always probing questions. Nor did she know how to segue from that conversation to *Oh yes, and I'm pregnant, which you haven't heard yet, but Bobby Dodge knows all about, having been informed by a female murder suspect.*

These were exactly the kind of situations that made D.D. a workaholic. Because finding Sophie and nailing Tessa would make her feel better. While talking to Alex about the new world order would only be falling deeper and deeper down the rabbit's hole.

'What you need is a falafel,' Bobby said now.

'*Gesundheit*,' D.D. answered.

'Annabelle loved them when she was pregnant. It's meat, isn't it? You can't stand the smell of meat.'

D.D. nodded. 'Eggs don't do wonders for me either.'

'Hence, Mediterranean food, with its many and varied vegetarian dishes.'

'Do you like falafels?' D.D. asked suspiciously.

'No, I like Big Macs, but that's probably not going to work for you right now — '

D.D. shook her head.

'So falafels it is.'

Bobby knew a place. Apparently a favorite of Annabelle's. He went inside to order, D.D. stayed in the car to avoid kitchen odors and catch up on voice mail. She started by returning Phil's call, asking him to rerun Brian Darby's financials, while digging deeper for other accounts or transactions, possibly under a family name or an alias. If Darby had a gambling habit, they should be able to see its impact on his bank account, with large sums of money coming and going, or perhaps a series of cash withdrawals from ATMs at Foxwoods, Mohegan Sun, or other casinos.

Then she transferred to Neil, who'd been working the hospital beat. Neil had been asking about Tessa's medical history. Now D.D. wanted to know about Brian's. In the past twelve months, any incidents of broken kneecaps (maybe a ski injury, D.D. mused) — or, say, a fall down a long flight of stairs. Neil was intrigued, saying he'd start right on it.

The hotline was receiving fewer Sophie sightings, but more calls concerning the white Denali. Turned out the city was filled with white SUVs, meaning the taskforce needed additional manpower to chase down all leads. D.D. suggested that the hotline squad pass all vehicle sightings to the three-man team currently tracing the truck's final hours. Which, she informed them, should be working 24/7, all OT requests automatically approved and if they needed more bodies, then snag more officers.

Tracking down the final drive of Brian Darby's SUV was a clear priority — pinpoint where the Denali had gone Saturday afternoon, find Sophie's body.

The thought depressed D.D. She ended her calls and stared out the window instead.

Chilly night. Pedestrians hustled by on the sidewalk, collars turned up tight around their ears, gloved hands thrust deep into coat pockets. No snow yet, but it felt like it was coming. A cold raw night, which fit D.D.'s mood.

She didn't feel good about arresting Tessa Leoni. She wanted to. The female trooper bothered her. Both too young and too composed. Too pretty and too vulnerable. All bad combinations in D.D.'s mind.

Tessa was lying to them. About her husband, her daughter, and if Hamilton's theory was correct, about two hundred and fifty thousand dollars currently missing from the troopers' union. Had Tessa stolen the money? Was this part of her 'new life'? Steal a quarter of a million, eliminate the family, and ride off into the sunset, young, pretty, and rich?

Or did it come back to the husband? Had he accrued gambling debts no honest man could pay? Maybe embezzling state police monies was

267

his idea and she'd been pressured into going along. Stand behind your man. Except then, once she had the cash, realized the full risk she'd taken, and considered the lure of total freedom . . . Why hand over the ill-gotten gains if you could keep them all for yourself?

She'd had a pretty good plan, too. Set up her husband as a child murderer and wife beater. Then off him in self-defense. Once the dust settled, Tessa could quietly resign from the police and move to another state, where she could be a widow who'd inherited two hundred and fifty thousand in life insurance.

Plan would've worked, D.D. thought, if the ME hadn't noticed the cellular damage caused by freezing.

Maybe that's why Tessa had been putting pressure on Ben to release her husband's body. To try to avoid the autopsy altogether, or if it did happen, for it to be rushed. Ben would get in, out, done, and nobody would be the wiser.

Way to go, Ben, D.D. thought, then realized she was exhausted. She hadn't eaten today, she hadn't slept much last night. Her body was shutting down on her. She needed a nap. She needed to call Alex.

Dear God, what was she ever going to say to Alex?

Car door popped open. Bobby climbed in. He was holding a brown paper bag that wafted all sorts of curious scents. D.D. inhaled, and for once, her stomach didn't rebel. She breathed in deeper, and just like that, she was starving.

'Falafel!' she ordered.

Bobby patted her hand, already digging out the wrap. 'Now, who was saying men shouldn't fuss . . . '

'Gimme, gimme, gimme!'

'Love you, too, D.D. Love you, too.'

★ ★ ★

They ate. Food was good. Food was energy. Food was power.

When they were done, D.D. demurely wiped her mouth, cleaned her hands, and returned the trash to the brown paper bag.

'I have a plan,' she said.

'Does it involve me going home to my wife and baby?'

'No. It involves going to Trooper Lyons's house, and questioning him in front of his wife and children.'

'I'm in.'

She patted his hand. 'Love you, too, Bobby. Love you, too.'

★ ★ ★

Lyons lived in a modest 1950s raised ranch, seven blocks over from Brian Darby. From the street, the house appeared dated but well maintained. Tiny front yard, currently cluttered with a collection of plastic snow shovels and sleek sleds. The remains of a snowman and what appeared to be a snow fort lined the driveway, where Lyons's cruiser was parked at attention.

Bobby had to circle the block a couple of

times for parking. When no spots became available, he parked illegally behind Lyons's cruiser. What was the point of being a cop if you couldn't bend a few rules?

By the time D.D. and Bobby got out of the car, Lyons was standing on the front porch. The burly trooper wore faded jeans, a heavy flannel shirt, and an unwelcoming scowl.

'What?' he asked by way of greeting.

'Got a couple of questions,' D.D. said.

'Not at my house you don't.'

D.D. eased back, let Bobby take the lead. He was a fellow state officer, not to mention better at playing good cop.

'Not intruding,' Bobby said immediately, tone placating. 'We were at the Darby house,' he lied, 'thought of a couple of things, and since you're right around the corner . . . '

'I don't bring work home.' Lyons's ruddy face was still guarded, but not as hostile. 'I got three kids. They don't need to be hearing about Sophie. They're freaked out enough as it is.'

'They know she's missing,' D.D. spoke up. He shot her a look.

'Heard it on the radio when their mother was driving them to school. Amber Alerts.' He shrugged his massive shoulders. 'Can't avoid 'em. Guess that's the whole point. But they know Sophie. They don't understand what could've happened to her.' His voice grew rougher. 'They don't understand why their father, the super-cop, hasn't brought her home yet.'

'Then we're all on the same page,' Bobby said.

He and D.D. had made it to the front stoop. 'We want to find Sophie, bring her home.'

Lyons's shoulders came down. He seemed to finally relent. After another moment, he opened the door, gestured them inside.

They entered into a small mudroom, wood-paneled walls covered in coats, ceramic-tiled floor overrun with boots. House was small, and it only took D.D. a minute to figure out who ran the roost, three young boys, ages five to nine, who rushed into the crowded space to greet the newcomers, talking over one another in their excitement, before their mother, a pretty thirty-something woman with shoulder-length brown curls, tracked them down, looking exasperated.

'Bedtime!' she informed the boys. 'To your rooms. I don't want to see you again until you've brushed your teeth and changed into pajamas!'

Three boys stared at her, didn't budge a muscle.

'Last one to the top of the stairs is a rotten egg!' the oldest boy suddenly yelled, and the three roared off like rockets, piling over one another in their haste to get to the stairs first.

Their mother sighed.

Shane shook his head.

'This is my wife, Tina,' he offered, making the introduction. Tina shook their hands, smiling politely, but D.D. could read tension in the fine lines bracketing the woman's mouth, the way she looked instinctively at her husband, as if for assurance.

'Sophie?' she whispered, the name hitching in her throat.

'No news,' Shane said softly, and he laid his hands on his wife's shoulders in a gesture D.D. found genuinely touching. 'Got some work to do here, okay? I know I said I'd put the boys to bed . . . '

'It's okay,' Tina said automatically.

'We'll be in the front room.'

Tina nodded again. D.D. could feel her eyes on them as they followed Shane from the mudroom into the kitchen. She thought the woman still looked worried.

Off the kitchen was a small front room. Looked like it had once been a three-season porch that Lyons had finished off with windows, installing a small gas-burning stove for heat. The room was decorated Rugged Male, with a big-screen TV, two oversized brown recliners, and a plethora of sports memorabilia. The Man Cave, D.D. deduced, where the stressed-out state trooper could retreat to recover from his day.

She wondered if the wife had an equivalent Crafts Room or Day Spa, because personally, she was betting life with three boys topped eight hours on patrol any day of the week.

Room didn't really offer seating for three, unless you counted the beanbags piled in the corner, so they stood.

'Nice home,' Bobby said, once again good cop.

Lyons shrugged. 'We bought it for the location. You can't see it right now, but the back lawn rolls down into a park, giving us plenty of green space. Great for barbecues. Essential for three boys.'

'That's right,' D.D. spoke up. 'You're known for your cookouts. That's how Tessa and Brian met.'

Lyons nodded, didn't say anything. He had his arms crossed over his chest, a defensive stance, D.D. thought. Or maybe an aggressive stance, given how it bulged the muscles of his shoulders and chest.

'We talked to Lieutenant Colonel Hamilton,' Bobby commented.

Was it D.D.'s imagination, or did Lyons just tense?

'He mentioned several of the outings you've organized, you know — boys' night out to Red Sox games, Foxwoods.'

Lyons nodded.

'Sounds like Brian Darby often joined.'

'If he was around,' Lyons said. Another noncommittal shrug.

'Tell us about Foxwoods,' D.D. said.

Lyons stared at her, then returned his gaze to Bobby. 'Why don't you just ask me the question.'

'All right. To your knowledge did Brian Darby have a gambling problem?'

'To my knowledge . . . ' The trooper suddenly sighed, uncrossed his arms, shook them out. 'Goddammit,' he said.

D.D. took that as a yes.

'How bad?' she asked.

'Don't know. He wouldn't talk about it with me. He knew I disapproved. But Tessa called me, 'bout six months ago. Brian was on tour, upstairs bathtub had sprung a leak. I gave her the name of a plumber, which she then contacted. Couple of pipes had to be replaced, some drywall patched. When all was said and done, guess it cost a good eight hundred, nine hundred bucks. Except when she went to withdraw it from savings, the money wasn't there.'

'It wasn't there?' D.D. repeated.

Lyons shrugged. 'According to Tessa, they should've had thirty grand in savings, except they didn't. I ended up loaning her the money to pay the contractors. Then, when Brian got back . . . '

'What happened?'

'We confronted him. Both of us. Tessa wanted me there. She said, if it was just her, it would sound like a nagging wife. But if it was both of us, Brian's wife and best friend, he'd have to pay attention.'

'You ran a gambling addiction 'intervention,'' Bobby said. 'Did it work?'

Lyons barked hollowly. 'Did it work? Hell, not only did Brian refuse to acknowledge he had a problem, he actually accused us of having an affair. We were in cahoots against him. Whole world out to get him.' Lyons shook his head. 'I mean . . . you think you know a guy. We'd been friends for how long? And then one day, he just goes off. It's easier for him to believe his best friend is fucking his wife than to accept that he has a gambling problem, and that liquidating his life savings to pay off loan sharks isn't a good way to live.'

'He took money from loan sharks?' D.D. asked sharply.

Lyons gave her a look. 'Not according to him. He said he'd taken the money to pay off the Denali. So, while we're all sitting there, Tessa, cool as a cucumber, picks up the phone and dials their bank. It's all automated systems these days, and sure enough, their vehicle loan still has a $34,000 balance due. Which is when he started yelling that we were obviously sleeping together. Go figure.'

'What did Tessa do?'

'Pleaded with him. Begged him to get help before he got in too deep. Which he refused to acknowledge. So finally she said, if he didn't have a problem, then it should be easy for him to agree not to gamble. At all. He'd stay out of Foxwoods, Mohegan Sun, everywhere. He agreed, after making her promise never to see me again.'

D.D. raised a brow, looked at him. 'Sounds like he really believed you and Tessa were too close.'

'Addicts blame everyone else for their problems,' Lyons replied evenly. 'Ask my wife. I told her all about it, and she can vouch for my time, both when Brian is home and when he's not home. We don't have secrets between us.'

'Really? Then why didn't you tell us this sooner?' D.D. said. 'Instead, I recall this whole little spiel on how you weren't too involved with Brian and Tessa's marriage. Now, twenty-four hours later, you're their personal intervention specialist.'

Lyons flushed. His fists were clenched at his side. D.D. glanced down, then . . .

275

'*Son of a bitch!*'

She grabbed his right hand, yanking it toward the light. Immediately, Lyons raised his left as if to shove her back, and in the next instant he had a loaded Sig Sauer dug into his temple.

'Touch her and die,' Bobby said.

Both men were breathing hard, D.D. sandwiched between them.

The state trooper had a solid fifty pounds on Bobby. He was stronger, and as a patrol officer, more experienced in a street fight. Maybe, if it had been any other officer, he would've been tempted to make a move, call the officer's bluff.

But Bobby had already earned his battle stripes — one shot, one kill. Other officers didn't ignore that kind of thing.

Lyons eased back, standing passively as D.D. jerked his bruised and battered fist under the overhead light. The knuckles on his right hand were purple and swollen, the skin abraded in several areas.

As Bobby slowly moved his firearm to his side, D.D.'s gaze went to the steel-toed boots on Lyons's feet. The rounded tip of the boot. The bruise on Tessa's hip her lawyer wouldn't let them examine.

'Son of a bitch,' D.D. repeated. 'You hit her. *You're* the one who beat the shit out of Tessa Leoni.'

'Had to,' Lyons replied in a clipped tone.

'Why?'

'Because she begged me to.'

★   ★   ★

276

In Lyons's new and improved story, Tessa had phoned him, hysterical, at nine a.m. Sunday morning. Sophie was missing, Brian was dead, some mystery man had done it all. She needed help. She wanted Lyons to come, alone, now, now, now.

Lyons had literally run to her place, as his cruiser would be too conspicuous.

When he'd arrived, he'd discovered Brian dead in the kitchen and Tessa, still in her uniform, weeping beside the corpse.

Tessa had told him some preposterous story. She'd arrived home from patrol, depositing her belt on the kitchen table, then walking upstairs to check on Sophie. Sophie's room had been empty. Tessa had just started getting nervous, when she heard a sound from the kitchen. She'd raced back down, where she'd discovered a man in a black wool trench coat holding Brian at gunpoint.

The man had told Tessa that he'd taken Sophie. The only way to get her back was to do as he said. Then he'd shot Brian three times in the chest with Tessa's gun and left.

'You believed this story?' D.D. asked Lyons incredulously. They were now sitting in the beanbags. It would almost appear cordial, except Bobby had his Sig Sauer on his lap.

'Not at first,' Lyons admitted, 'which became Tessa's point. If I didn't believe her story, then who would?'

'You think the man in black was an enforcer?' Bobby asked with a frown, 'sent by someone Brian owed money to?'

Lyons sighed, looked at Bobby. 'Brian muscled up,' he said abruptly. 'You asked about it, yesterday. Why'd Brian bulk up?'

Bobby nodded.

'Brian's gambling started a year ago. Three months into it, he has his first little 'episode.' Ran up a bit too much on tab, got roughed up by some casino goons till he worked out a payment plan. Next week, he joined the gym. I think Brian's bulking up was his own self-protection plan. Let's just say, *after* Tessa and I confronted him, he didn't quit the gym.'

'He was still gambling,' Bobby said.

'That's my guess. Meaning, he could've run up more debt. And the gunman came to collect.'

D.D. frowned at him. 'But he killed Brian. Last I knew, killing the mark made it difficult for him to pay up.'

'I think Brian was past that point. Sounds to me like he pissed off the wrong people. They didn't want his money, they wanted him dead. But he's the husband of a state police officer. Those kinds of murders can cause unwanted attention. So they came up with a scenario where Tessa herself became the suspect. Keeps all eyes off them, while getting the job done.'

'Brian's a bad boy,' D.D. repeated slowly. 'Brian is killed. Sophie is kidnapped, to keep Tessa in line.'

'Yeah.'

'This is what Tessa told you.'

'I already explained — '

D.D. held up a silencing hand. She'd already heard the story, she just didn't believe it. And the

278

fact it came from a fellow police officer who'd already lied to them once wasn't helping.

'So,' D.D. reviewed, 'Tessa is in a panic. Her husband has been shot with her gun, her daughter kidnapped, and her only hope of seeing her daughter alive is to plead guilty to her husband's murder.'

'Yes.' Lyons nodded enthusiastically.

'Tessa hatches a master plan: You'll beat the shit out of her. Then she'll claim Brian did it, and she shot him in self-defense. That way she can plead guilty — meeting the terms of her daughter's kidnappers — while keeping out of prison.' This part actually made some sense to D.D. Given past experience, Tessa Leoni had played to her strengths. Smart woman.

Bobby, however, had a question for Lyons. 'But you really, I mean *really* beat the shit out of her. Why?'

The trooper flushed, stared down at his mangled fist. 'I couldn't hit her,' he said in a muffled voice.

'Then how do you explain the fractured cheek?' D.D. asked.

'She's a girl. I don't hit girls. And she knew it. So she started . . . At the Academy, we had to pound one another. It was part of the self-defense training. And big guys like me struggled. We're interested in becoming cops because we have a sense of fair play — we don't hit women or pick on the little guy.' He eyed Bobby. 'Except at the Academy, where all of a sudden you had to.'

Bobby nodded, as if he understood.

'So, we trash-talked each other, right? Goaded each other into action, because the big guys had to start seriously hitting, if the little guys were going to seriously learn to defend.'

Bobby nodded again.

'Let's just say, Tessa was really good at goading. It had to be convincing, she said. Spousal abuse is an affirmative defense, meaning the burden of proof would be on her. I had to hit her *hard*. I had to make her . . . *fear*. So she started goading, and kept needling and needling and by the time she was done . . . Damn . . . ' Lyons looked off at something only he could see. 'I had a moment. I really did want her dead.'

'But you stopped yourself,' Bobby said quietly.

He drew himself upright. 'Yes.'

'Bully for you,' D.D. said dryly, and the state trooper flushed again.

'You did this on Sunday morning?' Bobby inquired.

'Nine a.m. You'll find a record of her call on my cell. I ran over, we did our thing . . . I don't know. It must've been ten-thirty. I returned home. She made the official call in, and the rest is what you already know. Other troopers arriving, the lieutenant colonel. That's all true. I think Tessa and I were both hoping the Amber Alert might shake things loose. Whole state's looking for Sophie. Brian's dead, Tessa's arrested. So the man can let Sophie go now, right? Just leave her at a bus stop or something. Tessa did what they asked of her. Sophie should be all right.'

Lyons sounded a little desperate. D.D. didn't

blame him. The story didn't make much sense, and as hour passed into hour, she was guessing Lyons was also coming to that realization.

'Hey, Lyons,' she said now. 'If you came to Tessa's house on Sunday morning, how come Brian's body was frozen before that?'

'What?'

'Brian's body. The ME ruled he was killed prior to Sunday morning, and put on ice.'

'I heard the DA . . . some comment . . . ' Lyons's voice trailed off. He gazed at them dully. 'I don't understand.'

'She played you.'

'No . . . '

'There wasn't any mystery man at Tessa's house Sunday morning, Shane. In fact, Brian was most likely killed Friday night or Saturday morning. And as for Sophie . . . '

The burly trooper closed his eyes, didn't seem to be able to swallow. 'But she said . . . For Sophie. We were doing this . . . Had to hit her . . . To save Sophie . . . '

'Do you know where Sophie is?' Bobby asked gently. 'Have any idea where Tessa might've taken her?'

Lyons shook his head. 'No. She wouldn't harm Sophie. You don't understand. There's no way Tessa would harm Sophie. She loves her. It's just . . . not possible.'

D.D. regarded him gravely. 'Then you're an even bigger fool than we thought. Sophie's gone, and given that you're now an accomplice to murder, looks to me like Tessa Leoni screwed you over good.'

25

Bobby and D.D. didn't arrest Lyons. Bobby felt it was more appropriate to let internal affairs kick into gear as state investigators could squeeze Lyons more effectively than the Boston police could. Plus internal affairs was in a better position to identify any links between Lyons's actions and their other major investigation — the missing funds from the troopers' union.

Instead, Bobby and D.D. returned to BPD headquarters, for the eleven p.m. debrief with the taskforce.

The falafel had done D.D. a world of good. She had that gleam in her eye and hitch in her step as they pounded up the stairs to the homicide unit.

They were closing in now. Bobby could feel the case building momentum, rolling them toward an inevitable conclusion: Tessa Leoni had murdered her husband and child.

All that remained was putting a few last pieces of the case in place — including locating Sophie's body.

The other taskforce officers were already seated by the time D.D. and Bobby walked through the door. Phil looked as jazzed as D.D., and sure enough, he went first.

'You were right,' he burst out as D.D. strode to the front of the room. 'They don't have fifty grand in savings — the entire sum was withdrawn Saturday morning. The transaction hadn't been posted when I got the initial report. And get this — the money had also been withdrawn twelve days prior, then returned six days after that. That's a lot of activity on fifty grand.'

'How was it finally taken out?' D.D. asked.

'Bank check, made out to cash.'

Bobby whistled low. 'Couple of pennies, available as hard currency.'

'Male or female closed the account?' D.D. asked.

'Tessa Leoni,' Phil supplied. 'Teller recognized her. She was still in uniform when she made the transaction.'

'Setting up her new life,' D.D. said immediately. 'If she ends up under investigation for killing her husband, joint assets might be frozen. So she got out the big money first, squirreled it away. Now, how much do you want to bet that if we find that fifty grand, there will be another quarter million sitting with it?'

Phil was intrigued, so Bobby related the state police's current investigation into embezzled funds. Best lead — the account had been closed out by a female wearing a red baseball cap and dark sunglasses.

'They needed the money,' Phil stated. 'Did a little more digging, and while Brian Darby and Tessa Leoni look good on paper, you won't believe the credit card debt six-year-old Sophie has run up.'

'What?' D.D. asked.

'Exactly. It would appear Brian Darby opened

283

half a dozen credit cards in Sophie's name, using a separate PO box. I found over forty-two grand in consumer debt, run up over the past nine months. Some evidence of lump sum payments, but inevitably followed by significant cash advances, most of which were at Foxwoods.'

'So Brian Darby does have a gambling problem. Putz.'

Phil grinned. 'Just to amuse myself, I correlated the dates of the cash advances with Brian's work schedule, and sure enough, Sophie only withdrew large sums of money when Brian was in port. So yeah, I'm guessing Brian Darby was gambling away his stepdaughter's future.'

'Last transaction?' Bobby asked.

'Six days ago. He made a payment before that — maybe the first time the fifty grand was taken out of savings. He paid off the credit cards, then he returned to the tables and either won big, or borrowed big, because he was able to replace the entire fifty grand to savings in six days. Wait a minute . . . ' Phil frowned.

'No,' the detective corrected himself. 'He borrowed big, because the latest credit card statements show significant cash advances, meaning in the past six days, Brian went deeper into debt, yet was able to replace fifty grand to his savings. Gotta be he took out a personal loan. Maybe to cover his tracks with his wife.'

Bobby looked at D.D. 'You know, if Darby was into it big with loan sharks, it's possible an enforcer might have been sent to the house.'

D.D. shrugged. She filled the taskforce in on Trooper Lyons's revised statement — that Tessa

Leoni had called him Sunday morning, claiming a mysterious hit man had kidnapped her child and killed her husband. She was to take the blame in order to get her child back. Shane Lyons had then agreed to assist her efforts by beating her to a pulp.

When she finished, most of her fellow investigators wore similar frowns.

'Wait a minute,' Neil spoke up. 'She called Lyons on Sunday? But Brian was dead at least twenty-four hours before then.'

'Something she neglected to tell him, and yet more evidence she's a compulsive liar.'

'I traced Darby's Friday night call,' Detective Jake Owens spoke up. 'Unfortunately, it went to a prepaid cellphone. No way to determine the caller, though a prepaid cellphone suggests someone who doesn't want his calls monitored — such as a loan shark.'

'And it turns out Brian suffered two recent 'accidents,'' Neil offered. 'In August, he received treatment for multiple contusions to his face, which he attributed to a hiking mishap. Let's see . . . ' Neil flipped through his notes. 'Worked with Phil on this one — yep, Brian shipped out September through October. Returned November three and November sixteen was in the ER again, this time with cracked ribs, which he said he received after falling from a ladder while patching a leak on his roof.'

'For the record,' Phil spoke up, 'Sophie Leoni's credit cards were all maxed out in November, meaning if Brian had accrued debt, he couldn't use her lines of credit to pay it off.'

285

'Any withdrawals from the personal accounts?' D.D. asked.

'I found a major one in July — forty-two grand. But that money was replaced right before Brian shipped out in September, and after that, I don't see any more significant lump sum transactions until the past two weeks.'

'The intervention,' Bobby commented. 'Six months ago, Tessa and Shane confronted Brian about his gambling, which Tessa had figured out due to the sudden loss of thirty grand. He replaced the money — '

'Winning big, or borrowing large?' D.D. muttered.

Bobby shrugged. 'Then he moved his habit underground, using a bunch of phony credit cards, with the statements mailed to a separate PO box, so Tessa would never see them. Until two weeks ago, when apparently Brian Darby fell off the wagon, this time withdrawing fifty grand. Which maybe Tessa found out about, which would explain its rapid replacement six days later.'

'And why she might have withdrawn it Saturday morning,' Phil pointed out. 'Forget starting a new life; seems to me Tessa Leoni was working pretty hard to save the old one.'

'All the more reason to kill her spouse,' D.D. declared. She moved to the whiteboard. 'All right. Who thinks Brian Darby had a gambling problem?'

Her entire taskforce raised their hands. She agreed, added the detail to their murder board.

'Okay. Brian Darby gambled. Apparently, not

successfully. He was in deep enough to run up debt, commit credit card fraud, and perhaps receive some poundings from the local goons. Then what?'

Her investigators stared at her. She stared back at them.

'Hey, don't let me have all the fun. We assumed Tessa Leoni's lover beat the crap out of her. Instead, it turns out it was a fellow police officer, who felt he was doing her a favor. Now we can corroborate half that story — Brian Darby did gamble. Brian Darby may have had debt worth an enforcer paying him a visit. So where does that leave us?'

D.D. wrote a fresh header: *Motive*.

'If I were Tessa Leoni,' she stated, 'and I discovered my husband was not only still gambling, but that the sorry son of a bitch had run up tens of thousands in credit card debt in my daughter's name, I'd kill him for that alone. Interestingly enough, my-husband-is-a-worthless-asshole is not an affirmative defense, meaning Tessa's still better off arguing battery and getting Lyons to beat the shit out of her.'

Several officers nodded agreeably. Bobby, of course, poked the first hole in the argument.

'So she loves her daughter enough to be offended by the credit card scam, but then kills her anyway?'

D.D. pursed her lips. 'Point taken.' She looked at the room. 'Anyone?'

'Maybe she didn't kill Sophie on purpose,' Phil suggested. 'Maybe, it was an accident. She and Brian were having a fight, Sophie got in the

287

way. Maybe, Sophie's death became one more reason to kill Brian. Except now her family's dead, her husband shot by her service weapon — automatic investigation right there,' Phil added, 'so Tessa panics. Gotta figure out a plausible scenario — '

'Self-defense worked for her once before,' Bobby commented. 'The Tommy Howe shooting.'

'She freezes her husband's body to buy her time, takes Sophie's body for a drive, and the next morning concocts a story to manipulate both Shane Lyons and us into believing what she needs us to believe,' D.D. finished. 'Sunday morning becomes showtime.'

'What if she withdrew the fifty grand Saturday morning because she discovered Brian was gambling again?' another officer spoke up. 'Brian found out, or she confronted him. Events escalated from there.'

D.D. nodded, wrote a new note on the board: *Where's the $$$?*

'Gonna be hard to trace,' Phil warned. 'Check's made out to cash, meaning it can be deposited at any bank under any name, or taken to a dealer and cashed.'

'Big check for most dealers,' Bobby said.

'Guaranteed percentage,' Phil countered. 'Especially if she called ahead, there are several check cashers who'd make that deal. Bank checks are good as gold and it's a tight financial market out there.'

'What if Tessa needed the money?' D.D. asked abruptly. 'What if she had a payment to make?'

Thirty pairs of eyes looked at her.

'It's another possibility,' she thought out loud. 'Brian Darby had a gambling problem. He couldn't control it, and like a sinking ship was taking Tessa and Sophie down with him. Now, Tessa is a woman who's already hit bottom once before. She knows better. In fact, she's worked doubly hard to rebuild a life, particularly for her daughter's sake. So what can she do? Divorce takes time, and God knows how much Brian will destroy their financials until it goes through.

'Maybe,' D.D. mused, 'maybe there was an enforcer. Maybe, Tessa Leoni *hired* him — a hit man to finally put her husband out of his misery. Except the man in black took out his own insurance policy — Sophie Leoni — so Tessa couldn't turn around and arrest him.'

Bobby looked at her. 'I thought you were convinced she'd killed her own daughter?'

D.D.'s hand was resting unconsciously across her stomach. 'What can I tell you? I'm getting soft in my old age. Besides, a jury will buy a wife killing her gambling-addicted husband. A mother killing her child, however, is a tougher sell.'

She glanced at Phil. 'We need to follow the money. Nail down that Tessa definitely took it out. See what else you can find in the financials. And tomorrow, we'll give Tessa's lawyer a call, see if we can arrange for a fresh chat. Twenty-four hours in jail has a tendency to make most people more talkative.

'Any other news from the hotline?' she asked.

Nothing, her taskforce agreed.

'Final drive of the white Denali?' she tried hopefully.

'Based on fuel mileage, it remained within a hundred miles of Boston,' the lead detective reported.

'Excellent. So we've narrowed it to, what, a quarter of the state?'

'Pretty much.'

D.D. rolled her eyes, set down the marker. 'Anything else we should know?'

'Gun,' spoke up a voice from the back of the room. Detective John Little.

'What about it?' D.D. asked. 'Last I knew, the firearms discharge investigation team had turned it over for processing.'

'Not Tessa's gun,' Little said. 'Brian's gun.'

'Brian had a gun?' D.D. asked in surprise.

'Took out a permit two weeks ago. Glock forty. I couldn't find it on the evidence logs as seized from either the house or his car.'

The detective gazed at her expectantly. D.D. returned his stare.

'You're telling me Brian Darby had a gun,' she said.

'Yes. Applied for the permit two weeks ago.'

'Maybe bulking up wasn't getting the job done anymore,' Bobby murmured.

D.D. waved her hand at him. 'Hello. Bigger picture here. Brian Darby had a Glock forty, *and we have no idea where it is*. Detective, that's not a small thing.'

'Gun permit just went through,' Detective Little countered defensively. 'We're a little backed up these days. Haven't you been reading the papers? Armageddon is coming and, apparently, half the city intends to be armed for it.'

'We need that gun,' D.D. said in a clipped voice. 'For starters, what if that's the weapon that killed Sophie Leoni?'

The room went silent.

'Yeah,' she said. 'No more talk. No more theories. We have a dead husband of a state police officer, and a missing six-year-old. I want Sophie Leoni. I want Brian Darby's gun. And if that evidence leads us where we think it's probably going to lead us, then I want us to build a case so fucking airtight, Tessa Leoni goes away for the rest of her miserable life. Get out. Get it done.'

Eleven o'clock Monday night, the detectives scrambled.

26

Every woman has a moment in her life when she realizes she genuinely loves a guy, and he's just not worth it.

It took me nearly three years to reach that point with Brian. Maybe there were signs along the way. Maybe, in the beginning, I was just so happy to have a man love me and my daughter as much as Brian seemed to love me and Sophie, I ignored them. Yes, he could be moody. After the initial six-month honeymoon, the house became his anal-retentive domain, Sophie and I receiving daily lectures if we left a dish on the counter, a toothbrush out of its holder, a crayon on the table.

Brian liked precision, needed it.

'I'm an engineer,' he'd remind me. 'Trust me, you don't want a dam built by a sloppy engineer.'

Sophie and I did our best. Compromise, I told myself. The price of family; you gave up some of your individual preferences for the greater good. Plus, Brian would leave again and Sophie and I would spend a giddy eight weeks dumping our junk all over the place. Coats draped over the back of kitchen chairs. Art projects piled on the corner of the counter. Yes, we were regular Girls Gone Wild when Brian shipped out.

Then, one day I went to pay the plumber and discovered our life savings was gone.

It's a tough moment when you have to confront the level of your own complacency. I knew Brian had been going to Foxwoods. More to the point, I knew the evenings he came home reeking of booze and cigarettes, but claimed he'd been hiking. He'd lied to me, on several occasions, and I'd let it go. To pry would involve being told an answer I didn't want to hear. So I didn't pry.

While my husband, apparently, gave in to his inner demons and gambled away our savings account.

Shane and I confronted him. He denied it. Not very plausibly. But at a certain point, there wasn't much more I could do or say. The money magically returned, and again, I didn't ask many questions, not wanting to know what I didn't want to know.

I thought of my husband as two people after that. There was Good Brian, the man I fell in love with, who picked up Sophie after school and took her sledding until they were both pink-cheeked from laughter. Good Brian fixed me pancakes and maple syrup when I got home from graveyard shift. He would rub my back, strained from the weight of carrying body armor. He would hold me while I slept.

Then there was Bad Brian. Bad Brian yelled at me when I forgot to wipe down the counter after doing the dishes. Bad Brian was curt and distant, not only turning the TV to whatever testosterone-bound show he could find, but turning up the volume if Sophie or I tried to protest.

Bad Brian smelled like cigarettes, booze, and sweat. He worked out compulsively, with the demons of a man with something to fear. Then he'd disappear for a couple of days at a time — time with *the guys*, Bad Brian would say, when we both knew he was going off alone, his friends having long since given up on him.

But that was Bad Brian for you. He could look his state police officer wife in the eye, and tell a lie.

It always made me wonder: Would he be a different kind of husband if I were a different kind of wife?

Bad Brian broke my heart. Then Good Brian would reappear long enough to patch it back together again. And around and around we would go, plummeting through the roller coaster ride of our lives.

Except all rides have to end.

Good Brian and Bad Brian's ride ended at exactly the same moment, on our kitchen's spotlessly clean floor.

Bad Brian can't hurt me or Sophie anymore.

Good Brian is going to take me a while to let go.

★　★　★

Tuesday morning, seven a.m.

The female CO started head count and the unit officially stirred to life. My roommate, Erica, had already been awake for an hour, curled up in the fetal position, rocking back and forth, eyes pinned on something only she could see, while muttering beneath her breath.

I would guess she'd retired to her bunk shortly after midnight. No watch on my wrist, no clock in the cell, so I had to gauge the time in my head. It gave me something to do all night long — I think it's . . . two a.m., three a.m., four twenty-one a.m.

I fell asleep once. I dreamt of Sophie. She and I were in a vast, churning ocean, paddling for all we were worth against steadily climbing waves.

'Stay with me,' I screamed at her. 'Stay with me, I'll keep you safe!'

But her head disappeared beneath the black water, and I dove and I dove and I dove, but I couldn't find my daughter again.

I woke up, tasting salt on my lips. I didn't sleep again.

The tower made noises in the night. Nameless women, goading nameless groaning men. The rattle of pipes. The hum of a huge facility, trying to settle its bones. It felt as if I were inside some giant beast, swallowed up whole. I kept touching the walls, as if the rough feel of cinder blocks would keep me grounded. Then I would get up and pee, as the cover of night was the closest to privacy I could get.

The female CO had reached our cell. She glanced at rocking Erica, then at me, and our eyes met, a flicker of recognition, before she turned away.

Kim Watters. Dated one of the guys in the barracks, had attended a couple of the group dinners. 'Course. CO at the Suffolk County Jail. Now I remembered.

She moved to the next cell. Erica rocked harder. I peered out the barred window and tried to convince myself that personally knowing my own prison guard didn't make things worse.

Seven-thirty. Breakfast.

Erica was up. Still muttering, not looking at me. Agitated. Meth had fried her brain. She needed rehab, and mental health services more than a jail sentence. Then again, welcome to most of the prison population.

We got limp pancakes, applesauce, and milk. Erica put the applesauce on her pancakes, rolled it all together, and ate it in three giant mouthfuls. Four gulps took care of the milk. Then she eyed my tray.

I had no appetite. The pancakes tasted like wet tissue on my tongue. I stared at her and slowly ate them anyway.

Erica sat on the toilet. I turned around to give her privacy.

She laughed.

Later, I used my hooter bag to brush my teeth and apply deodorant. Then . . . Then I didn't really know what to do. Welcome to my first full day in prison.

Rec time arrived. The CO opened our cell. Some women drifted out, some stayed inside. I couldn't take it anymore. The ten foot ceilings and yawning windows gave the illusion of space, but a jail cell was a jail cell. I already felt overflouresced, pining for natural sunlight.

I paced over to the sitting area at one end of the commons, where six ladies had gathered to watch *GMA*. The show was too happy for me.

Next, I tried the tables, four silver rounds where two women currently played hearts, while one more sat and cackled at something only she understood.

A shower went on. I didn't look. I didn't want to know.

Then I heard a funny sound, like a shivery gasp, someone trying to inhale and exhale at the same time.

I turned around. The CO, Kim Watters, looked like she was doing a funny dance. Her body was up in the air, her feet twitching as if reaching for the floor, except they couldn't find it. A giant black female with long dark hair stood directly behind her, heavily muscled arm cocked around Kim's windpipe, squeezing tight even as Kim's fingers scraped frantically at the massive forearm.

I stepped forward and in the next instant, my roommate, Erica, screamed, 'Get the fucking pig!' and half a dozen detainees rushed toward me.

I took the first blow in the stomach. I tightened my abs reflexively, rocked left and drove my fist into a soft, oomphing middle. Another careening blow. Ducking low, moving on instinct now, because that's why recruits trained. Do the impossible over and over and it becomes the possible. Better yet, it becomes routine, meaning one day, when you least expect it, months and years of training can suddenly save your life.

Another hard crack to my shoulder. They were aiming for my face, my swollen eye and shattered cheek. I brought up both hands in the classic pugilist stance, blocking my head, while driving myself toward the closest attacker. I caught her around the waist and flung her back at the rushing stampede, toppling two in a tangle of limbs.

Cries. Pain, rage, theirs, mine, didn't really matter. Moving, moving, moving, had to stay on my feet, confront the onslaught or be crushed by sheer numbers.

Sharp sting. Something cutting my forearm, while another fist connected with my shoulder. I sidestepped again, drove my elbow into the stomach of the attacker, then the side of my hand sharp into her throat. She went down and stayed there.

The remaining four finally backed up. I kept my gaze on them, trying to process many things at once. Other detainees, where? Back in their cells? Self-imposed confinement so they wouldn't be busted later?

And Kim? Gasping scuffle behind me. Officer down, officer down, officer down.

Panic button. Had to be one somewhere —

Fresh slice to my arm. I slapped at it, kicking out and catching the woman in the knee.

Then I screamed. I screamed and screamed and *screamed*, days' worth of rage and helplessness and frustration finally erupting from my throat, because Kim was dying and my daughter was probably already dead and my husband had died, right in front of my eyes, taking Good Brian with him, and the man in black had taken my daughter and left behind

298

only the blue button eye from her favorite doll and *I would get them. I would make them all pay*.

Then I moved. I was probably still screaming. A lot. And I don't think it was a sane sound because my attackers retreated until I was the one falling upon them, lips peeled back, hands fisted into hard balls.

I moved, I kicked, I jabbed, and I punched. I was twenty-three years old again. Behold the Giant Killer. Behold the Giant Killer really truly *pissed off*.

And my face dripped with sweat and my hands dripped with blood and the first two females were down and the third was running now, ironically toward the safety of her cell, but the fourth had a shank and she thought that would keep her safe. She'd probably fought off aggressive johns and pissed-off pimps. I was just a prissy white girl and no match for a genuine graduate of the school of hard knocks.

Rattling gasp from the CO's desk. The sound of a woman dying.

'Do it!' I snarled at her. 'Come on, bitch. Show me what you got.'

She charged. Stupid shit. I moved left, and straight-armed her in the throat. She dropped the shank and clutched at her crushed wind-pipe. I picked up the shank, and jumped over her body for central command.

Kim's toes weren't dancing anymore. She remained suspended in the air, black arm still twisted around her throat as her eyes glazed over.

I stepped around her.

I looked up at the large black female who turned out not to be a female at all, but a long-haired male who'd somehow infiltrated the unit.

He appeared startled to see me.

So I smiled at him. Then drove the shank through his ribs.

Kim's body dropped to the floor. The inmate staggered back, grabbing his side. I advanced upon him. He scrambled, twisting around trying to run for the unit door. I kicked him in the back of his right knee. He stumbled. I kicked him in the back of the left knee. He went down, then rolled over, hands coming up defensively.

I stood over him, holding the bloody shank. I must have looked fearsome, with my dripping hands, battered face, and one good eye, because large black male peed his orange prison jumpsuit.

I raised the shank.

'No,' he whispered hoarsely.

I brought it down into the meat of his thigh. He screamed. I twisted.

Then I sang for the entire unit to hear: 'All I want for Christmas is my two front teeth, my two front teeth, two front teeth . . .'

The inmate cried, as I leaned over, brushed back the long dark locks of his hair, and whispered like a lover in his ear: 'Tell the man in black I'm coming for him. Tell him he's next.'

I twisted the shank again.

Then I stood up, wiped the shank on my pant leg, and hit the panic button.

Do you mourn when your world has ended? When you have arrived at a destination from where there is no going back?

The SERT team descended as a stampede. The entire facility went to lockdown. I was shackled where I stood, legs swaying, arms lacerated, fresh bruises blooming down my sides and across my back.

They removed Kim on a stretcher, unconscious but breathing.

My fourth attacker, the one who'd brought the shank, left in a body bag. I watched them zip it up. I felt nothing at all.

Erica sobbed. Screamed and wailed and carried on to such an extent, they finally carted her off to Medical, where she would be heavily sedated and put under suicide watch. Others were questioned, but in the way these things worked, they had no idea what had just taken place.

'In my cell the whole time . . . '

'Never looked out . . . '

'Heard some noises, though . . . '

'Sounded like a lot of ass-whooping . . . '

'I slept through the whole thing, Officer. Really, I did.'

The male inmate, however, told anyone who would listen that I was the angel of death, and please God, please God, please God, keep me away from him.

The assistant deputy superintendent finally halted in front of me. He studied me for a long time, his expression judging me more trouble than I was worth.

He delivered my punishment as a single word. 'Segregation.'

'I want my lawyer.'

'Who attacked the CO, *detainee*?'

'Mrs. Doubtfire.'

'Mrs. Doubtfire, *sir*. Now, why did the inmate attack CO Watters?'

'Don't know, *sir*.'

'You've been in prison less than twenty-four hours. How'd you get a shank?'

'Took it off the ho' trying to kill me.' I paused. '*Sir*.'

'All six of them?'

'Don't fuck with the state police. *Sir*.'

He almost smiled. Instead, he jerked his thumb toward the ceiling and the multiple mounted cameras. 'Here's the thing about prison: Big Brother's always watching. So last time, *detainee*, anything you want to tell me?'

'Officer Watters owes me a thank you card.'

He didn't argue, so maybe he already knew more than he was letting on. 'Medical,' he said now, gesturing to my sliced-up forearms.

'Lawyer,' I repeated.

'The request will be sent through proper channels.'

'Don't have time.' I looked the assistant deputy superintendent in the eye. 'I have decided to cooperate fully with the Boston police,' I declared for all to hear. 'Call Detective D.D. Warren. Tell her I will take her to my daughter's body.'

27

'Fuck that!' D.D. exploded two hours later. She
was at BDP headquarters, in a conference room
with Bobby, the deputy superintendent of
homicide, and Tessa Leoni's lawyer, Ken Cargill.
Cargill had called the meeting twenty minutes
ago. Had a limited-time offer, he'd told them.
Needed D.D.'s boss in the room, because if a
decision was going to be made, it had to be
made fast. Meaning, he was planning on
negotiating for something above D.D.'s pay-
grade. Meaning, she should be letting the deputy
superintendent, Cal Horgan, respond to his
preposterous demand.

D.D. had never been good at keeping silent.

'We don't give guided tours!' she continued
hotly now. 'Tessa wants to finally do the right
thing? Good for her. Bobby and I can be
cell-side in twenty minutes, and she can draw us
a map.'

Horgan said nothing, so maybe he agreed with
her.

'She can't draw you a map,' Cargill answered
steadily. 'She doesn't remember the precise
location. She'd been driving for a bit before she
pulled over. As it is, she may not be able to get
you to the exact spot, but figures she can get
fairly close, by looking for familiar landmarks.'

'Can't even get us to the exact spot?' Bobby
spoke up, sounding as skeptical as D.D. felt.

'I would arrange for a dog team to assist,' Cargill replied.

'Cadaver team, you mean,' D.D. said bitterly. She sank back down in her chair, both arms crossed over her stomach. She had known, after the first twenty-four hours, that little Sophie Leoni with the curly brown hair, big blue eyes, and heart-shaped face was most likely dead. Still, to hear it said out loud, from Tessa's lawyer of all people, that it was time to recover the body . . .

There were days this job was just too hard.

'How did she say Sophie died again?' Bobby asked.

Cargill skewered him with a glance. 'She didn't.'

'That's right,' Bobby continued. 'She's not really telling us anything, is she? She's just demanding that we spring her from prison and take her for a drive. Imagine that.'

'She almost died this morning,' Cargill argued. 'Coordinated attack, six female detainees going after her, while a male inmate took out the CO. If not for the quick response by Trooper Leoni, Officer Watters would be dead and probably Tessa, as well.'

'Self-preservation,' Bobby said.

'Another fanciful story,' D.D. added harshly.

Cargill looked at her. 'Not fanciful. Caught on tape. I've watched the video myself. Male inmate attacked the CO first, then six females rushed Tessa. She's lucky to be alive. And you're lucky that the shock of said events has led her to want to cooperate.'

304

'Cooperate,' D.D. stated. 'There's that word again. 'Cooperate,' to me, means to assist others. For example, she could draw us a map, perhaps one based on recalled landmarks. That would be cooperating. She could tell us how Sophie died. That would be cooperating. She could also tell us, once and for all, what happened to her husband and child, yet another form of cooperation. Somehow, she doesn't seem to be getting it.'

Cargill shrugged. He stopped studying Bobby and D.D. and turned his attention to the deputy superintendent instead. 'Like it or not, I don't know how long my client is going to continue to want to *cooperate*. This morning she suffered a traumatic experience. By this afternoon, certainly by tomorrow morning, I can't guarantee the impulse will remain. In the meantime, while my client may not feel like answering all your questions, I would imagine that the recovery of Sophie Leoni's body would answer a great deal of them for you. You know — by supplying evidence. Or are you people still in the business of gathering evidence?'

'She goes back to jail,' Horgan said.

'Oh please.' D.D. blew out a puff of breath. 'Never negotiate with terrorists.'

Cargill ignored her, attention still on Horgan. 'Understood.'

'Shackled at all times.'

'Never assumed otherwise.' Short pause. 'You might, however, want to coordinate with the Suffolk County Sheriff's Department. From a legal perspective, she is under their custody, meaning they may want to be the ones providing escort.'

Horgan rolled his eyes. Multiple law enforcement agencies, just what they needed.

'How long a drive to the site?' Horgan asked.

'No more than one hour.'

D.D. glanced at the clock on the wall. It was ten-thirty a.m. Sun set by five-thirty. Meaning time was already of the essence. She stared at her boss, not sure what she wanted anymore. Hating to give in to a suspect's demands, and yet . . . She wanted to bring Sophie home. Yearned for that small piece of closure. As if it might ease some of the ache in her heart.

'Pick her up at noon,' Horgan said abruptly. He turned to regard D.D. 'Get a dog team. Now.'

'Yes, sir.'

Horgan, turning back to Cargill. 'No runarounds. Your client cooperates, or all her existing prison privileges vanish. She'll not only return to jail, but it'll be hard time now. Understood?'

Cargill smiled thinly. 'My client is a decorated member of law enforcement. She understands. And may I congratulate you on getting her out of jail, while she's still alive to assist in your efforts.'

*　*　*

There were a lot of things D.D. wanted to do right now — kick, storm, rage. Given the day's tight time frame, however, she restrained herself

306

and contacted the Northern Massachusetts Search & Recovery Canine Team.

Like most canine teams, the Mass. group was comprised of all volunteers. They had eleven members, including Nelson Bradley and his German shepherd, Quizo, who was one of only several hundred trained cadaver dogs in the world.

D.D. needed Nelson and Quizo and she needed them now. Good news, team president Cassondra Murray agreed to have the whole crew mobilized within ninety minutes. Murray and possibly Nelson would meet the police in Boston, and follow caravan style. Other members of the team would arrive once they had a location, as they lived too far outside the city to make it downtown in a timely manner.

That worked for D.D.

'What d'ya need?' D.D. asked by phone. She hadn't worked with a dog team in years and then it'd been a live rescue, not a body recovery. 'I can get you clothing from the child, that sort of thing.'

'Not necessary.'

''Cause it's a body,' D.D. filled in.

'Nope. Doesn't matter. Dogs are trained to identify human scent if it's a rescue and cadaver scent if it's a recovery. Mostly, we need you and your team to stay out of our way.'

'Okay,' D.D. drawled, a bit testily.

'One search dog equals a hundred and fifty human volunteers,' Murray recited firmly.

'Will the snow be an issue?'

'Nope. Heat makes scent rise, cold keeps it

307

lower to the ground. As handlers, we adjust our search strategy accordingly. From our dogs' perspectives, however, scent is scent.'

'How about time frame?'

'If the terrain's not too difficult, dogs should be able to work two hours, then they'll need a twenty-minute break. Depends on the conditions, of course.'

'How many dogs are you going to bring?'

'Three. Quizo's the best, but they're all SAR dogs.'

'Wait — I thought Quizo was the only cadaver dog.'

'Not anymore. As of two years ago, all our dogs are trained for live, cadaver, and water. We start with live searches first, as that's the easiest to teach a puppy. But once the dogs master that, we train them for cadaver recovery, then, water searches.'

'Do I want to know how you train for cadaver?' D.D. asked.

Murray laughed. 'Actually, we're lucky. The ME, Ben — '

'I know Ben.'

'He's a big supporter. We give him tennis balls to place inside the body bags. Once the scent of decomp has transferred to the tennis balls, he seals them in airtight containers for us. That's what we use to train. It's a good compromise, as the fine state of Massachusetts frowns on private ownership of cadavers, and I don't believe in synthetic 'cadaver scent.' Best scientists in the world agree that decomp is one of the most complicated scents on earth. God knows what the dogs are honing in on, meaning man shouldn't tamper with it.'

'Okay,' D.D. said.

'Do you anticipate a water search?' Murray asked, 'because that poses a couple of challenges this time of year. We take the dogs out in boats, of course, but given the temperatures, I'd still want them in special insulated gear in case they fall in.'

'Your dogs work in boats?'

'Yep. Catch the scent in the current of water, just like the drift of the wind. Quizo has found bodies in water a hundred feet deep. It does seem like voodoo, which again, is why I don't like synthetic scent. Dogs are too damn smart to train by lab experiment. Do you anticipate water?'

'Can't rule anything out,' D.D. said honestly.

'Then we'll bring full gear. You said search area was probably within an hour drive of Boston?'

'Best guess.'

'Then I'll bring my book of Mass. topographic maps. Topography is *everything* when working scents.'

'Okay,' D.D. said again.

'Is the ME or a forensic anthropologist gonna be on-site?'

'Why?'

'Sometimes the dogs hit on other remains. Good to have someone there who can make the call right away that it's human.'

'These remains . . . less than forty-eight hours old,' D.D. said. 'In below freezing conditions.'

A moment of silence. 'Well, guess that rules out the anthropologist,' Murray said. 'See you in ninety.'

Murray hung up. D.D. went to work on assembling the rest of the team.

28

Tuesday, twelve p.m. I stood shackled in the processing area of the Suffolk County Jail. No sheriff's van parked in the garage this time. Instead, a Boston detective's Crown Vic had rolled into the secured loading bay. Despite myself, I was impressed. I had assumed the Suffolk County Sheriff's Department would be in charge of transport. I wonder how many heads had rolled and markers had been called in to place me in Detective D.D. Warren's custody.

She got out of the car first. Derisive glance flicked my way, then she approached the command center, handing over paperwork to the waiting COs. Detective Bobby Dodge had opened the passenger's door. He came around the vehicle toward me, his face impossible to read. Still waters that ran deep.

No pedestrian clothes for my road trip. Instead, my previously issued pants and top had been replaced with the traditional orange prison jumpsuit, marking my status for the world to see. I'd asked for a coat, hat, and gloves. I'd been granted none of the above. Apparently, the sheriff's department worried less about frostbite and more about escape. I would be shackled for the full length of my sojourn into society. I would also be under direct supervision of a law enforcement officer at all times.

I didn't fight these conditions. I was tense

enough as it was. Keyed up for the afternoon events to come, while simultaneously crashing from the morning's misadventures. I kept my gaze forward and my head down.

The key to any strategy is not to overplay your hand.

Bobby arrived at my side. The female CO who'd been standing guard relinquished my arm. He seized it, leading me back to the Crown Vic.

D.D. had finished the paperwork. She arrived at the cruiser, staring at me balefully as Bobby opened the back door and I struggled to slide gracefully into the backseat with my hands and legs tied. I tilted back too far, got stuck like a beetle with its legs in the air. Bobby had to reach down, place one hand on my hip, and shove me over.

D.D. shook her head, then took her place behind the steering wheel.

Another minute and the massive garage door slowly creaked up. We backed up, onto the streets of Boston.

I turned my face to the gray March sky and blinked my eyes against the light.

Looks like snow, I thought, but didn't say a word.

★ ★ ★

D.D. drove to the nearby hospital parking lot. There, a dozen other vehicles, from white SUVS to black-and-white police cruisers were waiting. She pulled in and they formed a line behind us.

312

D.D. looked at me in the rearview mirror.

'Start talking,' she said.

'I'd like a coffee.'

'Fuck you.'

I smiled then, couldn't help myself. I had become my husband, with a Good Tessa and a Bad Tessa. Good Tessa had saved Kim Watters's life. Good Tessa had fought off evil attacking inmates and had felt, for just one moment, like a proud member of law enforcement.

Bad Tessa wore prison orange and sat in the back of a police cruiser. Bad Tessa . . . Well, for Bad Tessa, the day was very young.

'Search dogs?' I asked.

'*Cadaver* dogs,' D.D. emphasized.

I smiled again, but it was sad this time, and for a second, I felt my composure crack. A yawning emptiness bloomed inside. All the things I had lost. And more I could still lose.

All I want for Christmas is my two front teeth . . .

'You should've found her,' I murmured. 'I was counting on you to find her.'

'*Where?*' D.D. snapped.

'Route two. Westbound, toward Lexington.'

D.D. drove.

★ ★ ★

'We know about Trooper Lyons,' D.D. said curtly, talking from the front seat. We'd taken Route 2 past Arlington, exchanging urban jungle for suburban pipe dreams. Next up, the old money of Lexington and Concord, to be followed by the quaint, country charm of Harvard, Mass.

'What do you know?' I asked. I was genuinely curious.

'That he beat you up, in order to substantiate your claim of spousal abuse.'

'Have you ever hit a girl?' I asked Detective Dodge.

Bobby Dodge twisted in his seat. 'Tell me about the hit man, Tessa. Find out how much I'm willing to believe.'

'Can't.'

'Can't?'

I leaned forward, best I could with my hands tied. 'I'm going to kill him,' I said somberly. 'And it's not nice to speak ill of the dead.'

'Oh please,' D.D. interjected crossly. 'You sound like a Looney Tune.'

'Well, I have taken some blows to the head.'

The eye roll again. 'You're no more crazy than I'm kindhearted,' D.D. snapped. 'We know all about you, Tessa. The gambling-addicted husband who cleaned out your savings accounts. The horny teenage brother of your best friend, who figured he might get lucky one night. You seem to have a history of attracting the wrong men, then shooting them.'

I didn't say anything. The good detective did have a way of cutting to the heart of the matter.

'But why your daughter?' she asked relentlessly. 'Trust me, I don't fault you for plugging Brian with three in the chest. But what the hell made you turn on your own kid?'

'What did Shane have to say?' I asked.

D.D. frowned at me. 'You mean before or after

314

your loser friend tried to deck me?'

I whistled low. 'See, this is what happens. You hit your first woman, and it gets easier after that.'

'Were you and Brian arguing?' Bobby spoke up now. 'Maybe the fight turned physical. Sophie got in the way.'

'I reported for duty Friday night,' I said, looking out the window. Fewer houses, more woods. We were getting close. 'I haven't seen my daughter alive since.'

'So Brian did it? Why not just blame him? Why cover it up, concoct such an elaborate story?'

'Shane didn't believe me. If he couldn't, then who would?'

Red-painted apple stand, off to the left. Empty now, but sold the best glasses of cider in the fall. We had come here just seven months ago, drinking apple cider, going on a hay ride, then visiting the pumpkin patch. Is that what had brought me back, Saturday afternoon when my heart had been pounding and the daylight fading and I *had* felt like a Looney Tune, crazed by grief and panic and sheer desperation? I'd had to move, fast, fast, fast. Less thinking. More doing.

Which had brought me here, to the place of our last family outing before Brian shipped out for the fall. One of my last happy memories.

Sophie had loved this apple stand. She'd consumed three cups of cider and then, hopped up on fermented sugar, had run laps in the pumpkin patch before picking out not one pumpkin, but three. A daddy pumpkin, a mommy pumpkin, and a girl pumpkin, she'd declared. A whole entire pumpkin *family*.

315

'Can we, Mommy? Can we can we can we? Please, please, please.'

'Sure, sweetheart, you're absolutely right. It would be a shame to separate them. Let's save the whole family.'

'Yippee! Daddy, Daddy, Daddy, we're gonna buy a pumpkin family! Yippee!'

'Turn right up ahead,' I murmured.

'Right?' D.D. braked hard, made the turn.

'Quarter mile up, next left, onto a rural road . . . '

'Three pumpkins?' Brian shaking his head at me. 'Softy.'

'You bought her the donuts to go with the cider.'

'So three donuts equals three pumpkins?'

'Apparently.'

'Okay, but dibs on carving the daddy pumpkin . . . '

'The tree! Turn here. Left, left. Now, thirty yards, road on the right.'

'Sure you couldn't have drawn a map?' D.D. scowled at me.

'I'm sure.'

D.D. turned right onto the smaller, rural road, tires spinning on the hardpacked snow. Behind us, one, two, three, four cars labored to follow suit, then a couple of white SUVs, then the line of police cruisers.

Definitely going to snow, I decided.

But I didn't mind anymore. Civilization was long gone. This was the land of skeletal trees, frozen ponds, and white barren fields. The kind of place lots of things could happen before the general population noticed. The kind of place a desperate woman might use for her last stand.

Bad Tessa, rising.

'We're here,' I said.

And Detective D.D. Warren, heaven help her, pulled over.

'Get out,' she said crossly.

I smiled. I couldn't help myself. I looked the fine detective in the eye and I said, 'Words I've been waiting to hear all day.'

29

'I don't want her walking the woods!' D.D. was arguing with Bobby ten minutes later, off to one side of the stacked-up vehicles. 'Her job was to get us here. Now her job is done, and our job is beginning.'

'The canine team wants her help,' Bobby countered. 'There's no wind, meaning it'll be hard for the dogs to catch the open cone of the scent.'

D.D. stared at him blankly.

'Scent,' he tried again, forming a triangular shape with his hands, 'radiates from the target in the shape of an expanding cone. For the dog to catch the scent, it has to be downwind, in the opening of the cone, or the dog can be two feet from the target and still miss it.'

'When did you learn about dogs?' D.D. demanded.

'Thirty seconds ago, when I asked Nelson and Cassondra what they needed us to do. They're concerned about the conditions. Terrain's flat, which I guess is good, but it's open, which is more complicated — '

'Why?'

'Scent pools when it hits a barrier. So if this were a fenced-in field or brush-lined canyon, they'd start at the edges. But no fence or brush. Just big open . . . this . . . '

Bobby waved his hand around them. D.D. sighed heavily.

Tessa Leoni had brought them to one of the few half-forested, half-fielded, all-in-the-middle-of-nowhere places left in Massachusetts. Given Sunday night's fresh snowfall, the fields were a flat white expanse of sheer nothingness — no footprints, no tire tracks, no drag marks, interspersed with dark patches of skeletal trees and shaggy bushes.

They were lucky they'd been able to drive in, and D.D. still wasn't sure they'd be able to get back out. Snowshoes would be a good idea. A vacation even better.

'Dogs are gonna tire faster,' Bobby was saying, 'trudging through fresh snowfall. So the team wants to start with the smallest search area possible. Which means having Tessa get us as close to the target as possible.'

'Maybe she can point us in the right direction,' D.D. muttered.

Bobby rolled his eyes. 'Tessa's shackled and trying to walk through four inches of powder. Woman's not running away any time soon.'

'She doesn't have a jacket.'

'I'm sure someone has a spare.'

'She's playing us,' D.D. said abruptly.

'I know.'

'Notice how she answered none of our questions.'

'I noticed.'

'While doing her best to milk us for information.'

'Yep.'

'Did you hear what she did to the male inmate who attacked the CO? She didn't just take him

319

out. She drove a shank into his thigh and twisted it. Twice. That's a little beyond professional training. That's personal satisfaction.'

'She seems . . . edgy,' Bobby agreed. 'I'm thinking life hasn't gone too well for her the past few days.'

'And yet here we are,' D.D. said, 'dancing to the beat of her different drummer. I don't like it.'

Bobby thought about it. 'Maybe you should stay in the car,' he said at last. 'Just to be safe . . . '

D.D. fisted her hands to keep from hitting him. Then she sighed and rubbed her forehead. She hadn't slept last night, hadn't eaten this morning. Meaning she'd been tired and cranky even *before* receiving the news that Tessa Leoni was willing to take them to her daughter's body.

D.D. didn't want to be here. She didn't want to be trudging through snow. She didn't want to come to a faint mound and brush it back to find the frozen features of a six-year-old girl. Would it look like Sophie was sleeping? Wrapped up in her pink winter coat, clutching her favorite doll?

Or would there be bullet holes, red droplets giving testimony to a last moment filled with violence?

D.D. was a professional who didn't feel professional anymore. She wanted to crawl into the backseat and wrap her hands around Tessa Leoni's throat. She wanted to squeeze and shake and scream, *How could you do such a thing! To the little girl who* loved *you!*

D.D. probably should stay behind. Which meant, of course, that she wouldn't.

'The SAR team is requesting further assistance,' Bobby was stating quietly. 'We have four hours of daylight left, in less than ideal conditions. Dogs can only walk so fast. Same with the handlers. What do you suggest?'

'Shit,' D.D. murmured.

'My thoughts exactly.'

'Any funny business, I'm going to have to kill her,' D.D. said after another moment.

Bobby shrugged. 'Don't think too many people out here will argue with that.'

'Bobby . . . if we find the body . . . If I can't handle it . . . '

'I'll cover for you,' he said quietly.

She nodded. Tried to thank him, but her throat had grown too tight. She nodded again. He clasped her shoulder with his hand.

Then they returned to Tessa Leoni.

★   ★   ★

Tessa had left the Crown Vic. No coat, shackled at the wrists and ankles, she'd still managed to make it over to one of the SAR trucks, where she was watching Nelson unload his canines.

First two pet carriers contained smaller dogs, who were twirling in excited circles while barking maniacally.

'Those are search dogs?' Tessa was asking skeptically, as Bobby and D.D. approached.

'Nope,' Nelson said, opening a third, much larger carrier to reveal a German shepherd. 'Those are the reward.'

'What?'

Having released the German shepherd, who loped around him in a tight circle, Nelson bent down to open the other two carriers. The smaller, shaggier dogs were out like twin shots, leaping at the German shepherd, Nelson, Tessa, Bobby, D.D., and everyone else in a twenty foot square radius.

'Meet Kelli and Skyler,' Nelson drawled. 'Soft Coated Wheaten Terriers. Definitely smart as whips, but a little high strung for SAR work. On the other hand, Quizo thinks they're the best playmates in the whole world, and I'll be damned if he didn't choose them for his reward.'

'He doesn't eat them, does he?' Tessa asked skeptically. She appeared as a stain of orange against bright white snow, shivering from the cold.

Nelson was grinning at her, obviously amused by her statement. If talking to a murder suspect bothered him, D.D. thought, he didn't show it. 'Most important part of training a dog,' he said now, unloading more supplies from the back of his covered truck bed, 'is learning the dog's motivation. Each pup is different. Some want food. Some affection. Most hone in on a particular toy that becomes *the* toy. As a handler, you gotta pick up on those signals. When you finally figure out what the reward is, the single item that truly motivates your dog, that's when the serious training begins.

'Now, Quizo, here' — he gave the shepherd a quick pat on the head — 'was a tough nut to crack. Smartest damn dog I ever saw, but only when he felt like it. 'Course, that doesn't work. I need a dog who searches on command, not when he's in the mood. Then one day, these two' — he flicked a hand toward the bouncing, barking terriers — 'showed up. Had a friend who couldn't keep 'em anymore. Said I'd help out for a bit, till he could make better arrangements. Well, damned if it wasn't love at first sight. Miss Kelli and Mr. Skyler ran all over Quizo like twin rugrats and he chased them right back. Which got me to thinking. Maybe playtime with his best buds could be a reward. Tried it out a few times, and bingo. Turns out, Quizo is a bit of a show-off. He doesn't mind working, he just wants the right audience.

'Now when we arrive on-scene, I bring all three. I'm giving Quizo a moment here to interact with his buds, know they're on-site. Then Kelli and Skyler will have to be put away — or they'll be underfoot the entire time, let me tell you — and I'll give Quizo the command to work. He'll get right to it, as he understands the sooner he's completed his mission, the sooner he gets to return to his friends.'

Nelson looked up, regarded Tessa squarely in the eye. 'Skyler and Kelli will also help cheer him up,' the canine handler said levelly. 'Even SAR dogs don't like finding bodies. Depresses 'em, making it doubly important for Skyler and Kelli to be here today.'

Was it D.D.'s imagination, or did Tessa finally flinch? Maybe a heart still beat under that façade after all.

D.D. stepped forward, Bobby beside her. She

addressed Nelson first. 'How much more time do you need?'

He glanced at his dogs, then the rest of the SAR team, unloading in the vehicles strung out behind his. 'Fifteen more minutes.'

'Anything more you need from us?' D.D. asked.

Nelson cracked a thin smile. 'An X to mark the spot?'

'How do you know when the dogs have found it, made a hit?' D.D. asked curiously. 'Quizo will bark . . . louder?'

'Three-minute sustained bark,' Nelson supplied. 'All SAR dogs are trained a little different — some sit to indicate a hit, others have a particular woofing pitch. But given our team specializes in search and rescue, we've gone with a three-minute sustained bark, assuming our dogs might be out of sight, behind a tree or boulder, and we might need three minutes to catch up. Works for us.'

'Well, I can't supply a marked X,' D.D. said, 'but we do have one way of getting started.'

D.D. turned to Tessa. 'So let's take a trip down memory lane. You drove this far?'

Tessa's expression had gone blank. She nodded.

'Park here?'

'Don't know. The road was better formed, packed down. I drove to the end.'

D.D. gestured around. 'Trees, fields, anything look familiar?'

Tessa hesitated, shivering again. 'Maybe that copse of trees over there,' she said at last, pointing vaguely with two hands bound on the wrists. 'Not sure. The fresh snowfall . . . it's like someone wiped the chalkboard clean. Everything is both the same and different.'

'Four hours,' D.D. said crisply. 'Then one way or another, you're back behind bars. So I suggest you start studying the landscape, because if you really want to bring your daughter home, this is the only chance you're gonna get.'

Something finally moved in Tessa's face, a spasm of emotion that was hard to read, but might have included regret. It bothered D.D. She turned away, both arms wrapped around her middle now.

'Get her a coat,' she muttered to Bobby.

He was already holding an extra jacket in his hands. He held it out and D.D. almost laughed. It was a down-filled black coat emblazoned *Boston PD*, no doubt from the trunk of one of the patrol officers. He draped it around Tessa's shoulders, as she could not slide her shackled arms into the sleeves, then zippered up the front to hold it in place.

'What's more incongruous?' D.D. murmured out loud. 'A state trooper in a Boston PD field coat, or a Suffolk County Jail inmate in a Boston PD field coat? Either way,' her voice dropped, sounding dark, even nasty, 'it just doesn't fit.'

D.D. stalked back to her car. She stood alone, huddled against the cold and her own feeling of impending doom. Dark gray clouds gathered on the horizon.

Snow's coming, she thought, and wished again that none of them were here.

They set out twelve minutes later, a shackled Tessa in the lead, Bobby and D.D. on either side, with the canine team and an assortment of officers bringing up the rear. The dogs remained leashed. They hadn't been given the work command yet, but strained against their leads, clearly anxious.

They'd made it only twenty feet before having to stop for the first time. No matter how vindictive D.D. was feeling, Tessa couldn't walk shackled in four inches of fresh snow. They released the binds at her ankles, then finally made some progress.

Tessa led the group to a first copse of trees. She walked around it, frowning as if studying hard. Then she entered the cluster of bare-branched trees, making it ten feet before shaking her head and withdrawing again. They explored three more patches of woods in a similar fashion, before the fourth spot appeared to be the charm.

Tessa entered and kept on walking, her footsteps growing faster, surer now. She came to a massive gray boulder jutting up from the landscape and seemed to nod to herself. They veered left around the rock, Quizo whining low in his throat, as if already on scent.

No one spoke. Just the squeaky crunch of footsteps trampling snow, the panting of dogs, the muffled exhalations of their handlers and officers, bundled up in neck warmers and wool scarves.

They exited the copse of trees. D.D. paused,

thinking that must be a mistake, but Tess kept moving forward, crossing an open expanse of snow, fording a small, trickling stream just visible between fluffy white banks, before disappearing into a more serious line of woods.

'Awfully far to walk with a body,' D.D. muttered.

Bobby shot her a glance, seeming to think the same thing.

But Tessa didn't say a word. She was walking faster now, with purpose. There was a look on her face that was almost uncanny to see. Grim determination rimmed with ragged desperation.

Did Tessa even register the dog team, her entourage of law enforcement handlers? Or had she gone back somewhere in her mind, to a cold Saturday afternoon. Neighbors had seen the Denali depart around four p.m., meaning there hadn't been much daylight left by the time she made it all the way out here.

What had Tessa Leoni been thinking in those last thirty minutes of twilight? Struggling with the weight of her daughter's body as she careened through the woods, across flat white fields, heading deeper and deeper into the dense underbrush.

When you buried your child, was it like imparting your greatest treasure into the sanctity of nature? Or was it like hiding your greatest sin, instinctively seeking out the darkest bowels of the forest to cover your crime?

They came to another collection of moss-covered rocks, this time with a vague man-made shape. Rock walls, old foundations, the remnants

327

of chimneys. In a state that had been inhabited as long as Massachusetts, even the woods were never totally without remnants of civilization.

The trees gave way to a smaller clearing and Tessa stopped.

Her throat worked. It took her a couple of times, then the word came out as a whisper: 'Here,' Tessa said.

'Where?' D.D. asked.

'There was a fallen tree. Snow had collected in front of it, forming a snowbank. Seemed . . . like an easy place to dig.'

D.D. didn't say anything right away. She peered at the clearing, smothered with fresh white flakes. Over to her left, there appeared to be a gentle rise, like what might be formed by a toppled tree. Of course, there was another such rise a few feet in front of that, while she made a third on the other side of the clearing, next to a patch of stray trees. Still, she was gazing at three hundred square yards of space, give or take. Given a team of three experienced SAR dogs, the search area was highly manageable.

Bobby was studying the landscape as well, going over it with his fine sniper's eye. He looked at D.D., pointed out the first couple of swells, then an even broader rise next to the far edges of the woods. D.D. nodded.

Time to release the hounds.

'You will return to the car now,' D.D. said, not looking at Tessa.

'But — '

'*You will return to the car!*'

Tessa shut up. D.D. turned back to the

assembled team. She spotted an officer in the back, same one who'd worked the murder book at the original crime scene. She waved him over. 'Officer Fiske?'

'Yes, ma'am.'

'You will escort Inmate Leoni back to your cruiser and wait with her there.'

The kid's face fell. From active search to passive babysitting. 'Yes, ma'am,' he said.

'It's a big responsibility, escorting a prisoner alone.'

He perked up a little, taking up position at Tessa's side, one hand on his holster.

Tessa didn't say anything, just stood there, her face expressionless once more. A cop's face, D.D. thought suddenly, and for some reason, that made her shiver.

'Thank you,' D.D. said abruptly.

'For what?' Tessa asked.

'Your daughter deserves this. Children shouldn't be lost in the woods. Now we can bring her home.'

Tessa's expression cracked. Her eyes went wide, endlessly stark, and she swayed on her feet, might have even gone down, except she shifted her stance and caught herself.

'I love my daughter.'

'We'll treat her with respect,' D.D. replied, already gesturing to the SAR team, which was starting to re-form itself into a search line at the closest edge of the woods.

'I love my daughter,' Tessa repeated, her tone more urgent. 'You think you understand that now, but it's just the beginning for you. Nine months from now, you'll be amazed by how little you loved before that, and then a year after that, and then a year after that. Imagine six years. Six whole years of that kind of love . . . '

D.D. looked at the woman. 'Didn't save her in the end, did it?'

D.D. deliberately turned away from Tessa Leoni and joined the cadaver dogs.

30

Who do you love?

That was the question, of course. Had been from the very beginning — but, of course, Detective D.D. didn't know that. She thought she was dealing with a typical case of child abuse and homicide. Can't say that I blame her. God knows, I was called out to enough houses where wan-faced five-year-olds tended their passed-out mothers. I've watched a mother slap her son with no more expression than swatting a fly. Seen children bandage their own scrapes because they already knew their mothers didn't care enough to do it for them.

But I'd tried to warn D.D. I'd rebuilt my life for Sophie. She wasn't just my daughter, she was the love that finally saved me. She was giggles and joy and pure, distilled enthusiasm. She was anything that was good in my world, and everything worth coming home to.

Who do you love?

Sophie. It has always been Sophie.

D.D. assumed she was seeing the worst a mother could do. She hadn't realized yet that she was actually witnessing the true lengths a mother would go to for love.

What can I tell you? Mistakes in this business are costly.

I'd returned to Officer Fiske's police cruiser. Hands shackled at my waist, but legs still free.

He seemed to have forgotten that detail, and I didn't feel compelled to remind him. I sat in the back, working on keeping my body language perfectly still, nonthreatening.

Both doors were open, his and mine. I needed air, I'd told him. I felt sick, like I might vomit. Officer Fiske had given me a look, but had consented, even helped unzip the heavy BPD coat that pinned my arms to my torso.

Now, he sat in the front seat, obviously frustrated and bored. People became cops because they wanted to play ball, not sit on the bench. But here he was, relegated to listening to the game in the distance. The echoing whines of the search dogs, the faint hum of voices in the woods.

'Drew the short straw,' I commented.

Officer Fiske kept his eyes straight ahead.

'Ever done a cadaver recovery?'

He refused to speak; no consorting with the enemy.

'I did a couple,' I continued. 'Meticulous work, holding the line. Inch by inch, foot by foot, clearing each area of the grid before moving to the next, then moving to the next. Rescue work is better. I got called up to help locate a three-year-old boy lost by Walden's Pond. A pair of volunteers finally found him. Unbelievable moment. Everyone cried, except the boy. He just wanted another chocolate bar.'

Officer Fiske still didn't say anything.

I shifted on the hard plastic bench, straining my ears. Did I hear it yet? Not yet.

'Got kids?' I asked.

'Shut up,' Officer Fiske growled.

'Wrong strategy,' I informed him. 'As long as you're stuck with me, you should engage in conversation. Maybe you're the lucky one who will finally earn my trust. Next thing you know, I'll confide to you what actually happened to my husband and child, turning you into an overnight hero. Something to think about.'

Officer Fiske finally looked at me.

'I hope they bring back the death penalty, just for you,' he said.

I smiled at him. 'Then you're an idiot, because death, at this point, would be the easy way out.'

He twisted around till he was staring out the front of the parked cruiser, falling silent once more.

I started humming. Couldn't help myself. Bad Tessa rising.

'*All I want for Christmas is my two front teeth, my two front teeth, my two front teeth.*'

'Shut up,' Officer Fiske snapped again.

Then we both heard it: The sudden excited barks of a dog catching scent. The cry of the handler, the corresponding rush of the search team, closing in on target. Officer Fiske sat up straighter, leaned over the steering wheel.

I could feel his tension, the barely repressed urge to abandon the cruiser and join the fray.

'You should thank me,' I said from the back.

'Shut up.'

The dog, barking even louder now, honing in. I could picture Quizo's path, across the small clearing, circling the gentle rise of snow. The fallen tree had created a natural hollow, filled with lighter, fluffier flakes, not too big, not too small. I'd been staggering under the weight of my burden by the time I'd found it, literally swaying on my feet from exhaustion.

Setting down the body. Taking out the collapsible shovel strapped around my waist. My gloved hands shaking as I snapped the pieces of handle together. My back aching as I bent over, punching my way through the thin outer layer of ice to the softer snow underneath. Digging, digging, digging. My breath in short, frosty pants. The hot tears that froze almost instantaneously on my cheeks.

As I carved out the hollow, then gently placed the body inside. Moving slower now as I replaced scoop after scoop of snow, then carefully patted it all back into place.

Twenty-three scoops of snow to bury a grown man. Not nearly so many for this precious cargo.

'You should thank me,' I said again, slowly sitting up straight, uncoiling my body. Bad Tessa rising.

Dog was on it. Quizo had done his job and was letting his handler know it with his sustained bark.

Let him go play with his friends, I thought, tense now in spite of myself. Reward the dog. Take him away to Kelli and Skyler. Please.

Officer Fiske was finally staring at me.

'What's your problem?' he asked crossly.

'What's *your* problem? After all, I'm the one who just saved your life.'

'Saved my life? What the hell — '

Then, staring at my impassive face, he finally

connected the dots.

Officer Fiske jumped from the car. Officer Fiske scrambled for the radio on his duty belt. Officer Fiske turned his back to me.

What can I tell you? Mistakes in this business are costly.

I sprang from the rear of the cruiser, fisted both of my shackled hands together and cracked him over the skull. Officer Fiske stumbled forward. I got my arms over his head, around his neck, and yanked hard.

Officer Fiske gasped, made a funny rattling hum, which come to think of it was a lot like CO Kim Watters. Or maybe Brian, dying on the spotless kitchen floor.

I am not sane. That was my last thought. *I can't possibly be sane anymore.*

Officer Fiske's knees buckled. We both went down, while a quarter mile ahead, the snow blew up and screams split the sky and the first dog began to howl.

⋆ ⋆ ⋆

When Officer Fiske's legs finally stopped churning, I gasped three times, inhaling shocks of cold air that forced me back to the present. So much to do, so little time to do it.

Don't think, don't think, don't think.

I unwrapped my hands, fumbling with the keys at Officer Fiske's waist, then remembered to snatch his cellphone. Had a very important call to make in the next thirty seconds.

I could hear cries in the distance. More dogs

howling. Four vehicles over, Kelli and Skyler picked up the message of distress, their higher-pitched barks joining the fray.

Don't think, don't think, don't think.

I glanced at the sky, calculating remaining hours of daylight.

Looks like snow, I thought again.

Then, clutching keys and cellphone, I ran for it.

31

When the first explosion rocked the sky, D.D. was halfway across the clearing, striding toward the snowy mound where Quizo barked with excited intent. Then the world went white.

Snow sprayed up and out in a giant concussive boom. D.D. just got her arms up and it still felt like being hit by a thousand stinging needles. Quizo's deep bark turned into an immediate bay of distress. Someone screamed.

Then, another rocking explosion and several more cries, while D.D. was knocked back on her ass, head buried behind both arms to shield herself.

'Quizo, Quizo,' someone was crying. Probably Nelson.

'D.D., D.D., D.D.,' someone else was crying. Probably Bobby.

She got her eyes open in time to see Bobby charging across the clearing, legs plunging through the snow, face ashen with panic. 'Are you all right? Talk to me, D.D. Talk to me, dammit.'

'What, what, what?' She blinked. Shook ice and snow from her hair. Blinked again. Her ears were ringing, filled with a sense of pressure. She cracked her jaw, trying to release it.

Bobby had reached her side, clutching her shoulders.

'Are you okay are you okay are you okay?' His

lips moved. It took another second for his words to penetrate the buzz in her head.

She nodded weakly, pushing him back so she could inventory her arms, legs, and most importantly, her torso. By and large, she appeared to be in one piece. She'd been far enough away and the snow had cushioned her fall. She wasn't hurt, just dazed and confused.

She let Bobby help her to her feet, then triaged the rest of the damage.

The snowy rise targeted by Quizo's keen nose had disintegrated. In its place was a brown hollow of earth, covered in shredded bits of tree, leaves, and — heaven help them — pink fabric.

Quizo was off to one side, muzzle buried in the snow, whimpering and panting. Nelson stood over his dog, hands gently holding the shepherd's ears as he whispered low, soothing sounds to his distressed pet.

The other search dogs had halted in their tracks and were howling at the sky.

Officer down, D.D. thought. The dogs were telling the world. She wanted to bay with them, until this terrible feeling of rage and helplessness eased in her chest.

Cassondra Murray, team leader, already had her cellphone out and in clipped tones was summoning a vet. Other BPD officers were swarming the scene, hands on holsters, searching for signs of immediate threat.

'Stop!' Bobby yelled suddenly.

The officers stopped. The dog handlers froze.

He was looking around them in the snow. D.D., still cracking her jaw against the ringing in

338

her ears, did the same.

She saw pieces of hot pink fabric, a shred of blue jeans, what might have been a child's tennis shoe. She saw red and brown and green. She saw . . . Pieces. That was the only word for it. Where there had once been the buried remains of a body, there were now pieces, sprayed in all directions.

The entire clearing had just become a body recovery site. Meaning every single person needed to evacuate in order to limit cross-contamination. They needed to contain, they needed to control. And they needed to immediately contact the ME's department, let alone busloads of crime-scene techs. They had bits of human remains, they had hair and fiber, they had . . . they had so much work to do.

Dear God, D.D. thought vaguely, her ears still ringing, her arms still stinging. The dogs howling, howling, and howling.

She couldn't . . . It couldn't . . .

She looked down and realized there was a puff of pink now stuck to her boot. Part of a coat maybe, or a girl's favorite blanket.

Sophie Leoni with big blue eyes and a heart-shaped face. Sophie Leoni with brown hair and a gap-tooth smile who loved to climb trees and hated to sleep in the dark.

Sophie Leoni.

I love my daughter, Tessa had stood here and said. *I love my daughter.*

What kind of mother could do such a thing?

Then, all of a sudden, D.D.'s brain fired to life and she realized the next piece of the puzzle:

'Officer Fiske,' she yelled urgently, grabbing Bobby's arm. 'We need to alert Officer Fiske. Get him on the radio, *now*!'

Bobby already had his radio out, hit the button to transmit. 'Officer Fiske. Come in, Officer Fiske. Officer Fiske.'

But there was no reply. Of course there was no reply. Why else would Tessa Leoni demand to personally escort them to the body? Why else rig her own child with explosives?

D.D. turned to her fellow investigators.

'Officer down!' she shouted, and as a group they plunged back through the woods.

★ ★ ★

Afterward, it all seemed so obvious, D.D. couldn't believe she hadn't seen it coming. Tessa Leoni had frozen her husband's body for at least twenty-four hours. Why so long? Why such an elaborate plan to dispose of her daughter's remains?

Because Tessa Leoni hadn't been just dumping a corpse. She'd been planting her get-out-of-jail-free card.

And D.D. had played right into her hand.

She'd personally checked Tessa Leoni out of the Suffolk County Jail. She'd personally driven a suspected double-murderer to a remote location in central Mass. Then she'd personally escorted a canine team to a body rigged with explosives, allowing Tessa Leoni to disappear into the wild blue yonder.

'I am such a fucking idiot!' D.D. exclaimed

340

two hours later. They remained at the wilderness site, Boston police and local sheriff's department vehicles stacked up for a good three hundred yards.

Ambulance had arrived first, EMTs attempting to treat Officer Fiske, but then, when he waved them off, embarrassed, ashamed, and otherwise not ready to play well with others, they'd tended to Quizo instead. Poor dog had suffered a ruptured eardrum and singeing to the muzzle from being closest to the blast. Eardrum would heal naturally, just as it would in humans, the EMTs assured Nelson.

In the meantime, they'd be happy to drive the dog to his vet. Nelson had taken them up on that deal, obviously very shaken. The rest of the SAR team packed up his truck, including the mournful Kelli and Skyler. They would debrief with D.D. in the morning, team leader Cassondra had assured her. But for now, they needed to regroup and decompress. They were accustomed to searches that ended in tangible discoveries, not homemade explosives.

With the SAR team departing, D.D. got on the phone to Ben, the state medical examiner. Had body parts, definitely needed assistance.

So it went. Officers had withdrawn. Evidence techs had advanced.

And the search for former state police trooper Tessa Leoni, now officially a fugitive from justice, kicked into high gear.

According to Fiske, he'd forgotten to reshackle her ankles (another shamefaced admission that would no doubt lead to a pint of whiskey later

341

tonight). Tessa had also grabbed his keys, meaning there was a good chance she'd freed her wrists.

She'd taken his cellphone, but not his sidearm, which was good news for the fugitive recovery team, and probably a narrow escape from death for Fiske (a second pint of whiskey, probably tomorrow night). Tessa was last seen in an unzippered black BPD jacket, and a thin orange jumpsuit. On foot, no supplies, no hat or gloves, and in the middle of nowhere to boot, no one expected the woman to get far.

Adrenaline would carry her over the first mile or two, but soft snowfall made for exhaustive running, while providing a trail a blind man could follow.

Fugitive recovery team geared up, headed out. An hour of daylight left. They expected it to be enough, but were armed with searchlights in case it was not. Twenty officers against one desperate escapee.

They would get the job done, the lead officer had promised D.D. No child killer would be running on his watch.

D.D.'s turn to be shamefaced, but no pint of whiskey for her later tonight. Just another crime scene to process and a taskforce to debrief and a boss to update, who was probably going to be very unhappy with her, which was okay, because currently, she was very unhappy with herself, as well.

So she did what she always did: headed back to the scene of the crime, with Bobby at her side.

The ME had his staff on-site, suited up and

delicately depositing body parts into red-marked biohazard bags. Evidence techs followed in their wake, collecting other detritus, which hopefully included pieces of the incendiary device. Not too hard to rig homemade explosives in this day and age. Took about ten minutes on the Internet and a quick trip to the local hardware store. Tessa was a bright woman. Assemble a couple of pressure-sensitive devices, then place them in the snowy hollow with the body. Cover and wait.

Dogs and police arrive. Tessa retreats. Bombs go ka-boom. Her guard goes Say What? And Tessa seizes the opportunity to take down a fellow officer and hit the road.

Hello, injured search party. Goodbye, BPD.

As far as D.D. was concerned, each piece of evidence now recovered was another nail in Tessa Leoni's coffin, and she wanted them all. She wanted them *all*.

Ben looked up at Bobby and D.D.'s approach. He handed over his bag to one of his assistants, then crossed to them.

'Well?' D.D. asked immediately.

The ME, mid-forties, stoutly built, with buzz-cut steel gray hair, hesitated. He crossed his arms over his burly chest. 'We have recovered organic matter and bone consistent with a body,' he granted.

'Sophie Leoni?'

In answer, the ME held out his gloved hand, revealing a slender fragment of white bone, approximately two inches long and smeared with dirt and bits of leaves. 'Rib bone segment,' he said. 'Full length would be consistent with a six-year-old.'

D.D. swallowed, forced herself to briskly nod her head. Bone was smaller than she would've imagined. Impossibly delicate.

'Found a clothing tag, size 6T,' Ben continued. 'Fabric remnants are mostly pink. Also consistent with a female child.'

D.D. nodded again, still eyeing the rib bone.

Ben moved it to one side of his palm, revealing a smaller, corn-sized kernel. 'Tooth. Also consistent with a prepubescent girl. Except . . . no root.' The ME sounded puzzled. 'Generally when you recover a tooth from remains, the root is still attached. Unless, it was already loose.' The ME seemed to be talking more to himself than to D.D. and Bobby. 'Which I suppose would be right for a first-grader. A loose tooth, coupled with the force of the blast . . . Yes, I could see that.'

'So the tooth most likely came from Sophie Leoni?' D.D. pressed.

'Tooth most likely came from a prepubescent girl,' Ben corrected. 'Best I can say at this time. I need to get the remains back to my lab. Dental X-ray would be most helpful, though we have yet to recover a skull or jawbone. Bit of work still to be done.'

In other words, D.D. thought, Tessa Leoni had rigged an explosive powerful enough to blow a tooth right out of her daughter's skull.

A flake of snow drifted down, followed by another, then another.

They all peered up at the sky, where the

looming gray snow clouds had finally arrived.

'Tarp,' Ben said immediately, hurrying toward his assistant. 'Protect the remains, now, now, *now.*'

Ben rushed away. D.D. retreated from the clearing, ducking behind a particularly dense bush, where she leaned over and promptly dry-heaved.

What had Tessa said? The love D.D. currently felt for her unborn child was nothing compared to the love she'd feel a year from now, or a year after that or a year after that. Six years of that love. Six years . . .

How could a woman . . . How could a mother . . .

How did you tuck in your child one moment, then search out the perfect place to bury her the next? How did you hug your six-year-old good night, then rig her body with explosives?

I love my daughter, Tessa said. *I love my daughter.*

What a fucking bitch.

D.D. dry-heaved again. Bobby was beside her. She felt him draw her hair back from her cheeks. He handed her a bottle of water. She used it to rinse her mouth, then turned her flushed face to the sky, trying to feel the snow upon her cheeks.

'Come on,' he said quietly. 'Let's get you to the car. Time for a little rest, D.D. It's going to be okay. Really. It will be.'

He took her hand, pulling her through the woods. She trod dispiritedly behind him, thinking that he was a liar. That once you saw the body of a little girl blow up in front of your

345

eyes, the world was never okay again.

They should head for HQ, get out before the rural road became impassable. She needed to prepare for the inevitable press conference. *Good news, we probably found the body of Sophie Leoni. Bad news, we lost her mother, a distinguished state police officer who most likely murdered her entire family.*

They reached the car. Bobby opened the passenger-side door. She slid in, feeling jumbled and restless and almost desperate to escape her own skin. She didn't want to be a detective anymore. Sergeant Detective D.D. Warren hadn't gotten her man. Sergeant Detective D.D. Warren hadn't rescued the child. Sergeant Detective D.D. Warren was about to become a mother herself, and look at Tessa Leoni, trooper extraordinaire who'd killed, buried, and then blown up her own kid, and what did that say about female police officers becoming parental units, and what the hell was D.D. thinking?

She shouldn't be pregnant. She wasn't strong enough. Her tough veneer was cracking and beneath it was simply a vast well of sadness. All the dead bodies she'd studied through the years. Other children who'd never made it home. The unrepentant faces of parents, uncles, grandparents, even next door neighbors who'd done the deed.

The world was a terrible place. She solved each murder only to move on to the next. Put away a child abuser, watch a wife beater get released the next day. And on and on it went. D.D., sentenced to spend the rest of her career roaming backwoods for small lifeless bodies who'd never been loved or wanted in the first place.

She'd just wanted to bring Sophie home. Rescue this one child. Make this one drop of difference in the universe, and now . . . Now . . .

'Shhh.' Bobby was stroking her hair.

Was she crying? Maybe, but it wasn't enough. She pressed her tearstained cheek into the curve of his shoulder. Felt the shuddering heat of him. Her lips found his neck, tasting salt. Then it seemed the most natural thing in the world to lean back and find his lips with her own. He didn't pull back. Instead, she felt his hands grip her shoulders. So she kissed him again, the man who'd once been her lover and one of the few people she regarded as a pillar of strength.

Time suspended, a heartbeat or two when she didn't have to think, she only had to feel.

Then, Bobby's hands tightened again. He lifted her up and gently set her back, until she sat squarely in the passenger seat and he sat in the driver's seat and at least two feet loomed between them.

'No,' he said.

D.D. couldn't speak. The enormity of what she'd just done started to penetrate. She glanced around the small car, desperate for escape.

'It was a moment,' Bobby continued. His voice sounded rough. He paused, cleared his throat, said again: 'A moment. But I have Annabelle and you have Alex. You and I both know better than to mess with success.'

D.D. nodded.

'D.D. — '

Immediately, she shook her head. She didn't want to hear anything more. She'd fucked this up enough. A moment. Like he said. A moment. Life was filled with moments.

Except she'd always had a weakness for Bobby Dodge. She'd let him go, then never gotten over him. And if she spoke now, she was going to cry and that was stupid. Bobby deserved better. Alex deserved better. They all did.

Then, she found herself thinking of Tessa Leoni and she couldn't help but feel the connection again. Two women, so capable in their professional lives, and such total fuckups in their personal ones.

The radio on the dash crackled to life. D.D. snatched it up, hoping for good news.

It was the search team, Officer Landley reporting in. They'd followed Tessa's trail for two and half miles, as she'd run down the snow-packed rural road to the larger intersecting street. Then her footsteps had ended and fresh tire tracks had begun.

Best guess: Tessa Leoni was no longer alone and on foot.

She had an accomplice and a vehicle.

She had disappeared.

32

When Juliana and I were twelve years old, we developed a catchphrase: 'What are friends for?' We used it like a code — it meant that if one of us needed a favor, most likely something embarrassing or desperate, then the other had to say yes, because that's what friends were for.

Juliana forgot her math homework. What are friends for, she'd announce at our lockers, and I'd hastily share my answers. My father was being an asshole about letting me stay after school for track. What are friends for, I'd say, and Juliana would have her mother notify my father that she'd bring me home, because my father would never argue with Juliana's mom. Juliana developed a crush on the cute boy in our biology class. What are friends for? I'd sidle up to him during lunch and find out if my friend stood a chance.

Get arrested for murdering your husband. What are friends for?

I looked up Juliana's number Saturday afternoon, as my world was imploding and it occurred to me that I needed help. Ten years later, there was still only one person I could trust. So after the man in black finally departed, leaving my husband's body down in the garage, buried in snow, I looked up the married name, address, and phone number of my former best friend. I committed the information to memory, in order to eliminate the paper trail.

Shortly thereafter I built two small explosive devices, then loaded up the Denali and went for a drive.

My last acts as a free woman. I knew it even then. Brian had done something bad, but Sophie and I were going to be the ones punished. So I paid my own husband's murderer fifty thousand dollars in order to gain twenty-four hours' lead time. Then I used that time to desperately get two steps ahead.

Sunday morning, Shane had arrived and the games had begun. One hour later, beat within an inch of my life, head concussed, cheek fractured, I went from brilliant strategist to genuinely battered woman, dazed, confused, and somewhere in the back of my scrambled head, still dimly hoping that I'd been wrong about everything. Maybe Brian hadn't died in front of my eyes. Maybe Sophie hadn't been snatched out of her bed. Maybe next time I woke up, my world would be magically whole again and my husband and daughter would be by my side, holding my hands.

I never got that lucky.

Instead, I was confined to a hospital bed until Monday morning, when the police arrested me, and plan B kicked into gear.

All prison calls start with a recorded message to the receiver that the collect call has originated from a correctional institute. Would the other party accept the charges?

Million dollar question, I thought Monday night, as I stood in the commons area of the detainee unit and dialed Juliana's number with shaking fingers. I was as surprised as anyone when Juliana said yes. Bet she surprised herself, too. And bet she wished, within thirty seconds, that she'd said no instead.

Given that all outgoing calls are recorded, I kept the conversation simple.

'What are friends for?' I stated, heart hammering. I heard Juliana suck in her breath.

'Tessa?'

'I could use a friend,' I continued, quickly now, before Juliana did something sensible, such as hang up. 'Tomorrow afternoon. I'll call again. What are friends for.'

Then I hung up, because the sound of Juliana's voice had brought tears to my eyes, and you can't afford to cry in prison.

Now, having just taken out Officer Fiske, I snatched his cellphone. Then I sprinted one hundred yards down the hardpacked snow of the rural road until I came to an enormous fir tree. Ducking underneath its canopy of green branches I quickly dialed Juliana's number while withdrawing a small waterproof bag I'd previously tucked beneath the branches.

'Hello?'

I talked fast. Directions, GPS coordinates, and a list of supplies. I'd had twenty-four hours in prison to plan my breakout, and I'd put it to good use.

On the other end of the cellphone, Juliana didn't argue. What are friends for?

Maybe she would call the cops the second she hung up. But I didn't think so. Because the last time that phrase was spoken between us, Juliana had uttered the words, while handing me the gun that had just taken her brother's life.

I put down Officer Fiske's cellphone and opened up the waterproof bag. Inside was Brian's Glock .40, which I'd removed from our gun safe.

He didn't need it anymore. But I did.

★ ★ ★

By the time the silver SUV slowed to a halt on the main road, my confidence had fled and I was jumpy with nerves. Gun tucked into the pocket of my black coat, arms wrapped tight around me, I kept to the fringes of the bordering woods, feeling conspicuous. Any second now, a police car would roar by. If I didn't duck for cover in time, the alert officer would spot me, execute a tight one-eighty and that would be that.

Had to pay attention. Gotta run. Gotta hide.

Then, another vehicle looming in the distance, headlights bright against the thickening gloom. Vehicle was moving slower, more uncertainly, as if the driver was looking for something. No roof rack bearing sirens, meaning a pedestrian vehicle versus a cop car. Now or never.

I took a deep breath, stepped toward the asphalt. The headlights swept across my face, then the SUV braked hard.

Juliana had arrived.

I clambered quickly into the backseat. Second I closed the door, she was off like a shot. I hit the floor and stayed there.

Car seat. Empty, but half-covered in a baby blanket, so recently occupied. Don't know why that surprised me. I had a child. Why not Juliana?

When we were girls we planned to marry twin brothers. We would live in houses side by side and raise our kids together. Juliana wanted three children, two boys and one girl. I planned on having one of each. She was going to stay home with her kids, like her mom. I was going to own a toy store, where of course her kids would receive a family discount.

Next to the car seat was a dark green duffel bag. I got on my knees, keeping out of sight of the windows, and unzipped the bag. Inside I found everything I'd requested — a change of clothes, all black. Fresh pair of underwear, two additional tops. Scissors, makeup, black cap and gloves.

Hundred and fifty in cash, small bills. Probably the best she could scrounge up on short notice.

I wondered if that was a lot of money for Juliana these days. I only knew the girl she'd been, not the wife and mother she'd become.

I started by taking out all items in black and laying them on the backseat. It took a bit of wiggling, but I finally managed to shed the orange jumpsuit and redress in the black jeans and a black turtleneck. I twisted my hair up onto the top of my head and covered it with the dark baseball cap.

Then I turned around to study myself in the rearview mirror.

Juliana was staring at me. Her lips were pressed into a thin line, her hands white-knuckled on the steering wheel.

Newborn, I thought immediately. She had that look about her — the frazzled new mom, still not sleeping at night and frayed around the edges. Knowing the first year would be difficult, surprised to discover it was even harder than that. She glanced away, eyes on the road.

I sat down on the rear bench seat.

'Thank you,' I said at last.

She never answered.

★ ★ ★

We drove in silence for another forty minutes. The snow had finally started, lightly at first, then falling heavily enough that Juliana had to reduce her speed.

At my request, she turned the radio to the news. No word of any officers involved in a situation, so apparently D.D. Warren and her team had survived my little surprise, and had chosen to keep a lid on things.

Made sense. No cop wanted to admit she'd lost a prisoner, especially if she believed she would recapture the inmate shortly. Last Detective Warren knew, I was alone and on foot, meaning D.D. probably had believed she'd round me up within an hour.

Not sorry to disappoint her, but relieved everyone was okay. I'd done my best to rig the twin pressure-sensitive devices to blow back, away from the recovery team and into the

354

relative shelter of the fallen tree. But given that it was a rookie effort, I had no way of knowing how successful I'd be.

I'd sat behind Officer Fiske, both hoping and dreading what would happen next.

SUV slowed again. Juliana had her blinker on, was preparing to exit the highway for Route 9. She'd driven under the speed limit the entire way, eyes straight ahead, two hands on the wheel. The conscientious getaway driver.

Now our adventure was almost over, and I could see her lower lip trembling. She was scared.

I wondered if she thought I'd killed my husband. I wondered if she thought I'd murdered my own daughter. I should protest my innocence, but I didn't.

I thought she of all people should know better.

Twelve more minutes. All it took to travel back in time, to return to the old neighborhood. Past her old house, past my parents' shabby home.

Juliana didn't look at any of the buildings. Didn't sigh, wax nostalgic, say a single word.

Two final turns and we were there, at my father's garage.

She pulled over, killed the lights.

Snow was falling heavily now, blanketing the dark world in white.

I gathered up the last of my things, tucked them into the duffel bag, which I would take with me. Leave no evidence behind.

'When you get home,' I said now, my voice surprisingly loud in the silence, 'mix ammonia with warm water, and use it to wipe down the car. That will erase any fingerprints.'

Juliana looked at me in the review mirror again, but remained silent.

'The police are going to find you,' I continued. 'They'll hone in on the call I placed to you last night from jail. It's one of the only leads they have, so they're going to follow up on it. Just tell the truth. What I said, what you said. The whole conversation was recorded, so you're not telling them anything they don't already know, and it's not like we said anything incriminating.'

Juliana looked at me, remained silent.

'They shouldn't be able to trace today's call,' I told her. 'Our only point of contact has been someone else's cellphone, and I'm about to take an acetylene torch to it. Once I've melted its circuits, there's nothing it can give away. So you went for a drive this afternoon. I deliberately chose a location that didn't involve any toll roads, meaning there's no way for them to trace where you went. You could've gone anywhere and done anything. Make them work for it.'

It went without saying that she would hold up under police questioning. She had before.

'We're even.' She spoke up suddenly, her voice flat. 'Don't call again. We're even.'

I smiled, sadly, with genuine regret. For ten years, we'd kept our distance. And would've continued if not for Saturday morning and my stupid husband dying on our stupid kitchen floor.

Blood is thicker than water. Actually, friend-ship was, and so I had honored what I'd known Juliana had needed. Even when it hurt me.

'I would do it again,' I murmured, my eyes locking on hers in the rearview mirror. 'You were my best friend, and I loved you and I would do it again.'

'Did you really name her Sophie?'

'Yeah.'

Juliana Sophia MacDougall nee Howe covered her mouth. She started to cry.

I slung the duffel bag over my shoulder and stepped out into the snowy night. Another moment, the engine started up. Then the headlights flicked on and Juliana drove away.

I headed toward my father's shop. I could tell from the light burning inside that he was already waiting.

33

Bobby and D.D. headed back to HQ in silence. Bobby drove. D.D. sat in the passenger's seat. She had her hands fisted on her lap, trying not to think, her mind racing anyway.

She hadn't eaten all day and last night her sleep had been marginal at best. Combine that with the all-time shittiest day of her career and she was entitled to go a little nuts and kiss a married man while carrying another man's baby. Made total sense.

She leaned her forehead against the cool window, stared at the snow. The frozen flakes were falling heavily now. Obliterating Tessa Leoni's trail. Snarling traffic. Complicating an already complicated investigative operation.

She'd contacted her boss before leaving the crime scene. Better Horgan hear the news from her than the latest media report, where it was bound to break at any time. D.D. had lost a suspected double-murderer. Taken her out to middle-of-nowhere Mass., where her entire team had fallen victim to a rookie booby trap.

The BPD looked like a bunch of idiots. Not to mention, the violent fugitive apprehension unit — a state operation — was most likely going to take the entire case from them, given the steadily growing size of the search operation. So the BPD would appear incompetent and be denied any chance to redeem themselves. Talk about a one-way ticket to Asshole Avenue. Let alone a punch line in all future media reports — *suspected double-murderer Tessa Leoni, who escaped while in the custody of the Boston police . . .*

She'd better hope she was pregnant, D.D. thought. Then, instead of getting fired, she could take maternity leave.

She ached.

She did. Her head hurt. Her chest, as well. She mourned for Sophie Leoni, a sweet-faced child who'd deserved better. Had she looked forward to her mommy coming home from work each morning? Hugs and kisses, while snuggling close for stories or showing off her latest homework? D.D. would think so. That's what children did. They loved and loved and loved. With their entire hearts. With every fiber of their being.

Then the adults in their lives failed them.

And the police failed them.

And so it went.

I love my daughter.

'Gonna stop ahead,' Bobby spoke up, flipping on the right turn signal. 'Need food. Want anything?'

D.D. shook her head.

'How about some dry cereal? Gotta eat something, D.D. Low blood sugar has never been your strong suit.'

'Why do you do that?'

'Do what?'

'Take care of me.'

Bobby took his eyes off the road long enough

to regard her evenly. 'Bet Alex would, too. If you'd let him.'

She scowled. Bobby shrugged off the glare, attention back on the treacherous highway. It took a bit to ease the Crown Vic over, find the exit, then work their way into the parking lot of a small shopping plaza. D.D. noted a dry cleaner's, a pet supply store, and a mid-sized grocery store.

The grocery store appeared to be Bobby's target. They parked up front, most customers scared off by the wintry conditions. When D.D. got out of the car, she was surprised to see how much snow had already accumulated. Bobby came around the vehicle, wordlessly offering his arm.

She accepted his help, making her way gingerly along the snow-covered sidewalk into the brightly lit store. Bobby headed for the deli. She lasted five seconds before the smell of rotisserie chicken proved too much. She left him to wander on her own, commandeering an apple from produce, then a box of Cheerios from the cereal aisle. Maybe one of those fancy organic fruit drinks, she thought, or a premade protein shake. She could live on Ensure, next logical stage of the life cycle.

She found herself in the small pharmacy section, and that quickly knew what she was going to do.

Fast, before she could change her mind, before Bobby could appear: family planning section, condoms, condoms, and of course, when the condoms broke, home pregnancy kits. She snatched the first box she found. Pee on a stick,

360

wait to see what it tells you. How hard could it be?

No time to pay. Bobby would spot her for sure. So she high-tailed it for the restroom, apple, cereal box, and home pregnancy test clutched tight against her chest.

A green sign declared that no merchandise was allowed in the restroom.

Tough shit, D.D. thought, and pushed through the door.

She commandeered the handicap stall. Turned out it had a changing station bolted to the wall. She unfolded the plastic table and used it as a workbench. Apple, Cheerios, pregnancy kit.

Her fingers were shaking. Violently. To the point she couldn't hold the box and read the words. So she flipped the box over on the changing table, reading the directions as she worked the button on her pants, finally shoving her jeans down to her knees.

Probably this was the kind of thing women did at home. Surrounded by the cozy comfort of their favorite towels, peach-painted walls, maybe some floral potpourri. She squatted in an industrial gray tiled public restroom and did the deed, fingers still shaking as she tried to position the stick and pee on command.

Took her three tries to get it done. She set the stick on the changing table, refusing to look at it. She finished peeing. She pulled up her pants. She washed her hands at the sink.

Then she returned to the stall. Outside, she could hear the bathroom door opening. Footsteps as another woman entered, headed for the neighboring stall. D.D. closed her eyes, held her breath.

She felt naughty, the bad schoolgirl caught smoking in the loo.

She couldn't be seen, couldn't be discovered. For her to look at the stick, she needed absolute privacy.

Toilet flushing. Stall door opening. Sound of water running at the sink, then the blast from the automatic hand dryer.

Outside door opened. Outside door closed.

D.D. was alone again.

Slowly she cracked one eye. Then the other. She stared at the stick.

Pink plus sign.

Sergeant Detective D.D. Warren was officially pregnant.

She sat back down on the toilet, put her head in her hands, and wept.

* * *

Later, still sitting on the edge of the toilet, she ate the apple. The rush of sugary fruit hit her bloodstream, and suddenly, she was ravenous. She consumed half a box of Cheerios, then abandoned the bathroom in search of a protein bar, mixed nuts, potato chips, yogurt, and bananas.

When Bobby finally caught up with her, she was standing in the checkout line with her apple core, opened Cheerios box, opened pregnancy kit box, and half a dozen other groceries. The checkout girl, who sported three facial piercings and a constellation of star tattoos, was regarding her with clear disapproval.

'Where'd you go?' Bobby asked with a frown. 'Thought I'd lost you.'

Then his gaze fell upon the pregnancy test kit. His eyes widened. He didn't say another word.

D.D. handed over her credit card, accepted her grocery bags. She didn't say a word either.

They'd just made it out to the car when her cellphone rang. She checked the caller ID — Phil from headquarters.

Work. Just what she needed.

She punched Talk, listened to what Phil had to say, and whether from his news or her feeding frenzy, she finally felt better about the day.

She put away her phone, turned back to Bobby, who stood beside his car in the snow.

'Guess what? Tessa Leoni placed a phone call while under the fine care of the Suffolk County Sheriff's Department. Nine p.m. last night, she contacted her childhood BFF, Juliana Sophia Howe.'

'Sister of the guy she shot?'

'Exactly. Now, if you were arrested for murdering your spouse, what are the odds you'd call a family member of the last person you killed?'

Bobby frowned. 'Don't like it.'

'Me either.' D.D.'s face lit up. 'Let's go get her!'

'Deal.' Bobby opened his door, then paused. 'D.D. . . . ' His gaze flickered to her grocery bags. 'Happy?'

'Yeah,' she said, nodding slowly. 'I think I am.'

When Bobby and D.D. finally completed the treacherous drive to Juliana's house, they discovered the small home lit up bright as day against fat, slow falling snowflakes. A silver SUV and darker sedan were parked in the driveway.

As Bobby and D.D. approached, the front door opened and a man appeared. He wore a suit, still dressed for his workday, but now lugging a baby and a diaper bag. He met Bobby and D.D.'s gaze as they stepped onto the front porch.

'I already told her to call a lawyer,' he said.

The caring husband, D.D. deduced. 'She need one?'

'She's a good person and a great mother. You want someone to prosecute, go back and shoot her brother again. He deserves this abuse. Not her.'

Having said his piece, Juliana's husband pushed past both of them and strode through the snow for the dark blue sedan. Another minute to strap the baby in the back, then Juliana's family was out of the way.

'Definitely expecting our visit,' Bobby murmured.

'Let's go get her!' D.D. said again.

Caring husband hadn't fully closed the door behind him, so Bobby finished pushing it open. Juliana was sitting on the couch directly across from the door. She didn't get up, but regarded them evenly.

D.D. entered first. She flashed her creds, then

introduced Bobby. Juliana didn't rise. Bobby and D.D. didn't sit. The room was already humming with tension, and it made it easy for D.D. to reach the next logical conclusion:

'You helped her out, didn't you? You picked up Tessa Leoni this afternoon and drove her away from her daughter's burial site. You aided and abetted a fugitive. Why? I mean seriously.' D.D. gestured around the cute home with its fresh paint and cheerful collection of baby toys. 'Why the hell would you risk all this?'

'She didn't do it,' Juliana said.

D.D. arched a brow. 'Exactly when did you take the stupid pill and how long before it wears off?'

Juliana's chin came up. 'I'm not the idiot here. You are!'

'Why?'

'It's what you do,' Juliana burst out in a bitter rush. 'Police. Cops. Looking but never seeing. Asking but never hearing. Ten years ago they fucked up everything. Why should now be any different?'

D.D. stared at the young mom, startled by the violence of the outburst. At that moment, it came to D.D. What the husband had said outside. Juliana's inexplicable agreement to aid the woman who'd destroyed her family ten years ago. Her lingering rage with the police.

D.D. took the first step forward, then another. She squatted down until she was eye level with Juliana, seeing the tear tracks on the woman's cheeks.

'Tell us, Juliana. Who shot your brother that

365

night? It's time to unload. So you talk, and I promise, we'll listen.'

'Tessa didn't have the gun,' Juliana Howe whispered. 'She brought it for me. Because I asked her to. She didn't have the gun. She never had the gun.'

'Who shot Tommy, Juliana?'

'I did. I shot my brother. And I'm sorry, but I'd do it all over again!'

Now that the dam had finally broken, Juliana confessed the rest of the story in a sobbing rush. The first night her brother had come home and sexually assaulted her. How he'd cried the next morning and begged her forgiveness. He'd been drunk, hadn't known what he was doing. Of course he'd never do it again . . . please just don't tell Mom and Dad.

She'd agreed to keep his secret, except after that he'd raped her again and again. Until it'd been half a dozen times, and he was no longer drunk and he no longer apologized. He told her it was her fault. If she didn't wear those kind of clothes, if she wouldn't flaunt herself right under his nose . . .

So she started to wear baggier clothes and stopped doing her hair and makeup. And maybe that helped, or maybe it was just because he went away to college, where it turned out he'd found lots of other girls to rape. Mostly, however, he left her alone. Except for the weekends.

She lost her ability to concentrate at school, always had dark shadows under her eyes, because if it was Friday, then Tommy might come home so she had to be vigilant. She added a lock to her room. Two weeks later, she came home to find her entire bedroom door splintered into bits.

'Terribly sorry,' Tommy had said over dinner. 'Shouldn't have been running in the hall like that.' And her parents had beamed at him because he was their oldest son and they adored him.

One Monday morning Juliana broke. Went to school, started to cry, couldn't stop. Tessa tugged her into the end stall of the girl's restroom, then stood there until Juliana stopped weeping and started talking.

Together, the two girls had devised a plan. Tessa's father had a gun. She would get it.

'Not like he's ever paying attention,' Tessa had said with a shrug. 'How hard can it be?'

So Tessa would get the gun and bring it over on Friday night. They would have a sleepover. Tessa would stand guard. When Tommy showed up, Juliana would produce the weapon. She'd point the gun at him and tell him if he ever touched her again, she would shoot off his balls.

The girls practiced the phrase several times. They liked it.

It had made sense, huddled in a bathroom stall. Tommy, like any bully, needed to be confronted. Then he would back down, and Juliana would be safe again.

It had all made perfect sense.

By Thursday, Tessa had the gun. Friday night, she came over to the house and gave it to Juliana.

Then they sat together on the sofa and, a bit nervously, started their movie marathon.

Tessa had fallen asleep on the floor. Juliana on the couch. But both had woken up when Tommy came home.

For a change, he didn't look at his sister. Instead, he'd kept his eyes glued on Tessa's chest.

'Like ripe apples,' he'd said, already lurching for her when Juliana triumphantly whipped out the handgun.

She pointed it at her brother. Screamed at him to go away. Leave her and Tessa alone, *or else*.

Except Tommy had looked right at her and started laughing. 'Or else *what*? Do you even know how to shoot that thing? I'd check the safety if I were you.'

Juliana had immediately raised the gun to check the safety. At that moment Tommy had lunged for her, going after the weapon.

Tessa was screaming. Juliana was screaming. Tommy was snarling and pulling Juliana's hair and making grabby grabby.

The gun, squished between them. The gun, going off.

Tommy staggering back, gaping at his leg.

'You bitch,' her brother had said. Those were the last words he'd spoken to her. 'You bitch,' he'd said again, then he'd fallen down and, slowly but surely, died.

Juliana had panicked. She hadn't meant . . . Her parents, dear God her parents . . .

She'd thrust the gun at Tessa. Tessa had to take it. Tessa had to . . . run . . . just get out. *Get out get out get out.*

So Tessa did. And those words were the last Juliana had spoken to her best friend. *Get out get out get out.*

By the time Tessa had arrived at her house, the police were arriving at Juliana's. Juliana could've admitted what she'd done. She could've confessed what her brother was really like. But her mother was screaming hysterically and her father was shell-shocked and she couldn't do it. She just couldn't do it.

Juliana had whispered Tessa's name to the police and, that quickly, fiction became fact. Tessa had shot her brother.

And Tessa never said otherwise.

'I would have confessed,' Juliana said now. 'If it had gone to trial, if it looked like Tessa was really going to get into trouble . . . I would've confessed. Except the other women started coming forward and it became clear that Tessa would never face charges. The DA himself said he felt it was justifiable use of force.

'I figured she'd be okay. And my father . . . by then, he was a wreck. If he couldn't accept Tommy had ever assaulted other women, how could he believe what Tommy had done to *me*? It seemed better to just keep my mouth shut. Except . . . the longer you go without speaking, the harder it becomes. I wanted to see Tessa, but I didn't know what to say. I wanted my parents to know what happened, but I didn't know how to tell them.

'I stopped speaking. Literally. For an entire year. And my parents never even noticed. They

369

were too busy with their own nervous break-downs to bother with mine. Then Tessa disappeared — I heard her father had kicked her out. She never told me. Never stopped by to say goodbye. Maybe she couldn't speak either. I never knew. Until you showed up yesterday morning, I didn't know she'd become a cop, I didn't know she'd gotten married, and I didn't know she had a little girl named Sophie. That's my middle name, you know. She named her daughter for me. After everything I did to her, she still named her daughter for me . . . '

'The daughter who's now dead,' D.D. said bluntly.

'You're wrong!' Juliana shook her head.

'You're wrong, Juliana: We saw the body. Or at least the pieces after she blew it up.'

Juliana paled, then shook her head again. 'You're wrong,' the young woman insisted stubbornly.

'Once again, from the woman whose family could give lessons in denial . . . '

'You don't know Tessa.'

'For the past ten years, neither have you.'

'She's clever. Self-sufficient. But she wouldn't harm a child, not after what happened to her brother.'

Bobby and D.D. exchanged glances. 'Brother?' D.D. said.

'Stillborn baby. That's what tore her family apart, years before I knew her. Her mother fell into a deep depression, probably should've been institutionalized, except what did people know back then? Her mom lived in the bedroom.

370

Never came out, certainly never cared for Tessa. Her father did the best he could, but he was not exactly nurturing. But Tessa loved them. She tried to take care of them, in her own way. And she loved her baby brother, too. One day, we had a funeral for him, just she and I. And she cried, she truly cried, because that's the one thing in her house you were never allowed to do.'

D.D. stared at Juliana. 'You know, you could've told me this sooner.'

'Well, you could've figured it out sooner. Cops. Must the victims do all the work for you?'

D.D. bristled. Bobby promptly placed a settling hand on her arm.

'Where did you take her?' he asked quietly.

'I don't know what you're talking about,' Juliana said primly.

'You picked Tessa up. You already admitted that.'

'No. I did not. Your partner stated I picked her up. I never said any such thing.'

D.D. ground her teeth. 'So that's the way you want to play it?' She swept her arm across the toy-strewn floor. 'We can take you down to HQ. Seize your car. We'll tear it apart while you rot behind bars. How old's your kid again? Because I don't know if babies are even allowed to visit prison.'

'Tessa called me Monday evening shortly after nine p.m.,' Juliana stated defiantly. 'She said, what are friends for? I said, Tessa? Because I was surprised to hear her voice after all these years. She said she wanted to call me again. Then she hung up. That's what we said, and the only interaction I have had in the past ten years with Tessa Leoni. If you want to know why she called, what she meant, or if she intended any further contact, you'll have to ask her.'

D.D. was flabbergasted, honestly flabbergasted. Who knew Tessa's suburbanite playmate had it in her?

'One hair in your car, and you're screwed,' D.D. said.

Juliana made a show of slapping her cheeks. 'OhmyGod, so sorry. Did I mention that I vacuumed? Oh, and just the other day, I read the best trick for washing your car. It involves ammonia . . . '

D.D. stared at the housewife. 'I'm going to arrest you for that alone,' she said finally.

'Then do it.'

'Tessa shot her husband. She dragged his body down into the garage, and she buried it in snow,' D.D. snapped angrily. 'Tessa killed her daughter, drove her body out to the woods, and rigged it with enough explosives to take out the recovery team. This is the woman you're trying to protect.'

'This is the woman you *thought* killed my brother,' Juliana corrected. 'You were wrong about that. Not so hard to believe you're wrong about the rest of it, too.'

'We are not wrong — ' D.D. started, but then she stopped. She frowned. Something occurred to her, the niggling doubt from earlier in the woods. Oh, crap.

'I've gotta make a phone call,' she said abruptly. 'You. Sit. Take even one step from that sofa and I'll arrest your sorry ass.'

Then she nodded at Bobby and led him to the front porch, where she whipped out her cellphone.

'What — ' he started, but she held up a silencing hand.

'Medical examiner's office?' she spoke into the receiver. 'Get Ben. I know he's working. What the hell do you think I'm calling about? Tell him it's Sergeant Warren, because I bet you a hundred bucks he's standing over a microscope right now, thinking *Oh shit.*'

34

My father's garage had never been very impressive, and ten years hadn't improved it any. A squat, cinder-block building, the exterior paint was the color of nicotine and peeling off in giant flakes. Heating had always been unreliable; in the winter, my father would work under cars in full snow gear. Plumbing wasn't any better. Once upon a time, there'd been a working toilet. Mostly, my father and his male friends peed on the fence line — men, marking turf.

Two advantages of my father's shop, however: first, a bullpen of used cars awaiting repair and resell; second, an acetylene torch, perfect for cutting through metal and, coincidentally, melting cellphones.

The heavy front door was locked. Ditto with the garage bay. Back door, however, was open. I followed the glow of the bare bulb to the rear of the garage, where my father sat on a stool, smoking a cigarette and watching my approach.

A half-empty bottle of Jack sat on the workbench behind him. It'd taken me years to realize the full extent of my father's drinking. That we didn't go to bed by nine p.m. just because my father got up so early in the morning, but because he was too drunk to continue on with his day.

When I gave birth to Sophie, I'd hoped it would help me understand my parents and their endless grief. But it didn't. Even mourning the loss of an infant, how could they fail to feel the love of their remaining child? How could they simply stop seeing me?

My father inhaled one last time, then stubbed out his cigarette. He didn't use an ashtray; his scarred workbench got the job done.

'Knew you'd come,' he said, speaking with the rasp of a lifetime smoker. 'News just announced your escape. Figured you'd head here.'

So Sergeant Warren had copped to her mistake. Good for her.

I ignored my father, heading for the acetylene torch.

My father was still dressed in his oil-stained coveralls. Even from this distance I could tell his shoulders remained broad, his chest thickly muscled. Spending all day with your arms working above your head will do that to a man.

If he wanted to stop me, he had brute strength on his side.

The realization made my hands tremble as I arrived at the twin tanks of the acetylene torch. I took the safety goggles down from their nearby hook and set about prepping for business. I wore the dark gloves Juliana had supplied for me. I had to take them off long enough to dismantle the cellphone — slide off the cover, remove the battery.

Then I slipped the black gloves back on, topping them with a heavy-duty pair of work gloves. I set the duffel bag next to the wall, then placed the cellphone in the middle of the cement floor, the best surface when working with a torch

375

that can cut through steel like a knife through butter.

When I was fourteen, I'd spent an entire summer working at my father's shop. Helped change oil, replace spark plugs, rotate tires. One of my misguided notions, that if my father wouldn't take an interest in my world, maybe I should take an interest in his.

We worked side by side all summer, him barking out orders in his deep, rumbling voice. Then, come break time, he'd retreat to his dust-covered office, leaving me alone in the garage to eat. No random moments of comfortable silence between father and daughter, no spare words of praise. He told me what to do. I did what he said. That was it.

By the end of the summer, I'd realized my father wasn't a talker and probably never would love me.

Good thing I had Juliana instead.

My father remained on the stool. Cigarette done, he'd moved on to the Jack Daniel's, sipping from an ancient-looking plastic cup.

I lowered my safety goggles, lit the torch, and melted Officer Fiske's cellphone into a small, black lump of useless plastic.

Hated to see the thing go — never knew when the ability to make a call might come in handy. But I couldn't trust it. Some phones had GPS, meaning it could be used to track me. Or if I did make a call, they could triangulate the signal. On the other hand, I couldn't risk just tossing it either — if the police recovered it, they would trace my call to Juliana.

Hence, the acetylene torch, which, I have to say, got the job done.

I turned it off. Closed the tanks, rewrapped the hose, and hung up the work gloves and safety goggles.

I tossed the melted cellphone, now cooled, inside my duffel bag to reduce my evidence trail. Police would be here soon enough. When chasing fugitives you always visited all past haunts and known acquaintances, which would include my father.

I straightened and, my first order of business completed, finally faced my dad.

The years were catching up with him. I could see that now. His cheeks were turning into jowls, heavy lines creasing his forehead. He looked defeated. A formerly strong young man, deflated by life and all the dreams that never came true.

I wanted to hate him, but couldn't. This was the pattern of my life: to love men who didn't deserve me, and, knowing that, to yearn for their love anyway.

My father spoke. 'They say you killed your husband.' He started to cough, and it immediately turned phlegmy.

'So I've heard.'

'And my granddaughter.' He said this accusingly.

That made me smile. 'You have a granddaughter? That's funny, because I don't remember my daughter ever receiving a visit from her grandfather. Or a gift on her birthday, or a stocking stuffer at Christmas. So don't talk to me about grandchildren, old man. You reap what you sow.'

'Hard-ass,' he said.

'I get it from you.'

He slammed down his cup. Amber liquid sloshed. I caught a whiff of whiskey and my mouth watered. Forget a circular argument that would get us nowhere. I could pull up a chair and drink with my father instead. Maybe that's what he'd been waiting for the summer I'd been fourteen. He hadn't needed a child to work for him, he'd needed a daughter to drink with him.

Two alcoholics, side by side in the dim lighting of a run-down garage.

Then we would've both failed our children.

'I'm taking a car,' I said now.

'I'll turn you in.'

'Do what you need to do.'

I turned toward the Peg-Board on the left side of the workbench, dotted with little hooks bearing keys. My father climbed off his stool, standing to his full height before me.

Tough guy, filled with the false bravado of his liquid buddy Jack. My father had never hit me. As I waited for him to start now, I wasn't afraid, just tired. I knew this man, not just as my dad, but as half a dozen jerks I confronted and talked down five nights a week.

'Dad,' I heard myself say softly. 'I'm not a little girl anymore. I'm a trained police officer, and if you want to stop me, you're going to have to do better than this.'

'I didn't raise no baby killer,' he growled.

'No. You didn't.'

His brow furrowed. In his fuzzy state, he was having problems working this out.

'Do you want me to plead my innocence?' I continued. 'I tried that once before. It didn't work.'

'You killed that Howe boy.'

'No.'

'Police said so.'

'Police make mistakes, as much as it pains me to say that.'

'Then why'd you become a cop, if they're no good?'

'Because.' I shrugged. 'I want to serve. And I'm good at my job.'

'Till you killed your husband and little girl.'

'No.'

'Police said so.'

'And round and round we go.'

His brow furrowed again.

'I'm going to take a car,' I repeated. 'I'm going to use it to hunt down the man who has my daughter. You can argue with me, or you can tell me which of these clunkers is most prepared to log a few miles. Oh, and fuel would help. Stopping at a gas station isn't gonna work for me right now.'

'I got a granddaughter,' he said roughly.

'Yes. She's six years old, her name is Sophie and she's counting on me to rescue her. So help me, Dad. Help me save her.'

'She as tough as her mom?'

'God, I hope so.'

'Who took her?'

'First thing I have to figure out.'

'How you gonna do that?'

I smiled, grimly this time. 'Let's just say, the Commonwealth of Massachusetts invested a lot of resources into my training, and they're about to get their money's worth. Vehicle, Dad. I don't have much time, and neither does Sophie.'

He didn't move, just crossed his arms and peered down at me. 'You lying to me?'

I didn't feel like arguing anymore. Instead, I stepped forward, wrapped my arms around his waist, and leaned my head against the bulk of his chest. He smelled of cigarettes, motor oil, and whiskey. He smelled of my childhood, and the home and mother I still missed.

'Love you, Dad. Always have. Always will.'

His frame shook. A slight tremor. I chose to believe that was his way of saying he loved me, too. Mostly because the alternative hurt too much.

I stepped back. He unfolded his arms, crossed to the Peg-Board, and handed me a single key.

'Blue Ford truck, out back. Gotta lotta miles, but its heart's good. Four-wheel drive. You're gonna need that.'

For navigating the snowy road. Perfect.

'Gas cans are against the outside wall. Help yourself.'

'Thank you.'

'Bring her,' he said suddenly. 'When you find her, when you . . . get her back. I want . . . I want to meet my granddaughter.'

'Maybe,' I said.

He startled at my hesitation, glared at me.

I took the key, returning his look calmly.

'From one alcoholic to another — gotta stop drinking, Dad. Then we'll see.'

'Hard-ass,' he muttered.

I smiled one last time, then kissed him on his leathery cheek. 'Get it from you,' I whispered.

I palmed the key, picked up my duffel bag, then I was gone.

35

'Why was the scene in the woods so horrific?' D.D. was saying fifteen minutes later. She answered her own question: 'Because what kind of mom would kill her own child, then blow up the body? What kind of woman could do such a thing?'

Bobby, standing beside her on Juliana Howe's front porch, nodded. 'Diversion. She needed to buy time to escape.'

D.D. shrugged. 'Except not really. She was already alone with Officer Fiske and they were a quarter of a mile away from the search team. She could've easily jumped Fiske without the diversion, and still had a solid thirty minutes head start. Which is why exploding the child's remains seems so horrifying — it's gratuitous. Why do such a terrible thing?'

'Okay, I'll bite: Why do such a thing?'

'Because she needed the bones fragmented. She couldn't afford for us to find the remains *in situ*. Then it would've been obvious the body didn't belong to a child.'

Bobby stared at her. 'Excuse me? The pink bits of clothing, blue jeans, rib bone, tooth . . . '

'Clothing was planted with the body. Rib bone is approximately the right size for a six-year-old — or a large breed of dog. Ben just finished spending some quality time studying bone fragments in the lab. Those bones aren't human.

They're canine. Right size. Wrong species.'

Bobby did a little double-take. 'Fuck me,' he said, a man who hardly ever swore. 'The German shepherd. Brian Darby's old dog that passed away. Tessa buried *that* body?'

'Apparently. Hence the strong scent of decomp in the white Denali. Again, according to Ben, the size and length of many bones in a large dog would match a six-year-old human. Of course, the skull would be all wrong, as well as minor details like tail and paws. An intact canine skeleton, therefore, would never get confused for a human one. Scrambled pieces of bone fragments, however . . . Ben apologizes for his error. He's a bit embarrassed to tell you the truth. It's been a while since he's had a crime scene mess this much with his head.'

'Wait a second.' Bobby held up a cautioning hand. 'The cadaver dogs, remember? They wouldn't hit on nonhuman remains. Their noses and training are better than that.'

D.D. suddenly smiled. 'Fucking clever,' she muttered. 'Isn't that what Juliana said? Tessa Leoni is very clever, gotta give her that.

'Two front teeth,' she filled in for Bobby. 'Also three bloody tampons, recovered from the scene after we left. Ben supplies some of the training materials used by the SAR teams. According to him, dog handlers are fairly creative at finding sources of 'cadaver,' since owning actual dead people is illegal. Turns out, teeth are like bone. So search handlers get teeth from a local dentist's office, and use them to train the dogs. Same with used tampons. Tessa hid a dog body, but scattered the site with 'human cadaver' — her daughter's baby teeth topped with a dash of feminine hygiene.'

'That's disgusting,' Bobby said.

'That's ingenious,' D.D. countered.

'But why?'

D.D. had to think about it. 'Because she knew we'd blame her. That's been her experience, right? She didn't shoot Tommy Howe, but the cops assumed she did. Meaning we were right before — the first experience ten years ago has informed her experience now. Another terrible thing happened in Tessa Leoni's world. Her first instinct is that she will be blamed. Except this time she'll probably be arrested. So she stages an elaborate scheme to get out of jail.'

'But why?' Bobby repeated. 'If she didn't do anything, why not tell us the truth? Why . . . such a complicated ruse? She's a cop now. Shouldn't she have more faith in the system?'

D.D. arched a brow.

He sighed. 'You're right. We're born cynics.'

'But why not talk to us?' D.D. was continuing. 'Let's think about that. We assumed Tessa shot Tommy Howe ten years ago. We were wrong. We assumed she shot her husband, Brian, Saturday morning. Well, maybe we're wrong about that, too. Meaning, someone else did it. That person shot Brian, took Sophie.'

'Why kill the husband, but kidnap the child?' Bobby asked.

'Leverage,' D.D. supplied immediately. 'This does go back to gambling. Brian owed too much. Instead of shaking him down, however — the weak link — they're going after Tessa instead. They shoot Brian to show they mean business, then grab Sophie. Tessa can have her daughter back if she pays up. So Tessa heads to the bank, takes out fifty grand — '

'Clearly not enough,' Bobby commented.

'Exactly. She needs more money, but also has to deal with the fact that her husband's dead, shot by her gun, as ballistics was a match.'

Bobby's eyes widened. 'She was home,' he said suddenly. 'Only way they could've shot Brian with her gun. Tessa was home. Maybe even walked into the situation. Someone's already holding her child. What can she do? Man demands that she turn over her Sig Sauer, then . . . '

'Shoots Brian,' D.D. said softly.

'She's screwed,' Bobby continued quietly. 'She knows she's screwed. Her husband is dead by her service weapon, her child has been kidnapped, and she already has a previous history of shooting to kill. What are the odds of anyone believing her? Even if she said, *Hey, some mobster offed my gambling-addicted husband with my state sidearm, and now I need your help to rescue my kid . . .* '

'I wouldn't buy it,' D.D. said flatly.

'Cops are born cynics,' Bobby repeated.

'So she starts thinking,' D.D. continued. 'Only way to get Sophie back is to get the money, and only way to get the money is to stay out of jail.'

'Meaning, she needs to start planning ahead,' Bobby filled in.

D.D. frowned. 'So, based on the Tommy

shooting, option A is to plead self-defense. That can be tricky, however, as spousal abuse is an affirmative defense, so she decides she needs a safety net, as well. Option A will be self-defense, and option B will be to hide dog bones in the woods, which she'll claim are her daughter's remains. If self-defense doesn't work and she ends up arrested, then she can escape utilizing plan B.'

'Clever,' Bobby commented. 'As Juliana said, self-sufficient.'

'Complicated.' D.D. was scowling. 'Especially given that she's now on the run, making it that much harder for her to get money and rescue Sophie. Would you risk that much when it's your daughter's life at stake? Wouldn't it still be cleaner to fall on her sword and beg for our help? Get us tracking mobsters, get us to rescue Sophie, even if we arrest her first?'

Bobby shrugged. 'Maybe, like Juliana, she's not impressed by other cops.'

But D.D. suddenly had another thought. 'Maybe,' she said slowly, 'because another cop is part of the problem.'

Bobby stared at her, then she could see him connect the dots.

'Who beat her up?' D.D. asked now. 'Who hit her so hard that for the first twenty hours she couldn't even stand? Who was present the entire time we were at her house on Sunday morning, his hand on her shoulder? I thought he was showing his support. But maybe, he was reminding her to shut up.'

'Trooper Lyons.'

'The helpful 'friend' who fractured her cheekbone, and got her husband hooked on gambling in the first place. Maybe because Lyons was already spending a lot of quality time at Foxwoods.'

'Trooper Lyons isn't part of the solution,' Bobby muttered. 'Trooper Lyons is the heart of the problem.'

'Let's get him!' D.D. said.

She was already taking the first step off the front porch when Bobby grabbed her arm, drawing her up short.

'D.D., you know what this means?'

'I finally get to break Trooper Lyons?'

'No, D.D. Sophie Leoni. She could still be alive. And Trooper Lyons knows where she's at.'

D.D. stilled. She felt a flare of emotion. 'Then listen to me, Bobby. We need to do this right, and I have a plan.'

36

The old Ford didn't like to shift or brake. Thankfully, given the winter storm alert and the late hour, the roads were mostly empty. I passed several snowplows, a couple of emergency vehicles, and various police cruisers tending to business. I kept my eyes forward and the speedometer at the exact speed limit. Dressed in black, baseball cap pulled low over my brow, I still felt conspicuous heading back into Boston, toward my home.

I drove slowly by my house. Watched my headlights flash across the yellow crime-scene tape, which stood out garishly against the clean white snow.

The house looked and felt empty. A walking advertisement for Something Bad Happened Here.

I kept going until I found parking in an empty convenience store parking lot.

Shouldering my bag, I set out the rest of the way on foot.

Moving quickly now. Wanting the cover of darkness and finding little in a busy city liberally sprinkled with streetlights and brightly lit signs. One block right, one block left, then I was honing in on target.

Shane's police cruiser was parked outside his house. It was five till eleven, meaning he'd be appearing any time for duty.

I took up position, crouched low behind the

trunk, where I could blend into the shadow cast by the Crown Vic in the pool of streetlight.

My hands were cold, even with gloves. I blew on my fingers to keep them warm; I couldn't afford for them to be sluggish. I was going to get only one shot at this. I would either win, or I wouldn't.

My heart pounded. I felt a little dizzy and it suddenly occurred to me I hadn't eaten in at least twelve hours. Too late now. Front door opened. Patio light came on. Shane appeared.

His wife, Tina, stood behind him in a fluffy pink bathrobe. Quick kiss to the cheek, sending her man off for duty. I felt a pang. I squashed it.

Shane came down the first step, then the second. Door closed behind him, Tina not waiting for the full departure.

I released the breath I didn't realize I'd been holding and started the countdown in my head.

Shane descended all the steps, crossing the driveway, keys jingling in his hand. Arriving at his cruiser, inserting the key in the lock, twisting, popping open the driver-side door.

I sprung out from behind the cruiser and rammed my Glock .40 into the side of his neck.

'One word and you're dead.'

Shane remained silent.

I took his duty weapon. Then we both climbed into his police cruiser.

★ ★ ★

I made him sit in the back, away from the radio and the instrument panel. I took the driver's

389

seat, the sliding security panel open between us. I kept the Glock on this side of the bulletproof barrier, away from Shane's lunging reach, while pointing squarely on target. Normally, officers aimed for the subject's chest — the largest mass. Given that Shane was already wearing body armor, I trained on the solid block of his head.

At my command, he passed me his cellphone, his duty belt, then his pager. I piled it all in the passenger's seat, helping myself to the metal bracelets, which I then passed back and had him place around his own wrists.

Subject secured, I pulled my gaze from him long enough to start the car engine. I could feel his body tense, preparing for some kind of action.

'Don't be stupid,' I said crisply. 'I owe you, remember?' I gestured to my battered face. He sagged again, cuffed hands flopping back down onto his lap.

Car engine roared to life. If Shane's wife happened to glance out the window, she would see her husband warming up his cruiser while checking in with dispatch, maybe tending to a few messages.

A five- to ten-minute delay wouldn't be too unusual. Anything more than that, she might grow concerned, might even come out to investigate. Meaning. I didn't have much time for this conversation.

Still had to get a few digs in.

'Shoulda hit me harder,' I said, turning back around, giving my former fellow officer my full attention. 'Did you really think a concussion would be enough to keep me down?'

Shane didn't say anything. His eyes were on the Glock, not my bruised face.

I felt myself growing angry. Like I wanted to crawl through the narrow opening in the security shield and pistol-whip this man half a dozen times, before beating him senseless with my bare hands.

I had trusted Shane, a fellow officer. Brian had trusted him, a best friend. And he had betrayed us both.

I'd called him Saturday afternoon, after paying off the hit man. My last hope in a rapidly disintegrating world, I'd thought. Of course I'd been told not to contact the police. Of course I'd been told to keep quiet *or else*. But Shane wasn't just a fellow officer. He was my friend, he was Brian's closest friend. He'd help me save Sophie.

Instead, his voice cold, totally devoid of emotion on the other end of the phone: 'You don't take instruction too well, do you, Tessa? When these boys tell you to shut up, you *shut up*. Now stop trying to get us all killed, and do what they told you to do.'

Turned out, Shane already knew Brian was dead. He'd received some instructions of his own over the matter, and now he spelled it all out for me: Brian was a wife beater. In the heat of the moment, he'd gone too far and I'd discharged my weapon in self-defense. No evidence of physical assault? Don't worry, Shane would assist with that. I babbled that I'd been granted twenty-four hours to prepare for Sophie's return. Fine, he'd said curtly. He'd be over first thing in

391

the morning. A minor pummeling, then we'd contact the authorities together, Shane by my side every step of the way. Shane, keeping watch and reporting back.

Of course, I'd realized then. Shane wasn't just Brian's friend, he was his partner in crime. And now he had to protect his own hide at any cost. Even if that involved sacrificing Brian, me, and Sophie.

I was screwed and my daughter's life hung in the balance. It's amazing how clear-eyed you can suddenly become when your child needs you. How covering your husband's dead body with snow makes all the sense in the world. As well as fetching Duke's corpse from underneath the back deck, where Brian had stored the body while waiting for the spring thaw. And looking up bombs on the Internet . . .

I let go of my denial. I embraced the chaos. And I learned that I was a much more ruthless person than I'd ever believed.

'I know about the money,' I told Shane now. Despite my best intentions for calm, I could feel my rage bubble up again. I remembered the first eye-shattering impact of Shane's fist connecting with my face. The way he'd towered above me as I went down on the bloody kitchen floor. The endless minute, when I'd realized he could kill me, and then there would be no one to save Sophie. I'd cried. I'd begged. That's what my 'friend' had done to me.

Now Shane's gaze flickered to mine, his eyes rounding in surprise.

'Did you think I'd never connect the dots?' I

said. 'Why did you demand this whole farce that I claim to have killed my own husband? Because you and your partners wanted me out of the way. You wanted to destroy my credibility, then frame me for the theft. Your mobster friends aren't interested in shaking me down for money. You're using me to cover your tracks, letting me take the fall for all the money *you* stole from the troopers' union. You were gonna blame me for everything. *Everything!*'

He didn't say a word.

'You goddamn bastard!' I exploded. 'If I went to prison, what would happen to Sophie? You signed her death warrant, you prick. You basically killed my daughter!'

Shane blanched. 'I didn't . . . I wouldn't. It never would've gone that far!'

'*That far?* You *stole* from the troopers' union. You screwed your friends, your career, and your family. That wasn't letting things go too far?'

'It was Brian's idea,' Shane said automatically. 'He needed the money. He'd lost a little too much . . . They'd kill him, he said. I was just trying to help. Honest, Tessa. You know how Brian can be. I was just trying to help.'

In response, I grabbed his duty belt with my left hand, unclipped the Taser, and held it up.

'One more lie, and you're gonna dance. Do you understand me, Shane? Stop *lying!*'

He swallowed, tongue darting out nervously to lick the corner of his mouth.

'I don't . . . Ah Christ,' he blurted out suddenly. 'I'm sorry, Tessa. I don't know how it came to this. At first, I'd go with Brian to

Foxwoods to keep *him* under control. Which meant, of course, that sometimes I'd play, too. Then, coupla of times, I won. I mean, I *won*. Five grand, just like that. Bought Tina a new ring. She cried. And it felt . . . great. Wonderful. Like I was Superman. So, of course, I had to play again, except we didn't always win. So then you play more because now you're due. It's your turn. One good hand, that's all you need, one good hand.

'That's what we told ourselves, these past few weeks. One solid afternoon at the tables and it would all turn around. We'd be okay. Couple of hours even. Just the right coupla hours and we would've been fine.'

'You embezzled money from the troopers' union. You sold your soul to mobsters.'

Shane looked at me. 'Gotta have money to make money,' he said simply, as if this were the most logical explanation in the world.

Maybe to a gambler, it was.

'Who did you borrow the money from? Who shot Brian? Who took my daughter?'

Shrug.

'Fuck you, Shane! They have my little girl. You will talk or I will blow off your head!'

'They'll kill me anyway!' he fired back, eyes finally blazing to life. 'You don't mess with these guys. They already sent me pictures — Tina in the grocery store, Tina going to yoga, Tina picking up the boys. I'm sorry about Brian. I'm sorry about Sophie. But I gotta protect my own family. I might be a fuckup, but I'm not a total failure.'

'Shane,' I said crisply. 'You're not getting it yet. I'm going to kill you. Then I'm going to pin the word 'snitch' to your chest. I give Tina and the boys about forty-eight hours to live beyond that. Probably less.'

He blinked. 'You wouldn't . . . '

'Think of how far you'd go for your sons, and know that I would, too.'

Shane exhaled sharply. He stared at me, and I could tell in his gaze he'd finally figured out how this was all going to go down. Maybe, like me, he'd spent the last few days figuring out there really were multiple layers of Hell, and no matter how deep you'd thought you'd fallen, there was still someplace deeper and darker to go.

'If I give you a name,' he said abruptly, 'you gotta kill him. Tonight. Swear to me, Tessa. You'll get him, before he gets my family.'

'Done.'

'I love them,' Shane whispered. 'I'm a fuckup, but I love my family. I just want them to be okay.'

My turn not to talk.

'I'm sorry about Brian, Tessa. Really, didn't think they'd do that. Didn't think they'd harm him. Or go after Sophie. I never shoulda gambled. Never shoulda picked up one fucking card.'

'The name, Shane. Who killed Brian? Who took my daughter?'

He studied my battered face, finally seemed to wince. Then he nodded, sat up a little straighter, squared his shoulders. Once, Shane had been a good cop. Once, he'd been a good friend. Maybe he was trying to find that person again.

'John Stephen Purcell,' he told me. 'An enforcer. A guy who works for guys. Find Purcell, and he'll have Sophie. Or at least know where she is.'

'His address?'

Slight hesitation. 'Take off the cuffs and I'll get it.'

His pause was enough warning for me. I shook my head. 'You never should've harmed my daughter,' I said softly, bringing up the Glock.

'Tessa, come on. I told you what you needed to know.' He rattled his cuffed wrists. 'Jesus Christ, this is crazy. Let me go. I'll help you get your daughter back. We'll find Purcell together. Come on . . . '

I smiled, but it was sad. Shane made it all sound so easy. Of course, he could've made that offer on Saturday. Instead, he'd informed me to sit down, shut up, and oh yeah, he'd be by in the morning for my beating.

Good Brian. Bad Brian.

Good Shane. Bad Shane.

Good Tessa. Bad Tessa.

Maybe for all of us, that line between good and bad is thinner than it ought to be. And maybe for all of us, once that line's been crossed, there's no going back. You were who you were, and now you are who you are.

'Shane,' I murmured. 'Think of your sons.'

He appeared confused, then I saw him connect the dots. Such as cops who died in the line of duty received death benefits for their families, while cops who went to jail for embezzling funds and engaging in criminal activities didn't.

As Shane had said, he was a fuckup, but not a total failure.

Good Shane thought of his three sons. And I could tell when he reached the logical conclusion, because his shoulders came down. His face relaxed.

Shane Lyons looked at me one last time.

'Sorry,' he whispered.

'Me, too,' I said.

Then, I pulled the trigger.

* * *

Afterward, I drove the cruiser out of the driveway and onto the street, eventually pulling in behind a darkened warehouse, the kind of place a cop might go if he spotted suspicious activity. I climbed into the back, ignoring the stench of blood, the way Shane's body still felt warm and pliable.

I dug through his pockets, then his duty belt. I discovered a scrap of paper with digits that resembled GPS coordinates tucked beside his cellphone. I used the computer in the front seat to look up the coordinates, then wrote down the corresponding address and directions.

I returned to the backseat, uncuffing Shane's hands, then placing his duty belt back around him. I'd done him a favor, shooting him with Brian's Glock. I could've used his own Sig Sauer, raising the possibility that his death was suicide. In which case, Tina and the boys would've received nothing.

I'm not that hard yet, I thought. Not that stone cold.

My cheeks felt funny. My face curiously numb.

I kept myself focused on the business at hand. The night was young yet, and I had plenty of work to do.

I moved around the cruiser and popped the trunk. State troopers believed in being prepared and Shane did not disappoint. A case of water, half a dozen protein bars, and even some MREs lined one side. I dumped the food in my duffel bag, half a protein bar already stuffed into my mouth, then used Shane's keys to open the long metal gun locker.

Shane stocked a Remington shotgun, M4 rifle, half a dozen boxes of ammo, and a KA-BAR knife.

I took it all.

37

Bobby and D.D. were halfway to Trooper Lyons's house when they heard the call — *Officer down, officer down, all officers respond* . . .

Dispatch rattled off an address. D.D. plugged it into her computer. She paled as the local map appeared on the screen in front of her.

'That's right by Tessa's house,' she murmured.

'And Trooper Lyons's,' Bobby said.

They stared at each other.

'Shit.'

Bobby hit the lights, floored the gas. They sped toward the address in utter silence.

* * *

By the time they arrived, ambulances and police cruisers had already bottlenecked the scene. Lots of officers milling about, no one really doing anything. Which meant only one thing.

Bobby and D.D. climbed out of the car. The first officer they came to was a state trooper, so Bobby did the honors.

'Situation?' he asked.

'Trooper Shane Lyons, sir. Single GSW to the head.' The young trooper swallowed hard. 'Deceased, sir. Declared at the scene. Nothing the EMTs could do.'

Bobby nodded, glancing in D.D.'s direction.

'Was he on a call?' she asked.

'Negative. Hadn't reported in yet to the duty desk. Detective Parker' — the kid gestured to a man dressed in a gray heavy wool coat and standing inside the crime-scene tape — 'is leading the investigation. Might want to talk to him, sir, ma'am.'

They nodded, thanked the kid, and moved forward.

Bobby knew Al Parker. He and D.D. flashed their creds for the uniformed officer handling the murder log, then they ducked under the yellow tape and approached the lead detective.

Parker, a thin, gangly man, straightened at their arrival. He shook Bobby's hand with his leather gloves still on, then Bobby introduced D.D.

The snow was finally slowing down. A couple of inches remained on the pavement, revealing a churn of footprints as officers and EMTs had rushed to assist. Only one set of tire tracks, though. That was D.D.'s first thought. Another vehicle would've left some kind of imprint behind, but she didn't see anything.

She related this to Detective Parker, who nodded.

'Appears Trooper Lyons drove behind the building,' he said. 'Not officially on duty yet. Nor did he notify dispatch that he was responding to signs of suspicious activity . . . '

Detective Parker let that statement explain itself.

Officers on duty always called in. It was imprinted into their DNA. If you grabbed coffee, peed, or spied a burglary in progress, you called it in. Meaning whatever had brought Trooper Lyons to this remote destination hadn't been professional, but personal.

'Single GSW,' Detective Parker continued. 'Left temple. Shot fired from the front seat. Trooper Lyons was in the back.'

D.D. startled. Bobby, as well.

Seeing their looks, Detective Parker waved them over to the cruiser, which sat with all four doors open. He started with the bloodstain in the backseat, then worked backwards for the trajectory of the shot.

'He was wearing his duty belt?' Bobby asked with a frown.

Parker nodded. 'Yes, but there are marks on his wrists consistent with restraints. Bracelets were no longer present when the first officer arrived, but at some point this evening, Trooper Lyon's hands were cuffed.'

D.D. didn't like that image — a bound officer, sitting in the back of his cruiser, staring down the barrel of a gun. She hunkered deeper inside her winter coat, feeling cold snowflakes whisper across her eyelashes.

'His weapon?' she asked.

'Sig Sauer is in his holster. But check this out.'

Parker led them around to the rear of the cruiser, where he popped the trunk. It was empty. D.D. instantly understood the significance. No cop, uniformed or otherwise, had an empty trunk. There should be some basic supplies, not to mention at least a rifle or shotgun or both.

She glanced at Bobby for confirmation. 'Remington shotgun and M4 rifle are standard issue,' he muttered, nodding. 'Somebody was looking for weapons.'

Parker studied both of them, but neither she nor Bobby said another word. It went without saying between them who that somebody was, a person who knew Trooper Lyons, could lure him out to his cruiser, and desperately needed fire power.

'Trooper Lyons's family?' Bobby asked now.

'Colonel went over to notify.'

'Shit,' Bobby murmured.

'Three boys. Shit,' Parker agreed.

D.D.'s cellphone rang. She didn't recognize the number, but it was local, so she excused herself to answer.

A minute later, she returned to Bobby and Parker.

'Gotta go,' she said, tapping Bobby lightly on the arm.

He didn't ask, not in front of the other detective. He simply shook Parker's hand, thanked him for his time, then they were off.

'Who?' Bobby asked, once they were out of hearing.

'Believe it or not, Shane's widow. She has something for us.'

Bobby arched a brow.

'Envelope,' D.D. clarified. 'Apparently, Shane handed it to her Sunday evening. Said if anything happened to him, she was to call me, and only me, and hand it over. Colonel has just left. The widow is now complying with her husband's final wishes.'

★ ★ ★

Every light blazed in Shane Lyons's house. Half a dozen cars crowded the street, including two parked illegally on the front yard. Family, D.D. guessed. Wives of other troopers. The support system, kicking into gear.

She wondered if Shane's boys had woken up yet. She wondered if their mother had already broken the news that their father would never again be coming home.

She and Bobby stood shoulder to shoulder at the front door, faces carefully schooled, because that's how these things worked. They mourned the passing of any law enforcement officer, felt the pain of the officer's family, and tended to duty anyway. Trooper Shane Lyons was a victim who was also a suspect. Nothing easy about this kind of case or this kind of investigation.

An older woman came to the door first. Judging by age and facial features, D.D. pegged her to be Tina Lyons's mom. D.D. flashed her credentials; Bobby, too.

The older woman appeared confused. 'Surely you don't have questions for Tina right now,' she said softly. 'At least give my daughter a day or two — '

'She called us, ma'am,' D.D. said.

'What?'

'We're here because she asked us to come,' D.D. reiterated. 'If you could just let her know Sergeant Detective D.D. Warren is here, we don't mind waiting outside.'

Actually, she and Bobby preferred outside.

403

Whatever Tina had for them was the kind of thing best not shown in front of witnesses.

Minutes passed. Just when D.D. was beginning to think that Tina had changed her mind, the woman appeared. Her face was haggard, her eyes red-rimmed from weeping. She wore a fluffy pink bathrobe, the top clutched closed with one hand. In the other, she held a plain white catalog-sized envelope.

'Do you know who killed my husband?' she asked.

'No, ma'am.'

Tina Lyons thrust the envelope toward D.D. 'That's all I want to know. I mean it. That's *all* I want to know. Find that out, and we'll speak again.'

She retreated back to the tenuous comfort of her family and friends, leaving D.D. and Bobby on the front stoop.

'She knows something,' Bobby said.

'She suspects,' D.D. corrected quietly. 'She doesn't want to know. I believe that was the whole point of her statement.'

D.D. clutched the envelope with gloved hands. She looked around the snowy driveway. After midnight in a quiet residential area, the sidewalk studded with streetlights, and yet pools of darkness loomed everywhere.

She felt suddenly conspicuous and overexposed.

'Let's go,' she muttered to Bobby.

They moved carefully down the street toward their parked car. D.D. carried the envelope in her gloved hands. Bobby carried his gun.

404

Ten minutes later, they'd conducted basic evasive maneuvers around a maze of Allston-Brighton streets. Bobby was content no one had followed them. D.D. was dying to know the contents of the envelope.

They found a convenience store buzzing with college students, not deterred by either the weather or the late hour. The cluster of vehicles made their Crown Vic less conspicuous, while the students provided plenty of eyewitnesses to deter ambush.

Satisfied, D.D. exchanged her winter gloves for a latex pair, then worked the flap of the envelope, easing it carefully open in order to preserve evidence.

Inside, she found a dozen five-by-seven color photos. The first eleven appeared to be of Shane Lyons's family. Here was Tina at the grocery store. There was Tina walking into a building holding a yoga mat. Here was Tina picking up the boys from school. There were the boys, playing on the school playground.

It didn't take a rocket scientist to get the message. Someone had been stalking Shane's family and that person wanted him to know about it.

Then D.D. came to the last photo. She sucked in her breath, while beside her, Bobby swore.

Sophie Leoni.

They were staring at Sophie Leoni, or rather, she was staring directly at the camera, clutching a doll with one mangled blue button eye.

Sophie's lips were pressed together, the way a child might do when trying hard not to cry. But she had her chin up. Her blue gaze seemed to be trying for defiance, though there were streaks of dirt and tears on her cheeks and her pretty brown hair now looked like a rat's nest.

The photo was cropped close, providing only the hint of wood paneling in the background. Maybe a closet or other small room. A windowless dark room, D.D. thought. That's where someone would imprison a child.

Her hand started to tremble.

D.D. flipped over the photo, looking for other clues.

She found a message scrawled in black marker: *Don't Let This Be Your Kid, Too.*

D.D. flipped the photo back over, took one more look at Sophie's heart-shaped face, and her hands now shook so badly she had to set the photo on her lap.

'Someone really did kidnap her. Someone really did . . . ' Then her next jumbled thought. 'And it's been more than three fucking days! What are our odds of finding her after *three fucking days!*'

She whacked the dash. The blow stung her hand and didn't do a thing to dampen her rage.

She whirled on her partner. 'What the fuck is going on here, Bobby? Who the fuck kidnaps one police officer's child, while threatening the family of a second officer? I mean, *who the hell does that?*'

Bobby didn't answer right away. His hands were clutching the steering wheel, and all his knuckles had turned white.

'What did Tina say when she called?' he demanded suddenly. 'What were Shane's instructions to her?'

'If something happened to him, she was to give this envelope to me.'

'Why you, D.D.? With all due respect, you're a Boston cop. If Shane needed help, wouldn't he turn to his own friends in uniform, his supposed brothers in blue?'

D.D. stared at him. She remembered the first day of the case, the way the state police had closed ranks, even against her, a city cop. Then her eyes widened.

'You don't think . . . ' she began.

'Not that many criminals have the cajones to threaten one, let alone two, state troopers. But another cop would.'

'Why?'

'How much is missing from the troopers' union?'

'Quarter mil.'

Bobby nodded.

'In other words, two hundred and fifty thousand reasons to betray the uniform. Two hundred and fifty thousand reasons to kill Brian Darby, kidnap Sophie Leoni, and threaten Shane Lyons.'

D.D. considered it. 'Tessa Leoni shot Trooper Lyons. He betrayed the uniform, but even worse he betrayed her family. Now the question is, did she get from Lyons the information she was after?'

'Name and address of the person who has her

daughter,' Bobby filled in.

'Lyons was a minion. Maybe Brian Darby, too. They pilfered the troopers' union to fund their gambling habit. But somebody else helped them — the person calling the shots.'

Bobby glanced at Sophie's photo, seemed to be formulating his thoughts. 'If it was Tessa Leoni who shot Trooper Lyons, and she's made it this far, that means she must have a vehicle.'

'Not to mention a small arsenal of weapons.'

'So maybe she did get a name and address,' Bobby added.

'She's going after her daughter.'

Bobby finally smiled. 'Then for the criminal mastermind's sake, the bastard better hope that we find him first.'

38

Some things are best not to think about. So I didn't. I drove. Mass Pike to 128, 128 southbound to Dedham. Eight more miles, half a dozen turns, I was in a heavily wooded residential area. Older homes, larger properties. The kind of place where people had trampolines in the front yard and laundry lines in the back.

Good place to hold a kid, I thought, then stopped thinking again.

I missed the address the first time. Didn't see the numbers in the falling snow. When I realized I'd gone too far, I hit the brakes, and the old truck fishtailed. I turned into the spin, a secondhand reflex that calmed my nerves and returned my composure.

Training. That's what this came down to.

Thugs didn't train.

But I did.

I parked my truck next to the road. In plain sight, but I needed it accessible for a quick getaway. I had Brian's Glock .40 tucked in the back waistband of my pants. The KA-BAR knife came with a lower leg sheath. I strapped it on.

Then I loaded the shotgun. If you're young, female, and not terribly large, shotgun is always the way to go. You could take down a water buffalo without even having to aim.

Checking my black gloves, tugging down my black cap. Feeling the cold, but as something abstract and far away. Mostly, I could hear a rushing sound in my ears, my own blood, I supposed, powered through my veins by a flood of adrenaline.

No flashlight. I let my eyes adjust to the kind of dark that exists only on rural roads, then I darted through the woods.

Moving felt good. After the first twenty-four hours, confined to a hospital bed, followed by another twenty-four hours stuck in jail, to finally be out, moving, getting the job done, felt right.

Somewhere ahead was my daughter. I was going to save her. I was going to kill the man who had taken her. Then we were both going home.

Unless, of course . . .

I stopped thinking again.

The woods thinned. I burst onto a snowy yard and drew up sharply, eyeing the flat, sprawling ranch that appeared in front of me. All windows were dark, not a single light glowing in welcome. It was well after midnight by now. The kind of hour when honest people were asleep.

Then again, my subject didn't make an honest living, did he?

Motion-activated outdoor lights, I guessed after another second. Floodlights that would most likely flare to life the second I approached. Probably some kind of security system on the doors and windows. At least basic defensive measures.

It's like that old adage — liars expect others to lie. Enforcers who kill expect to be killed and plan appropriately.

Getting inside the house undetected probably was not an option.

Fine, I would draw him out instead.

I started with the vehicle I found parked in the driveway. A black Cadillac Esplanade with all the bells and whistles. But of course. It gave me a great deal of satisfaction to drive the butt of the shotgun through the driver's-side window.

Car alarm whistled shrilly. I darted from the SUV to the side of the house. Floodlights blazed to life, casting the front and side yard into blinding white relief. I tucked my back against the side of the house facing the Cadillac, edging as close as I could toward the rear of the home, where I guessed Purcell would ultimately emerge. I held my breath.

An enforcer such as Purcell would be too smart to dash out into the snow in his underwear. But he would be too arrogant to let someone get away with stealing his wheels. He would come. Armed. And, he probably thought, prepared.

It took a full minute. Then I heard a low creak of a back screen door, easing open.

I held the shotgun loosely, cradled in the crook of my left arm. With my right hand, I slowly withdrew the KA-BAR knife.

Never done wet work. Never been up this close and personal.

I stopped thinking again.

My hearing had already acclimated to the shrill car alarm. That made it easier for me to pick up other noises: the faint crunch of snow as the subject took his first step, then another. I took one second to check behind me, in case there were two of them in the house, one creeping from the front, one stalking from the back, to circle around.

I heard only one set of footsteps, and made them my target.

Forcing myself to inhale through my nose, take the air deep into my lungs. Slowing my own heartbeat. What would happen would happen. Time to let go.

I crouched, knife at the ready.

A leg appeared. I saw black snow boots, thick jeans, the red tail of a flannel shirt.

I saw a gun held low against the man's thigh.

'John Stephen Purcell?' I whispered.

A startled face turning toward me, dark eyes widening, mouth opening.

I stared up at the man who'd killed my husband and kidnapped my child.

I slashed out with the knife.

Just as he opened fire.

★ ★ ★

Never bring a knife to a gunfight.

Not necessarily. Purcell hit my right shoulder. On the other hand, I severed the hamstring on his left leg. He went down, firing a second time, into the snow. I kicked the gun out of his hand, leveled the shotgun, and except for thrashing wildly in pain, he made no move against me.

Up close and personal, Purcell appeared to be mid-forties to early fifties. An experienced enforcer, then. Kind of guy with some notches on his brass knuckles. He obviously took some pride in his position, because even as his jeans darkened with a river of blood, he set his lips in a hard line and didn't say a word.

'Remember me?' I said.

After a moment, he nodded.

'Spend the money yet?'

He shook his head.

'Shame, because that was the last shopping trip you had left. I want my daughter.'

He didn't say a word.

So I placed the end of the shotgun against his right kneecap — the leg I hadn't incapacitated. 'Say goodbye to your leg,' I told him.

His eyes widened. His nostrils flared. Like a lot of tough guys, Purcell was better at dishing it out than taking it.

'Don't have her,' he rasped out suddenly. 'Not here.'

'Let's see about that.'

I ordered him to roll over on his stomach, hands behind his back. I had a pocketful of zip ties from Shane's supplies. I did Purcell's wrists first, then his ankles, though moving his injured left leg made him moan in pain.

I should feel something, I thought idly. Triumph, remorse, something. I felt nothing at all.

Best not to think about it.

Purcell was injured and restrained. Still, never underestimate the enemy. I patted down his pockets, discovering a pocketknife, a pager, and a dozen loose cartridges he'd stuck in his pants for emergency reloading. I removed all items and stuck them in my pockets instead.

Then, ignoring his grimace, I used my left arm to drag him several feet through the snow to the back stoop of his house, where I used a fresh zip tie to bind his arms to an outside faucet. With enough time and effort, he might be able to free himself, even break off the metal faucet, but I wasn't planning on leaving him that long. Besides, with his arms and legs bound and his hamstring severed, he wasn't making it that far, that fast.

My shoulder burned. I could feel blood pouring down my arm, inside my shirt. It was an uncomfortable sensation, like getting water down your sleeve. I had a vague impression that I wasn't giving my injury proper significance. That probably, I hurt a great deal. That probably, losing this much blood was worse than a bit of water down a sleeve.

I felt curiously flat. Beyond emotion and the inconvenience of physical pain.

Best not to think about it.

I entered the house cautiously, knife returned to its sheath, leading with the shotgun. I had to cradle the barrel against my left forearm. Given my condition, my aim would be questionable. Then again, it was a shotgun.

Purcell hadn't turned on any lights. Made sense, actually. When preparing to dash out into the dark, turning on interior lights would only ruin your night vision.

I entered a heavily shadowed kitchen that smelled of garlic, basil, and olive oil. Apparently, Purcell liked to cook. From the kitchen, I passed into a family room bearing two hulking recliners and a giant TV. From that room, into a smaller den with a desk and lots of shelves. A small bathroom. Then, a long hallway that led to three open doorways.

I forced myself to breathe, walking as stealthily as possible toward the first doorway. I was just easing the door open wider when my pants began to chime. I ducked in immediately, sweeping the room with the shotgun, prepared to open fire on any lunging shapes, then flattening my back against the wall and bracing for the counterattack.

No shadows attacked. I dug my right hand frantically into my pocket and pulled out Purcell's pager, fumbling for the Off button.

At the last second, I glanced at the screen. It read: *Lyons DOA. BOLO Leoni.*

Shane Lyons was dead. Be on the lookout for Tessa Leoni.

'Too little, too late,' I murmured. I jammed the pager back in my pocket and finished clearing the house.

Nothing. Nothing, nothing, nothing.

By all appearances, Purcell lived a bachelor life with a big screen TV, an extra bedroom, and a den. Then I saw the door to the basement.

Heart spiking again. Feeling the world tilt dizzily as I took the first step toward the closed door.

Blood loss. Getting weak. Should stop, tend the wound.

My hand on the knob, turning.

Sophie. All these days, all these miles.

I pulled open the door, stared down into the gloom.

39

By the time D.D. and Bobby arrived at Tessa Leoni's father's garage, they found the back door open, and the man in question slumped over a scarred workbench. D.D. and Bobby burst into the space, D.D. making a beeline for Mr. Leoni, while Bobby provided cover.

D.D. raised Leoni's face, inspecting him frantically for signs of injury, then recoiled from the stench of whiskey.

'Holy crap!' She let his head collapse back against his chest. His whole body slid left, off the stool, and would've hit the floor if Bobby hadn't appeared in time to catch him. Bobby eased the big man down, then rolled Leoni onto his side, to reduce the odds of the drunk drowning in his own vomit.

'Take his car keys,' D.D. muttered in disgust. 'We'll ask a patrol officer to come over and make sure he gets home safely.'

Bobby was already going through Leoni's pockets. He found a wallet, but no keys. Then D.D. spied the Peg-Board with its collection of brass.

'Customers' keys?' she mused out loud.

Bobby came over to investigate. 'Saw a bunch of old clunkers parked in the back,' he murmured. 'Bet he restores them for resell.'

'Meaning, if Tessa wanted quick access to a vehicle . . . '

'Resourceful,' Bobby commented.

D.D. looked down at Tessa's passed-out father, shook her head again. 'He could've at least put up a fight, for God's sake.'

'Maybe she brought him the Jack,' Bobby said with a shrug, pointing to the empty bottle. He was an alcoholic; he knew these things.

'So she definitely has a vehicle. Description would be nice, but somehow I don't think Papa Leoni's talking anytime soon.'

'Assuming this isn't a chop shop, Leoni should have papers on everything. Let's check it out.'

Bobby gestured to the open door of a small back office. Inside, they found a tiny desk and a battered gray filing cabinet. In the back of the top file was a manila folder marked 'Title Work.'

D.D. pulled it and together they walked out of the garage, leaving the snoring drunk behind them. They identified three vehicles sequestered behind a chain link fence. The file held titles for four. By process of elimination, they determined that a 1993 dark blue Ford pickup truck was missing. Title listed it as having over two hundred thousand and eight miles.

'An oldie but a goodie,' Bobby remarked, as D.D. got on the radio and called it in.

'License plate?' D.D. asked.

Bobby shook his head. 'None of them have any.'

D.D. looked at him. 'Check the front street,' she said.

He got what she meant, and jogged a quick tour around the block. Sure enough, half a block down, on the other side of the street, a car was missing both plates. Tessa had obviously pilfered from it to outfit her own ride.

Resourceful, he thought again, but also sloppy. She was racing against the clock, meaning she'd grabbed the nearest plates, instead of burning time with the safer option of snatching plates from a vehicle blocks away.

Meaning she was starting to leave a trail and they could use it to find her.

Bobby should feel good about that, but he felt mostly tired. He couldn't stop thinking what it must've been like, returning home from duty, walking through the front door, to discover a man holding her daughter hostage. *Give us your gun, no one will get hurt.*

Then the same man, shooting Brian Darby three times before disappearing with Tessa's little girl.

If Bobby had ever walked through the door, found someone with a gun at Annabelle's head, threatening his wife and child . . .

Tessa must've felt half-crazed with desperation and fear. She would've agreed to anything they wanted, while maintaining a cop's inherent mistrust. Knowing her cooperation would never be enough, of course they'd betray her first chance they got.

So she desperately needed to get one step ahead. Cover up her own husband's death to buy time. Plant a corpse with baby teeth and homemade explosives as a macabre backup plan.

Shane had originally stated Tessa had called him Sunday morning and requested that he beat her up. Except now they knew Shane had most

418

likely been part of the problem. Made sense — a friend 'helping' another friend would just smack her around a little, not deliver a concussion requiring an overnight hospital stay.

Meaning it had been Shane's idea to beat Tessa. How would that play out? *Let's drag your husband's dead body up from the garage to defrost. Then, I'm going to pound the shit out of you for kicks and giggles. Then, you'll call the police and claim you shot your dirtbag husband because he was going to kill you?*

They'd known she'd get arrested. Shane, at the very least, should've figured out how thin her story would sound, especially with Sophie missing and Brian's body having been artificially maintained on ice.

They'd wanted her arrested. They'd needed her behind bars.

It all came down to the money, Bobby thought again. Quarter mil missing from the troopers' union. Who'd stolen it? Shane Lyons? Someone higher in the food chain?

Someone smart enough to realize that sooner or later they'd have to supply a suspect before internal affairs grew too close.

Someone who realized that another discredited officer, a female, as seen on the bank security cameras — say, Tessa Leoni — would make the perfect sacrificial lamb. Plus, her husband had a known gambling problem, making her an even better candidate.

Brian died because his out-of-control habit made him a threat to everyone. And Tessa was packaged up with a bow and handed over to the powers that be as their own get-out-of-jail-free card. We'll say she stole the money, her husband gambled it away, and all will be accounted for. Investigation will be closed and we can ride off into the sunset, two hundred and fifty thousand dollars richer and no one the wiser.

Brian dead, Tessa behind bars, and Sophie . . .

Bobby wasn't ready to think about that. Sophie was a liability. Maybe kept alive in the short term, in case Tessa didn't go along with the plan. But in the long term . . .

Tessa was right to be on the warpath. She'd already lost one day to planning, one day to hospitalization, and one day to incarceration. Meaning this was it. She was running out of time. In the next few hours, she'd find her daughter, or die trying.

A lone trooper, going up against mobsters who thought nothing of breaking into police officers' homes and shooting their spouses.

Who would have the balls to do such a thing? And the access?

Russian mafia had sunk huge tentacles into the Boston area. They were widely acknowledged to be six times more ruthless than their Italian counterparts, and were swiftly becoming the lead players in all things corrupt, drug-fueled, and money-laundered. But a quarter mil defrauded from the state troopers' union sounded too small time in Bobby's mind.

The Russians preferred high risk, high payoff. Quarter mil was a rounding error in most of their undertakings. Plus, to steal from the state police, to actively summon the wrath of a powerful law enforcement agency upon your head . . .

It sounded more personal to Bobby. Mobsters wouldn't seek to embezzle from a troopers' union. They might, however, apply pressure to an insider who then determined that was the best way to produce the necessary funds. An insider with access to the money, but also with the knowledge and foresight to cover his own trail . . .

All of a sudden, Bobby knew. It horrified him. Chilled him to the bone. And made complete sense.

He raised his elbow and drove it through the passenger-side window of the parked car. Window shattered. Car alarm sounded. Bobby ignored both sounds. He reached inside, popped the glove compartment, and helped himself to the vehicle registration info, which included record of the license plate now adorning Tessa Leoni's truck.

Then he trotted back to D.D. and the garage, armed with new information as well as their final target.

40

People were brought down here to die.

I knew that from the smell alone. The deep, rusty scent of blood, so deeply soaked into the concrete floor, no amount of bleach or lime would ever make it go away. Some people had workshops in the basements of their homes. Apparently, John Stephen Purcell had a torture chamber.

I needed overhead light. It would destroy my night vision, but also disorient any gangsters waiting to pounce.

Standing on the top step, my hand on the left-hand wall switch, I hesitated. I didn't know if I wanted light in the basement. I didn't know if I wanted to see.

After hours of blessed numbness, my composure was starting to crack. The smell. My daughter. The smell. Sophie.

They wouldn't torture a little girl. What would they have to gain? What could Sophie possibly tell them?

I closed my eyes. Flipped up the switch. Then, I stood in the deep quiet that falls after midnight, and waited to hear the first whimper of my daughter waiting to be saved, or the rush of an attacker about to ambush.

I heard nothing at all.

I unpeeled my right eye, counted to five, then opened the left. The glare from the bare bulb didn't hurt as much as I'd feared. I kept the shotgun cradled in my arms, and dripping blood from my wounded right shoulder, I started to descend.

Purcell maintained a clutter-free basement. No stored lawn furniture or miscellaneous boxes of junk or bins of Christmas decorations for a man in his line of work.

The open space held a washer, dryer, utility sink, and massive stainless steel table. The table was rimmed with a trough, just like the ones found in morgues. The trough led to a tray at the bottom of the table, where one could attach a hose to drain the contents into the nearby utility sink.

Apparently, when breaking kneecaps and slicing off fingertips, Purcell liked to be tidy. Judging by the large pink blush staining the floor, however, it was impossible to be totally spill-proof about these things.

Next to the stainless steel table was a battered TV tray bearing various instruments, laid out like a doctor's operating station. Each stainless steel piece was freshly cleaned, with an overhead light winking off the freshly sharpened blades.

I bet Purcell spent a lot of time staging his equipment just so. I bet he enjoyed letting his subjects take in the full array of instruments, their terrified minds already leaping ahead and doing half of his work for him. Then he would strap them to the table.

I imagined most of them started babbling before he picked up the first pair of pliers. And I bet talking didn't save them.

I passed the table, the sink, the washer and dryer. Behind the stairs I found a door leading to the utility room. I stood to one side, reaching around with my hand to pop the door open, with my back still pressed to the wall.

No one burst out. No child cried a greeting.

Still jittery from nerves, fatigue, and a low throbbing sense of dread, I crouched down, bringing up the shotgun to shoulder level, then darting into the gloom.

I encountered an oil tank, a water heater, the utility box, and a couple of plastic shelves weighed down with various cleaning products, zip ties, and coiled rope. And a thick coiled hose, perfect for spraying down the last of the mess.

I rose slowly to my feet, then surprised myself by swaying and nearly passing out.

The floor was wet. I looked down, vaguely surprised to see a pool of my own blood. Pouring down my arm now.

Needed help. Should go to the ER. Should . . .

What, call the cavalry?

The bitterness of my thoughts pulled me back together. I left the basement, returning to the gloom upstairs, except this time I snapped on every light in the house.

As I suspected, I found a small battery of first-aid supplies in Purcell's bathroom. Guy in his line of work no doubt expected injuries he couldn't report, and had outfitted his medicine cabinet accordingly.

I couldn't pull my black turtleneck over my head. Instead, I used surgical shears to cut it off. Then, leaning over the sink, I poured the hydrogen peroxide straight into the bloody hole.

I gasped in shocked pain, then bit down hard on my lower lip.

If I were a true tough guy — say, Rambo — I would dig out the bullet with chopsticks, then stitch up the hole with dental floss. I didn't know how to do any of those things, so I shoved white gauze into the wound, then taped the bloody bundle with white strips of medical adhesive.

I washed down three ibuprofen with water, then helped myself to a dark blue flannel shirt from Purcell's closet. The shirt was two sizes too big and smelled of fabric softener and male cologne. The hem fell to midthigh and I had to roll up the cuffs awkwardly to free my hands.

I'd never worn the shirt of a man I was going to kill. It struck me as oddly intimate, like sprawling in bed in your lover's button-up Oxford after the first time you'd had sex.

I have gone too far, I thought, *lost some piece of myself.* I was looking for my daughter, but discovering an abyss I'd never known existed inside of me. Would finding Sophie ease the pain? Would the light of her love chase the darkness back again?

Did it even matter? From the moment she was born, I would've given my life for my child. What's a little sanity instead?

I picked up the shotgun, and retreated outside, where Purcell remained slumped against the house, eyes closed. I thought he'd passed out, but when my feet crunched through the snow, his eyes opened.

His face was pale. Sweat dotted his upper lip,

425

despite the freezing temperature. He'd lost a lot of blood. He was probably dying and seemed to know it, though it didn't appear to surprise him.

Purcell was old school. Live by the sword, die by the sword.

That would make my next job tougher.

I squatted down beside him.

'I could take you down to the basement,' I said.

He shrugged.

'Let you sample a taste of your own medicine.'

He shrugged again.

'You're right: I'll bring the equipment up here. Save me the trouble of lugging your sorry ass around.'

Another shrug. I wished suddenly that Purcell had a wife and kid. What would I do if he did? I didn't know, but I wanted to hurt him as much as he'd hurt me.

I placed the shotgun behind me, out of Purcell's reach. Then I slid out the KA-BAR knife, hefting it lightly in the palm of my left hand.

Purcell's gaze flickered to the blade. Still, he said nothing.

'You're going to die by a woman's hand,' I told him, and finally had the satisfaction of seeing his nostrils flare. Ego. Of course. Nothing hurt a man quite as much as being one-upped by a woman.

'Do you remember what you told me that morning in the kitchen?' I whispered. 'You told me as long as I cooperated no one would get hurt. You told me as long as I handed over my service weapon, you'd let my family go. Then you turned and murdered my husband.'

I ran the knife down the front of his shirt. The blade popped off the first button, the second, the third. Purcell wore a dark T-shirt underneath, topped by the requisite gold chain.

I planted the tip of the knife at the top of the thin cotton fabric and began to tear.

Purcell stared at the blade in rapt fascination. I could see his imagination kicking into gear, starting to realize everything such a large, well-honed blade could do to him. While he sat with his hands tied on his very own property. Helpless. Vulnerable.

'I'm not going to kill you,' I said, slicing down the black T-shirt.

Purcell's eyes widened. He stared at me uncertainly.

'That's what you want, isn't it? Dying in the line of duty. A suitable end to an honorable gangster.'

Last shirt button. Pop. Last inch of T-shirt. Shred.

I used the blade to peel back his shirts. His stomach was unexpectedly pale, a little thicker around the waist, but defined. He trained. Not a big guy. Maybe a boxer. He understood fitness mattered in his line of work. Got to have some muscle to lug unconscious bodies down to the basement and strap them to the table.

Gotta have some size to snatch a struggling six-year-old girl.

The knife eased back his shirts, exposing his left side. I stared at his bare shoulder in

427

fascination. The goose pimples that rippled across his flesh in the cold. The way his nipple formed a round bud right over his heart.

'You shot my husband here,' I murmured, and I used the blade to mark the spot. Blood welled up, forming a perfect red X against Purcell's skin. The razor-sharp blade made for a nice, clean cut. Shane had always taken his equipment seriously.

'Next shot was right here.' I moved the blade again. Maybe I cut deeper this time, because Purcell hissed low, quivering beneath me.

'Third shot, right here.' This time, I definitely went deep. When I raised the KA-BAR knife, the blood welled at the edge of the blade and dripped down onto Purcell's stomach.

Blood in the clean white snow.

Brian dying in the clean bright kitchen.

The mobster was shaking now. I gazed into his face. I let him see the death in my eyes. I let him see the killer he helped make.

'Here's the deal,' I informed him. 'Tell me where my daughter is, and in return, I'll remove your restraints. I'm not giving you a knife or anything that crazy, but you can take a shot at me. Maybe you can overpower me, in which case, my bad. Maybe you can't. In which case, at least you go down swinging instead of dying trussed up like a pig in your own front yard. You have until the count of five to decide. *One*.'

'I don't snitch,' Purcell snarled.

I shrugged, reached up, and mostly because I felt like it, lopped off a giant piece of his thick brown hair. '*Two*.'

428

He flinched, didn't back down. 'Gonna fucking kill me anyway.'

Another section of hair, maybe even a bit of ear. '*Three.*'

'Fucking cunt.'

'Stick and stones may break my bones . . . ' I wadded up a big fistful of dark hair at the top of his forehead. Getting into the spirit of things now, I pulled up hard, so I could see his scalp lift. '*Four.*'

'I don't have your daughter!' Purcell exploded. 'Don't do kids. Told them in the beginning, don't do kids.'

'Then where is she?'

'You're the fucking cop. Don't you think you should know?'

I whacked with the blade. I got a lot of hair and definitely some scalp. Blood bubbled up red. Dripped onto the icy ground, turned pink against the snow.

I wondered if I would ever make it through another winter, where fresh snowfall wouldn't make me want to vomit.

Purcell howled, shuddering against his restraints. 'You trusted all the wrong people. Now you hurt me? I did you a favor! Your husband was no good. Your police officer friend even worse. How'd I even get into your house, you stupid cunt? Think your old man would just let me in?'

I stopped. I stared at him. And I realized, in that instant, the one piece of the puzzle I'd been missing. I'd been so overwhelmed by the trauma of Saturday morning, I'd never contemplated the logistics. I'd never analyzed the scene as a cop.

For example, Brian already knew he was in trouble. His weight lifting, the recent purchase of the Glock .40. His own jumpy mood and short temper. He knew he'd waded in too deep. And yeah, he'd never open the door to a man like John Stephen Purcell, especially with Sophie in the house.

Except Sophie hadn't been in the house when I'd returned home.

She was already gone. Purcell had been standing in the kitchen alone, holding Brian at gunpoint. Sophie had already been taken, by a second person who must've come with Purcell. Someone Brian would feel safe greeting at the door. Someone who had access to the troopers' pension. Who knew Shane. Who felt powerful enough to control all the parties involved.

My face must have paled, because Purcell started to laugh. The sound rattled in his chest.

'See? I tell the truth,' he growled. 'I'm not the problem. The men in your life are.'

Purcell laughed again, the blood dripping down his face and making him look as crazy as I felt. We were two peas in a pod, I realized abruptly. Soldiers in the war, to be used, abused, and betrayed by the generals involved.

Others made the decisions. We just paid the price.

I set the knife down behind me, beside the shotgun. My right arm throbbed. Using it so much had caused the gunshot wound to bleed again. I could feel fresh moisture trickling down my arm. More pink stains in the snow.

Not much longer now, I knew. And like

Purcell, I was not afraid. I was resigned to my fate.

'Trooper Lyons is dead,' I said.

Purcell stopped laughing.

'Turns out, you killed him two hours ago.'

Purcell thinned his lips. He was no fool.

From the back waistband of my pants, I pulled out a .22 semiauto I'd found taped to the back of the toilet tank in Purcell's bathroom. Strictly a backup weapon for a guy like him, but it would still get the job done.

'I'm guessing this is a black market weapon,' I stated. 'Serial number filed off. Untraceable.'

'You promised a fair fight,' Purcell said suddenly.

'And you promised to let my husband go. Guess we're both liars.'

I leaned close. 'Who do you love?' I whispered in the bloody snow.

'No one,' he replied tiredly. 'Never did.'

I nodded, unsurprised. Then I shot him. Double tap to the left temple, classic gangland hit. Next, I picked up the KA-BAR knife and matter-of-factly carved the word 'snitch' into the dead man's skin. Had to obliterate the three Xs I'd formed earlier in his chest, which would've led a savvy detective such as D.D. Warren straight to my doorstep.

My face felt strange. Hard. Grim, even for me. I reminded myself of that tidy basement with its lingering scents of bleach and blood, of the pain Purcell would've happily inflicted upon me, if I'd given him the chance. It didn't help. I was meant to be a cop, not a killer. And each act of violence

431

took something from me that I would not get back again.

But I kept moving, because like any woman, I was good at self-inflicted pain.

Final details: I returned to the house long enough to help myself to Purcell's cleaning supplies. Working with paper towels and bleach, I obliterated all traces of my blood inside the home. Then I traded my boots for his, tramping around in the mud and snow until my footprints were gone and only Purcell's remained.

Lastly, I retrieved Brian's Glock .40 from my duffel bag and wrapped Purcell's right hand around the pistol grip to transfer his prints. Purcell's .22 went into my duffel bag, to be tossed in the first river I passed. The Glock .40 went inside Purcell's house, taped to the back of the toilet as he'd done with the first firearm.

Sometime after the sun rose, the police would find Purcell's body tied to the house, obviously tortured, now deceased. They would search his house, they would discover his basement, and that would answer half their questions — a guy in Purcell's line of work was bound to die badly.

While searching Purcell's house, they would also discover Brian's Glock .40. Ballistics would match the slug that killed police officer Shane Lyons to that firearm, providing a theory that Purcell had once entered my home and stolen my husband's gun, which he later used to kill a highly respected state trooper.

Purcell's murder would go to the back burner — just another thug meeting a violent end. Shane would be buried with full honors and his family would receive benefits.

The police would search for the weapon that shot Purcell, of course. Wonder about his murderer. But not all questions were meant to be answered.

Just like not all people were meant to be trusted.

One-seventeen a.m. I staggered to my feet, made my way back to the truck. I downed two bottles of water and ate two power bars. Right shoulder burned. Tingling in my fingers. A hollow sensation in my gut. A curious numbness to the set of my lips.

Then I was on the road again, shotgun on my lap, bloody hands at the wheel.

Sophie, here I come.

41

'It's Hamilton,' Bobby said, pulling D.D. out of Leoni's garage and already jogging back to their car.

'Hamilton?' D.D. narrowed her eyes. 'As in State Police Lieutenant Colonel?'

'Yep. Has access, has opportunity, and knows all the players involved. Maybe Brian's gambling problem started the ball rolling, but Hamilton was the brains of the operation — *You guys need money? Hey, I happen to know where there's a huge pot of cash, just sitting there . . .* '

'Between him and Shane . . . ' D.D. murmured. She nodded, feeling the first tinge of excitement A name, a suspect, a target. She climbed into the car and Bobby pulled away from the curb, already racing toward the highway.

'Yep,' he said now. 'Easy enough to work out the logistics of setting up a shell company, with Hamilton pulling strings to cover their tracks from the inside. Except, of course, all good things must come to an end.'

'Once the internal investigation kicks into gear . . . '

'Their days are numbered,' Bobby filled in for her. 'They have state investigators sniffing around, plus, thanks to Shane and Brian continuing to gamble excessively, they also have various mobsters wanting a piece of the pie.

Hamilton, of course, grows concerned. And Brian and Shane go from being partners in crime to highly expendable liabilities.'

'Hamilton killed Brian, then kidnapped Sophie so Tessa would confess to shooting her own husband and be framed for defrauding the troopers' union?' D.D. frowned, then added, 'Or an enforcer did it. The kind of mobster Brian had already pissed off. The kind of guy willing to do one last piece of wet work in order to get his money back.'

'The kind of guy who'd mail photos of Shane's family as a warning,' Bobby agreed.

'That's the thing about the brass,' D.D. said with a shake of her head. 'They're big on ideas, but don't like to get their own hands dirty during implementation.' She hesitated. 'Following that logic, where is Sophie? Would Hamilton risk personally holding a six-year-old girl?'

'Don't know,' Bobby said. 'But I'm betting if we drop on him like a ton of bricks, we can find that out. He should be downtown, at the scene of Lyons's shooting, hanging out with the colonel and other brass.'

D.D. nodded, then suddenly grabbed Bobby's arm. 'He's not downtown. Bet you anything.'

'Why not?'

'Because Tessa is on the loose. We know it. He knows it. Furthermore, he would've heard by now that Trooper Lyons's shotgun and M4 rifle are missing. Meaning he knows Tessa is armed, dangerous, and desperate to locate her daughter.'

'He's on the run,' Bobby filled in, 'from his own officer.' But then it was his turn to shake his

435

head. 'Nah, not a guy as experienced and wily as Hamilton. Best defense is a good offense, right? He's going for Sophie. If she's still alive, he's gonna get his hands on her. She's the only bargaining chip he's got left.'

'So where's Sophie?' D.D. asked again. 'We've had a statewide Amber Alert for three days. Her picture is plastered all over the TV, her description on the radio. If the girl's around, we should've gotten a lead by now.'

'Meaning she's someplace buttoned up tight,' Bobby mused. 'Rural, no close neighbors. With someone assigned to keep her under lock and key. So a place that is inaccessible, but well supplied. A location Hamilton trusts not to be compromised.'

'He'd never stash Sophie in his own house,' D.D. said. 'Too close to him. Maybe she's at a friend of a friend? Or a second home? We saw the pictures of him hunting deer. Does he have a hunting lodge, a cabin in the woods?'

Bobby suddenly smiled. 'Bingo. Hamilton has a hunting cabin near Mount Greylock in western Mass. Two and half hours away from state headquarters, tucked in the foothills of the Berkshires. Isolated, containable, and distant enough to provide him with plausible deniability — even if he owns it, he can say he hasn't been there in days or weeks, particularly given all the activity that's required his attention in Boston.'

'Can you get us there?' D.D. asked immediately.

Bobby hesitated. 'I've been there a couple of times, but years ago. Sometimes he invites

436

troopers over for hunting weekends, that kind of thing. I can picture the roads . . . '

'Phil,' D.D. stated, pulling out her cellphone. 'You get on the Pike. I'll get us the address.'

Bobby hit the lights, roaring for the Mass Pike, the quickest route for cutting across the state. D.D. dialed BPD headquarters. It was after midnight, but nobody in the state or Boston force was sleeping tonight; Phil answered on the first ring.

'You heard about Trooper Lyons?' Phil stated in way of greeting.

'Already been there. Got a sensitive request for you. Want full background on Gerard Hamilton. Search under his family members' names, too. I want all known property addresses, and after that, a full financial workup.'

There was a pause. 'You mean the lieutenant colonel of the state police?' Phil asked carefully.

'Told you it was sensitive.'

D.D. heard a tapping sound. Phil's fingers, already flying across the computer keyboard.

'Ummm, if you want some unofficial info, not even water cooler talk, more like urinal gossip . . . ' Phil started, as he typed away.

'By all means,' D.D. assured him.

'Heard Hamilton's got himself a mistress. A hot Italian spitfire.'

'Name?'

'Haven't a clue. Guy only mentioned her . . . derriere.'

'Men are pigs.'

'Personally, I'm a pig who's in love with his wife and needs her to survive four kids, so don't look at me.'

'True,' D.D. granted. 'Start digging, Phil. Tell me what I need to know, because we think he might have Sophie Leoni.'

D.D. hung up. Bobby came to the exit for the Mass Pike. He careened up it at seventy miles per hour and they went squealing around the corner. Roads were finally clear of snow and there wasn't much traffic at this time of night. Bobby hit one hundred on the broad, flat highway as they soared toward western Mass. They had a hundred and thirty miles to cover, give or take, D.D. thought, not all of which could be traveled at top speed. Two hours, she decided. Two hours till finally rescuing Sophie Leoni.

'Do you think she's a good cop?' Bobby asked suddenly.

D.D. didn't have to ask who he was talking about. 'I don't know.'

Bobby took his gaze off the fast flying darkness just long enough to glance at her. 'How far would you go?' he asked softly, his eyes dropped to her belly. 'If it were your child, how far would you go?'

'I hope I never have to find out.'

'Because I would kill them all,' Bobby said flatly, his hands flexing and unflexing on the wheel. 'If someone threatened Annabelle, kidnapped Carina. There wouldn't be enough ammo left in this state for what I would do to them.'

D.D. didn't doubt him for a minute, but she still shook her head.

'It's not right, Bobby,' she said quietly. 'Even if you're provoked, even if the other guy started it . . . Criminals resort to violence. We're cops. We're supposed to know better. If we can't live up to that standard . . . Well then, who can?'

They drove in silence after that, listening to the throaty growl of a flat-out engine and watching city lights wink by like bolts of lightning.

Sophie, D.D. thought, *here we come.*

42

Lieutenant Colonel Gerard Hamilton was my commanding officer, but I would never say I knew him well. For one thing, he was several levels above me in the food chain. For another, he was a guy's guy. When he did hang out with the troopers, it was with Shane, and he often included Shane's partner in crime, my husband, Brian.

They'd catch Red Sox games, maybe a hunting weekend, or a field trip to Foxwoods.

In hindsight, it all made perfect sense. Shane's little excursions. My husband tagging along. Hamilton, too.

Meaning, when Brian started to gamble too much, get in too deep . . . Who would know how badly he needed money? Who would know another option for getting rich quick? Who would be in the perfect position to prey on my husband's weakness?

Shane had never been big in the brains department. Lieutenant Colonel Hamilton, however . . . He'd know how to bring Shane and Brian along. Skim a little here, then a little there. It's amazing how people can rationalize doing bad things when at first you start out small.

For example, I didn't plan on killing Shane when I got out of jail, or murdering a gangster named John Stephen Purcell, or driving through the freezing night to my superior officer's hunting cabin with a shotgun on my lap.

Maybe Brian and Shane told themselves they were merely 'borrowing' that money. As union rep, Shane would know all about the pension account and available balance. Hamilton probably knew how to get access, what kind of shell company would be most appropriate for defrauding retired state cops. In the old boys' network, it was probably a matter of a single phone call.

They'd set up a dummy company and they were off and running, billing the pension fund, collecting the funds, and hitting the tables.

How long had they planned on running the racket? A month? Six months? A year? Maybe they didn't think that far ahead. Maybe it hadn't mattered to them at the time. Eventually, of course, internal affairs had figured out the fraud and launched an investigation. Unfortunately for Brian and Shane, once such an investigation started, it didn't end until the taskforce got answers.

Is that when Hamilton had decided to turn me into the sacrificial lamb? Or had that been part of the domino effect? When, even after stealing from the troopers' pension, Brian and Shane had continued to be short on funds, borrowing from the wrong players until they had both internal investigators and mob enforcers breathing down their necks?

At some point, Hamilton had realized that Shane and Brian might crack under the pressure, might confess their crimes to save their own necks and deliver up Hamilton on a platter.

Of the two, Brian was definitely the bigger liability. Maybe Hamilton had negotiated a final deal for the mob. He'd pay off the last of Brian and Shane's bad debts. In return, they'd eliminate Brian and help frame me for all the crimes.

Shane would remain alive but too terrified to speak, while Hamilton and his cohorts could keep their illicit gains.

Brian would be dead. I would be in prison. Sophie . . . well, once I'd done everything they asked, they wouldn't need her anymore, would they?

So my family would be destroyed, for Shane's survival and Hamilton's greed.

The rage helped keep me awake as I drove three hours west, toward Adams, Mass., where I knew Hamilton kept a second home. I'd been there only once, for a fall barbecue several years ago.

I remembered the log cabin as being small and isolated. Perfect for hiking, hunting, and holding a young child.

The fingers on my right hand wouldn't work anymore. The bleeding had finally slowed, but I suspected the bullet had damaged tendons, maybe even nerves. Now inflammation had further compromised the injury and I couldn't form a fist. Or pull a trigger.

I would proceed left-handed. With any luck, Hamilton wasn't around. One of his officers had been killed in the line of duty tonight, meaning Hamilton should be in Allston-Brighton, tending to official matters.

I would park at the bottom of the long dirt drive that led to the cabin. I would hike in through the woods, bringing the shotgun, which I could fire left-handed from my hip. Aim would be lousy, but that was the joy of a shotgun — impact area was so large, your aim didn't have to be any good.

I would scope out the cabin, I rehearsed in my mind. Discover it deserted. Use the butt of the shotgun to break out a window. Climb in, then locate my daughter sound asleep in a darkened bedroom.

I would rescue her and we would run away together. Maybe flee to Mexico, though the sensible thing would be to head straight back to BPD headquarters. Sophie could testify that Hamilton had kidnapped her. Further investigation into the lieutenant colonel's affairs would reveal a bank balance far greater than it had any right to be. Hamilton would be arrested. Sophie and I would be safe.

We would move on with our lives and never be frightened again. Someday, she'd stop asking for Brian. And someday I'd stop mourning him.

I needed to believe it would be that easy.

I hurt too badly for it to be otherwise.

Four thirty-two in the morning, I found the dirt road that led to Hamilton's cabin. Four forty-one, I pulled off the road and parked behind a snow-covered bush.

I climbed out of the car.

Thought I smelled smoke.

I hefted up the shotgun.

And heard my daughter scream.

43

Bobby and D.D. had just turned off the Mass Pike for the dark ribbon of rural US 20 when her cellphone rang. The loud chime jerked D.D. out of her groggy state. She hit answer, held the phone to her ear. It was Phil.

'D.D., you still headed west?'

'Already here.'

'Okay, Hamilton has two property addresses. First one's in Framingham, Mass., near state HQ. I'm assuming the primary home, as it's listed jointly under Gerard and Judy Hamilton. But there's a second home, in Adams, Mass., solely under his name.'

'Address?' D.D. demanded crisply.

Phil rattled it off. 'But get this: Police scanner just picked up a report of a residential fire in Adams, near the Mount Greylock State Reservation. Maybe it's a coincidence? Or possibly Hamilton's cabin is the one on fire.'

'Shit!' D.D. jerked to attention, fully awake. 'Phil, contact local authorities. I want backup. County and town officers, but no state troopers.' Bobby shot her a look, but didn't argue. 'Now!' she stated urgently, ending the call, then immediately plugging the Hamilton's address into the vehicle's navigation system.

'Phil got us the address, which apparently is

near the scene of a fire.'

'Dammit!' Bobby pounded the steering wheel with his hand. 'Hamilton's already there and covering his tracks!'

'Not if we have anything to say about it.'

44

Sophie screamed again, and I jerked into action. I grabbed both the shotgun and the rifle, pouring shotgun shells and rounds of .223 ammo into my pants pockets. The fingers on my right hand moved sluggishly, dumping more ammo onto the snow covered ground than into my pockets. I didn't have time to pick it up. I moved, relying on adrenaline and desperation to get the job done.

Weighed down with a small arsenal of weapons and ammo, I careened into the snowy woods, heading toward the smell of smoke and the sound of my daughter.

Another scream. An adult cursing. The sizzling sound of wet wood catching flame.

Cabin was straight up. I bounced from tree to tree, struggling for footing in the fresh snow, breathing shallowly. Didn't know how many people might be present. Needed the advantage of surprise if Sophie and I were going to get through this. Don't give away my position, find the higher ground.

My professional training counseled a strategic approach, while my parental instincts screamed for me to charge in and grab my daughter *now, now, now.* The air grew denser with smoke. I coughed, feeling my eyes burn as I finally crested a small knoll on the left side of the property. I discovered Hamilton's cabin on fire and my daughter struggling with a woman in a thick black parka. The woman was trying to drag Sophie into a parked SUV. My daughter, wearing nothing but the thin pink pajamas I'd put her to bed in four nights ago and still clutching her favorite doll, Gertrude, was thrashing wildly.

Sophie bit the woman's exposed wrist. The woman jerked back her arm and slapped her. My daughter's head rocked sideways. She stumbled, sprawling backward into the snow and coughing raggedly from the smoke.

'No, no, no,' my daughter was crying. 'Let me go. I want my mommy. *I want my mommy!*'

Shotgun on the ground — couldn't risk it with my child so close to the target. Finding the rifle instead, yanking out the magazine, fumbling in my left pocket. Always load an M4's stack magazine minus two in order to keep it feeding evenly, my police training dictated.

Kill them all, my mother's instinct roared.

I hefted up the rifle, racked the first round.

Fresh blood oozing from my shoulder. Sluggish fingers curling laboriously around the trigger.

The woman towered over Sophie. 'Get in the car, you stupid little brat,' she screeched.

'Let me go!'

Another scream. Another smack.

Anchoring the butt of the assault rifle against my bleeding shoulder and sighting the dark-haired woman now beating my child.

Sophie crying, arms curled around her head, trying to block the blows.

I stepped clear of the woods. Zeroed in on my target.

'Sophie!' I called out loudly across the crackling, acrid night. 'Sophie. *Run!*'

As I'd hoped, the unexpected sound of my voice captured their attention. Sophie turned around. The woman jerked sharply upright, trying to pinpoint the intruder.

She looked right at me. 'Who the — '

I pulled the trigger.

Sophie never glanced behind her. At the body that dropped suddenly, at the head that exploded beneath the onslaught of a .223 slug and turned into a puddle of crimson snow.

My daughter never turned. She heard my voice and she ran to me.

Just as a gun cocked in my ear, and Gerard Hamilton said, 'You fucking bitch.'

* * *

D.D. and Bobby followed the GPS system through a winding maze of rural roads, until they came to a narrow dirt road lined by fire trucks and grim-faced firefighters. Bobby killed the lights. He and D.D. bolted out of the car, flashing their creds.

News was short and bad.

Firefighters had arrived just in time to hear screams followed by gunshots. Residential home was an eighth of a mile straight up, surrounded by deep woods. Judging by smoke and heat, the building was probably fully engulfed in flames. Firefighters were now waiting for police to secure the scene, so they could get in there and do their thing. Waiting was not something any of them were good at, particularly as one of the guys swore the screaming came from a kid.

Bobby told D.D. to stay in the car.

In response, D.D. stalked to the rear of her vehicle, where she donned her Kevlar vest, then pulled out the shotgun. She handed the rifle to Bobby. After all, he was the former sniper.

He scowled at her. 'I go first. Recon,' he snapped.

'I'll give you six minutes,' she retorted just as sharply.

Bobby donned his vest, loaded the M4, and walked the edge of the steep property. Thirty seconds later, he disappeared into the snowy woods. And three minutes after that, D.D. hit the trail right behind him.

More sirens in the distance.

Local officers finally arriving at the scene.

D.D. focused on following Bobby's footsteps.

Smoke, heat, snow. A winter inferno.

Time to find Sophie. Time to get the job done.

* * *

Hamilton yanked the rifle from my injured arm. The M4 fell bonelessly from my grasp and he scooped it up. The shotgun was at my feet. He ordered me to pick it up, hand it over.

From the top of the knoll, I could see Sophie running toward me, sprinting across the property below, framed in white-dusted trees and bright red flames.

449

While the barrel of Hamilton's gun dug into the sensitive hollow behind my ear.

I started to bend down. Hamilton relented an inch to give me room, and I hurled myself backward into him, yelling wildly, 'Sophie, get away! Into the woods. Get away, get away, get away!'

'Mommy!' she screamed, a hundred yards back.

Hamilton pistol-whipped me with his Sig Sauer. I went down hard, my right arm collapsing beneath me. More searing pain. Maybe the sound of something tearing. I had no time to recover. Hamilton hit me again, looming over me, slicing open my cheek, my forehead. Blood pouring down into my face, blinding my eyes as I curled up in the fetal position in the snow.

'You should've done what you were told!' he screamed. He was wearing his dress uniform, topped with a knee-length black wool coat, his wide-brimmed hat pulled low over his eyes. Probably donned the ensemble upon receiving news that an officer had been killed in the line of duty. Then, when he realized it was Shane, and that I'd escaped, was still on the loose . . .

He'd come to get my daughter. Dressed in the official uniform of a Massachusetts State Police lieutenant colonel, he'd come to harm a child.

'You were a trained police officer,' he snapped now, looming over me, blocking out the trees, the fire, the night sky. 'If you'd just done what you were told, no one would've gotten hurt!'

'Except Brian,' I managed to gasp. 'You

450

arranged his death.'

'His gambling problem was out of control. I did you a favor.'

'You kidnapped my daughter. You sent me to prison. Just to make a few extra bucks.'

In response, my commanding officer kicked me full-force in the left kidney, the kind of kick that would have me peeing up blood, assuming I lived that long.

'Mommy, Mommy!' Sophie cried again. I realized with horror that her voice was closer. She was still running toward my voice, clambering over the snowbank.

No, I wanted to cry. *Save yourself, get away.*

But my voice wouldn't work anymore. Hamilton had knocked the air from my lungs. My eyes burned with smoke, tears pouring down my face as I gasped and heaved against the snow. Shoulder burned. Stomach cramped.

Black dots dancing before me.

Had to move. Had to get up. Had to fight. For Sophie.

Hamilton reared back with his foot again. He lashed out to hit me square in the chest. This time, I dropped my left arm, caught his foot midkick, and rolled. Caught off guard, Hamilton was jerked forward, falling to one knee in the snow.

So he stopped hitting me with the Sig Sauer and pulled the trigger instead.

The sound deafened me. I felt immediate searing heat, followed by immediate searing pain. My left side. My hand falling down, clutching my waist, as my gaze went up, toward my commanding officer, a man I'd been trained to trust.

Hamilton appeared stunned. Maybe even a little shaken, but he recovered quickly enough, finger back on the trigger.

Just as Sophie crested the knoll and spotted us.

I had a vision. My daughter's pale, sweet face. Her hair a wild tangle of knots. Her eyes, a bright, brilliant blue as her gaze locked on me. Then she was running, the way only a six-year-old could run, and Hamilton did not exist for her and the woods did not exist for her, nor the scary fire, or the threat of night or the unknown terrors that must have tormented her for days.

She was a little girl who'd finally found her mother and she tore straight toward me, one hand clutching Gertrude, the other arm flung open as she threw herself on top of me and I groaned from both the pain and the joy that burst inside my chest.

'I love you I love you I love you,' I exhaled.

'Mommy, Mommy, Mommy, Mommy, Mommy.'

'Sophie, Sophie, Sophie . . . '

I could feel her tears hot against my face. It hurt, but I still brought up my hand, cradling the back of her head. I looked at Hamilton, and then I tucked my daughter's face into the crook of my neck. 'Sophie,' I whispered, never taking my gaze off him, 'close your eyes.'

My daughter clung to me, two halves of a whole, finally together again.

She closed her eyes.

And I said, in the clearest voice I could muster, 'Do it.'

The darkness behind Hamilton materialized into a man. At my command, he raised his rifle. Just as Hamilton placed the barrel of his Sig Sauer against my left temple.

I concentrated on the feel of my daughter, the weight of her body, the purity of her love. Something to carry with me into the abyss.

'You should've done what I said,' Hamilton hissed above me.

While in the next heartbeat, Bobby Dodge pulled the trigger.

45

By the time D.D. made it to the top of the property, Hamilton was down and Bobby stood over the lieutenant colonel's body. He looked up at her approach and shook his head once.

Then she heard crying.

Sophie Leoni. It took D.D. a second to spot the child's small, pink-clad form. She was on the ground, covering another dark-clad figure, skinny arms tangled around her mother's neck as the girl sobbed wildly.

Bobby dropped to one knee beside the pair as D.D. approached. He placed his hand on Sophie's shoulder.

'Sophie,' he said quietly. 'Sophie, I need you to look at me. I'm a state policeman, like your mother. I'm here to help her. Please look at me.'

Sophie finally raised her tearstained face. She spotted D.D. and opened her mouth as if to scream. D.D. shook her head.

'It's okay, it's okay. My name is D.D. I'm a friend of your mom's, too. Your mom led us here, to help you.'

'Mommy's boss took me away,' Sophie said clearly. 'Mommy's boss gave me to the bad woman. I said no. I said I wanted to go home! I said I wanted Mommy!'

Her face dissolved again. She started to cry, soundlessly this time, still pressed against her mother's unmoving body.

'We know,' D.D. said, crouching down beside them, placing a tentative hand on the girl's back. 'But your mother's boss and the bad woman can't hurt you anymore, okay, Sophie? We're here, and you're safe.'

To judge by the look on Sophie's face, she didn't believe them. D.D. couldn't blame her.

'Are you hurt?' Bobby asked.

The girl shook her head.

'What about your mommy?' D.D. asked. 'Can we check her, make sure she is okay?'

Sophie moved slightly to one side, enough so D.D. could see the dark stain on the left side of Tessa's dark flannel shirt, the red blood in the snow. Sophie saw it, too. The girl's lower lip started to tremble. She didn't say another word. She simply lay down in the snow beside her unconscious mother and held her hand.

'Come back, Mommy,' the girl said mournfully. 'Love you. Come back.'

Bobby scrambled down the slope for the EMTs.

While D.D. peeled off her own coat and used it to cover both mother and child.

★ ★ ★

Tessa regained consciousness as the EMTs went to load her. Her eyes popped open, she gasped sharply, then reached out frantically. The EMTs tried to hold her down. So D.D. did the sensible thing, grabbing Sophie and lifting the child onto the edge of the gurney.

Tessa clutched her daughter's arm, squeezed

455

hard. D.D. thought Tessa might be crying, or maybe it was the tears in her own eyes. She couldn't be sure.

'I love you,' Tessa whispered to her daughter.

'Love you more, Mommy. Love you more.'

The EMTs wouldn't let Sophie remain on the gurney. Tessa required immediate medical attention and the child would only be in the way. After thirty seconds of negotiation, it was determined that Sophie would ride in the front of the ambulance, while her mother was tended in the back. The EMTs, moving quickly, started to hustle the girl to the front.

She twisted around them long enough to race back to her mother, and tuck something beside her, then ran for the passenger's seat.

When D.D. looked again, Sophie's one-eyed doll was tucked beside Tessa's unmoving form. The EMTs loaded her up.

The ambulance whisked them away.

D.D. stood in the middle of the snowy dawn, hand on her own stomach. She smelled smoke. She tasted tears.

She looked up to the woods, where a fire was now burning down to ash. Hamilton's last bid attempt to cover his tracks, which had cost both him and his female companion their lives.

D.D. wanted to feel triumphant. They'd saved the girl, they'd vanquished the evil foe. Now, except for a few days of excruciating paperwork, they should be riding off in the sunset.

It wasn't enough.

For the first time in a dozen years, D.D. Warren had reached the successful conclusion of a case, and it wasn't enough. She didn't feel like reporting the good news to her superiors, or supplying self-gratifying answers to the press, or even grabbing a couple of beers to wind down with her taskforce.

She wanted to go home. She wanted to curl up with Alex and inhale the scent of his aftershave, and feel the familiar comfort of his arms around her. And she wanted, heaven help her, to still be at his side the first time the baby moved, and be looking into his eyes when the first contraction hit, and be holding his hand when their baby slid into the world.

She wanted a little girl or a little boy who would love her as much as Sophie Leoni obviously loved her mother. And she wanted to return that love tenfold, to feel it grow bigger and bigger every single year, just as Tessa had said.

D.D. wanted a family.

She had to wait ten hours. Bobby couldn't work — having used deadly force, he was forced to sit on the sidelines and await the arrival of the firearms discharge investigation team, which would formally investigate the incident. Meaning D.D. was on her own as she notified her boss of the latest developments, then secured the scene and began processing the outer fringes, while waiting for the last embers of the fire to cool. More officers and evidence techs arrived. More questions to answer, more bodies to manage.

She worked through breakfast. Bobby brought her yogurt and a peanut butter sandwich for lunch. She worked. She smelled of smoke and sweat, of blood and ash.

Dinner came and went. Sun set again. The life of a homicide detective.

She did what she had to do. She tended what needed tending.

And then, finally, she was done.

Scene was secured, Tessa had been airlifted to a Boston hospital, and Sophie remained safely at her mother's side.

D.D. got in her car and headed back to the Mass Pike.

She phoned Alex just as she reached Springfield. He was cooking chicken parm and delighted to hear she was finally coming home.

She asked if he could change the chicken parm to an eggplant parm.

He wanted to know why.

Which made her laugh, then made her cry, and she couldn't get the words out. So she told him she missed him and he promised her all the eggplant parm in the world, and that, D.D. thought, was love. His love. Her love. Their love.

'Alex,' she finally managed to gasp. 'Hey, Alex. Forget dinner. I've got something I need to tell you . . . '

*   *   *

I was in the hospital for nearly two weeks. I got lucky. Hamilton's shot was a through and through that missed most major organs. Hit man Purcell, however, had been a pro to the bitter end. He'd shattered my rotator cuff, resulting in numerous surgeries and endless months of PT.

458

I'm told I'll never regain full range of movement in my right shoulder, but I should get finger function back once the swelling goes down.

I guess we'll find out.

Sophie stayed with me in the hospital. She wasn't supposed to. Hospital policy said children should only be there during visiting hours. Within hours of my arrival, Mrs. Ennis had received word and shown up to assist. But she couldn't peel Sophie off me, and after another ten minutes, the head nurse waved her off.

Sophie needed her mother. I needed Sophie.

So they let us be, two girls in our private room, an unbelievable luxury. We slept together, ate together, and watched SpongeBob Squarepants together. Our own little form of therapy.

Day nine or so, we took a little walk to my former hospital room, where lo and behold, tucked in the back of the bottom drawer, we found Gertrude's missing button eye.

I sewed it on that afternoon with surgical thread, and Sophie made Gertrude her own hospital bed for recovery.

Gertrude would be okay, she informed me solemnly. Gertrude had been a very brave girl.

We watched more SpongeBob after that, and I kept my arm around my little girl and her head upon my shoulder even though it ached.

The hospital arranged for a pediatric psych specialist to visit with Sophie. She wouldn't talk about her captivity and hadn't mentioned Brian's name at all. The doctor advised me to keep 'the channels of communication open' and to let Sophie come to me. When she was ready, the doctor said, she would talk. And when she did, I must keep my face neutral and my comments nonjudgmental.

I thought this was funny advice to give a woman who'd committed three murders to save her daughter, but I didn't volunteer that.

I held Sophie. We slept, by mutual consent, with the lights on, and when she drew pictures filled with black night, red flames, and exploding guns, I complimented her level of detail and promised to teach her how to shoot the moment my arm healed.

Sophie liked that idea very much.

Detectives D.D. Warren and Bobby Dodge returned. They brought Mrs. Ennis with them, who took Sophie to the hospital cafeteria so I could answer the last of their questions.

No, Brian had never hit me. My bruised ribs were because I had fallen down icy steps, and, being late for patrol, tended the injury myself. Shane, however, had beat me on Sunday morning, in an attempt to make it look like Brian's death was self-defense.

No, I didn't know Trooper Lyons had been shot. What a terrible tragedy for his family. Did they have any leads at this time?

They showed me photos of a thin-faced man with blazing dark eyes and thick brown hair. Yes, I recognized the man as the one I'd discovered in my kitchen on Saturday morning, holding my husband at gunpoint. He'd told me that if I would cooperate, no one would get hurt. So I had taken off my duty belt; at which time, he'd pulled my Sig Sauer and shot my husband three times in the chest.

Purcell then explained that if I wanted to see my daughter alive again, I had to do exactly what he said.

No, I'd never seen Purcell before that morning, nor did I know of his reputation as a professional hit man, nor did I know why he had my husband at gunpoint or what had happened to Sophie. Yes, I'd known my husband had a gambling problem, but I did not realize it had grown so bad that an enforcer had been hired to deal with the problem.

After Purcell had shot Brian, I'd offered him fifty thousand dollars in return for more time before reporting his death. I'd explained I could freeze Brian's body, then thaw it and call the cops on Sunday morning. I'd still do whatever Purcell wanted, I just needed twenty-four hours to prepare for Sophie's return, as I'd be in jail for shooting my husband.

Purcell had accepted the deal, and I'd spent Saturday afternoon covering Brian's body in snow, then retrieving the dog's body from under the deck, and building a couple of incendiary devices. I tried to rig them to blow back so no one would get hurt.

Yes, I had planned my escape from jail. And no, I hadn't felt it was safe to disclose to anyone, even to the Boston detectives, what was really going on. For one thing, I didn't know who'd taken Sophie and I genuinely feared for her life. For another, I knew at least one fellow officer, Trooper Lyons, was involved. How could I know the taint didn't extend to Boston cops? Or, as the case turned out, to a superior officer?

At the time, I was acting on instinct, carefully trying to do as I'd been instructed, while also realizing that if I didn't escape and find my daughter myself, chances were she was as good as dead.

D.D. wanted to know who had given me a lift from the search and recovery site. I stared her straight in the eye and told her I'd hitchhiked. She wanted a description of the vehicle. Sadly, I didn't remember.

But I'd ended up at my father's garage, where I helped myself to a vehicle. He'd been passed out at the time, in no shape to agree or protest.

Once I had the Ford truck, I'd driven straight to western Mass. to confront Hamilton and rescue Sophie.

No, I didn't know what happened to Shane that night, or how he came to be shot by Brian's Glock .40. Though, if they'd retrieved the Glock .40 from the hit man's house, didn't that imply that Purcell had done the deed? Maybe someone viewed Shane as another loose end that needed to be wrapped up. Poor Shane. I hoped his wife and kids were doing okay.

D.D. scowled at me. Bobby said nothing at all. We had something in common, he and I. He knew exactly what I'd done. And I think he accepted that a woman who'd already killed three people probably wasn't going to magically crack and confess, even if his partner used her angry voice.

I did shoot and kill Hamilton's mistress,

462

Bonita Marcoso. The woman had been assaulting my child. I had to use deadly force.

As for the lieutenant colonel . . . In killing him, Bobby Dodge had saved my life, I informed D.D. And I wanted to go on record with that. If not for the actions of state detective Bobby Dodge, Sophie and I both would probably be dead.

'Investigated and cleared,' Bobby informed me.

'As it should be. Thank you.'

He flushed a little, not liking the attention. Or maybe he simply didn't want to be thanked for taking a life.

I don't think about it much myself. I don't see the point.

So there you have it, I wrapped up for D.D. My husband was not a wife beater or child abuser. Just a gambling addict who'd gotten in way over his head. And maybe I should've done more about that sooner. Cut him off. Kicked him out.

I hadn't known about the credit cards he'd opened in Sophie's name. I hadn't known about his skimming of union funds. There was a lot I hadn't known, but that didn't make me culpable. Just made me a typical wife, wishing fruitlessly that my husband would walk away from the card tables and come home to me and my child instead.

'Sorry,' he'd told me, dying in our kitchen. 'Tessa . . . love you more.'

I dream of him, you know. Not something I can tell Detective Warren. But I dream of my

463

husband, except this time he is Good Brian, and he is holding my hand in his and Sophie is riding ahead of us on her bike. We walk. We talk. We are happy.

I wake up sobbing, which makes it just as well that I don't sleep much anymore.

Want to know how much the lieutenant colonel made in the end? According to D.D., internal affairs recovered one hundred thousand dollars in his account. Ironically, a mere fraction of what he would've received in legitimate retirement benefits if he'd just done his job conscientiously, then taken up fishing in Florida.

The lieutenant colonel had ordered my husband's death, and lost money in the process.

They hadn't been able to recover the rest of the funds. No record in Shane's accounts and no record in Brian's. According to D.D., internal affairs believed that both men had gambled away their illicit gains at the casino, while Hamilton had saved his share of the scam. Ironically, their bad habit meant Shane and Brian would never be charged in the crime, while Hamilton and his girlfriend Bonita — who'd been positively ID'd as the female who'd closed out the shell company's bank account — would posthumously shoulder the blame.

Good news for Shane's widow, I thought, and good news for me.

I heard later that Shane was buried with full honors. The police determined that he must have agreed to meet with Purcell in the back alley. Purcell had overpowered him, then killed him, maybe to eliminate Shane, just as he'd eliminated Brian.

Purcell's murder remains open, I've been told, the weapon having yet to be recovered.

As I explained to Detective D.D. Warren, I don't know nothing about anything, and don't let anyone tell you otherwise.

★ ★ ★

Sophie and I live together now in a two-bedroom apartment just down the street from Mrs. Ennis. We've never returned to the old house; I sold it in about three hours, because even if it was once a crime scene, it still has one of the largest yards in Boston.

Sophie does not ask for Brian, nor speak of him. Nor does she talk about the kidnapping. I believe she feels she's protecting me. What can I tell you — she's a chip off the old block. She sees a specialist once a week. He advises me to be patient and so I am. I view my job now as building a safe place to land for when my daughter inevitably lets go.

She will fall, and I will catch her. Gladly.

I made Brian's funeral arrangements alone. He's buried with a simple granite marker bearing his name and relevant dates. And maybe it was weakness on my part, but given that he died for Sophie, that he knew, standing there in our kitchen, the decision I would have to make, I added one last word. The highest praise you can give a man. I had etched, under his name: *Daddy*.

Maybe someday Sophie will visit him. And maybe, seeing that word, she can remember his love and she can forgive his mistakes. Parents aren't perfect, you know. We're all just doing the best we can.

I had to resign from the state police. While D.D. and Bobby have yet to connect me to Shane Lyons's or John Stephen Purcell's deaths, there's still the small matter of me breaking out of jail and assaulting a fellow officer. My lawyer is arguing that I was operating under extreme emotional duress, given my superior officer's kidnapping of my child, and should not be held responsible for my actions. Cargill remains optimistic that the DA, wanting to avoid too much bad publicity for the state police, will agree to a plea where I serve a probationary sentence, or at worse, house arrest.

Either way, I understand my days as a police officer are over. Frankly, a woman who's done the things I've done shouldn't be an armed protector of the public. And I don't know — maybe there is something wrong with me, an essential boundary missing, so that where other mothers would've cried for their child, I armed myself to the teeth and hunted down the people who took her instead.

Sometimes, I'm scared by the image that greets me in the mirror. My face is too hard, and even I realize it's been a long time since I've smiled. Men don't ask me out. Strangers don't strike up conversations with me on the subway.

Bobby Dodge is right — killing someone is not something to be thankful for. It's a necessary evil that costs you a piece of yourself and a connection to humanity you never get back.

But you don't need to feel sorry for me.

I recently started with a global security firm, making more money while working better hours. My boss read my story in the paper and called me with the job offer. He believes I have one of the finest strategic minds he's ever encountered, with an uncanny ability to foresee obstacles and anticipate next steps. There's a demand for those kinds of skills, especially in this day and age; I've already been promoted twice.

Now I drop off Sophie at school each morning. I go to work. Mrs. Ennis picks Sophie up at three. I join them at six. We eat dinner together, then I take Sophie home.

She and I tend the apartment, do homework. Then, at nine, we go to bed. We share a room. Neither of us sleeps much, and even three months later, we're still not ready for the dark.

Mostly, we snuggle together, Gertrude nestled between us.

Sophie likes to rest with her head on my shoulder, her fingers splayed in the palm of my hand.

'Love you, Mommy,' she tells me each and every night.

And I say, my cheek pressed against the top of her dark hair: 'Love you more, baby. I love you more.'

Author's Note And Acknowledgments

With all due respect to Detective D.D. Warren, my favorite part of embarking on a new novel isn't spending time with old characters, but rather, researching new and inventive ways to commit murder and mayhem. Oh, and, um, also spending quality time with law enforcement professionals who remind me why a life of crime really isn't a good idea, and thus I should continue to hope the whole writing gig pans out.

For *Love You More*, I got to fulfill one of my lifelong dreams of conducting research at the University of Tennessee Anthropology Research Facility, aka the Body Farm. I am deeply indebted to Dr. Lee Jantz, who is one of the smartest people I know, working one of the coolest jobs on the planet. She can look at a pile of cremated bones and tell you within thirty seconds pretty much everything about the person, including gender, age, chronic health issues, and what kind of dental floss he/she used. I had many moments with Dr. Jantz I would've liked to have put in the novel, but I didn't think anyone would believe me.

Readers interested in morbid things like decomp, identifying skeletal remains, and post-mortem insect activity should absolutely check out *Death's Acre*, by Dr. Bill Bass, creator of the

Body Farm, and coauthor Jon Jefferson. You can also visit my Facebook page for photos from my very informative research trip.

Oh, this is the part where I add anthropologists are trained professionals, whereas I just type for a living, meaning all mistakes in the novel are mine and mine alone. Plus, just as an FYI, I would never accuse Dr. Jantz, who has a T-shirt reading *Don't piss me off — I'm running out of places to hide the bodies*, of having made a mistake.

I am also deeply indebted to Cassondra Murray, Southern/Western Kentucky Canine Rescue & Recovery Task Force, for her insights into training cadaver dogs and life as a volunteer dog handler. I had no idea that most canine SAR teams are volunteer organizations. These groups and their dogs do amazing work, and we are indebted to them for their hard work, dedication, and sacrifice.

Again, all mistakes are mine, so don't even think about it!

Next up: Officer Penny Frechette, as well as several other female police officers who preferred to remain off the record. I appreciate the time and candor shared by these women, and enjoyed my first ride-along in a police cruiser. I was nervous! She was not. For those of you into police procedure, my character Tessa Leoni's experiences are an amalgamation of different jurisdictions, and not necessarily representative of the life of a Massachusetts State Trooper. The Massachusetts State Police is a fine, upstanding organization and I appreciate their patience with

469

suspense authors who exercise plenty of fictional license.

Under other nerve-wracking and noteworthy experiences, I must thank Superintendent Gerard Horgan, Esquire, and Assistant Deputy Superintendent Brian Dacey, both of the Suffolk County Sheriff's Department for a fun-filled day at the Suffolk County Jail. It's not every day I drive all the way to Boston just to be incarcerated, but boy did I learn a lot (basically, stick to writing fictional crimes, because let me tell you, I wouldn't last a day behind bars). They showed me a first-class operation. I, of course, used the facility for yet more murder and mayhem, because hey, that's what I do best.

Also, my deepest appreciation to Wayne Rock, Esquire, for legal advice and various insights into the BPD. A retired Boston detective, Wayne is always very patient when answering my questions and no longer seems startled when I lead with things like, *So I want to kill a guy but not have it be my fault. What's my best option?* Thank you, Wayne!

I am also indebted to Scott Hale, third generation merchant mariner, for his insights into the life. He agreed to help me out, even after knowing I was going to kill the merchant marine character. Thanks, Scott!

And wrapping things up in the research department, my endless gratitude to gifted doctor and fellow suspense author C.J. Lyons for her medical expertise. Let's face it, not just anyone will respond to e-mails with subject headings such as 'Need Advice for Maiming.' Thanks, C.J.!

Since writing novels isn't all touring jails and hanging out with cops, I must also thank David J. Hallett and Scott C. Ferrari, who outbid all rivals with a generous donation to our local animal shelter, for the right to include their Soft Coated Wheaten Terriers Skyler and Kelli in the novel. I hope you enjoy Skyler and Kelli's star-making turn, and thanks for supporting our local shelter.

I couldn't let animals have all the fun. Congrats to Heather Blood, winner of the 6th Annual Kill a Friend, Maim a Buddy Sweepstakes, who nominated Erica Reed to die. Also, Canadian Donna Watters for winning the international edition, Kill a Friend, Maim a Mate. She sacrificed her sister, Kim Watters, for a grand end.

I hope you enjoyed your literary immortality. And for those of you hoping to get in on the action, please check out www.LisaGardner.com.

Of course, I couldn't do this without my family. From my own darling child, who quizzed me every day on whether I had saved the little girl yet, to my extremely patient husband, who's gotten so used to having a wife who takes off for prison, he doesn't even ask what time I'll be home anymore. That's love, I tell you.

Finally, for Team Gardner. My supportive agent, Meg Ruley; my brilliant editor, Kate Miciak; and my entire Random House publishing team. You have no idea how many talented and hardworking people it takes to produce a novel. I am indebted to each and every one. Thanks for being on my side, and helping to make the magic happen.

* * *

This book is dedicated in loving memory to Uncle Darrell and Aunt Donna Holloway, who taught us laughter, love and, of course, cribbage strategy.

Also, to Richard Myles, aka Uncle Dick, whose love of great books, beautiful gardens, and a good Manhattan will not be forgotten.

We love you, and we remember.

We do hope that you have enjoyed reading this large print book.

Did you know that all of our titles are available for purchase?

We publish a wide range of high quality large print books including:
Romances, Mysteries, Classics
General Fiction
Non Fiction and Westerns

Special interest titles available in large print are:
The Little Oxford Dictionary
Music Book
Song Book
Hymn Book
Service Book

Also available from us courtesy of Oxford University Press:
Young Readers' Dictionary
(large print edition)
Young Readers' Thesaurus
(large print edition)

For further information or a free brochure, please contact us at:
Ulverscroft Large Print Books Ltd.,
The Green, Bradgate Road, Anstey,
Leicester, LE7 7FU, England.
Tel: (00 44) 0116 236 4325
Fax: (00 44) 0116 234 0205

Other titles published by
The House of Ulverscroft:

LIVE TO TELL

Lisa Gardner

In Boston, four members of a family have been brutally murdered. The father is now in intensive care — a possible suspect. Murder-suicide? Or something worse? Police detective D.D. Warren knows there's more to this case. Danielle Burton is a dedicated children's nurse in a locked-down paediatric psych ward. But she's haunted by the family tragedy that shattered her life twenty-five years ago. The dark anniversary is approaching, and when D.D. Warren and her partner show up at the facility, Danielle realizes: it has started again. A devoted mother, Victoria Oliver will do anything to ensure that her troubled son has some semblance of a childhood. She will love him no matter what — keep him safe — even when the threat comes from within her own house.